THE
LAST
GIRL

ALSO BY JOE HART

NOVELS
Lineage
Singularity
EverFall
The River Is Dark
The Waiting
Widow Town
Cruel World

NOVELLAS
Leave the Living
The Exorcism of Sara May

SHORT STORY COLLECTIONS
Midnight Paths: A Collection of Dark Horror

SHORT STORIES
"The Line Unseen"
"The Edge of Life"
"Outpost"
"And The Sea Called Her Name"

THE LAST GIRL

BOOK ONE
THE DOMINION TRILOGY

JOE HART

THOMAS & MERCER

Published by Thomas & Mercer, Seattle

www.apub.com

Amazon, the Amazon logo, and Thomas & Mercer are trademarks of Amazon.com, Inc., or its affiliates.

ISBN-13: 9781503952089
ISBN-10: 1503952088

Cover design by M.S. Corley

Printed in the United States of America

*To my wife, my mother, my daughter, and my sister,
the strongest women I know.*

The savage in man is never quite eradicated.

—*Henry David Thoreau*

BEFORE . . .

"As of today we don't have any solid factual data or numbers to speak of concerning the phenomena. We are working tirelessly with the World Health Organization as well as the Attorney General's office. Everyone can rest assured that we will issue a statement soon, and in the meantime we're doing everything we can to identify the cause."

—Cameron West, United States Secretary of Health and Human Services, January 2017

"I think what most people are missing is the fact that this isn't a localized event. This is global, and it happened overnight. To my knowledge no one—not a scientist, not a government official, and not a single news source—has come up with a satisfying explanation for what's happening."

—Ramona Chandler, independent journalist for The Underground, May 2017

"The National Obstetric Alliance that was formed early last year has made significant progress in determining the cause of the so-called 'drought of female births.' I can honestly say that we are on the verge of understanding the origin of this occurrence, and we implore the American people as well as citizens throughout the world to remain calm and strong in the face of this unprecedented challenge. An answer is very near."

—Benson Andrews, 45th President of the
United States of America, February 2018

NT: In your opinion, what truly caused the uprising in Harrisburg?

FW: (draws on cigarette) Limits.

NT: Limits?

FW: Yeah, limits. Everyone has theirs, you know? When the induction into NOA's research program went from voluntary to mandatory, that's what did it. It pushed people past their limits. This is America, for God's sake, the land of the free. But suddenly we're being told that all women who've given birth to baby girls in the last five years have to report to one of NOA's reception complexes, or else? (shakes his head) No way. No way were people going to put up with that.

Listen, I've heard stories of armed raiding groups taking entire families from their beds at night. There is a woman in

New York who said her eight-month-old daughter was taken from her crib and that a government official contacted her the next morning warning her not to take action. And then of course there was the Divinity cult that Senator Jesperson was associated with in Texas that was exterminating newborn boys in its membership. They thought that this was all God's work, and if they kept killing male infants the females would start being born again. I mean, this doesn't sound like the United States at all, at least not the one that I'm familiar with.

NT: There hasn't been a female birthrate report released in over six months now. The last one put the percentage at one in one hundred thousand. Would you say that's correct?

FW: (laughs) Are you kidding? One in a hundred thousand? Try one in ten million. That's the last statistic I saw before resigning, and by all accounts it was getting worse. I wouldn't be surprised if the new data shows one in a hundred million. When the masses start to realize what's happening, there's going to be war.

NT: You predict there will be more uprisings like in Pennsylvania?

FW: Slaughter. Call it what it was. A slaughter of American citizens by their government. And yes, this is only the beginning.

—Excerpt from NewsTime interview with
Foster White, former Undersecretary to the
Attorney General's office, ten days before his
disappearance, June 2018

"The rebellion's a tide, just like whatever the hell happened to the baby girls. You can't stop it."

—Anonymous rebel soldier, November 2018

No women

No babies

No hope

—Graffiti on the Washington Monument,
December 2018

AFTER . . .

1

A flash of light against her closed eyelids brings Zoey up out of the limbo between sleep and waking.

If she could stay there, in between dreams and reality, she would, but there is no use trying. She stands, stretching her arms above her head, feeling the coldness of the concrete floor begin to leach the heat she's gathered while sleeping. A hint of sickness roils in the base of her stomach. Her slippers are under the bed, and she puts them on before moving to the window.

It rained again in the night. A few streaks made it past the stark overhang that juts above the unbreakable glass, staining its exterior in slashes of transparent scars. The concrete beyond the window is dark gray, moist but already drying into pooled splotches dotting the promenade that circles the building. Beyond the walkway's gap is the curving wall that stretches up and nearly out of sight from her third-floor view. Atop the wall, a sniper shifts in his nest, readjusting himself to a more comfortable position, his rifle scope a bright wink of light as he turns. A flash like that is what woke her. She wonders if sometimes they look in the women's windows, trying to catch sight of them changing, perhaps. It is forbidden, but the thought of the possibility lingers like a bad dream.

Zoey swallows, placing her hands against the glass that's as cold as the concrete floor. Her breath fogs the area in front of her face, and she draws a circle there. Inside the circle she makes seven dots with the tip of her finger, one for each of the remaining women, then swipes the last dot away. Tomorrow, only six.

She turns from the glass, surveying the room. The softness of her bed is incongruent with the rest of the space. There are no gentle lines anywhere else. Everything is ninety-degree angles and harsh edges. The corners of the small desk bolted to the wall. The solid steel door leading into the tiny bathroom—no lock on it, of course. The windows to the outside shaped in a T, breaking the drabness of the room by letting in the gray light of day. Everything sharp and unforgiving.

The shower is hot, the water the only thing that's ever warm except for Lee's hands. Zoey recalls the times he's touched her back, so discreetly, always at a perfect angle to avoid the cameras. She thinks of his face, the freckles sprinkled across his nose and cheeks like the constellations in the sky at night. The thought of his smile creates a warmth that blooms inside her and grows with the fantasy of his hands on her skin, teasing, caressing. She stiffens with the memory of what is to come today, and the flame inside her cools.

She tugs at the rubber bracelet around her wrist, washing beneath it with soap because at times it can begin to smell of sweat. It gives only enough for her to get a single finger beneath it. She's pulled on it before, hard, and knows there are wires hidden within the rubber casing that assist whatever mechanism unlocks the door to her room when entering, but there is no scanner on the inside that allows her to leave.

Zoey steps from the tiny shower and dries herself on one of the towels that she's folded countless times. She brushes her teeth, scrubbing away the sour taste and replacing it with the bitter tang of something that's supposed to be mint but isn't. She knows what mint tastes like, from the chewing gum she's not supposed to have.

She wipes the steam from the small mirror over the sink and sighs. Her hair. What to do with it? "Unmanageable" is a kind term for the long, dark curls that seem to have a mind of their own. She tries sweeping it to one side and securing it with a thin clasp, but it pulls free and dangles over her face almost immediately. She frowns, changing tactics, and draws it straight back, tightening it into a ponytail before winding an elastic tie around it. She gives herself a last look and leaves the bathroom.

Zoey dresses in rough cotton pants the color of the early morning light, then pulls on a shapeless top, which hangs down to her narrow hips. She's given up looking in the mirror in the bathroom in regards to her clothing. There are only two styles to choose from. She has one on and knows she'll wear the other later that day.

A tremble runs through her that ends in her center and curls there, making the slight nausea she woke with worsen. She tries not to look at the digital calendar above her desk but does anyway. It's the brightest and most prominent object in the room, with its glowing numbers that shine too bright even when the contrast has been turned down.

The date is important, almost as important as the rules. It's the first thing that is taught: the months and days, numbers to form dates, those are what are supposed to be remembered. She can still hear Miss Gwen's voice through the years that have passed since their very first lesson. She remembers standing before her, no more than four years old and afraid, the instructor's pert dress like a bell above her flat-soled, black shoes. The older woman seems not to have changed at all in the last sixteen years. Miss Gwen is like the calendar, a constant fixture, always reminding, chiding, telling them that they are special, that they are hope. Telling them that their lives are not their own but belong to the greater good.

How much is a life worth?

This question is the first that enters Zoey's mind each morning, and it is the last she thinks before falling off to sleep every night. Can a price be put on such a thing? And if it could be, would one ever be able to pay it?

She reaches out, wishing she could smash the protrusion of the calendar off the wall but knows they'll just put another up, and an act like that would earn her time in one of the boxes. She's never had to go inside but knows she doesn't want to. There are some things in life that don't have to be experienced to form an opinion of.

A quiet scratching comes from the window and she spins, her breath catching in her chest. Zoey hurries across the room, grabbing the chair from her desk to set it beside the glass. She peers out at the closest sniper, but the angle is enough to hide her from his sight. She places her fingers in the joint of the right side of the smallest pane that creates the top of the T. It is only eight inches tall by two feet long, but it is heavy, bonded in place by some material that has hardened over the years since the Advance Research Compound was built. But with the time, like most things, it has cracked around its border. Enough so that a fingernail can be inserted, causing the gap to widen over weeks and weeks of worrying.

Zoey listens for sounds of footsteps in the hall outside her door, over the thud of her excited heartbeat, but there is only silence. It's still early, and Simon won't be waiting for her for another half hour. She has time.

She presses against the right side of the pane, and there's a soft squeak as the entire piece of composite glass shifts. She turns it until she can grasp its closest end before drawing it out of its frame. Cool spring air courses into the room, bathing her face with dampness left over from the night. She shivers, partially from the cold but mostly from happiness. *Could he finally be back?* She tosses the glass onto her bed, where it bounces once without a sound, and leans forward to gaze into the small alcove set outside her room on the face of the compound.

The space isn't large, barely ten inches across and five inches deep, but it is recessed in such a way that it stays dry from the rain and can't be seen unless someone were to remove the window just as she has. And since the bedrooms are the only places in the compound that don't have cameras, no one knows that the window can be extracted.

Zoey stretches up farther on the chair, tilting her head so that she can see the entirety of the alcove.

A lone, dry leaf scratches against the concrete, nudged by the wind.

Disappointment courses through her. There is no downy, brown owl waiting for her, and there hasn't been for several months.

◆　◆　◆

When she first found the owl huddled in the alcove nearly a year ago, his wing cocked away from his body at a strange angle, she was sure the bird would die, either by starvation or by the hands of one of the guards. There are no pets allowed within the walls of the ARC. She could hear Miss Gwen's high, nasally voice telling them that the virus could be carried not only by people, but by animals as well, and if they were to ever find one to notify a Cleric or a guard immediately.

It was two months after Zoey found the owl that he flew again. Two months of sneaking bits of bread hidden in the collar of her shirt, of keeping stringy chunks of meat tucked next to her molars in the back of her cheek until she returned to her room each day, always worried that someone would hear a slight slur in her speech and ask her to open her mouth for an inspection. Slowly the owl mended and became more and more tolerant of her company, the gentle touch of her hands, her low words to him each night before she retired to bed.

One day while the women were out for their daily exercise, a starling had swooped low past their heads, and Simon had laughed as they ducked, saying that the songbird was "quite a zipper."

And so she had found a name for the owl, because something as precious as a secret should always have a name.

In the last light of a day several months ago, Zipper had swooped away into the deepening night and never returned. The ache at his absence was a nearly constant pain in her center, and each time she took the window out, the hope rose that he would be there staring back at her with his luminous, yellow eyes, and then it fell when she saw that he wasn't. But why would he stay when he could leave?

◆　◆　◆

She reaches out and pulls the wayward leaf from the alcove, tossing it away to reveal what does still reside in the small space.

The books. One of the many mysteries within the ARC. She found one of them a year ago, tucked away at the very bottom of her bed, her toes touching it when she climbed in to sleep. *The Count of Monte Cristo*. The title itself raised goose bumps on her arms as she read it over and over. It was the first book she'd ever seen that hadn't been printed by the National Obstetric Alliance.

Three weeks later another book appeared once again beneath her covers. *The Scarlet Letter*. She had already devoured *Monte Cristo* twice in that time, her heart pounding so hard as she turned the pages, eyes wide as Edmond endured unspeakable torture and eventually seized the day when his escape presented itself. Hawthorne's book was much different, but the same in some ways because she realized Hester was trapped in a prison as well. One of love, and honor, and faith.

She'd considered throwing the books out more times than she could count. If anyone were to find them, she would surely spend time in the box. She imagined herself locked away in the infinite darkness, but there was something indefinable about being punished for such a thing as imagination. She thought that the discipline might fan the flames that had begun to burn within her instead of snuff them out.

But the electrifying question was, who had left them for her?

She had questioned Lee in a roundabout way, never alluding to the fact that she had the books, but instead prying at him, attempting to see a chink in the cheerful armor he wore as he squinted at her with confusion. She so wanted to tell him, but secrets were heavy, and Simon might notice him carrying such a weight. Such was the way with fathers and sons, it seemed. Whoever it had been, they were telling her something, encouraging her in a way that would bring swift and terrible punishment if spoken aloud.

She shakes herself free of her thoughts and considers taking a piece of chewing gum from the dwindling package that was left in her bed the same way as the books over a month ago. No, she'd better not; she doesn't have enough time to savor the sweet and spicy mint until it fades to nothing. *Maybe tonight.*

She replaces the glass carefully, the persistent fear of losing her grip on it and seeing it plummet into open air washing over her. As soon as it's in place, footsteps begin to echo down the hallway, coming closer and closer to her door. Zoey hurries, securing the glass before climbing down to replace the chair beneath her desk. She stands near her bed, sliding on her worn shoes as the footsteps stop before her door.

A knock.

"Come in," she says. The door opens, and Simon stands there in the hallway. He wears his usual Cleric uniform—a black button-up shirt, closed tight at the throat, and dark cargo pants above hiking boots. His handsome features are wrinkled by lines on his forehead as well as on either side of his thin mouth. His dark hair, always combed so carefully to the side, seems to have grayed more at the temples overnight. He looks at her with eyes very blue against the slate concrete, though there's a softness to them that always reassures her no matter what's happening at the moment.

"Good morning, Zoey."

"Good morning, Simon."

"You rested well?"

She nods.

"Good. Are you ready for breakfast?"

"Sure."

He holds the door open for her, letting it coast shut when she steps into the hall, the lock hidden in the frame snapping quietly. They walk slowly down the hallway, their steps nearly matched. *How many times have we done this?* She could do the math, she supposes, but what purpose would it serve? Because she knows why they do it. It's the same reason for the calendars in all the rooms, it's why they're taught to read the months and days only after the rules are memorized. It's to add another wall around them, knowing how long they've been here doing the same thing day after day.

They near the end of the hall and turn a corner. Zoey glances at their strange, bulbous reflections in the curved mirror mounted near the ceiling. She makes a face at herself. The stairs are ahead of them, but she slows as she sees another Cleric standing outside one of the last doors on the left. He's younger than Simon, but not by much. He has close-cropped blond hair that reveals his scalp beneath the fluorescent lighting. She knows him as Abbot, but most call him Abe. Zoey stops, and Simon halts as well.

"What's wrong?" Simon asks.

"I was wondering . . ." She blinks and licks her lips. "I wanted to talk to her before she goes."

Simon tips his head back, his mouth thinning until it's only a bloodless line. "Zoey, you know you're not supposed to speak with her in her room. Especially today."

"I know. But what will it hurt? She'll be gone this afternoon, and I won't see her—" She starts to say *ever again* but corrects herself. "—for quite a while." Abe has overheard them talking and is watching Simon, unmoving, unaffected. Simon frowns and glances down the hallway at the domed shape jutting from the ceiling. The cameras are everywhere, their opaque eyes always watching, judging.

"Please," she says, surprising herself. Simon returns his gaze to her before looking at Abe. Abe shrugs, as if to say *Fine with me.*

"Only a few minutes," Simon says.

Abe turns and knocks twice on the door. A murmured reply comes from within, and he holds his bracelet up to the reader beside the lock. The door clacks, and he opens it for Zoey as she steps past him.

The room is a duplicate of her own. There is the desk, the chair, the hateful calendar, and the room's sole occupant sitting on the bed.

Zoey's struck, as she always is, by how beautiful Terra can be. Her hair is long and blonde, bordering on white. It is straight and will do almost anything Terra wants it to. Now it's pulled back from her face, accentuating her long nose, high cheekbones, and dark eyes that Zoey has never seen shine with true surprise until now.

"Zoey, what are you doing here? You're not supposed to be in my room." Her voice is commanding and powerful. She stands from the bed and rises a full three inches above Zoey's height. It's not so much that Zoey's short, but more that Terra is tall. Everything about her cries *leader*, and that's why Zoey is so afraid.

"I needed to talk to you. Before the ceremony."

"About what?"

Zoey hesitates, hovering on the brink of an abyss before stepping off.

"Pretend you're sick," she says in a low voice. Terra tips her head and squints at her as if she didn't hear what Zoey said.

"What? Why?"

"So you don't have to go."

Terra sighs. "Zoey, we've talked about this. You know it's what we all want. I've been waiting for this day for years and years. For . . ." Terra's voice falters, and Zoey sees a sheen appear in her eyes. ". . . for as long as I can remember. The Program isn't something to be afraid of, it's something to embrace. It's for the greater good of—"

Zoey turns from her, staring down at the floor, and moves to the desk. "Please don't say that to me."

"Say what?"

"'The greater good.' Please don't say that."

Terra comes up behind her, places her hands on Zoey's shoulders. They are strong and sure, radiating strength that seems to be the only thing other than kindness that Terra can produce.

"It's true, Zoey. Today isn't something I'm afraid of, and you shouldn't be afraid either. I'm going to get to see them today. I'm going to see my parents." Terra's voice falters again, and Zoey knows that she's crying behind her, but she can't bring herself to look at her friend. "There's a place outside of these walls that's safe for us, and after the waiting period I'm going to see it with them."

Zoey turns then, gazing up at Terra's tear-streaked face. "I don't believe it. I think they're lying to us."

"How can you say that? They've always kept us safe here, sheltered from the plague, those that would hurt us. Why would they protect us if they were lying?"

Zoey ignores the question. "Pretend to trip, to fall down the stairs. If you're injured even a little, they'll send you to the infirmary, and we'll have a few more days." Zoey can't stand the pleading in her voice, but there's no straining it out.

Terra smiles, and Zoey suddenly hates the expression. It's full of knowing, and comfort, and regal condescension. "You know I won't do that. I can't. Don't worry, it will only be a little while, and we'll be in the safe zone together. We'll get to see Grace and Halie, and we'll be able to meet each other's parents."

Zoey steps away from Terra. "It's a lie," she hisses, unable to contain the sudden fury that's bloomed within her. "I don't know what's after induction, but it's not what they say. It's all a lie. I can see it on

Miss Gwen's face whenever she tells us about the safe zone. She's lying, and so is the Director."

Terra looks like she's been slapped. One of her hands reaches up to cover her mouth, which has dropped partially open. "Zoey, stop. You don't know what you're saying. That's heresy."

Zoey shakes her head and realizes she's trembling all over, like after a long run. "Please, Terra, don't go."

Terra draws herself up, becoming once again the leader, the keeper of order that she's been for the last decade among the other women. Her eyes harden, and she blinks away the last of her tears.

"I love you, Zoey. You'll see soon that everything is okay. Everything is going to be all right." Zoey looks at her and feels something shrivel in on itself within her chest.

"Goodbye, Terra," she says, and moves to the door without looking back.

2

The cafeteria is quiet as usual, only the tinkle and scrape of a spoon or fork on plastic breaking the silence.

The room will easily seat over three hundred people elbow to elbow at the long, low tables that are attached to the plastic stools lining their sides. But only one table is occupied.

The other women sit in two different groups, dotting the stools. There are only five of them altogether. When Zoey enters along with Simon, several sets of eyes glance up at them, Rita's cruel, green orbs holding the longest before she sneers and returns her attention to her plate. Sherell and Penny, the two women on either side of her, give Zoey only a cool glare, though Penny's gaze never fails to make Zoey squirm internally no matter where she is. It's as if the other woman is dissecting her with her eyes, taking pieces of her off and enjoying it.

Zoey moves past the table to where the plates are kept warm beneath low-hanging lights. There are three meals left sitting on the steel serving tray, hers separated by nearly three feet from Simon's and Abe's. Her plate and bowl are red, while the Clerics' are dark gray. She picks up her food without really looking at it, knowing it will be the

same mixture of vegetables, the same pallid oat cereal, the same puri-
fied water that's so clean it is as tasteless as air.

Zoey sits down beside Lily, the smallest and youngest of them at
only sixteen. Lily has a spoon in one hand and a fork in the other. She is
struggling to bring the cereal to her mouth. Her hand shakes, and most
of it slides off into her bowl. A spray of frizzy, light brown hair obscures
the right side of her face. No one has helped her tie it back today.

"Good morning, Lily," Zoey says.

Lily shifts awkwardly on the stool, one shoulder raised above the
other. When she sees Zoey she smiles, drawing up the features that
appear smeared on her face. One of her eyes lazes to the side.

"Hi, Zee," she says enthusiastically. "Hi," she adds, leaning forward,
still smiling. There is cereal stuck to the corners of her mouth and bits
clinging to her loose hair. Zoey returns her smile before throwing a deep
look of hate at Steven, Lily's Cleric. He stares back at her from the opposite end of the table before taking a long drink of water.

Zoey returns her attention to Lily, wiping her hair clean first before
dabbing at her mouth. Lily laughs quietly and bangs one hand on the
table.

"Will you shut that retard up?" Rita says, without looking away
from her plate. Zoey glances at the bigger woman. "It makes me sick
watching her eat."

Zoey opens her mouth to say something, but Crispin, the guard on
duty, steps forward, putting a gloved hand on the table. "I won't allow
that kind of talk," he rumbles, his baritone voice coming from deep in
his chest. Rita glances at him, giving him a smirk before pushing a lank
tendril of her red hair behind one ear. Zoey quivers with rage but nods
a thank-you to Crispin as he steps back, tucking his thumbs beneath
the wide leather belt he wears across his uniform.

"Don't listen to her," Zoey whispers to Lily as she strips off an extra
elastic band from her wrist. Lily doesn't look at her but blinks rapidly
and begins to wave her fingers in front of her face. Zoey gently ties the

girl's hair back, smoothing it from her brow before helping her eat the last of her cereal. When Lily's done, Zoey starts on her own food.

"You aren't going to have time to finish eating now," says a voice from across the table.

Zoey looks up at Meeka, who is leaning casually on one elbow, her hand propped beneath her jaw. Meeka's slanted, almond-shaped eyes are almost black, matching her hair. Today her tresses descend from her sharp widow's peak and hang down on either side of her oval face.

"I don't care," Zoey says, taking a bite of carrot. The vegetable snaps between her teeth.

"You will when they haul you up to the infirmary for being malnourished and plug you into one of the feeding machines. I mean, look at you. If you fell down in the hallway, you'd slip under a door."

"Like you have any room to talk," Zoey says. "You weigh about five pounds more than I do."

"Yeah, but it's pure muscle, and you know it." Zoey can't help but smile.

"Meeka," says Thomas, her Cleric, from where he's finishing his meal. "That's enough."

"We're still allowed to talk to one another, right? Or did they add that to the list of the damn rules while we were all sleeping?" Meeka's voice rises, and all heads in the room turn toward her.

"Meeka . . ." Thomas begins, standing partially from his seat.

"Yeah, yeah, I know. Stow it, or I'll get tossed in the box." She rolls her eyes at Zoey and pulls a face for Lily that makes her laugh again and begin to rock on her stool. Thomas grumbles something and returns to his seat.

"You are going to get yourself time in there if you keep up your attitude," Zoey says. "You can only push them so far."

"When was the last time someone got sent to the box? Hmm? I'll tell you. It was over a year ago, right before Halie was inducted. Remember how she quit eating and they force-fed her up in the infirmary?"

Zoey sets her fork down, suddenly not hungry anymore. "Yeah, I remember."

"When she attacked that guard, they tossed her in the box for two days. You remember what she looked like when she came out?"

Zoey meets Meeka's hard gaze, and her jaw clenches. "Yes, I do. You can stop."

"It looked like something had burned out in her head. Like whatever happened to her in there was beyond terrible. She never spoke again before they inducted her."

"I remember!" Zoey nearly yells. Lily jumps and puts her hands to her ears, rocking harder on the stool. Zoey glances around, meeting Simon's frown. He shakes his head once. "I'm sorry," she says before picking up her tray to dump the food, mostly untouched, into the large garbage bin beside the shuttered serving window. A short chime intones from all of the speakers mounted throughout the ARC. It echoes down the empty corridors and vacant rooms, and the women rise along with the Clerics.

Meeka takes a step toward Zoey but hesitates and continues through the doorway and into the hall. Steven assists Lily with her tray and helps lead her out as well, her hitching gait making Zoey's throat tighten as it always does. Simon appears at Zoey's side but says nothing, waiting as she looks down at the floor, until the lunchroom is silent once again.

"Okay. Let's go," she finally says.

◆　◆　◆

The lecture hall is on the same floor as the cafeteria and is equally large. It is centered in the building so that it has no windows to distract from the lessons. The footsteps of the women echo as they file in, the space meant for so many more bodies. The emptiness of it holds a disappointing air as if the room itself is disgusted with their lack of numbers.

The Clerics take seats near the door while the women cross the room to where a makeshift partition has been set up. The sound-deadening boards that make up the walls of their cubicle stretch nearly to the fifteen-foot ceilings. Inside the space is still enough room for at least fifty desks, but only six wait for them near the very front. Zoey pauses as she rounds the corner, unable to keep her eyes from traveling to the place where Terra's desk has sat for as long as she can remember. Now there is only a stark void, four abrasions on the floor the only sign that anything has ever rested there.

Zoey takes her seat directly in front of the empty spot, all the while trying to ignore the absence at her back that is like a chill wind.

Miss Gwen is at her desk, as usual. She smiles at them all as they file past like this is the first day she's ever met them. She is a pretty woman, perhaps in her late forties, with dirty blonde hair and a short forehead above hazel eyes tucked behind dark-rimmed glasses. Her cheeks are round and always red, as if she has either been outside in brisk weather or just heard some bit of inflammatory gossip. Zoey knows it is neither.

When they are all seated, Miss Gwen continues to smile at them for another moment before standing and rounding her long, old desk that looks to be from another era when everything wasn't made of plastic or concrete. She wears her usual dress, the same color as their own clothes. It reaches down below her knees, stopping above her flat-soled shoes. The smile on the instructor's face is as artificial as the plants that adorn the hallways in some places.

"Good morning," Miss Gwen says.

"Good morning, Miss Gwen," the women reply in unison, except for Meeka. She hasn't said good morning to the instructor in two weeks. Lily makes an excited sound from the back row where she's been placed, and Miss Gwen's smile falters. There is a tinge of disdain in her eyes as Lily quiets, so quick that Zoey's not sure if any of the others even notice.

"How are we this morning?" the instructor asks.

"Very well, thank you," they intone again. Miss Gwen beams.

"We will all rise now and recite the creed."

There is a shuffling of feet, and all the women stand. The instructor returns to the side of her desk, picking up a narrow, wooden pointer and jabbing it at a brass plaque affixed to the wall.

They begin to recite the words, none of them needing to read what is etched into the brass and inlaid with black paint.

"We are of the greater good. We live for the chance to rebuild the world that is no longer. We are one in our knowledge and stand steady before the challenges that face us. We give thanks for our shelter and for the guidance of the Director. We will not stray from the path."

Miss Gwen smiles at them and taps the separate list of words below the creed, each line numbered and set in bold, capital print. They begin to speak again.

"The greater good is more important than any one life. We obey the Director and his edicts. We do not disobey the Clerics or the guards, for their words are the Director's. We will not make a decision lightly, for everything we do affects everyone else. If we break a rule, the woman closest to us will receive the same punishment as the offender. For we are never alone. All of the commune that is left of the world depends upon us."

"Very good. Your voices are so beautiful together. You may sit," Miss Gwen says. They all slide into their chairs. Zoey notices Meeka looking at her, but when she turns to meet her gaze she sees that Meeka's eyes rest not on her, but the vacant space where Terra's desk used to be. Meeka looks back to the front of the lecture hall. After a moment Zoey follows suit.

"Now, before we continue," Miss Gwen says. "I'm sure you're all aware that this is a very special day for one of us. As you know, it is Terra's twenty-first birthday today and she will be inducted into the Program this afternoon. This is momentous because it's been over a year now since Halie left us for the safe zone with her parents." Miss Gwen clasps her hands before her and shivers. "Soon all of us will be there with them and as sad as it will be to leave our home here, it will be an unparalleled occasion! I hope you've all reflected on how to say goodbye to Terra in your own way this afternoon and take comfort in knowing that soon it will be your turn to travel with the Director as well." She gazes at them all, hesitating for a brief moment on Meeka's stony profile before nodding. "Now, if we can all open our texts to chapter twenty-two, page one hundred three."

There is a rattle and thump as the desks open and each woman pulls out the single textbook inside. The books are hardcovers and glossy black. The silver letters N, O, and A in the center shine as Zoey flips to the correct page. "Now. Who would like to read first?" Miss Gwen says, as if it is the greatest honor she can think of. Lily's hand rises immediately, and she breathes heavily through her nose. Zoey watches a look of disgust ripple across Miss Gwen's pretty features before she shifts her attention to Penny, who raises her hand nonchalantly, her bobbed, greasy hair swinging above her narrow shoulders.

"I will, Miss Gwen," Penny says.

"Excellent, Penny. You may begin."

Lily lowers her hand, blinking, and begins to run her fingers over the text of the page as if she is reading through them. Zoey stares at Miss Gwen's frozen smile and has the insatiable urge to run forward and drive the older woman into the wall hard enough to break her back, crack her skull—anything to wipe that incessant grin off her face.

"The Dearth," Penny reads from the chapter heading. "Late in the year two thousand sixteen, a noticeable drop in female births became apparent across the globe. At first it was by only several percent but soon after, in mid–two thousand seventeen, the rate dropped to well below half of the previous year's. By fall of the year two thousand eighteen, despite an unprecedented, scientific undertaking by the National Obstetric Alliance, female births were recorded at less than one in one hundred million.

"During this time, a rebel force consisting of several militant groups rose up against the United States government as well as the National Obstetric Alliance and waged open war on those that were trying to find a cure for the Dearth, see chapter forty-three for more information on the rebellion. For five years a civil war unlike any the world had seen before raged until an astonishing discovery was made. NOA scientists pinpointed the source of the Dearth as a singular virus that attacks embryonic nucleotides within pairings of X chromosomes, thus halting the births of females. This same virus then mutated and became deadly to all who encountered it. The greatest nation, and soon the world, became plague-ridden and fell into complete and utter chaos."

Penny's words drone on in a dreary tone that starts the inkling of a headache in the back of Zoey's skull. She gazes down at the neat paragraphs within the textbook, the pages beginning to wear at their edges from being turned. This is how she learned to read, how they all learned to read. It is from the text in the front of the book that they learned English, math, and science, while the second, much larger portion holds the knowledge of what was and is outside the walls. How many times have they finished the entire book, only to start once again the next day? Because what else is there to learn here? What other purpose but to wait and believe in the day when they will be inducted and leave forever?

Zoey rubs the back of her neck, blocking out Penny's voice in favor of reliving Edmond's daring escape from his cell. Even after reading *Monte Cristo* more times than she can remember, it is still magical each time she opens to the first page. She closes her eyes and is there with him on the sea, moments away from finding the treasure, moments away from becoming something new, something powerful and full of vengeance.

"Zoey!"

Zoey comes awake, only then realizing she was dreaming. Miss Gwen is several steps away, glaring, mouth turned sour at the corners.

"Yes, ma'am?"

"You were sleeping," Miss Gwen says, spitting out the words as if they were curses.

"I'm sorry. I didn't . . ."

"Didn't what?"

"I . . ." Zoey's throat is closing up under the instructor's relentless gaze. Rita snickers. Penny grins. "I didn't sleep well last night because I was so excited for the ceremony today." The lie rolls off her tongue like water.

Miss Gwen straightens, some anger draining from her eyes as her mouth evens. "Well, I suppose I can understand that, what with your induction coming very soon as well." She gives what Zoey guesses is the closest thing to a sympathetic expression she's capable of before nodding to the open textbook on Zoey's desk. "Regardless, it's your turn to read. At the bottom of page one hundred six, second-to-last paragraph."

Zoey clears her throat and reads.

The rest of the morning passes with the monotony of lecture. They take turns reading, and Miss Gwen asks them her questions that have been answered again and again.

Why do we obey the rules?

Because they keep us safe.

Why must we remain here inside the walls?

Because beyond them is ruin.

How can we rebuild the world?

By being part of the greater good.

The chime sounds, and they rise from their desks. Zoey's stomach gurgles as hunger pangs roll through her from her lack of breakfast. Meeka hangs back when Zoey waits for Lily to gain her feet.

"I shouldn't have said those things," Meeka says. She puts out a hand and Lily grasps it, making a delighted sound.

"It's okay. I overreacted," Zoey responds. They walk past Miss Gwen's desk, the instructor's eyes following them like two blades. They wait until they're outside the cubicle before speaking again.

"It's not okay," Meeka says. "I say things before I think them through."

"You're not telling me anything I don't know." Zoey casts a sidelong glance at her friend, her mouth curling up a little. Meeka shoots her a poisonous look.

"Last time I'm nice to you."

"Oh, was that you being nice?"

"You're quite the bitch, you know?" Meeka says, but her eyes are smiling.

"Bish, bish, bish, bish," Lily begins to chant.

"Lily, that's not okay," Zoey says, stopping their progress across the wide lecture hall. "You can't say that, okay?"

Lily smiles, dropping her chin to her chest. "Kay." They begin walking again. "Bish," Lily whispers. Meeka's laughter peals out and echoes off the concrete walls. Her Cleric squares himself toward them, tilting his head to one side. Meeka rolls her eyes and lets go of Lily's hand.

The Clerics fall in beside them as they walk down the hallway, the sound of footfalls loud in the closed space. Zoey hangs at the very back of the group, Simon at his usual place on her left. As they move toward the cafeteria and the smell of lunch permeates the air, Simon surprises her by speaking.

"I heard you get reprimanded this morning," he says.

She glances at him, but he doesn't look at her. "Yes. I fell asleep."

"You should take care not to do that."

"I will. I was tired."

"You're not sleeping well?"

"No. I'm sleeping fine."

He grunts. "You need to pay attention in lecture."

"I know. I do." The anger rises again within her, and she grits her teeth. *Why?* She thinks. *Why should I pay attention? So I can read all of the edicts and rules that have been stamped in my brain over and over again? So I don't incur the wrath of that woman in there who hides her true feelings behind a fake smile?* Because Miss Gwen hates them, Zoey knows. She can see it every time the older woman gazes at them, the way her hands flit at her sides sometimes like she yearns to do something terrible with them.

Zoey is snapped from her thoughts as she sees Lee round the corner ahead.

Lee. His sandy hair, always messy as if he's recently woken up. The carefree smile on his face that never seems to leave. His freckles, that she's studied up close more times than she can count . . . He sees her and his simmering grin widens, flashing bright teeth. But his gaze only hovers on her for a second before he turns it to his father beside her.

"Hi, Dad. I was looking for you," Lee says, striding up to them.

"You know you're not supposed to stop us in the halls," Simon says, glancing past his son to the receding line of women and their Clerics.

"I wouldn't have, but Assistant Carter found me this morning on my way to breakfast. He wanted me to tell you to report to him after your shift tonight." Simon squints and glances at the floor before shooting a look at the nearest camera in the ceiling.

"Okay. Thank you."

"You're welcome." Lee turns and moves past them, brushing against Zoey so lightly she barely feels it, and knows that even on the camera the movement would look innocent.

She doesn't turn her head or acknowledge anything. Instead she fixes a blank expression on her face as they continue down the hall to the cafeteria, slowly letting her hand travel into her pocket to feel the folded scrap of paper there.

"I need to go to the bathroom," she says, gesturing to one of the doorless rooms on the right as they near it. Simon glances at his watch and nods.

"Hurry."

Zoey steps into the bathroom, a wave of elation sliding over her as she sees it's empty. There is a camera mounted in the far corner of the room, but it cannot see into the many stalls that line the wall. Slight means of privacy seem to be the only power the women have over the rest of the ARC's inhabitants.

She steps into the stall, lowering her pants to complete the charade, but not before she draws out the note. As she sits on the cold plastic seat she unfolds the piece of paper that is not over a half-inch in diameter. There is only one word written in its center.

Tonight.

She allows herself a smile before putting the paper in her mouth. She chews it into a ragged, pulpy lump before swallowing it.

3

"I wonder what the princess is eating right now," Meeka says, picking at the boiled vegetables and canned meat that were already cold by the time they sat down at their places.

Zoey eats hungrily, downing the pasty meat without wondering what animal she might be ingesting. She shrugs. "Something special, I suppose."

"I've heard you get whatever you want," Mecka says, sipping her water.

"You can't have whatever you want if they don't have it."

"That's the thing. I think they do. I mean, a lot of these veggies are fresh, right? So they're growing them somewhere, and I don't know about you, but I haven't seen any dirt or plots of land within the ARC." It is an old discussion between them, but Zoey indulges her to help patch over their earlier spat.

Zoey chews, thinking. "Might be on the roof."

"Maybe. But I doubt it."

"You think they grow them outside the walls?"

"Have to."

"The only ones who go outside the walls are Reaper and the Redeyes." Zoey forces down the shiver that tries to rise in her from speaking the name of the reclamation unit.

"They're the only ones we *see* go outside. We can't see in the dark," Meeka says, widening her eyes comically.

"No, but . . ." Zoey frowns.

"What?"

She shakes her head. "Nothing. We're going to get in trouble talking like this."

Meeka shrugs. "We get in trouble for everything. Don't speak to the Clerics' sons, don't have impure thoughts. We're not even supposed to touch ourselves—like I'm gonna follow that rule . . ."

"Meeka!"

"Well, it's true. It's really all we've got. Remember when they caught Kelli in the bathroom with that one Cleric's son? What was his name?"

"Andrew," Zoey says in a quiet voice.

"She went in the box for a day and we never saw him or his father again."

"I remember. That's why you should keep your voice down."

"I really don't care anymore. I've got another six months, and then I'll see whatever they've got planned for us. In the face of that, nothing really seems very frightening." They both fall quiet for a time, concentrating on their meals. "I bet Terra got chicken and mashed potatoes," Meeka says quietly. "With butter."

The mention of butter floods Zoey's mouth with saliva, and suddenly her meal tastes more bland than ever. They only have butter once a year, on New Year's Eve.

Zoey sighs and sets her fork down. "Why can't you ever be quiet?"

"Not in my nature."

Lily rocks beside Zoey, humming something out of tune under her breath. She watches her movements, dread rippling through her like water disturbed by a storm. Who will watch after Lily when she's gone?

The chime sounds and makes Zoey jump, her hand slashing out, knocking a spoon flying to the other side of the table. Meeka grabs it up, her reflexes so fast Zoey doesn't even see her hand move.

"You okay?" Meeka asks, handing the spoon back as the table begins to empty.

"I'm fine," Zoey says.

They file back down the different hallways to their rooms. Zoey watches Lily and her Cleric disappear into the closest chamber to her own before scanning the strap on her wrist.

She enters her room, leaving Simon to stand beside the entry in the hall, his hands folded neatly behind his back. His stance is a holdover from being in the military, she knows. She suspects that all the Clerics are former military, chosen for their assignments to the women for sometimes obvious, sometimes cryptic reasons.

She recalls the night she knew for sure that Simon had been a soldier . . .

◆　◆　◆

She'd been no more than seven years old. The auto-guns woke her. Their chatter was muted somewhat by the walls and the building around her, but it was still loud enough to drag her up from sleep and send her halfway across the room, wide-eyed and staring before she'd even known she'd left the bed. A red glow had filled her room. It had been so beautiful, the color deeper than any she'd ever seen before, deeper than the most brilliant sunrise. She'd gone to the window and peered out, no longer flinching at the thunder of heavy gunfire.

The night had been alive with color.

Streaks of white phosphorus cut the air above the ARC, while a red falling star trailed down toward the compound, its light bathing everything below. The snipers on the wall began shooting then, their gun barrels spraying fire over and over at something below. She could hear screams too, long and loud. Bellows and curses that curdled her insides. But she couldn't look away. She pressed her eyes to the glass and stared, finding the zips of light she knew must be bullets flying, but even then the fear was overshadowed by the awe of something beautiful in the chaos.

An explosion shook the entire ARC, sending her vibrating away from the window. A ball of fire as wide as her room rose above the wall, flames licking over its side like water. The fire reached out and touched one of the snipers in his nest, setting him alight. He burned and spun, a sound coming from him that nearly made her clamp her hands over her ears. He had leapt from the wall then. Not inside, toward the track of concrete that surrounded the building, but out into the open air. He had jumped outside. And this fact alone somehow terrified her more than anything else she'd seen. Because at that moment in her early years, nothing was more frightening than being outside the walls.

Simon had burst into her room, eliciting a short cry from her before she realized who it was. She ran to him, clutched at his waist, and he embraced her, one of the last times he had ever done so. His voice was low and calm, but there was something in it that made her look up into his face. He was scared, too.

In the excitement she didn't notice that Lee was with him until the boy touched her hand. Simon told them to go sit in the bathroom and not to talk, to be quiet. Lee led her there but she glanced back at Simon as he closed the door, one hand pressed to it as if to keep it firmly shut, the other holding a pistol like the ones that hung on the guards' belts.

They sat together in the darkness of the bathroom, Lee holding her hand, saying things that didn't make sense at the time. Later she realized he was telling her a story to keep her calm, all the while his arm trembled beside her own. Only several months older than she was, and already he was trying to take care of her.

They stayed that way as the night wore on, the red light coming and going as if the world were spinning so fast that the sun rose and set over and over. Slowly the gunshots lessened, the silences between them growing after each concussion. Soon there was only the quiet crackle of flames, barely audible over their breathing in the enclosed space . . .

◆　◆　◆

Zoey catches herself staring out the window at the curving, impassive wall and casts off the memory. It had been a battle, she knows that now, but what for and with whom, she can only guess.

She moves to the narrow closet set beside the bathroom and draws the doors open. In it hangs a dress made from the same rough material as her current clothes, the color an identical gray. She takes it down, hating the feel of the fabric more than the uniform she wears. She takes the dress into the bathroom and changes into it, only looking at herself to make sure the neckline is straight and the shoulders are even.

It's an ugly thing, lumpy and rough. It isn't made to be beautiful. It's made to remind the wearer of her place and of what will come.

She turns off the light, liking the darkness better, and stands there in the silence, bathing in it like a healing balm.

◆　◆　◆

Zoey and Simon travel up the stairway to the fourth level, stopping to wait for the rest of the women outside the assembly. The hallway is quiet except for the footsteps that gradually come nearer from several directions. There are workers in their bright yellow coveralls, cooks wearing green aprons, several guards who are either off duty or unneeded for the moment, adorned in the customary black vests and cargo pants. Their prods hang from their belts, the long burnished composite tubes reflecting the light with a promise of violence, two electrodes protruding from their ends like silver fangs.

Zoey eyes the weapons and wonders what it would be like to be beaten with one of them, to be shocked. She's seen it only a handful of times. Once, when a worker seemingly lost his mind and had stripped a guard of his prod, screaming incoherent threats and obscenities. Four other guards had surrounded him, diving in at once, their prods blazing white electricity. The worker hadn't even been able to scream, he simply stiffened, his mouth opening, and she had seen pale fire jumping from tooth to tooth within.

They wait outside the assembly, the women all in their identical gray dresses, their Clerics beside them, the Clerics' sons standing in another group. The boys are all close in age, some tall, some short, some with cocky grins and looks to boot, all wearing pale blue shirts over dark pants. Zoey finds Lee in their midst and he winks, barely keeping his smile in check. She frowns and looks away.

The sound of booted feet come from the far end of the corridor, and her heart nearly stops.

Reaper and six Redeyes march toward them. Their uniforms are black with matching boots polished to dark mirrors. In their hands they carry short, powerful-looking machine guns. They walk in time to a pace set by their leader. Reaper is a head taller than almost all the other soldiers. He is broad across the shoulders with a growth of dark hair cut close to his skull. A long scar slices through his hairline, streaking down in an ugly, rippling mass to the mask he wears on his lower face. The black fabric covers his nose, mouth, and jaw. Two straps run from it around the back of his skull to hold it in place.

The gathering of people in the hall splits like water as the men near. The Clerics stand at attention while the women press themselves to the wall. Zoey is no exception. She tells herself she won't look as they move by, knowing what she will see, but in the end she can't help herself. She glances up as Reaper passes.

He is looking directly at her.

His eyes are nearly colorless in the artificial light. The slightest shade of gray tinges them with a frigid clarity of complete inhumanity. There is no emotion in them. They have been burned cold.

Zoey shudders and looks away until they pass, the sound of their boots fading to nothing. It is only minutes before the sound of helicopter rotors rise somewhere above them. Even through the thick layers of concrete the motor's voices are clear.

"Must've got a tip on a baby girl," Meeka whispers.

"They've never brought one back since Lily," Zoey says.

"Doesn't mean they're going to quit looking."

A bleep comes from the intercom, and Assistant Carter's weak voice slithers after it.

"You may enter."

There is a click, and the double doors before them unlock.

The assembly is a circular room with tiered seating. It is meant, like so many other places in the ARC, to hold vast crowds. But there is only the short filing of people that fill the bottommost rows, their numbers barely rising past sixty. The women move to the very first row that sits below a platform where a podium has been placed. A banner emblazoned with the NOA seal, a wreath of red flames surrounding the dark acronym, hangs from the podium's front. A larger banner extends from the ceiling. To the far right is a set of doors that Zoey knows lead to the infirmary. She's looked at them from the opposite side before when having her monthly checkup. She imagines the other set of doors on the far side of the infirmary, the ones that are solid steel, always locked, a guard permanently stationed beside them.

She swallows the lump in her throat.

Everyone takes their seats and the auditorium quiets. Without flourish, the doors to the infirmary open and a pair of doctors, garbed in their white scrubs, take positions on either side of the entry. Assistant Carter is next.

He is a direct representation of his voice.

Carter is in his late thirties with shining hair slicked tight against his oblong skull. His nose is long and pointed, nearly hooked at the end above two bright red lips. He is thin and swims in his three-piece suit, the only thing she's ever seen him dressed in. The ridiculous yellow tie he wears hangs almost to his belt. His eyes flow over the women first, and a sneer that Zoey supposes is his best smile crawls onto his face. He moves to the edge of the low stage and waits, rubbing his palms together as if he's touched something wet and is drying them, or enjoying the feel of the moistness.

Two guards appear in the doorway a second later, followed by the Director himself.

He is a tall man, well built, with stately, iron-gray hair raked back from a wide brow. His face is ruddy, akin to the snipers' visages she's seen, as if he spends most of his time outside in the wind rather than within the walls. His eyes are a crisp blue, so sharp and piercing they remind her of pinpoints. The Director walks with a casual air to the stage and gives them all a smile as he takes his place behind the microphone. Up close, he appears younger rather than older, his healthy color glowing beneath the powerful lights.

"Good afternoon, everyone," the Director says into the small microphone growing from the podium. "Thank you all for coming."

"As if we had a choice," Meeka breathes out of the side of her mouth. Zoey bites the inside of her lip.

The Director seems to pause to collect his thoughts. His bright eyes focus on the podium top before he gazes out at them. "The Phoenix is a mythical creature from Greek lore often portrayed as a fiery and noble bird. It is said the Phoenix could live thousands of years before succumbing to death, and typically it died and was reborn through fire. The sentiment is not uncommon. The idea of a second chance, of rebirth, of renewing one's hopes and dreams. One could say it is our destiny, our fate within the human condition to always hold onto hope of redemption even if it is the last thread that connects us to life."

The Director pauses, scanning the faces of the women. Zoey looks past him when his eyes stop on her, letting her gaze rest on the blankness of the wall behind him. Someone coughs quietly. "You women are that thread. You are our hope for rebuilding the world that once was. The world itself, you see, was a Phoenix. For millions of years mankind built upon the bones of his ancestors, toiling away for a better future. The fire of industry burned bright, and we reveled in our discoveries. You've seen in your texts that man has stepped upon the moon. As unbelievable as that may be, it's true. There were countless honorable endeavors created in the minds of geniuses that alas, will never be."

The Director's face darkens, and Zoey wonders where he learned this showmanship. She's read the definition of a politician, and if there is one left in the world, he's standing before her now.

"Because we were struck down as one by a virus of most vile design, whether it is natural or manmade, we do not know. In the beginning it did not take our lives firsthand, but in the darkness of women's bodies, it did its horrid work. It undermined the very fabric of life, its effects robbing the world of procreation by burning out the possibility of female existence. And so, when all seemed lost and we were at our final thread, the brave scientists and researchers of NOA, who dedicated their lives to the betterment of our species, held onto that last hope. That hope was planted here within this Advance Research Compound as a seed that they dreamed would one day grow into new life. And that is why we are gathered here today."

The Director looks down, waiting for the applause he knows will come, and it does. Zoey hears a clapping much louder than the rest and turns her head to see Miss Gwen on her feet, lower lip trembling, palms flaming red from her effort. The Director lets it roll over him for a moment before holding up a hand.

"The safe zone built outside the walls is becoming more so each day. Soon all of you will travel there and life will begin anew. Hope will be restored not by governments or by battles, but by all of the brave young women I see before me, along with the one who is about to join us."

The Director raises a hand, gesturing to the entrance that they'd come through earlier, and Terra is there with Abe. She wears a flowing white gown studded with reflective points that glitter in the light, making her appear as if she is emanating some of the glow within the room. Her hair is swept back from her brow, and she is smiling, eyes already wet with tears of joy.

The crowd begins to applaud, but Zoey can't muster the energy. She watches Terra approach the podium, her gown swishing along the floor, trailing behind her like a comet's tail. Terra reaches the Director and he embraces her lightly, whispering something in her ear. She lets out a quiet sob that doesn't rise above the continued applause and nods. The Director motions for silence, and the clapping fades away.

"Today, Terra will leave you behind—friends who've been here since birth. But this is not the end. Such is the nature of a Phoenix. Today may seem to be ash for some, but know that with our continued effort and unified bond, we will rise again and see a future steeped in glory."

The Director takes a step back from the microphone and holds out his hands toward Terra, palms up, as if to display her. Terra, still crying, makes a small bow, sweeping her gaze across the other women. She smiles at them through her tears. Zoey feels a prickling behind her eyes but blinks rapidly before Terra looks at her. She simply stares up at her friend, knowing what Terra wants, but gives her not the slightest smile of approval. Terra hesitates as the Director begins to usher her away, her eyes locked on Zoey. There is a flicker of something there in her expression. Doubt? Zoey holds her gaze as long as she can, but finally the Director leads Terra away.

There is a last swish of white fabric, and then Terra is through the double doors of the infirmary, applause still clouding the air like gunfire.

They file out of the assembly into the hall, the women first and then the rest of the crowd. Miss Gwen is crying, and Zoey has to grip the fabric of her dress with balled fists to keep her hands from flying to the older woman's throat. Simon walks beside her and pauses in the hallway, tilting his head back toward the assembly where the weasel-form of Carter is standing beside the doors.

"I have to speak to Assistant Carter. Wait here for me, okay?"

"Okay."

Simon walks away, his normally fluid stride somewhat stilted as he approaches Carter. She wonders if Simon dislikes the man as much as she does. There's a poke to her ribs and she grunts as Meeka steps from behind her.

"Quite the show, huh?"

Zoey nods. "Always is."

Meeka stiffens and turns a little to one side. "I was hoping he wouldn't be here today."

"Who?" Zoey asks, scanning the crowd that is slowly moving off in their separate directions, the excitement of the ceremony over.

"Dellert and his crony over there by the wall."

Zoey glances to her left and sees the young guard at once. He leans against the concrete as if he's holding it in place, his hands clasped before him, one long leg crossed over the other. Dellert Crosby is perhaps four years their senior, with short, dark hair and a moon of a face below it. The roundness of his head is incongruent with the rest of his gangly body and sits atop it like a melon perched on a stake. There is a shadow of a mustache above his heavy upper lip, and the collar of his uniform is undone, a few straggly chest hairs peeking from the gap. His brown eyes flick from Meeka to Zoey, his gaze lurid and slow as he runs it down her length, focusing on the exposed skin of her calves. His tongue appears and flicks once at the corner of his mouth. He seems utterly oblivious to the other workers and guards that clutter the hall and flow through the space separating them. Zoey thinks she sees him mouth a word but can't be sure. Her skin crawls.

"God, what a sicko," Meeka says, shooting a look in Dellert's direction. "And Baron's following right in his footsteps."

Zoey throws a glance at the younger guard beside Dellert. Baron Garrison is smiling, his boyish good looks giving way to the handsome shadow of manhood that he'll enter into soon. His blond hair is a shock of gold that hangs at an angle off the top of his head. His eyes dance across her face and he snickers a little, saying something low to Dellert, who acts like he hasn't heard.

Zoey turns and takes a few steps down the hall, pulling Meeka with her. "Don't look at them," she says as they walk, Thomas falling in behind them several strides back.

"They're really pushing it. It only takes one wrong person to see them looking at us like that," Meeka says.

"I guess Dellert's forgotten whatever punishment they doled out to him after he touched Halie."

"Looks like it."

"You think they threw him in the box?"

Meeka shakes her head. "They've got other ways of dealing with the guards who step out of line."

"Well, whatever it was, I think it's worn off. He's so disgusting."

"We can't all have guys like Lee swooning over us."

"Meeka," Zoey hisses, swiveling her eyes around. "Lee doesn't swoon."

"Mmmhmm. Right."

"Zoey, you need to wait for Cleric Asher," Thomas says. "And Meeka, you need to change and get to the supply room. Your shift's about to start."

"I know what time it is, Thomas, thanks," Meeka says, rolling her eyes in her usual way to Zoey. "I'll see you at dinner."

"Sure." Zoey watches Meeka and Thomas move away as she runs through the Director's words. There is always a speech at an induction, something supposed to be moving, inspiring, uplifting, but the words have always been like a hazy gauze wrapped around something amorphous and dark. It has become more apparent in the last several years as she's watched woman after woman, friend after friend whom she's known since birth, disappear behind those doors.

Never to be seen again.

Footsteps coming closer snap her from her thoughts. Dellert and

Baron are approaching, and the hallway seems to shrink. There isn't enough space to let them pass comfortably. Dellert looms closer and closer, his height more pronounced the nearer he comes. His lip twitches in a smile, the thin mustache wriggling like some poisonous caterpillar. The fear is irrational—she knows he can't touch her or do anything that his leering stare is suggesting—but it is there nonetheless. She feels the concrete behind her and realizes she's pressed her back against it. She hates herself a little for it. Zoey can smell him now, an acrid tang of body odor mixed with the last tinges of vanilla that all the clothes are washed in. The scent makes her want to vomit.

"Pretty," Dellert whispers as he passes in a rush of air. He doesn't look back, but she hears Baron snicker, a low, furtive sound that could be passed off as a cough. She's trembling and she grits her teeth as Simon steps out of the assembly, his head snapping around when she isn't standing where he left her. He sees her, and she feels a rush of appreciation for him in that moment. He would kill for her, die for her. She knows this though it's never been said. It's simply his job, among other things that are less appealing.

When he nears her, he sees there's something wrong. He stops a short distance away, eyes questioning. *Are you okay?*

Yes.

You're sure?

Yes.

I don't believe you.

I'm fine.

"Let's go," she says aloud. Simon nods slowly, and she leads the way down the hall.

◆　◆　◆

Zoey changes clothes in her room quickly, tossing the dress onto the floor in an angry display of defiance that gives her a fleeting second of triumph before she concedes that she'll be the one that will have to pick it up. But she leaves it there for now, crumpled and misshapen, something ugly. She grinds her heel on it as she leaves the room.

When Zoey steps from her room, the corridors are deserted save for Lily and Steven. Lily hurries toward her, her hitching gait and lopsided smile both raising and lowering Zoey's mood at the same time. She grasps the girl's hand.

"Ready to go to work, Lily?"

"Ayeah. Worr!" Lily says, and tries to dance ahead, but Zoey keeps a firm grip on her. They move down the halls until the stairway comes into view. Their Clerics talk in low voices behind them and only catch up when they reach the first-floor entrance at the base of the stairs. Simon scans his bracelet and opens the steel door.

This level hums.

The walls seem to vibrate with the power of the machines that reside behind them. The mechanical room, on their left, is by far the largest area on the first floor. Zoey has been inside only a handful of times, always accompanied by Simon and a guard. There are motors twice as tall as she is hidden behind enormous casings. The air is constantly moving there, hot and sour with the smell of burning dust. Even the foam earplugs that can be retrieved from a station inside the door can't block out all of the sound, the high whining and thrumming bass that froths the blood within her veins.

Zoey and Lily move on, the loudest area falling behind them. To the right is the sprawling exercise facility that the women are allowed to use on days when the weather is too inhospitable for walks outside. They can use the aerobic machines but aren't permitted to touch the many free-weights or pieces of machine-weight apparatus. *It's because they don't want us to be strong*, Meeka told her once. *Healthy, yes. Strong, no.* Meeka always seems to voice Zoey's own thoughts.

At the very end of the hallway two doors sit perpendicular to one another. The first, straight ahead, leads outside to the promenade. A guard stands beside it with his hand resting casually on the butt of his handgun. She can't remember his name, but she gives him a quirked glance. She's never seen a guard use a handgun. As far as she knows, it's forbidden. That's why they carry the prods. There's something in his stance that tells her he hopes she tries to run for it. She grips Lily's hand tighter and heads toward the other door.

It is set in the left wall and Zoey doesn't wait for Simon to scan his bracelet—she simply flashes her own across the reader. This is the only other door in the facility that opens for her and Lily.

"Hey, let's stay out here. Those machines give me a fuckin' headache," Lily's Cleric says to Simon. "They're not goin' anywhere."

"That's not protocol," Simon says.

"There's a camera in there with them, and this is the only way in or out. We'll be right here."

"It's okay, Simon," Zoey says. "We'll be fine." She nods once at him, and before he can protest, she and Lily enter the laundry.

The ceiling is well over twelve feet high with no handholds anywhere on the bare walls, which are painted a dingy yellow. Or maybe they were white once and gave up the fight to stay so. The washing machine and dryer are stainless steel giants, their squared shoulders touching in the center of the room. Three seamless chutes protrude from the ceiling at the far end. Beneath them are wide cloth baskets heaped with clothing of different colors. The black eye of the camera in the middle of the room stares down. Zoey stares back.

"Come on, Lily, let's get to work."

They begin sorting the laundry and hauling it from beneath the tubes to the washing machine. It is painfully dull work that lost its excitement after folding the very first load of garments so many years ago.

They start the washing machine, and the entire room comes alive with sound. It's not so loud that they need earplugs, and she's gotten used to it over the years. They spend the twenty minutes it takes for the load to wash sitting on the floor drawing letters in the dust. Lily rocks beside her and shrieks with delight every time she completes an entire word correctly.

Zoey draws a circle over and over. It is the wall outside. But really does it matter if the walls are square or round? They are walls and do their job well.

She stands and moves to the laundry chutes. Their dark hollows run straight up and out of sight. Even if Lily were able to give her a boost, how would she climb up the slick sides of the metal? And if she were able to shimmy up to a different level, what then? The walls would still be there, the guards, the cameras. Nothing would change, except she would be punished.

The washing machine signals its completion with a buzz and they switch the load to the dryer beside it. After they repeat the cycle a half hour later, they take their heavy baskets around the wall beside the dryer and set their burdens at the foot of the folding table.

The table is eight feet long and four feet wide. Beyond it is the garment elevator, an apparatus built into its own shaft that runs all the way to the fourth floor. It has three extendable trays spaced ten inches from one another. The clothing is folded and stacked on the appropriate tray. When the elevator is full, a button is pushed on the wall and the doors before it slide shut. It stops at each level, depositing the garments into storage closets before returning empty. Zoey has considered climbing inside the elevator time and time again. First off, she doesn't think she can fit between the shelves, she's been too afraid to try—and this is the first time in months that their Clerics haven't been right on the other side of the little wall. No, she doesn't think she can get inside unless she were able to unfasten one of the trays. And again, what would it solve?

Nothing.

She's in this room for a single purpose—to clean the clothes and return them. People wear the clothes, dirty them, send them down the chutes, and it starts all over again.

Zoey hears a strained creaking and looks down at her hands. She's wringing the collar of a guard's uniform so hard the material squeaks. She releases it, her bloodless fingers throbbing.

"Do you like birds, Lily?" she says in a low voice, loud enough to be heard only by the girl beside her. She glances in the direction of the camera and is reassured as always that they are shielded from view. This is the only place within the ARC she knows of besides her room and the bathroom stalls that is hidden.

"Burrs?" Lily says.

"Yes, birds. Do you like how they fly? How they're . . ." She hesitates. ". . . free?" There, she's said it. Free. What a magical word, and how wonderful it feels on her tongue.

"Fee?" Lily asks. She continues to fold the shirt she's holding. Its edges aren't even. It will have to be fixed. Zoey snatches the shirt away from her and grabs her wrists, yanking Lily around. Lily's eyes are wide, and even the one that lazes to the side, unfocused, is filled with surprise and fear.

"Don't you want to be a bird, Lily? Don't you want to fly over the walls and away from here? Go somewhere where they can't tell us what to do? Where they can't keep us in a box?"

Lily's lower lip trembles, and tears begin to spill from her eyes. "Ow," she says through a sob, and Zoey sees she's gripping the other girl's wrists hard. Too hard.

She releases them and Lily steps back, crying fully now, her small shoulders shaking. Zoey sags, leaning on the folding table before reaching out gently to bring Lily into an embrace.

"I'm sorry, Lily. I'm so sorry."

"Ow, ow, ow," Lily says, hiccupping. "Zee, ow."

"I know, I'm sorry. Shh, I'm sorry." She strokes Lily's hair and closes her eyes.

Hours later, the tone sounds and they leave the laundry. Lily's eyes are red but dry, and Zoey knows her Cleric won't notice. Simon unlocks the door beside the guard, and they step through it.

The fresh air hits her as it always does. It's intoxicating to a point where her head lightens and she imagines it floating away over the walls. The sky is a faultless blue, distilled to a shade that hurts her eyes if she looks at it too long. As always there is the endless sound of wind, howling over the top of the walls. It growls in a monotone that rarely seems to change, like the hollow noise of air blown across an empty bottle. She and Meeka, and to an extent, Lee, have discussed where the ARC might be positioned that the sound of the wind would be so continuous. *We're on a mountain*, Zoey had told Meeka one afternoon. *There's no other explanation for it. It would make sense for them to put it there. Harder to get in, harder to get out.* Meeka had laughed, and when Zoey asked her what she thought was so funny, Meeka had simply said, *There is no getting out.*

The promenade is more than thirty feet wide and shaped in a constant bend. As much as the building in the center of the ARC is hard angles and flat edges, the outside is all curves. The soaring wall beside the track slopes outward and the top looks as if it curls over like the lip of a bowl. Not that she would know for sure, since she's never been high enough to see it, but it would make sense. The ARC was built for sustainability, a long-term facility meant to protect and contain. She's seen pictures of flowers in the NOA textbook. She imagines the circular walls resemble some of them in bloom.

The main building sits as a squat reminder of its power in the center of the promenade. Its height is only dwarfed by the walls around it, but its pure oppression can be felt even out in the open air. Zoey gazes up at its sides dotted with different-shaped windows. She spots her own and is, as always, relieved that the alcove beside it is completely hidden.

"Get moving," Steven says gruffly. "This is exercise hour, so exercise." Simon gives him a look, pursing his lips, but nods once at Zoey, who leads Lily away. The two Clerics sit on a small, steel bench that is built into the side of the wall.

Zoey leads Lily away as fast as the girl can manage. The track is easily a mile around, making it perfect for guards and Clerics to use for exercise as well. The only break from the monotony of smooth concrete on either side is the random bench or security door mounted in the main building. High above them, the snipers perch on the wall like giant birds of prey, their shadows cascading down in monstrous shapes to splatter on the promenade. Ahead, the narrow bridge extends from the roof of the main building to the edge of the wall. Its delicate structure looks weak enough to fold under the weight of a single man, but she's seen more than one sniper on it at a time, walking calmly to relieve the other men of their posts in the high wind.

A door on the building opens and two Clerics appear, followed by Sherell and Penny. They give Zoey and Lily a look before beginning their walk ahead of them. Their Clerics shoot several furtive glances around before lighting up cigarettes, the smoke sweet and pungent as it rides the air out of their lungs and away from their mouths.

"Burr, burr, burr," Lily intones, not looking up but studying the path before her.

"Shh," Zoey says, a ripple of fear running through her.

A gust of wind careens down off the walls and casts a cloud of dust and grit past them that stings her eyes. She watches Sherell and Penny walk ahead, their progress steady and even. They don't look back. Zoey shifts her gaze to the bridge more than seventy feet overhead as they pass beneath it. There must be some means of descending from the wall on the opposite side. Like Meeka said, they're not growing vegetables within the ARC.

Zoey is so entranced by her contemplations that she doesn't register Penny and Sherell stopped directly in their path.

She brings her eyes down in time to see Penny's knuckles fill up her vision.

The blow is whip-fast and hard. Zoey's neck pops as her head rocks back, and pain explodes on her cheek. She loses her grip on Lily's hand.

Blinking, she staggers backward, her feet scrambling to keep her upright as two hands shove her from behind, rocketing her forward again.

She stumbles, falls.

Her palms abrade on the rough concrete, pebbles engraining themselves in her skin. Her knee is bleeding, she can feel it beneath the untorn fabric of her pants. Her vision whipsaws, elongating before snapping back.

Lily releases a cry that is cut off abruptly.

Zoey looks up into Rita's wide face. Her red hair has come loose of its tie and hangs like bloody curtains beside her pale cheeks. Her eyes are alight with a storm of fury and excitement.

"Aww, you fell down, Zoey. Why'd you do that?" Rita says.

"What do you want?" Zoey asks, sitting up. The pain is ebbing slowly but not entirely away.

"I want you to know—now that the princess is gone, you're not safe anymore."

Zoey pushes herself to her feet. Her legs wobble and threaten to drop her again. Sherell is holding Lily from behind, one strong hand pressed firmly over her mouth. Lily is crying and swaying in the bigger woman's grasp. Rita must have waited for them to pass before following. Shooting a look over Rita's shoulder, Zoey sees that the closest sniper's back is to them and there are no Clerics in sight. They've planned this well.

"What have we ever done to you?" Zoey asks, curling her fingers into fists.

"You exist. How's that? You piss me off by being alive. And this one," Rita says, turning on Lily. "She makes me nauseous whenever I look at her. I can barely eat when she's in the cafeteria." Lily struggles harder as Rita approaches. Penny is entranced, her eyes half-lidded, lips parted in anticipation. Zoey sees her chance.

She moves.

She lashes out with a hard kick to the back of Rita's left leg. It folds, and the other woman goes down with a short cry. Rita tries to lift her stocky bulk up, but Zoey gets a handful of her hair and yanks her onto her back. The satisfaction at seeing Rita's head bounce off the concrete is short-lived as Penny's hand chops Zoey hard in the side of the throat.

Zoey goes down as if her legs have been cut from her. She doesn't register the impact. Pain, unlike any she's experienced so far in life, grows exponentially from the point of the blow down her shoulder and up the side of her face. Her throat is going to explode. She knows this and accepts the fact. Through her bleared vision she sees Rita rise and, in one motion, throw a kick at her midsection.

The toe of Rita's shoe is surprisingly hard, and for a moment Zoey thinks it's pierced her stomach. When the bigger woman retracts her foot, there will be blood and entrails extending from it in a gory line. She coughs out the last of her air, and the world wavers in shimmers of darkness.

"Now maybe they won't want you, bitch," Rita breathes. "Maybe I busted your fucking ovaries and you're as useless as I know you are." She spits, and the saliva speckles Zoey's face.

"Hey!" The shout comes from far away, or at least to Zoey it seems so. She knows the voice, and it triggers a burst of adrenaline that wipes away the shadows that are clouding her vision.

Simon is running toward them with Lily's Cleric directly behind him. Sherell has released Lily and stands several yards from her, hands in her pockets. Penny stands dead-eyed off to the side. A stricken look crosses Rita's face, and she starts to straighten before she's jerked away by Simon's strong hands. He flings her toward the wall of the main building, and his eyes are ablaze. He is no longer a Cleric, but the soldier he used to be.

Rita stumbles but manages to keep her feet. She turns, the panicked look gone from her face and replaced with indignity.

"You can't touch me!" she yells at him. Her cry brings Simon out of his fugue, and he stops stalking toward her. He stands, staring at her for a long moment, Lily's soft sobs the only other sound above the wind.

"You're going in the box," Simon says, so low it's hard to hear. He turns away from Rita as more Clerics round the next corner of the building. He comes to Zoey and kneels, reaching out to grasp her hand. "Are you okay?"

"Yeah, I'm fine," she manages, but tastes blood. Must've bit her tongue.

"Can you stand?"

"If you help me."

Simon raises her to her feet, letting her lean against his arm.

"Maybe you want to reconsider sending her to the box," Lily's Cleric says. "Zoey was the closest to Rita, so that means she'll go in as well."

"Zoey was being attacked," Simon says in a voice coated in ice. "*She* was the closest." He points at Penny, who merely stares back at him.

"I don't . . ." Steven begins again, but Zoey steps away from Simon, her anger boiling over.

"Why don't you help your ward, Cleric?" she says. Her stomach is on fire, the pain trying to double her over, but she won't let it. Steven scowls but slowly turns and begins to speak to Lily in a quiet voice. She continues to rock back and forth, her hands rubbing endlessly at one another.

The promenade is alive with movement, men streaming out of the building, all of them talking at once. The sniper is trained on their position now. The scope on his rifle flashes in the sun as he pans it over them all.

"Come on, let's go," Simon says, and leads her away from the throng. As they walk, Rita catches Zoey's eye. She bares her teeth and shakes her head. Zoey looks away and focuses on walking, one foot after the other on the concrete.

◆　◆　◆

The infirmary smells of disinfectant and vanilla linens. Zoey lies in a bed within one of the sectioned rooms that occupy an end of the medical area. Outside the open entrance there is another doorway as well as a hanging curtain around a large operating space. The tiled floor reflects cool light. Simon sits rigidly in a chair by the door. He stares at the wall beside her bed, not making a sound. A balding doctor with a long, clean-shaven face returns to the room and gives them both a quick smile.

"X-rays and MRI look normal," he says, pulling on a pair of latex gloves. "There seems to be only bruising to the abdomen and swelling around the zygomatic bone as well as the sternocleidomastoid muscle in the neck." He opens a slender packet and oozes a clear ointment onto one finger. "Here, this should ease the swelling and pain a bit." He dabs the gel onto Zoey's cheek and neck where Penny struck her. The effect is instantaneous. The throbbing pain recedes like dust before water. She can't help but sigh with relief.

"Can I put that on my stomach too?" she asks when the doctor steps back.

"No. It won't do a lot for a larger injury like that. I'll give you a painkiller before you leave." He looks coldly at her as if she is something inanimate before turning to Simon. "She's free to go."

"Thank you," Simon says. The doctor leaves and Simon rises, moving toward the door. "You can change. I'll get the pill for you."

He is nearly out the door when she speaks. "Simon?" He pauses. "Thank you."

"There's nothing to thank me for, Zoey." He hesitates. "I failed you today." She begins to tell him he's wrong, that the Clerics haven't accompanied the women around the track for many years now, but he's already gone, the door closing solidly behind him.

She stands and strips off the thin cotton gown she changed into for the examination and dons her clothes. The knees of her pants are dotted with crimson from the abrasions that still sting as she flexes her legs. She catches sight of herself in the long mirror beside the door. A skinny woman a year out of her teens with dark, unruly hair that's come loose from its binding. Her image, the weakness she exudes, sparks the anger within her once again, and she wants to smash the mirror into a thousand pieces. *But that would only make more reflections of me*, she thinks. She sighs and leaves the room, not looking at the mirror again.

After Zoey takes her pain pill under the scrutiny of the doctor, they leave the infirmary, but not before she sees the massive steel doors hiding the elevator at its far end. It's hard to believe that Terra disappeared through them only today. Zoey tries to imagine what is happening to her, but her thoughts are lost in the tumult between what she's been told and what she feels is true. The guard beside the doors studies her and Simon before returning his gaze straight ahead.

They walk down the hallway side by side but when they reach the stairs, Simon turns right instead of left. Zoey stops.

"Where are you going?" she asks.

"Not me. We. We're going to the boxes."

She shakes her head. "I don't want to go. I don't need to see."

"It's not optional, Zoey. We have to."

"Please, I just want to go to my room."

"Zoey." There's steel in his voice that holds no compromise. She stands at the head of the stairs for a moment before following him in the opposite direction.

They pass the assembly and turn down another, narrower corridor before stopping outside a windowless door. Simon scans his bracelet, and they pass through.

The room they enter is low-ceilinged and wide. It holds a sense of constriction, an air of suffocation that may partially have to do with the two separate facades that intrude on its far side.

The protrusions extend into the room several feet and line the entire length of the wall. It is like another room has been shoved into the current one but stopped short before its full bulk could be revealed. Two black doors are positioned on either end of the boxes.

The other women are already there, waiting in a half-circle of chairs, their Clerics standing behind them. Assistant Carter waits before the two boxes, his hands held behind his back. He nods to them as they enter, and Zoey takes her seat beside Lily. There is a long silence that draws out painfully before Carter finally steps forward and speaks.

"I'm disappointed in you," he says, looking down at his shoes. "There is order and disorder. Order breeds compliance, compliance begets tolerance, and tolerance brings peace." He flicks his ferret-like gaze across them all. "Disorder is unacceptable. The greater good depends upon all of you, and you quibble and fight like children!" His nasally voice tightens as it rises, and Zoey has to resist clamping her hands over her ears. "You should be ashamed," Carter says, spinning away from them, his tie swinging. Lily begins to rock in her seat, and Zoey places a hand gently on her arm. "Punishment is, at times, the only language that is understood, the only . . ." He pauses, a smile curling then fleeing from his face. ". . . voice that is heard. Clerics?"

Rita's and Penny's Clerics move around the row of chairs as the two women rise. Rita walks with sullen steps toward the right door, while Penny strides to the left. They turn when they reach the wall and stand looking out back at the group. Assistant Carter takes center stage between them.

"Rita and Penny, you are sentenced to twenty-four hours in containment. No food or water shall be given during this time. You shall not speak to anyone nor have any contact with the outside. Remember, and do not fall outside the rules again."

Carter nods to the Clerics, who each scan their bracelets. Zoey looks at Rita, their eyes meeting, and sees her lips are moving soundlessly, repeating words over and over.

You're dead, you're dead, you're dead you'redeadyou'redeadyou'redead.

The doors pop open as if pressurized. Inside, there seems to be nothing.

It's not simply dark within the boxes—the light from the room doesn't *penetrate* the blackness. The void is like something alive, churning just out of sight past the threshold. Rita doesn't move, struck by the sight as the rest of them are. Penny only hesitates a moment before stepping inside, disappearing as if she's been swallowed.

"Rita," Carter says. She looks at him, and there is hatred etched in her face, but also fear. She shoots one last look at Zoey before walking out of sight.

The doors clank shut, latches clacking louder than any Zoey's ever heard before.

"Take the punishment of others and use it to keep yourselves on the path," Carter says. "The greater good is more important than any one life."

They repeat his last words in unison, knowing it's expected. Then they are dismissed with a wave of Carter's pale hand.

The dinner chime rings as they move down the hallways, and Meeka shoots Zoey a look. Zoey shakes her head before hanging back behind the rest of the group.

"I don't want to go to dinner, Simon," she says.

"Zoey, you barely had anything today. You need to eat."

"I'm not hungry." She doesn't look at him, her eyes fastened on the tips of her shoes.

"Zoey, look at me." She does. "It is not your fault that Rita and Penny are being punished. You didn't do anything wrong. I'm the one that sent them there."

"It doesn't matter. They blame me."

"That's ridiculous. What they did was inexcusable; they could've truly hurt you. They could've—"

"Could've damaged me, you mean," Zoey says. "Could've made me sterile."

"That's not what I was going to say."

"You didn't have to."

A long, uncomfortable silence drifts between them. "They'll think twice before ever attacking you again," Simon finally says.

"Or they'll make sure they don't get caught next time."

"I'll protect you."

"You can't protect me from everything."

He opens his mouth to reply but stops. She follows his gaze over her shoulder and sees the digital calendar set in the wall.

"Take me to my room," she says after a moment. She leads the way and hears him follow a second later.

◆　◆　◆

Zoey watches the afternoon pass into evening and then into night. The sun slides on its track below the rim of the walls, fading to a glow before it winks out completely. The exterior lights come on, flashing to life one at a time to bathe the promenade in their radiance. But it's the walls they want seen, even at night. Always the reminder of where they are.

She takes out the window and chews a piece of gum to quell the hunger that's built upon itself over the last hours. She should've eaten something. Simon was right. Again. She chews until the flavor is completely gone before swallowing the stringy lump that is slowly dissolving on her tongue. She applies the last of the ointment to her bruised neck and face before lying back on her bed with the copy of *Monte Cristo*, reading in the dim light cast by the bulb built into the wall beside the headboard. The book seems to breathe the word that's been floating through her mind for years now. At first it was insubstantial and fluttering, like the wings of a moth disappearing into the night. But now it is a pounding insistence that won't disperse no matter what she tries to focus on.

Escape.

She comes awake to a sound, only then realizing that she had fallen asleep. The book is splayed on her chest, open to the page she stopped reading on. The light still glows beside her, the calendar minutes away from a new day.

Someone is standing at the foot of her bed.

4

Zoey inhales, a shriek building in her lungs, but the person steps forward, letting the light wash over his smiling features.

"Lee," she hisses.

"Hey."

"Don't hey me, you ass," she says, flinging her pillow at him before standing up. He catches it, flinching in a mockingly hurt way.

"You think I'd get a warmer welcome being in here for what, the fifth time ever?"

"I knew you were going to try to get in, I just thought I'd hear you." She eyes him. "How do you get in? Do you pick the lock?" The brightness of Lee's smile is only rivaled by his intelligence. Already he's found solutions for several issues regarding the ARC's mechanical maintenance that had baffled some of the best workers. It's rumored he'll be the head of the department before he's twenty-two.

He shakes his head, coming closer. His true grin is back, and she can see he's pleased with himself. "Told you before, I gotta keep some secrets from you." Lee stops inches away and gazes at her. His hand runs down her arm, leaving a trail of tingling warmth in its wake, before he grasps her fingers gently. The urge to lean fully into him, to press herself against him, is powerful, though the thought both thrills and frightens her in equal measure. Lee seems to sense what she's thinking and tips his head down toward her. His eyes flit to the book she holds in her free hand, and she glances at it before returning his gaze. "Where did you get that?"

"I . . ." *I found it. Someone must have dropped it.* "I don't know," she says. "It was left for me."

Lee steps back. "Left for you? By who?"

"I don't know, it was just in my room one day."

"Zoey, you can't have that, it's too dangerous."

"Why?"

"Because that's contraband. And whoever left it is probably trying to set you up, get you punished."

"My room's been inspected and they've never found it. Besides, you're telling me you haven't seen a book before outside of the NOA texts?"

He falters. "Well, no. But . . ."

"So you're saying you've seen them but never read any?"

His jaw works. "No, I've read a few, but—"

"So they're available to the men?"

"Yes, there's quite a few in a room attached to the guards' dorms."

"But *I'm* not supposed to have one, is that it?"

"I'm just worried that you'll get caught, that's all."

"Don't worry about me," she says. She sets the book on the covers. "I can take care of myself." She strides to the window and looks out at the wall. Lee sidles past her bed, careful to keep out of the sniper's view.

"Zoey, I'm sorry. You know they're not my rules. If I could choose, you'd have as many books as you want. You wouldn't be locked up in here, either. But I'm not in charge, not yet anyway." She watches his reflection in the window. He's fidgeting with something in his pocket. "I talked to Dad again about what will happen after your induction."

She lets the quiet of the room build for a moment. "What did he say?"

"He said it will be up to the Director whether or not we can go with you and your parents to the safe zone."

"That's never happened before, Lee, and you know it. Grace and Halie's Clerics are reassigned now, and so are their sons. What makes you think you and Simon will be any different?"

"There's no reason not to let us go. I'm working on getting a private audience with the Director. If I can, I'll make him understand."

She turns to face him. "He won't listen, Lee. Don't you get it? The system doesn't make allowances. Not for you, or your father, or for me. We're just pieces in a game."

"Listen—"

"What's your last name?"

Exasperation has finally stripped him of his cheerfulness. "You know what it is."

"Say it."

"Asher."

"And what's mine?"

He blinks, then sighs. "I don't know."

"I don't either. No woman here does. What purpose does that serve, Lee? What could possibly be gained by keeping our heritage from us?"

"I don't know."

"It's control. It's just another wall built to keep us in place." She glances away from him. He seems to struggle with something and looks down at the floor.

"I always told you I'd give you my last name."

She studies him and then slowly moves to stand before him. She puts a hand to his cheek, and he looks into her eyes. "I know you would. But I need my own. Do you understand?"

He nods. "It scares me a little when you talk like this. You sound like you're going to do something rash."

She is on the edge, the cliff beneath her feet once again. What to say? How much to tell him?

"If we were able to leave, would you come with me?" she asks, her foot hovering over the drop.

"What? What do you mean, leave?"

She looks around, knowing they are alone but unable to help herself. "I mean, escape."

It's like she's hit him with something. He steps back from her, and her hand that had fallen to his shoulder drops to her side.

"Zoey, think about what you're saying. The wrong person hears you even breathe that word, and you're in the box."

"I know, but there's something wrong. There's always been something wrong. This place isn't what they tell us, what they've pounded into our heads for years."

"Look, I know you're shook up. I heard about what happened today, but you have to think about this logically."

"I am. This has nothing to do with Rita." She stops herself. "You know, maybe it has a lot to do with Rita. You know why she's so angry? Because she's the only one of us who's ever seen her parents' faces. She came here when she was five, but that's enough time to remember. I can't forget how much she cried. Do you remember?"

He nods. He seems to have run out of words.

"That anger she has for everyone and everything, it's not a coincidence. She was taken, Lee, just like we all were. This isn't right."

"It's for the greater good."

"You don't even know what that means."

"I know Reaper and his men go out, week after week, hunting for another infant girl, and they never find one. I know my father has dedicated his life to protecting you, and soon he's going to have to let you go. He would never turn you over to any kind of danger."

"He has no idea what waits behind those steel doors in the infirmary." Their voices are barely above whispers, but the vehemence in them could cut flesh.

"And neither do you. There's no reason not to believe the Director and Miss Gwen. No one has ever hurt you besides Rita and the other two."

"See, that's where you're wrong," Zoey says, moving to her bed. She picks up the copy of *The Count of Monte Cristo*. "Maybe you should read this. Then you'll have an idea how much they've hurt me. Hurt all of us."

He doesn't take the book from her outstretched hand, instead glancing at the glowing calendar. Immediately he turns away, then shuffles to the door and pulls it open. He snatches something from the lock and pockets it. She expects him to say something more, some final retort, but there's nothing. He simply steps into the dim hallway, lets the door click shut behind him, and is gone.

◆ ◆ ◆

She watches the curved horizon of wall until the sky begins to pale in the east. The urge to cry comes and goes, as does the fury. There is something worse about being reprimanded by Lee. It's not only because he has been her closest friend for all the years she can remember. It's something else she can't put fully into words. He's told her before that he would give her his name, but never explained exactly what he means. As thrilling as the idea is to have something so precious, the odd independence she feels holds her back and drives her forward at the same time.

There is the swift flutter of feathers outside the window and her heart leaps in her chest. *Zipper?* She steps to the window, eyes searching the air outside her room. A small, dark shape swoops past the glass, and her hope flattens. It is a bird, but some species she can't identify, its outline too compact to be the owl. It glides over the top of the wall and disappears from sight.

"How does it feel to fly away?" she says, watching for the bird's shape to reappear. When it doesn't, she nods once to herself. "I thought so."

She dozes for several hours and wakes, groggy and sullen with sleep, to a sharp rap on her door.

"Zoey? Are you awake?" It's Simon.

"Yes. I need a few minutes."

A long pause. "Take your time."

She showers, dressing in clean clothes and making her bed afterward. She takes the cloth sack filled with that week's laundry with her when she leaves, stopping to deposit it down the third-level chute, knowing she will most likely be washing it herself later that day.

Simon says nothing other than "good morning" to her on the way to breakfast, and they encounter no one in the halls since they're running late.

The cafeteria is quiet as Zoey collects her plate and sits in her customary place beside Lily. Meeka nods from across the table, her mouth overly full of food. Zoey glances to her left, seeing Sherell seated by herself. The woman's ebony skin glows beneath the lights, almost as if she's lit from within. She looks up from her plate and catches Zoey staring. There is a hint of something in her gaze before Zoey looks away, but she can't determine if it is anger or simply a vague interest.

"How are you feeling?" Meeka murmurs, swallowing an enormous mouthful of cereal.

Zoey shrugs. "Sore. Tired. Other than that, fine."

"Total bitches," Meeka says, even lower. "I was late getting out from my shift. If I would've been there—"

"If you would've been there, we both would've taken a trip to the infirmary." It's their custom to rib one another, but she doesn't fully believe her words. She's never seen anyone with reflexes as fast as Meeka's. Perhaps if she had been there, they wouldn't have gone to the infirmary. Instead it might be them in the boxes right now.

Meeka seems to read her thoughts. She waves a spoon in Zoey's direction. "Whatever. It's probably better this way. Those two needed to be taken down a notch, along with someone else I know." She says the last words louder, turning her head to stare at Sherell. The other woman glances her way and smiles poisonously. Meeka raises her eyebrows and pulls a face. Zoey laughs a little under her breath, causing pain to slide across her stomach.

"Stop, you're only going to make things worse for me," Zoey says.

"Why do you say that?"

"Do you really think Rita and Penny are just going to apologize and leave it at that? The next chance they get, they're going to attack me again."

Meeka waves a dismissive hand. "They won't have the chance. Simon won't let you out of his sight now. He'll send them to the box for a week if they try it again."

"He doesn't have the power to do that," Zoey says, trying to eat her food.

"What do you mean? He just did it yesterday."

"I know he sent them there, but Assistant Carter is the one that decides the length of punishment. Lee told me," she adds.

"I didn't know that," Meeka says after a time. "Why have you never told me that?"

"No one has gone to the box since Halie and Grace. It didn't seem very important."

Meeka stirs the remainder of her food around before dropping her spoon. "He creeps me out almost as much as Dellert."

"Who? Carter?" Zoey asks.

Meeka nods. "It's like he's not really a person, just something wearing human skin as a disguise."

The image gives Zoey pause. She imagines Carter unzipping a hidden seam in his flesh to reveal a hideous sublayer of scales and glistening skin. She shivers.

The chime comes from the speakers and they rise, filing through to deposit their trays. Zoey follows Meeka through the hallways to the lecture hall. Miss Gwen is there, waiting beside her desk. Her eyes glide over them as they take their seats, her face tight, hands clamped together. When they've settled she steps forward, head tilted to the side.

"Good morning."

"Good morning, Miss Gwen."

"I'm sorry to see so few of you here today. Punishment is an ugly, but necessary, aspect of our lives. If the balance of the world were not so precarious, there might only be warnings for such transgressions. But alas, it is."

The speech sounds scripted. Zoey wonders who gave her the orders to write it.

"To renew humanity; what a purpose," Miss Gwen says, looking at each of them, a glaze of awe on her face. "To give birth to a new generation and drive away the shadows of extinction—what better cause do we have? We must coexist and work together for the greater good. Our differences must be put aside, our conflicts cast away." She stares solely at Zoey as she says this. "There is no one person more important than the fate of our species. We would all do well to remember that." Zoey holds her gaze until the instructor finally gives her a cold smile and turns away, saying over her shoulder, "Rise and recite the creed."

The women do as they are told. "We are of the greater good. We live for the chance to rebuild the world that is no longer. We are one in our knowledge and stand steady before the challenges that face us. We give thanks for our shelter and for the guidance of the Director. We will not stray from the path."

Zoey can barely finish the words with the dry, sour taste in her mouth. They continue to stand and chant the rules together and when they are done, Miss Gwen nods approvingly.

"Take out your texts and turn to page three hundred forty-four, please."

Zoey knows what part of the book this is before she even opens the cover. She finds the correct page and stares at the chapter title. The Fall.

"Zoey, will you read please?" Miss Gwen says.

Lily claps her hands and laughs. "Ya Zee, ree!"

"Quiet, Lily!" Miss Gwen nearly yells. Zoey jumps in her seat, shocked at the volume of the instructor's voice. Lily's smile vanishes and she cowers, flapping her fingers before her eyes. Zoey grits her teeth until they feel as if they'll shatter. Blood pounds in her ears. Her hands shake.

"Zoey? You may begin," Miss Gwen intones.

Zoey takes a breath and starts to read.

"In late two thousand eighteen, the patches of rebel factions that had skirmished with U.S. forces several times over the year unified and declared open war on the United States Government. Due to mass panic and the spread of propaganda concerning NOA's research, the factions grew until they numbered in the hundreds of thousands. Despite their advanced weaponry, the government forces that were deployed to help keep order were outnumbered three to one. They took heavy casualties as many of the battles were fought in urban settings that played to the rebels' advantage. At first President Andrews ordered only nonlethal measures be used, but when an entire battalion of Marines was overrun in the suburbs of Chicago, he had no choice but to employ air strikes as well as live rounds in all weapons.

"The war raged on for three years. Society as a whole was disrupted, and soon the entirety of the country fell into chaos. Schools were closed, as were most businesses. Families attempted to leave the war-torn country, and many refugees were executed by neighboring governments when they tried to cross borders of Canada and Mexico (see chapter forty-three, index nine for more information).

"In early two thousand twenty-one, the virus known as $TiF3$, which caused 'The Dearth,' became lethal to humans. It spread quickly and killed millions within several months. At this time, President Andrews and his cabinet, headed by Speaker of the House Steven Richton, were stationed in a remote, secure location outside Washington, D.C. It is estimated that only six members of the House of Representatives and two members of the Senate were present with him behind the most well-defended lines of government forces, the rest of the members of those governing bodies having either deserted or disappeared over the years of tumult.

"On the evening of April twelfth, two thousand twenty-one, an atomic device was detonated by rebel forces within the boundaries of the President's location. Though the bomb was believed to be of rudimentary construction and one-third the strength of those dropped on Hiroshima and Nagasaki during the Second World War, its blast killed over eight thousand government troops along with three hundred women and children being harbored there from rebel forces. The President and the Speaker of the House were killed in the blast, as well as General Franklin Harris, the supreme commander of the armed forces.

"This assassination succeeded in ending the war and caused mass desertion by the remaining U.S. military. It has been called 'the most cowardly act by American citizens since the murder of John F. Kennedy' by Dr. Howard Messing, the original leading scientist for the National Obstetric Alliance. Dr. Messing was later killed in a skirmish outside Denver when his caravan was ambushed by rebels."

Zoey stops reading at the end of the last paragraph and looks up at Miss Gwen, who is nodding.

"Thank you, Zoey." Miss Gwen stands, holding her hands out before her as if in supplication. "Do you see now what happens when individuals either can't see or plainly ignore the larger picture? Our great nation was toppled by a few people—no, that's not right—a few *cowards*, who decided the leader of the country should no longer live." Her face grows grave. "President Andrews helped initiate NOA's work in researching why the virus affected the female birthrate, and subsequently why it became deadly years later. He was a great man and died serving his country. We are beyond fortunate to have the life we do now within the safety of these walls. We are fortunate to have protection, and food, and the guidance of the Director—whose vision for the future, in my opinion, rivals the President's own."

Miss Gwen's cheeks are aglow with the fervor of her speech. She looks beseechingly at them and Zoey can only stare back. Something is rising within her mind, tugging at the weavings of an idea that is still indefinite. Someone speaks, and Meeka coughs loudly, bringing her back to the present. Meeka motions with her eyes to the front of the room where Miss Gwen waits.

"I'm sorry, Miss Gwen. What was the question?" Zoey says.

The instructor huffs impatiently. "Zoey, you will sit facing the corner of the room if you cannot hold attention in lecture from now on. Is that clear?"

"Yes, ma'am."

"Good. I asked, what does it mean to you to know that others sacrificed themselves for the greater good, and in turn, your life?"

Zoey hesitates only a moment. "Everything, ma'am. Everything."

◆　◆　◆

Lecture ends, and they return to the cafeteria for lunch. Meeka tries to engage her in conversation, mocking Miss Gwen, but Zoey is lost in thought. The sounds fade around her, the smells, even the walls become hazy and insubstantial. She eats robotically, shoving the food in even as her stomach revolts. She feeds Lily her lunch, which is soup today, a difficult thing for the girl to eat.

When the chime rings, they leave for their afternoon work stations. Zoey walks beside Lily, holding her hand as they move down the stairways to the lowest level. As they turn on the last landing and head down the final set of treads, she sees Crispin striding through the security door. He spots them and waits to let them pass, his smile shining bright against his dark skin.

"Well, hello, how are we today?" he says. Lily waves and laughs, jerking on the third step from the bottom. Her sudden movement throws Zoey's balance off. She tries to catch herself but the battered muscles in her abdomen shriek their protest and she misses the handrail by inches.

Zoey falls, letting go of Lily as she does.

Simon yells something.

She's going to break her neck.

As the hard edges of the stairs come up to meet her, Crispin steps forward. His hands snag her wrists and pull her up just as she's about to slam into the concrete.

"Whoa! You all right?" he says, standing her back on her feet. Her stomach throbs with exertion.

"Yes," she manages. "Sorry, I tripped."

"Looks like you kept little Lily here from falling," Crispin says. "And no need to be sorry. Accidents happen, am I right?"

"Yes." She smiles at him. He is the only guard in the ARC who acknowledges her presence outside of giving orders. Besides Dellert, that is. But the younger guard's body language and unsaid words in his looks are something predatory, so unlike Crispin's.

"Thank you, Crispin," Simon says, putting a hand on Zoey's arm. "Glad you were there at the right time."

"Me too, me too. You all have a nice afternoon, okay?"

"We will," Simon says.

"Thank you," Zoey calls after him as he climbs the stairs. He nods, shooting her a last smile that breaks apart before he looks away. There is something sorrowful in Crispin that she catches glimpses of from time to time, like a cloud crossing the sun.

"Bye!" Lily yells and laughs at how her voice echoes in the stairwell.

"Come on," her Cleric says, guiding them toward the security door.

As they pass through into the next corridor, a worker wearing the customary yellow jumpsuit steps in from the outside. He moves quickly toward them, glancing at the exercise facility as he walks.

"You, Clerics, I need your help. There's a relay box inside mechanical I need assistance moving," he says. The worker stops several steps away and points at the closest door.

"That's not our assignment," Simon replies. "Find another worker."

"They're all over at the . . ." The worker's eyes find Zoey and Lily. ". . . outside. This needs to be done now, I don't have time to go up to level two and find someone."

Simon shares a glance with Steven before turning back to the worker. "Five minutes."

"That's all it will take," the worker says, unlocking the mechanical room door.

The sound emerges like a beast from within. Heavy pounding and a high, incessant squealing. They file inside the massive room, and Zoey is struck again by how large the area is.

Ahead of them are rounded encasements, reaching almost to the fifteen-foot ceilings that hum with electrical power, their shapes like slumbering animals in the low light. To the right is a wide corridor lined with pipes and branching electric cables. On the left is a row of benches and storage units. Racks of various tools and yellow jumpsuits hang among the shadows.

The worker hands out foam earplugs, and Zoey helps Lily put hers in after prying her hands from the sides of her head. There is a four-foot steel box resting on the floor, with looping wire and several large handles protruding from its side. The worker points to it before motioning to somewhere in the rear of the room. The three men nod at one another before Simon glances in Zoey's direction. He points to her and Lily before jabbing a finger at the floor. *Stay here, don't move.* Zoey gives him a quick bob of her head.

The men bend at the knees, grasping the box's handles before lifting. Simon is very strong, but Zoey sees his back quiver with exertion as he stands. The other Cleric's face turns a bright shade of red, and spittle appears between his lips as the three men begin walking, disappearing behind one of the encasements in a slow procession of shuffling steps.

As soon as they're out of sight, Zoey turns and examines the door. It is the same as any other in the building. The scanner near the handle glows red, and even though she knows it's futile, she swipes her bracelet across it.

The red eye remains unblinking in the gloom.

Lily takes a step forward, looking at the dusty floor. She wipes the toe of her shoe through the grime, making a narrow, sweeping line. Zoey can't hear it, but sees Lily laugh before kneeling to draw in the filth. As gently as she can, Zoey brings her to her feet. There's a confused look on the girl's face. Zoey shakes her head and as she tries to figure out how to convey that it's not okay to play in the dirt, she spots a flash of movement to their left.

Zoey turns and stares where she saw it. She waits, holding tight to Lily's arm as the girl stretches toward the floor. There it is again—a shifting of gray between two of the cabinets, barely enough to see it is some sort of fabric moving. Lily tugs again, but Zoey straightens her up and holds her face still, shaking her own head from side to side. Lily says something that's lost in the cacophony of the room. When Zoey looks at the spot between the cabinets again, she spies a flash of pale flesh, there and gone.

There is no sign of the men and Zoey strains to the right, assuring that they aren't returning before leading Lily away from the door. Her shoes want to slide on the detritus covering the floor. They pass the long line of worker jumpsuits on pegs, most of them with long tears or scorched holes dotting their lengths. Zoey imagines one of the empty sleeves snapping out to wrap around her arm and takes a step away from them.

They make their way past the workbenches and come even with the cabinets. Zoey leads Lily down the closest row, stopping at the small gap between two of the tallest units. Her heart hammers as she leans to the side and peers between the metal lockers with one eye.

Beyond the cabinets is a short, clear area followed by stacks of boxes and rolls of wire. A heavy rope is coiled below another long bench, and two pieces of humming machinery block a portion of her view. She stands on tiptoe, pulling herself close to the cabinet, her eyes widening in the shadows.

Miss Gwen sits on the end of the long bench, and Zoey sees that it was the hem of the instructor's skirt and the white flesh of her leg that she saw from the doorway. Her dress is drawn up high over her thighs, and a guard stands before her, his hips thrusting in constant motion. It takes a split second for Zoey to see that his pants are crumpled at his ankles. Miss Gwen is reclined on the bench, her fingers laced around the back of the guard's neck, her mouth open in a jaw-cracking yawn. Her eyes are clenched shut, and even with the lack of light, Zoey can see beads of sweat running down the instructor's throat into her neckline.

Zoey blinks as a sickening weight plummets from her throat to the bottom of her stomach. She knows what this is, but the immensity of it flat-lines her thoughts. Lily tugs at her arm, bringing her back from the unreal sight beyond the cabinets. When she pulls her face away from the small gap, she sees Lily gesturing toward the door.

Between two of the enclosures there is the flare of yellow.

Zoey drags Lily back the way they came, nearly tripping over a wrench at the end of the aisle. She half runs to the door, weaving past the ruined jumpsuits before skidding to a stop in front of the entrance. A heartbeat later, Simon rounds the corner and stops in front of her. His eyes narrow. Zoey gives him a quick smile. *We've been here the whole time, don't worry about us!* The worker sidles past Simon's shoulder and moves to the door, scanning his bracelet. They file out into the hallway, removing their earplugs. Zoey takes Lily's earplugs out for her.

The air is blessedly cool compared to the mechanical room, and the slight scorched smell recedes as the door falls shut behind them.

"Thank you," the worker says, moving toward the outside door. "I appreciate the help."

"You're welcome," Simon replies. He holds out his hand to Zoey, and she drops the four earplugs into his palm. He studies her face, running his eyes over her as if he can see the image of Miss Gwen and the guard that's playing on a loop within her mind. "Let's get to work," he says after a long pause.

After checking to be sure the laundry is empty, Simon leaves them to their shift. They load the washing machine and set it in motion. The rhythmic chugging only aids in bringing Zoey back to the mechanical room.

Procreation. That's what they'd been doing. There were other words for it in the NOA textbook, but procreation is as close as the tome had ever gotten to describing it in terms of humans. Animals mated, or reproduced, and humans procreated. It had always seemed like such a cold and mechanized term for speaking of new life. And what Miss Gwen and the guard had been doing didn't seem cold or robotic whatsoever. The instructor had not only allowed the act, but she had seemed to be enjoying it.

The problem was, it was forbidden.

No one had ever said so much aloud, but it was abundantly clear. Males and females were not to spend time together alone. That was why Lee's appearance inside her room startled her so much. It was an offense punishable by death. But until that point, she had never considered Miss Gwen among the restricted. Besides being the only other woman outside of the younger group, she was a creature of authority, almost more so than some of the guards. Zoey had never wondered if the woman was also governed by the same set of rules they all were.

◆　◆　◆

It was Miss Gwen who had explained roughly what was happening years ago when, inexplicably and in silent horror, Zoey had begun to bleed during a morning shower. She had been almost too embarrassed to tell Simon, but the fear had finally won out and she had whispered it to him after padding her underwear with folded toilet paper. He had nodded, quickly leading her to Miss Gwen's quarters and then standing outside the door while the instructor spoke to Zoey. The entire conversation had been confusing and surreal. Inside her was life waiting to be born? Eggs? The possibility of rebuilding the human race if only she could give birth to a girl.

It was almost too much to comprehend.

And though Miss Gwen had been fairly patient with Zoey's questions, while still cagey when Zoey asked about certain things, there had been an air of coldness and detachment, possibly even resentment, in the instructor's eyes. Zoey had left the room with a handful of cylindrical objects, a vague understanding of what she was supposed to do with them, and a new monthly scheduled checkup at the infirmary. Afterward she had felt adrift and more alone than ever before. The sensation that she had done something wrong followed her like an awful miasma for weeks until Meeka revealed that the same thing had happened to her.

♦　♦　♦

Now, after seeing Miss Gwen and the guard, a clearer picture is forming about her unanswered questions.

The buzzer goes off, signaling that the load is done, and Zoey and Lily rise from the floor to switch the laundry. As Zoey sets the time for the dryer, a realization hits her so hard she nearly staggers.

There are no cameras in that part of the mechanical room.

Miss Gwen and the guard wouldn't have chosen an area that was easily observed, either by the naked eye or any of the artificial ones that hang from the ceiling.

Now Zoey knows of two blind spots in the ARC.

5

The day is chilly when they step outside for exercise, the air misted with fog.

Zoey and Lily begin their walk around the main building. Simon and Lily's Cleric follow a short distance behind. Sherell paces ahead of them, head down, not looking back. Zoey hopes she feels alone and vulnerable, maybe even a little frightened without the bolstering of her two friends. She wants to tell the other woman that no matter what she's feeling, it's nothing compared to the fear that Sherell instilled in Lily the day before.

As they walk, her thoughts drift to Rita and Penny for the innumerable time that day. *What are they going through right now? What will they look like when they come out?* Halie and Grace had been unresponsive and cagey in the days following their release from the boxes. Halie had only been able to tell them it was dark and would say nothing further, the brightness of her eyes dimmed to almost nothing by whatever she had seen.

Meeka joins them after a time but says nothing. The roar of the wind above them is louder than the day before, thicker somehow. Meeka seems to sense it too as she continues to glance up at the walls every few minutes.

They make several loops around the long promenade before the chime tones. When they approach the security entrance and wait for the Clerics to let them in, Zoey notices Simon staring at her. She tilts her head.

"What?" she asks him.

"How did your clothes get so dirty?" he says, pointing at her. A strand of dread laces her insides as she looks down.

There are long swatches of dirt and dust coating the front of her pants and the bottom of her shirt from where she leaned up against the cabinets in the mechanical room.

"Uh, must've brushed up against something in the mechanical room," she says. Simon frowns.

"You brushed up against something while standing still near the door?"

Her mind stutters. "Lily tried to get something on the closest bench and I had to stop her. I must've leaned against it." Simon's frown eases some and he nods slowly.

"Well, you better change before dinner."

"Definitely," she adds, her voice attempting to die in her throat.

"I not, Zee," Lily says, shaking her head. "I not duree."

"No, you're not dirty, I am," Zoey says, taking the girl by the hand. She bustles Lily away through the door when Simon holds it open for them, avoiding his gaze.

When the door to her room shuts behind her, she lets a sigh of relief escape. She looks down at the traitorous dirt gracing the front of her clothes and swats at it, knocking a plume of dust into the air. Her mouth is sour.

She moves to the bathroom, scooping water in her hand and drinking, but the alkaline taste won't go away. *You're tasting your lies*, she thinks. *You blamed Lily for something she didn't do. You're getting closer.*

How much is a life worth?

She shudders. The taste in her mouth is so sickening that she fears she will vomit. She breathes through her nose, holding herself steady on the edge of the sink. Slowly she straightens and moves to the window, carrying the chair with her.

She takes only a half-piece of gum from the wrapper, carefully placing the other half back. She chews, letting the mint flood away the taste in her mouth. When all hints of the sourness are gone, she swallows the gum and changes into fresh clothes before knocking on the door for Simon to let her out.

"Better?" he asks as they walk toward the cafeteria.

"Yes."

"Good." He says nothing for several paces, their footsteps echoing down the hall. Finally he glances sideways at her. "You're different lately, Zoey."

The same lace of dread weaves through her stomach. "Different?"

"You seem worried."

"I'm fine."

"Is it the induction?"

"No. I'm . . . I'm looking forward to it." She sees him glance at her again but can't meet his gaze.

They near the entrance to the cafeteria but he slows and stops outside the door. "Zoey, I—"

But his words are cut off as the doors open and Rita steps out.

There is a fog of predetermined violence in the air, surrounding them in its own atmosphere. The look in Rita's eyes says it all: *You will pay. You will hurt like I have.* Because she is smaller. She's lost weight in the day spent inside the box. Her face contains the same hollow, burned-out look that Halie's had after her punishment.

Zoey readies herself for a fight even though Simon is only a step away and Rita's Cleric is a shadow behind her. There will be no restraining Rita's rage.

Rita steps forward, but instead of throwing a punch, she bows her head.

"Zoey, I'm glad I saw you. I want to apologize for my unforgivable behavior yesterday. I don't know what came over me."

Zoey squints, sure she's heard the other woman wrong. "What?"

"I'm sorry for my actions and can only hope you'll be able to forgive me."

Rita takes another step and envelops Zoey in a gentle embrace.

It's like being hugged by a predator. Any moment she expects her throat to be torn out or her eyes gouged. Instead, Rita holds her lightly, but close. Her lips brush Zoey's ear.

"I'm going to kill you. I'll find a way," she whispers, almost too quietly for Zoey to hear.

Then Rita draws back, holds her at arm's length. She gives her a smile that would be at home on a snake, and moves away. Zoey stares after her, but Rita doesn't look back. She notices a slight limp in Rita's gait before she turns a corner in the hall and is gone.

"Are you okay?" Simon asks.

"Yes."

"She wouldn't have been able—"

"I'm fine," Zoey says. "Let's go."

As they enter the cafeteria a new sense of unease grips her. Rita's whispered threat replays endlessly in her head. She glances around to see if Penny is there, but her seat is empty, and Sherell is nearly finished with her dinner. Where will it come from? How? When? Zoey gathers her meal and goes to sit with Lily and Meeka.

"Did you see her?" Meeka asks before she can settle onto her stool.

"Who?"

"For God's sake, Zoey, the woman that tried to beat the hell out of you yesterday! The one that spent a day in the box."

"Yeah, I saw her."

"And?"

"And she hugged me."

Meeka couldn't look more surprised. Her mouth works for a moment before she shakes her head. "Yuck!" She sticks her tongue out and makes a gagging noise. "I'd rather she try to beat me."

"Yeah. She had ulterior motives."

"Like what?"

"She said she's going to kill me."

"Well, that's more like her, I guess."

Zoey sighs and picks at some gravy studded with vegetables and a few unidentifiable hunks of stringy meat. "I knew it would only make things worse."

Meeka takes a large bite and chews loudly. "I wouldn't be so sure. She looked like shit when she was in here. She couldn't eat anything. She just stared at her plate."

"Have you seen Penny?"

"No. She never showed up. Crazy bitch probably liked her time in the box. I bet it was like a treat for her."

"Maybe."

"So where did you get dirty like that?" Meeka asks. The sly tone of her voice speaks volumes.

"Like I said, must've brushed up against something."

"Umm-hmm. Well, if you want to be a real friend and actually tell me, I'll be waiting."

"Meeka . . ."

The other woman shrugs, concentrating on a gelatinous pudding. Zoey ponders telling Meeka what she saw in the mechanical room, but Meeka is like one of those small, oblong rocks they sometimes take turns kicking on the promenade; there is no way of telling which way she will bounce.

"I'm just glad Rita didn't change. I'd really miss her beautiful smile," Meeka says without looking up.

Zoey chuffs laughter through a bite of stew and nearly chokes. A moment later Meeka joins in, and soon Lily is giggling as well, shifting her gaze from one woman to the other.

"Quiet down," Thomas says from the other end of the table. So they laugh to themselves in silent gales.

◆　◆　◆

She is at the doors in the infirmary. The steel doors that she's never seen open before. They are miles tall, their tops lost in mist like mountains she's seen pictures of in the NOA texts. Her feet are wet and there is blood on her hands. She looks down, peering curiously, without the feeling of pain. She is wearing a dress of white, the ceremonial gown, yet it is crimson just below her waist, a blooming flower of blood. Her hands are sticky with it, and she hears crying. It is the cry of a baby. Her heart aches with it, and she tries to turn to see where the sound is coming from, but her feet are frozen in place, immovable as if she's slipped into the concrete and is moored there.

A low rumbling overtakes the crying child's voice. It is something inhuman, so deep and alien it must be a machine. But it isn't. There is a feral quality to it that tells her it is alive, and hungry. Another flood of wetness coats her feet, and she stares down.

A clear, viscous fluid is leaking from between the doors. It pools upon her bare feet and begins to burn. Zoey tilts her head back to release the scream in her chest, but all sensation is washed away by what she sees.

The doors are opening, and there is something between them. Jagged things and a lolling red shape beyond them.

Teeth.

There are teeth between the doors, and the saliva, the saliva on her feet is burning, burningburningburningburning . . .

She comes awake in a flurry of movement, within and without. Her heart thunders, lungs heave, eyelids flicker, arms strain to push her upright. Her teeth are clenched, holding back a scream, and she gazes down at her feet, sure that they'll be nothing but burnt and bloody stubs of bone, eaten away by the acidic drool of the doors. No, it was a mouth—the doors to the elevator were a mouth. It was going to swallow her whole.

She knows she's going to be sick only moments before it happens. She tries to run to the bathroom, but her feet are tingly and asleep. She trips, crawls forward to vomit over the lip of the shower. Her tasteless dinner spews out of her in a choking stream that runs toward the drain. Zoey coughs, tasting bile—and blood. She's bitten the same place on her tongue as the day before.

After many prolonged minutes, the clenching in her gut subsides. She turns on the hot water, letting it wash away her partially digested dinner. When it's swirled away she splashes cold water on her face until the skin there grows numb. She wishes she could wash her mind, scour away the images and the sound, the sound of the baby crying.

As she hobbles back toward the bed, a noise begins to grow in the hall. She freezes, arm outstretched toward the waiting blankets. Booted feet are coming closer and closer outside. Shadows darken the small gap below the door, and there is the clack of her lock releasing.

Dellert's face is the first thing she sees in the gap, followed by two other guards along with the crimson flash of a Redeye's goggles. Behind them is Simon, his face gray and stony.

Dellert steps fully into her room, a perversion of a smile on his lips as he looks around before focusing on her.

"Hello, Zoey. Mind if we come in?"

6

The words don't come to her, the ones she wants to say.

She wants to tell him no. She wants to say get out, to scream it at him. This is her place, her only sanctuary, the last space she has that she can call her own. Until now.

"What's going on?" she asks, casting her glance from Dellert to Simon, who still waits in the hall. Dellert takes several steps closer, examining the wall while he speaks.

"We've gotten a report of contraband in this room," Dellert says. "We're searching it. Please stand aside."

"I don't have anything," Zoey says, beseeching Simon with a look. *Do something.* But he is stoic and solemn.

"We'll be the judge of that," Dellert says, moving around the foot of her bed. He takes a flashlight from his pocket and shines it in the corners of the room while the other two guards begin their own searches along the floor and ceiling. The Redeye stands at the door, the lower part of his face not obscured by his thick goggles lineless and without expression. He's staring at her through the red lenses. She can feel it.

Dellert snaps the light on in the bathroom and curses, stepping back. "The hell is that smell?"

"I got sick."

"And you couldn't get to the toilet?"

She doesn't answer, only lowers herself to the bed, no longer trusting the strength of her legs. Dellert huffs another curse and returns to the bathroom. The other guards crawl over the floor, scuttling along like insects, fingers probing every seam of concrete. One of them leans under the desk, sliding his hand beneath its top. The sink runs in the bathroom, shuts off. The shower spurts to life. Off. The toilet flushes. The tank lid scraping open is like needles in her ears. After a long pause, Dellert comes back into the room, walking slowly. He stops by the calendar and presses on its sides, trying to shift it on the wall. He sniffs when it doesn't move.

"So where is it, Zoey?" Dellert asks. He doesn't look at her.

"I told you, I don't have anything."

Dellert smiles but still keeps his gaze on the red numbers. "You're lying. You should tell me and make it easy on yourself."

"I can't tell you about anything I don't have."

Dellert places his hand on the prod hanging from his belt. It sways in its loop. "You guys find anything?" The two guards shake their heads. "You check her bed?"

"The bottom," one guard offers.

"Check the whole thing," Dellert says.

"Excuse me," the closest guard says, not meeting her eyes as he drags down the covers on her bed. Zoey stands and moves to the farthest corner of the room. The Redeye's goggles follow her. The guards strip her bed. They shake her blankets out, pull up the mattress, feel along the bottom and sides. Dellert watches them, his gaze flicking to her every few seconds, waiting for some kind of reaction. She gives him nothing.

When they're done, the guard that asked her to move begins to remake her bed.

"What are you doing?" Dellert asks.

"I'm putting it back."

"Are you a guard or a maid?" Dellert sneers. The other man opens his mouth, then shuts it and drops her blankets back to the floor. Dellert paces past her bed, stepping on the sheets, and touches the small light built into the wall. He tries turning it.

"Big day coming soon," Dellert says, running his hand along the wall when the light doesn't budge. His fingertips rasp in a way that sets her teeth on edge. "Always so exciting. And two inductions this close together." He shakes his head. "Just beautiful." He stops near the window and raps once on the glass. Zoey's entire body tenses but she keeps her face placid, unmoving, even as something flexes within her, threatening to break. "You must miss her already."

Zoey shifts from one foot to the other. Her soles are freezing on the cold concrete. "I miss all that have gone before me."

"So patriotic," Dellert says. "You say all the right things, Zoey." He steps away from the window, scanning the walls and ceilings again. He taps the calendar as he passes. "Tick, tick, tick, tick," he says in a low voice.

"Guards, are you satisfied with your inspection?" Simon says, finally stepping into the room.

Dellert focuses on him, cocking his head.

"Cleric, tell me, are you ushering us away from our investigation for a reason?"

"I'm simply saying that it's late and we're all tired. Besides, I already told you I've always made my own inspections on time and never found a thing. If your suspicions have been allayed, I would suggest letting Zoey return to bed, especially since she's not feeling well." He keeps his eyes locked on Dellert as he says this and a surge of affection rises within her.

"I would suggest you keep track of your tongue, or else I'll report your interference to Assistant Carter," Dellert says. He holds Simon's gaze, and to Simon's credit he stares back without faltering. Finally Dellert looks away, shooting a last glance around. His mustached lip curls and he signals to the other guards. "Let's go."

They begin to file from the room, the Redeye stepping out first followed by the other two guards. Simon stays inside the door and doesn't seem willing to leave until Dellert has left the room. Dellert moves past him and is almost through the door when the wind rises outside the window and a whistling comes from the far side of the room.

Zoey's heart falters, forgetting its purpose. She quits breathing, hoping against hope she was the only one who heard the sound.

Dellert pauses and turns back, head cocked once again. "What was that?"

"What?" Simon says, frowning.

"I heard something," Dellert says, crossing the space again. The two guards linger in the doorway but the Redeye moves past them, fingering the handgun on his belt. He corners Zoey, making her retreat with his encroachment. The wall meets her shoulder blades as she backs up.

"It was the wind," Zoey says, and to her horror there is a pleading note in her voice. Dellert seems to hear it and moves closer to the far corner, closer to the loosened glass panel.

"Sure was, but it sounded strange," Dellert says. He feels along the glass, his movements faster, excited. He shines his flashlight along the floor and then across the top frame of the window.

The beam stops on the cracked casing around the right panel, and holds.

Dellert freezes and slowly turns his head to look at her over his shoulder. "Oh Zoey, you clever girl."

Zoey begins to move, but the Redeye's hand grips her arm and he shoves her back against the wall. Simon gives her a small shake of his head without looking her way.

"Bring me the chair," Dellert says. One of the other guards carries her desk chair to him, and he stands on it. There is a hanging moment that stretches and hope keeps the delicate thing in her chest whole for a moment before the glass panel shifts. Dellert pulls the piece away, his smile beyond joy as he hands it to the guard beside him. He turns back to the opening that floods the room with cool air and reaches into the darkness outside the window.

When his hand reappears, it is grasping her books and the package of gum.

"Well, look what we have here. Contraband." Dellert shakes his head and steps down from the chair. As he approaches her, he begins tearing out single pages from *The Count of Monte Cristo*. They fall gracefully to the floor and the guard steps on several of them as he nears her. "So where did you get all this, Zoey?"

She says nothing, only stares back at him with all the hatred she can muster. She wishes Zipper would have been in the alcove and torn his smug face completely off.

Dellert shifts his gaze to Simon. "Cleric, do you know anything about this?"

"No," Simon says. "But it needs to be reported to the Director."

"I couldn't agree more." Dellert gives the guard at the door a quick nod, and the other man moves away down the corridor. "You're in very big trouble, Zoey. This is quite the malfeasance. You'll be going to the box for this." He strips open one of her last pieces of gum and pops it in his mouth. Outside the room she hears something that lowers the temperature of her blood between heartbeats.

Lily, babbling in a frightened way.

A moment later the guard reappears, holding the girl by the arm, Lily's eyes frantic and bloodshot from being woken.

"What are you doing with her?" Zoey asks.

"Why Zoey, she's going into the box too. Don't you know the rules?"

"No, please, she didn't do anything."

"You're right, she didn't. But you should've thought about that before filling up your little hiding spot with contraband," Dellert says.

"You can't," Zoey whispers. "She won't make it."

"I guess we'll see, won't we?"

He grins.

The rage flash-boils within her and emerges as a scream. Ripping her arm away from the Redeye, she takes one step and rakes both hands down Dellert's face, feeling his skin peel beneath her fingernails. Fingers wrap in her hair and she's yanked back off her feet, but not before she sees what she's done.

Dellert's cheeks hang in tatters. Red, vertical mouths gape open below his eyes and course blood onto the floor. The guard's gaze is manic, insane. His lips part and he bellows, flecks of blood spraying in all directions.

The room falls silent so fast it's as if the air has been vacuumed out.

Zoey slams down, the floor biting into her spine. Her vision sways. The Redeye is above her, leaning in, and suddenly he's gone. There's a tug at her hair, and one of Simon's hiking boots steps past her. Someone issues a grunt of pain, and then the other two guards are shouting.

Zoey rolls over, cowering beside her bed. Simon is facing away, one hand locked around the Redeye's throat. His opposite hand holds the soldier's wrist at a painful angle. Simon shakes, his muscles trembling beneath his shirt, and when Zoey looks down she sees the Redeye's boots are an inch off the floor.

"Drop him!" one guard yells. His prod is charged, blue fire crackling on its end. He moves in behind Simon as the Cleric pulls his gaze from the man he's subduing. There is a beat before Simon drops the soldier. The Redeye makes no move for retaliation. He simply rubs his throat and twists his head once, an audible crack coming from his neck. Simon steps toward the door, hands held at shoulder height.

Dellert curses and steps up to Simon.

"You'll hang for that," Dellert says. His face is a mass of dripping ribbons, yellow teeth smeared with blood.

"No, I don't believe I will. But he might," Simon says, pointing at the Redeye. "No man is allowed to harm a ward unless suffering bodily injury himself. He wasn't being attacked, you were."

Dellert blinks, slowly bringing his gaze to the Redeye before looking down at Zoey. He licks his lip and spits a gob of blood onto *The Count of Monte Cristo* where it lies on the floor. "Check the space again outside the window," he says to the guard not holding Lily. Zoey stares down at her blood-caked fingernails before looking up into Dellert's leering, nightmarish face.

"I hope you like the dark," he says.

7

They stand before the gathered Clerics and women.

Assistant Carter, wearing his suit even at this hour, paces the floor. Zoey hovers in place, one moment sure that she'll faint while the next she wonders if she can somehow kill Carter before they can lock her inside the box. Her eyes burn from crying. She clenches her jaw.

Lily laughs loudly and Zoey glances her way. The girl stands in front of the opposite door, slowly turning in a circle before her Cleric. She wears the same clothing she had on the day before, Zoey can see the spatters where she spilled stew down the front of her shirt. Lily smiles and gives her a little wave before spinning around again.

"Unspeakable contraband," Carter says as he stops pacing. "I won't even begin to describe what Zoey had in her room. Needless to say, punishment is the least she deserves. What is it that makes her believe she is more important, more special than any of you?" Carter walks closer to the seated women. Penny and Sherell watch him pass, but Rita stares at Zoey, a hint of a smile poised at the corners of her mouth. Meeka looks at the floor between her feet, her narrow shoulders slumped.

"You are all beyond precious, but not one is more significant than the other," Carter continues before turning to look at Zoey. "That is something you'll learn very soon." He faces the cluster of women and Clerics again. "Zoey and Lily, you are both sentenced to seventy-two hours in confinement." There are gasps among the crowd, not only from the women but from the Clerics as well. Zoey feels as if she's been struck. Seventy-two hours? She must have heard him wrong. No one's ever been in the boxes for more than two days. She looks at Simon, but he doesn't return her gaze. Carter clasps his hands behind his back. "You will have no contact with the outside. Do not stray from the path again. Clerics?"

Simon hesitates only a split second before guiding Zoey toward the waiting door.

"Simon, please," Zoey whispers. Tears run from her eyes. "Please. At least spare Lily." Simon scans his bracelet and the door unlocks. Darkness washes out from the gap as it swings open. It is a solid thing, as corporeal as any person in the room. And she senses its intelligence, its *intent*. The darkness is alive.

"No, no, no, no, don' wanna go there," Lily says. The panic in her voice wrenches at Zoey's heart, and she wishes then that she would die, just to escape from hearing Lily sound like that again.

"It's okay, Lily, it's okay. I'll be with you," Zoey says, but her voice cracks. Lily's Cleric pushes the girl forward.

"Nah, nah, sta, sta, sta, no!" Lily cries, struggling away from the waiting dark.

"Cleric?" Carter says. His tone holds the promise of what will be done if Simon doesn't comply. Zoey tears her gaze away from Lily, resisting the urge to cover her ears, and steps into the box. She turns as Simon begins to shut the door.

"I'm sorry," he breathes. Beyond him Meeka is mouthing something to her, over and over. *Be strong, be strong, bestrongbestrongbestrong.*

Lily begins to scream, but the door closes and the sound is cut off. The darkness rushes in and is complete.

Zoey lets out a held breath and it is loud. Beyond loud. She can hear the thudding of her heart. She puts out a hand and touches the door, making sure it's still really there. Yes, she can feel its borders, but no light seeps from around its edges.

She's barefoot, and the floor is smooth and cold where she stands. She shivers and blinks. Never before has she experienced darkness like this. There has always been light available. Even a year ago when the power had suddenly faltered and failed in the middle of a huge lightning storm, the faint glow of emergency lights had shone in the hallway outside her room, filtering in beneath the door. The lightning had also kept the darkness away as it crawled in breathtaking pulses across the sky. She'd watched the storm for hours until the lights sprang on once again as quickly as they'd failed. She hadn't been afraid then. She'd been captivated, entranced.

But she is afraid now.

She breathes deeply, trying to stave off the panic that's threatening to overtake her like a drenching rain. It's only darkness, the absence of light. Nothing can hurt her here. She should explore the space, catalogue it, get to know every inch. She takes a step to the right, keeping her hand on the door.

The floor and ceiling change.

Her head bumps into something, and the floor becomes upraised and knobby beneath the sole of her foot. She curses, rubbing the blooming spot of pain on the side of her skull. She puts a hand out and feels the ceiling descend down in a sharp angle. She kneels, running her palm over the floor. The upraised bumps are perhaps an inch tall and rounded, the space between them wide enough to trace her fingertip through. She stretches out, unsure of what to make of the floor. The bumps continue in all directions. In fact, the only smooth space she feels is directly before the entrance to the box. The area without the bumps is only two feet square by her estimate.

She stands again and puts out a hand, finding the sloping ceiling. Zoey takes a step onto the nubs, their rounded forms immediately painful as she settles her full weight onto them. The ceiling forces her down farther and farther until she must crawl. The floor gouges her knees, her hands, but she continues. The ceiling barely clears her back but doesn't slant any lower. She moves forward until she senses the next wall ahead. She traces it with her hand, finding the nearest corner. It is smooth and unbroken. She turns and crawls on, trying to ignore the growing agony in her knees and palms. The back wall comes up to meet her after she has moved for thirty seconds. She turns again, trying to trace the wall with one hand as she crawls. The box is exactly that. A box. Unmarred by any entrances or holes that she can feel other than the door she entered through.

She is nearly back to her starting point when she hears a sound. It is a skittering that immediately rolls waves of goose bumps across her arms and back. She's heard it before.

Six months ago a black beetle emerged from the drain in her shower. Its head was blunted save for two flicking antennae, eyes as black and shiny as the guards' gun holsters. Its body was ponderously long, and it made short hissing sounds as its six legs dragged it forward. She hadn't been showering at the time but had heard the thing's progress long before it revealed itself. The revulsion she'd felt at the time had been a tangible thing. She'd crushed the insect with her shoe on pure instinct before it could trundle back down into the dark of its hole, scraping the remains onto a piece of toilet paper before flushing it away. It had taken her a full week to feel comfortable in the shower again. Each time she had to close her eyes to wash her hair, her imagination conjured the sound of the insect's body above the shower's cascade.

But now, alone and in the dark, she hears it once again.

Zoey stares into the black depths, eyes swimming with colors that aren't there. *Where is it coming from? From the left—no, the right end of the box. There's more than one of them.* She sidles toward the door until she feels the smooth patch of cement and stands. The chittering scrape of hard carapaces fills the room. Her breath heaves in and out. She can almost see them advancing toward her through the maze of knobs, turning corners and climbing over the small mountains, but always coming closer.

Zoey spins and slams the bottom of her fist on the door. "Hey! Help! There's something in here with me! There's bugs in here!" She hates the hysterical pitch of her voice, but there's nothing for it. The sound is louder, closer. "Help me! Please!" Her throat constricts with tears and a fear so consuming she thinks she'll go mad from it. Zoey turns, backing up as tight as she can against the door, trying to press herself through it. *Please, make it go away, please, let them leave me alone.*

Something grazes her foot and she screams.

Zoey lunges away, the cry of terror reverberating in the enclosed space. Her head meets the ceiling, and as the pain detonates in her skull she realizes she forgot about the slant.

She crumples to the ground, hard nubs embracing her knees, her hip, and finally her shoulder as she folds over. The floor seems to tilt. Maybe that's what this place is. Maybe it's not even part of the ARC. It's somewhere separate and moving, distant beyond the reach of all she knows and recognizes. As the wobbling in her head slowly stills, so do her thoughts. The bugs—one of them touched her. That's why she hit her head.

Zoey draws her knees up to her chest, making herself as small as possible, and listens.

The sounds are gone, vanished as if they never were.

She doesn't believe her ears, sure that something happened to her hearing when she bashed her head. She snaps her fingers. Yes, she can still hear. The bugs are gone. Or they're waiting, completely still and biding their time. She imagines them resting on the top of the nubs like kings on hills, long antennae flicking, tasting the air for her presence.

Zoey waits for many long minutes before sliding back to the smooth doorstep. That's what she's named the flat square, the doorstep. She feels around its entire area. Her hand encounters no thin feelers, no scrambling legs, no hard shells. How would they get into the box if it's a sealed container? And if they did, how would they get out again that quickly? Did she imagine it all? No. She heard them, heard their bodies sliding on the floor, she felt something touch her. Fear and darkness, no matter how thick, couldn't change her perception that much.

She sits in the same place for a long time, her back against the door. Or maybe it's a short time. Strangely, she feels like time passes differently without light to gauge it by. Three days. Seventy-two hours. Four thousand three hundred twenty minutes. She tries to do the calculation for seconds, but the math keeps getting jumbled in her head. She fingers the lump above her ear. It's enormous and still growing, but it isn't bleeding. Blood. Blood on her book, her ruined book. No, she's not going to think about that, not right now. She needs to heed Meeka's words. *Be strong, be strong, be strong.*

She's repeating the words like a mantra when a new sound begins to invade the box. It's a high, fluting noise with hitches and breaks punctuated by solid bangs. Zoey listens, unable to identify what it is until she makes out words among the flotsam of sound.

Out! Out! Wan out!

Lily.

Zoey's heart pummels the inside of her chest, and she leaves the sanctity of the doorstep to crawl across the torturous floor. How can she hear Lily now? How is it possible? She meets the wall that runs parallel to Lily's chamber and feels along it as the cries increase in volume.

"Lily! It's okay, I'm here! I'm right here!" But Lily continues to scream incoherently. Zoey scrambles the full length of the wall again. No breaks, no holes, but she can hear Lily as if she's only steps away.

Nah! Nah! Out!

"Stop! Stop it!" Zoey screams, not yelling at Lily but at those who put them here. "She didn't do anything! Let her out! Please, let her out!" She tries to yell more, but her voice withers to hoarseness. She lies on her side, the knobby floor nosing its way into her bones. She cries, hot tears flowing as she jerks with the fury of her sobs. "Please, God."

This is the first time she's ever truly prayed. The notion of a higher entity gathered by bits and pieces of conversation overheard and rumored throughout the years.

God is good. He watches over us.

God is old, so old, older than everything.

God lives in the sky. He is kind and has long white hair. He watches out for us.

God is cruel. All suffering is his doing.

God is dead.

God never was.

She has never believed in a higher power, and she still doesn't now. But Lily's pitiful cries have broken her last reserves. She is willing to try anything simply to help her friend.

But her prayers aren't answered. The wails go on and on until she's sure she will go insane from listening to them. There is no escaping it, not even if they stopped this second, because she will never forget the sound.

After a long time Lily's voice fades away and silence returns, broken only by the sound of her own weeping.

◆　◆　◆

Sleep finds her after a time. She's a husk of guilt, drained of any motivation to move. Her body aches from the floor, because even after she moves back to the doorstep and lies down, her upper body still rests on the nubs. She fades in and out of consciousness. No other sounds invade the box, and at times she doesn't know if her eyes are open or not.

Hours, or years, later, there is a clack and something hits the floor a few feet from her. Zoey pops into a sitting position, her arms in full revolt as blood attempts to reinvade them. She winces at the tingling until it recedes enough for her to move. Something dropped from the ceiling, she's sure of it, and judging by the sound it was something fairly small.

She stretches out, barely able to tolerate even a second's worth of pressure on her knees now. They are two pulsating masses of bruised skin, cartilage, and bone. She sweeps her hand out, afraid of encountering some horror in the darkness, but instead her fingers brush something cool and cylindrical. Zoey prods it, hearing the tinkle of steel and slosh of liquid. She picks the object up and brings it back to the doorstep.

It's a bottle of sorts, smooth metal with its top threaded on she realizes after several fumbling minutes. She unscrews the cap and finds an open mouth beneath it. She sniffs the liquid inside. It's sweet-smelling with a hint of musk, like the yellow fruit they serve every other week. Zoey puts it to her lips, the thought of poison crossing her mind, but of course, why go to all the trouble of putting her in here only to kill her? She sips. The flavor matches the scent but is also coupled with a strong salinity. Its viscosity is somewhere between water and gravy.

She drinks the entire serving in several long gulps before setting the container aside. The hunger that's been quietly growing inside her diminishes to a faint memory. Calorie-rich, she realizes. Something to keep her strength and health up even while they torture her. She should've refused it, flung it across the room. If she didn't eat and they saw it, maybe they'd let her out sooner. Because they are watching her— she can feel it. And this angers her more than anything else.

"Go to hell," she growls through her strained vocal cords. "Go right to fucking hell!" She tosses the empty canister to punctuate her yell. It clangs in the darkness at the far end of the box before falling silent. "Go to hell," she whispers. But this is hell, isn't it? She's living in it right now.

Zoey purses her lips and tips her head to the side, cracking the taut vertebrae in her neck. She stands, stretching out her legs, and they feel like separate pieces of something dying that she's vaguely aware of. She needs to move more, she can't sit in one place. Sitting still will kill her, break her mind.

She squats and rises several times, counting off reps until the muscles of her legs begin to burn past the ache from the floor. She extends her arms, grazing the slanted ceiling with her fingertips. After she's moved enough to assure she's still alive and not some bitter figment of a madman's dream, she sits again.

How long? How long has she been inside the box? The memory of Lily's cries comes to her again and she forces it away. She can't help Lily, not right now. But she will. She's going to help them all when she gets out.

How much is a life worth?

It is worth more than this. So much more.

A searing desire for vengeance sweeps through her, turning her blood molten hot within her veins and with it the will to exact revenge on those responsible, to destroy what should be obliterated. To reap justice.

Zoey drifts with the righteous thoughts, leaving her body moored in the creeping agony of the floor and its hold. She dreams of clawing at the walls around the ARC. Instead of her fingers shredding on the rough concrete, she gouges away heaping handfuls of the wall. She digs through it with a singular purpose, unbothered by the stinging of the sniper's bullets. They are nothing, nothing compared to the last seventeen-odd years she can truly remember. She claws the concrete away as if it is dirt. She's broken through. Light streams from the hole she's made, light and fragrant air that speaks promises of beauty beyond reason. She glances over her shoulder to smile back at the other women she knows are behind her, but the smile dies on her lips.

There is only darkness. And it is closing in.

Zoey comes awake as she slides to the side. She's still partially propped up against the door, and her legs are asleep. She stretches them and shivers. It seems colder than before. When the maddening prickle of blood subsides, she stands, the ache from sitting a deeper pain than she's ever felt before. She would gladly take another kick from Rita in the stomach before enduring this type of misery.

Rita. She'd forgotten that the other woman had been in this exact same place only hours ago. She'd probably lain on the same concrete, felt the same pain and disorientation of the dark. The callousness she'd harbored for Rita throughout the years begins to soften and is replaced with something resembling sympathy. She's not sure she could wish this on her worst enemy. But then the Director's ruddy, smiling face appears before her eyes in the darkness, and she reconsiders. Zoey's hands clench the cotton of her pants and she trembles, but not from the cold.

She's about to sit down again when a sound reaches from the rear of the box, a short grating like small rocks grinding beneath a boot. She stares into the uncompromising dark. Heart hammering. Waiting.

Two red points appear across the room. They are stationary for a moment and then begin to move and sway toward her.

Eyes.

Zoey's mouth falls open and she stumbles to the side, barely remembering the low ceiling. The eyes track her movement and adjust their course. It's coming toward her. She hears the scratch and rustle of its body. It's at least as big as she is, probably bigger. It makes a snuffling noise that is wholly inhuman, and she registers her bladder releasing. She crawls away, unable to tear her eyes from the shining points of light. They follow her, turning at first but then coming closer, a crazed panting overriding the sound of her own breathing. She's got to get away from it, get out, get out somehow.

That's it.

If it got in, she can get out. She scrambles toward the point where she first heard the sound of the thing's arrival. Behind her, the eyes dip and move slowly forward. It grunts, a hollow, metallic sound. Zoey ratchets her body across the knobs, their touch like small hammer blows each time she moves. She traces the low ceiling, fingertips searching for a break or gap in the cement. There's nothing.

Something grazes her foot.

Zoey shrieks, yanking her leg up and away from the thing's touch. She spins and retreats, entire body shaking. She's going to die, die from the fear. It will happen, and at least then she'll be free. The eyes sway, and the creature makes a wet, gnashing noise. A hungry sound.

Zoey backs up until her feet encounter the farthest wall. Through the blinding panic she focuses on the floor, trying to find a seam. The ceiling again. Nothing. The eyes are closer, brighter. She can smell it now. It carries the heady stink of the exercise room after the guards have been working out. She runs her feet along the wall, searching for a lever that she missed before, a button, anything that will get her away from the thing that's inching forward, so close now she's sure she can touch it. Her hand closes on something cold and hard beside her. The eyes loom as it slithers forward, fetid breath puffing against her face. She waits through a single heartbeat that lasts forever. Its hand touches her shoulder.

Zoey swings the steel bottle around as hard as she can.

She feels the canister connect with something solid, and the eyes tilt. She winds back her arm and swings again. Harder this time. Again the connection that reverberates through the bones of her hand. The thing releases a staticky mewling, like the sounds that come from the speakers in the corridors at times. Pebbled fingers graze her arm, and she cries out with revulsion. Zoey lunges forward, jabbing the solid bottle like a knife between the two glowing orbs. Something snaps in the darkness, and the worst noise yet comes from the thing. It's a long, baritone groan hitched with huffs of pain. The eyes slink lower to the floor and, unbelievably, it begins to retreat.

Zoey's eyes water and she wipes them, shaking so badly she smears the whole side of her face with their wetness. The creature slides backward, eyes angling as if it's lost its course. It's hurt, badly. Zoey wheezes, and her vision doubles. She swallows and brings herself back from the brink of unconsciousness with the thought of being completely defenseless in the dark with the thing. It continues to creep away from her, and she can hear its limbs struggling to move its weight. All at once she is consumed by rage. Like the flip of a switch the anger courses through her, accompanied by a realization.

They let it in here with her. They meant to torture her with it. This was designed. And worst of all, it might be happening to Lily right now.

The last thought breaks her paralysis and she crawls forward, bottle clanking against the floor in one hand. The thing whips its head toward her before sliding away faster, its sounds higher now, pleading.

Zoey catches up to it, terrified for a moment as her hand touches its body, afraid of how it will feel. But her fingers snag lumpy cotton, not unlike some of the medical jackets she's washed before. She swings her body around to get a better angle and whips the bottle toward the glow of the eyes. The solid thump that resounds above the thing's cries is beyond satisfaction. She hits it again, and again. Each time pouring more anger, more hatred into the blows. She is screaming now, not saying any words, simply releasing a fury that can't be expressed through violence. She wants to tear the thing apart with her bare hands, her teeth. She wants to taste blood.

A cool touch caresses the back of her neck and she pauses, turning to bat at the space behind her. The bottle swings, unchecked. There's nothing there. But she can feel it. Air. Cool air that smells slightly of chemicals. It rushes past her, blasting her sweat-matted hair away from her cheeks. A weakness invades her muscles, turning them to water even as she tries to hold her breath. She can't fall asleep, not now, not with the creature still beside her.

But as she collapses to the studded floor, she can't see its position anymore. Its eyes have gone out.

8

Zoey wakes as if slapped.

Her eyes open to blindness and she waits for the world to come flooding in, but there's nothing. No sight, no sound, nothing but thrumming pain in her back and skull. It coalesces until it becomes her new senses. She can see its dancing color of red, hear its humming in her bones, taste its metallic tang, smell its stench, and feel it, feel it beyond anything that's come before.

She manages to roll over to her side with a scream. She can't help it—there are holes in her back where she's lain on the nubs, she's sure of it. She gasps with the enormity of the pain and nearly vomits. She coughs, begins to crawl, and moves several feet before realizing there's nothing blocking her way.

The creature is gone.

Zoey fans her arm out, confirming that she's alone. She turns her head and looks around the box but sees no sign of the eyes anywhere. Feeling, beyond the pain, is slowly returning to her body. She wiggles her toes and crawls forward. After several long minutes of shuffling, her hands meet smooth concrete and she slides herself onto the small doorstep. The flat flooring is like balm to her flesh, and she revels in it before gradually hauling herself to her feet. Her stomach aches with hunger, and her mouth is paper-dry. She sways in place, urging the blood to do its work, to wash away the pain and begin to heal her. She stretches the corroded muscles in her back and legs before finally settling to the floor.

How long? How long has she been here? Certainly more than a day. More than two? Maybe it's been a week. Maybe they've forgotten her here. Perhaps something's happened outside the box and the ARC is empty now, silent spaces devoid of any life except her here in this room. It is the most horrifying yet exalting thing she's ever imagined. If she's been forgotten, then that means the other women have gotten out. They are somewhere safe, or they are dead.

And death is a sort of safety in itself.

Zoey scans the darkness again for the thing's eyes but there is nothing. She's sure she won't be able to quit looking for it until she's released. She laughs quietly. The idea of leaving the box is almost absurd now. The darkness is forever. It's inside her. No, not inside her. She is the darkness.

A loud crack jerks her upright, burning muscles taut, eyes wide, fists clenched for the fight she knows must come. Zoey waits. No more sound. She kneels and crawls forward, passing her palm over the studs until it encounters the cold steel of a full canister. She drags herself back to the doorstep and uncaps the sustenance, already tasting the fruity concoction. She tips her head back and lets it flood her mouth.

It is blood.

Zoey gags, spitting the mouthful beside her. The taste of blood invades her sinuses, crawls upward to her brain. *I drank someone's blood, they're feeding me blood, it's in my mouth!* She gags again but doesn't throw up. There's nothing left in her stomach. Her fingers are clenched around the bottle's cool sides and she brings her arm up to throw it in a fit of repulsion, but stops.

She breathes through her nose and works her tongue around her mouth. There's something wrong. The blood tastes strange, chalky and somewhat gritty. She swallows and moves her tongue again. Yes, the iron flavor is fading, leaving only a mellow undertone of yeast like the undercooked biscuits they sometimes have at lunch.

Zoey sits staring into the dark.

It's all been manufactured.

The sound of the bugs, the "touch" of one on her foot, the thing with red eyes, the blood in the canister. They're all tools to break her. She sits calmly, letting the pain in her back and legs ease with the coolness of the doorstep. After a time she brings the bottle to her mouth and drinks the camouflaged fluid. It goes down smooth. She screws the cap back on and sets it beside her, staring out across the room she cannot see. She smiles.

"Got anything else?" she asks. There is no reply. "Didn't think so." She curls in on herself, folding up so that only her lower legs rest on the knobs outside of the flat area, and falls asleep.

◆　◆　◆

Zoey rises from a dreamless slumber to the rasp of metal on metal. She sits up, reaching out for the bottle, finding it after a second of fumbling. Where had the sound come from? Across the box? Were they sending something else in an attempt to terrorize her?

Light cuts into the room from behind her and she gasps. The flare of it is astounding in its solidity. Even as she clenches her eyes shut she's sure she could grasp the light itself and hold it in her hands.

"Zoey. Are you okay?"

Simon.

She turns toward his voice and pries her eyelids up. He is a shadow encased by light. She can't see his face but feels his hand on her arm, helping her stand. She embraces him, uncaring that it's prohibited. The feel of his shirt, the strength of his arms as he hugs her is more than worth it. She begins to sob, and he whispers to her that it's all right, that everything will be okay.

There are other voices there, but she keeps her eyes closed, tears leaking from their corners to wet Simon's shirt. He guides her away from the box and across floors that have no torturous, upraised nubs. As they pass through the first door she stiffens and braces her feet, stopping their motion.

"Lily," she says, her voice still raw-edged.

"She's out. She's safe."

Zoey nearly crumples with relief, but Simon carries her along. The light beyond her eyelids is a red and painful haze as they move through the corridors. Then she smells the infirmary and is being helped onto a bed. Sinking into the thin mattress is another level of elation. The bed gives beneath her weight, embraces her. She sighs with the all-encompassing pleasure of it.

"Can you turn out the lights?" she asks. Immediately the redness darkens and she cracks her eyes open a little.

She is in the same exam room that she visited after being attacked by Rita. The same doctor is there and he's taking her blood pressure. He nods at Simon, who stands at her bedside, and pulls a blanket from a nearby cabinet before spreading it over her.

"She's stable, considering how long she was in there. Doesn't look too malnourished. She was fed, apparently. I'll start an IV, and then she should rest."

Zoey reaches out and finds Simon's hand, grips it. He squeezes her fingers back and gazes down at her. His eyes are awash with emotion. His jaw trembles.

"I'm okay," she says weakly. He nods and looks away as the doctor returns with the IV. The needle burns where he inserts it in her arm, but she doesn't flinch in the slightest. It is nothing compared to the ache from the floor.

"I'm administering some sedative along with the saline solution. It should help you sleep and will take the pain down quite a bit," the doctor says as he injects something into the IV. It enters her vein, warming her arm as it goes. The notion that she can feel the drug traversing her bloodstream is ridiculous, but it's there nonetheless.

"Simon, I—" she starts.

"Shh. You rest now. We can talk later. Plenty of time for talk."

Zoey opens her mouth to say something else, but she's sinking further and further into the bed. It envelops her and closes slowly like a set of doors until there is only silence and velvet darkness she is no longer afraid of.

◆　◆　◆

"Zoey."

Her name is like a switch that opens her eyes. She feels rested, her body only vaguely aching. She stares up at a shadowed, unfamiliar ceiling for several heartbeats before memories of the last three days come rushing in. She's out of the box. She's in the infirmary. And that voice, she knows that voice . . .

Zoey turns her head to the side and is met with Lee's cautious smile.

"Hi," he whispers.

"You," she says, trying to scoot away from him. His smile drops in an instant.

"What?"

"You . . . you told them about the books. You got us sent to the box."

"Zoey, no. I would never—"

"You wanted me in my place just like everyone else. Maybe you thought it would teach me a lesson." She restrains the urge to strike him, but there is open horror etched into his face as if she's already done so.

"No, God no, Zoey. Look at me, you know me. Could I ever, ever do anything like that? I would never in a thousand years betray you. I'd die before hurting you."

She hesitates, but slowly sinks back into the bed and blinks. "You're the only one who knew."

"Except for the person who left the books for you. Did you ever think it might've been Dellert himself? He would have access to them."

She shakes her head. "He was going to leave until he heard the wind whistling in the loose window." Lee looks past her at the wall before scooting closer to the bed.

"How do you feel?"

She licks her lips. Her tongue has become sandpaper. "Thirsty."

"I can fix that," Lee says. There is soft clinking and then he's holding a glass brimming with water. A plastic straw pokes from the top. He helps her shift closer to the edge of the bed and holds the glass and straw steady. She drinks, sucking the water down greedily. It is so cold, images of frosted steel tumble through her mind. She downs half the glass before Lee draws it away.

"Hey, I wasn't done yet," she says.

"You'll make yourself sick if you drink too much."

"I feel fine." She rolls to her back and winces at the flash of pain that recedes like fluttering lightning through clouds.

"Yeah, it looks like it."

She studies him in the dim light. "What are you doing here?"

"I came to see you."

"You're going to get caught."

He shakes his head. "It's exercise hour. Dad's sleeping. The doctors checked in on you fifteen minutes ago. No one's around."

"They'll see you on the cameras."

"Not with Becker working. He's not as observant as everyone thinks he is."

"What do you mean?"

"I'll tell you later." He shifts in his seat, and reaches out to grasp her hand. His palm is so warm. "I thought I'd lost you."

"You knew where I was."

"Yeah, but no one's ever been in the box that long."

She sees the swaying, red eyes in the darkness and shivers. "I made it."

"I know." Lee chews his lower lip. "I'm sorry. For what I said the other night. I've been thinking a lot and . . ." He lets his voice trail off before shooting a look at the partially open door.

"And?"

"And, you're right. There's . . ." He sighs. ". . . there's something wrong. I can feel it too."

"You're just realizing it now?"

"No. I've always felt it. That's why I got so upset the other night in your room. You said what's been in the back of my mind for a long time. I just never wanted to admit it." He rubs the back of her hand with his thumb and it causes a pleasurable flow of gooseflesh to shimmy up her arm. "I spoke with the Director."

Zoey's eyes open wide. "You did?"

"Yeah. He granted me an audience yesterday. I asked him to let you out early."

Zoey laughs. "That went well."

Lee smiles, but it's tinged with sadness. "I got a five-minute lecture on discipline and how contraband is dangerous. Then he told me that Dellert was petitioning to have you executed."

"You're kidding."

"No. His face is pretty tore up. He said that you were a menace to the ARC and all within it. Of course the Director said that your punishment was sufficient, but Dellert wasn't happy about it." Lee plays with the corner of her blanket, worrying it between his fingers.

"But that's not all you asked the Director, was it?" Zoey says.

"No. I asked him about Dad and me accompanying you to the safe zone. He did exactly what you said he would. He told me it was against protocol to release a Cleric or any other unauthorized personnel into the zone. Said it was a quarantine risk, whatever that means."

"Did you really expect anything different?"

"No. I guess not."

The weariness she's felt for the last few days is gradually lifting. The idea that's been growing ever more vivid in her subconscious is blooming into the brightness of reality. She feels it materialize even more with Lee's confession.

"I want to escape," she whispers, so quietly the sound barely carries across the short distance between them.

Lee blinks, and she worries that he'll recoil like last time, but after a long moment he nods. He starts to say something and falters before trying again. "Our choices can break us, Zoey."

She grasps his hand tighter. "They can set us free, too."

Something changes in Lee's eyes, and he swallows. His lips tremble, and she's about to ask him what's wrong when he leans forward and kisses her.

It's so unexpected she doesn't know what to do. His lips are warmer than his hands, softer, so gentle. Heat rolls outward from her chest to her extremities in a deliciously soft wave. Her eyes are as wide open as his are tightly shut, so she is the one who sees movement outside the door a split second before it is pushed inward.

Simon stands outlined in the doorway.

"Lee." His name sounds like a curse coming from his father. Lee snaps away from her as if thrown, dropping her hand and standing straight up. "What the hell are you doing?"

"I . . . I had to see Zoey."

Simon says nothing else. He moves with a frightening fluidity. And though Lee is strong, his father slings him into the hallway as if he weighs nothing. The door shuts behind them, and silence invades the room.

Zoey doesn't realize she's sitting up until the pain begins to pound through her back. A dizzying sense of falling washes over her.

She's going back in the box.

Simon saw them kissing. He *saw* them. Oh God, oh God, who's the closest woman to her right now? It's exercise hour, and she's on the fourth floor. It could be anyone, it could be . . .

No. No. Nonononono. Lily isn't at exercise hour. She's most likely in the next room recovering. Or she could be in her own quarters on the floor below, but either way the girl is the closest in proximity to her.

"No," Zoey breathes. Lily can't go back in the box. She can't. The room tilts and stretches around her. The building begins a slow turn as vertigo runs sickening tendrils through her head. Lily won't survive another moment in that hellhole of a room. Her screams were enough to tell her so.

They have to get out now. Or die trying.

The enormity of her decision nearly crushes her, but she slides to the edge of the bed and swings her feet to the floor. She's still wearing her soiled clothes, and she can smell herself. She pads to the door, moving on rusted joints. How, how, how to do it? How can she get them both out? She'll have to search the infirmary first, find Lily. Then . . . then what? Then take a doctor or guard by surprise. Get a weapon, force them to open doors and . . . and go where?

But she knows where.

Zoey swallows, searching the room for some kind of weapon. The cabinet in the corner only reveals more blankets and several wispy medical gowns. There's got to be something here. She picks up the chair Lee had been resting on, forcing away the protestations of her back and legs. No, it's too heavy. Something else. She'll have to find it outside the room.

She makes it to the door and is about to turn the handle when footsteps close in and stop outside. She leaps back as the door is pushed open. Simon stands there, startled at seeing her out of bed.

"Zoey, what are you doing?"

"What are you going to do?" she asks. Her hands are clenched into fists, and though she feels like she could faint at any time, she's willing to fight.

"Do? What do you mean?"

"What did you do with Lee?"

Simon sighs, glancing over his shoulder before shutting the door. "He's in his room, and you are forbidden from seeing one another."

A part of her crushes in on itself. "What are you going to do?" she repeats.

"If you mean, am I going to send you back to the box, the answer is no," he says, staying close to the door while speaking in a low voice. "No one saw Lee come here."

Zoey sags with relief and steadies herself on the bed frame. "Thank you."

"Don't thank me. You should be ashamed of yourself. I thought you were smarter than this."

She slowly lowers herself into the chair she'd considered using as a weapon minutes ago. "He just came to visit me."

"It is forbidden." Simon enunciates each word. "If I had been someone else, there would be worse punishment than the box again. And think of Lily. Are you so selfish that you've forgotten her?"

Zoey fixes him with a cold stare. "No. I haven't."

Simon heaves out another sigh and seems to deflate with it. "Get back into bed. We're going to pretend what I saw never happened, do you understand?"

"Yes."

"Good. You need rest."

Zoey stands and pauses by the bed, the promise of escape still singing in her blood even with Simon's reassurances. "Where is Lily?"

"She's in her room."

"You said she's okay?"

He hesitates. "Yes."

"How long was she in the box? Did they let her out early?"

"They let her out after ten hours."

"They did?"

"Yes."

The slight relief she feels goes cold when she sees Simon won't look at her. "Why? Why did they let her out so early? Simon?" She comes closer to him and he finally glances up.

"She started to hurt herself and wouldn't stop."

Zoey pushes past him and hurls the door open. She ignores the pain looping through her back and legs even as a gray mist settles at the corners of her vision.

"Zoey, stop," Simon says, grasping her arm. She yanks away, heading toward the door.

"Take me to her."

"Zoey—"

"Take me to her, Simon." She stands beside the door, waiting, not looking back. Just when she thinks he won't let her through, he comes forward and scans his bracelet. She hurries through the door and down the hallway, grimacing as she trundles down the stairs, her legs screaming. In a few moments she's within sight of Lily's door. Steven sits on a chair beside it, staring at his hands. He glances up in astonishment as she approaches.

"Open it," she says.

"What's the—"

"Do it. Right now." There must be something in her voice or expression that speaks to him past her words, because he rises and scans his bracelet.

The setting sun is still above the ARC's wall, and it floods the room with thick afternoon light. It covers the floor, the desk cluttered with wax markers, as well as the bed and the girl sitting upon it. Zoey stops short at the sight, her hand coming to her mouth as tears blur her vision.

Lily's hair is gone. It has been shaved away almost down to the scalp. There are angry, red patches, partially scabbed over in several places peeking through the soft down of hair that is left. Lily rocks slowly forward and back.

Zoey moves, as if in a dream, around the end of the bed and catches sight of Lily's face. The girl's cheeks are welted and scratched in downward lines. Her forehead is swollen and purple around a bandage that hangs precariously from her skin below several black-threaded stitches. Zoey softly puts the bandage back in place.

"She started banging her head on the floor and pulling her hair out," Steven says. "They had to cut it all off so she'd stop."

"Get out," Zoey hisses, dropping to her knees at Lily's bedside.

"That's—"

"Get out!"

The Cleric's face mottles, and he blinks before turning to the door. "I'm keeping it partially open," he mumbles and then is gone. Zoey scoots closer to Lily, but the girl's eyes are unfocused, seeing far beyond the walls of the room.

"Lily? Look at me." Nothing. "Lily, it's Zee." Zoey touches one of Lily's hands but she draws it away, her eyelids flutter. She continues to rock.

A tremble begins within Zoey, starting at her core and works itself outward. It is pure, undiluted hatred. It is murderous rage and a knowledge that she would tear the ones responsible apart with her hands if they were within reach. She swallows the hard knot of rage that's lodged in her throat and looks around the room. Nothing of comfort, nothing beautiful. Zoey stares at the floor where Lily's feet rest. There is a thin layer of dust on the concrete. She swipes at the remaining tears in her eyes and uses the moisture to draw a smiling face on the floor.

"Look at her, she's so happy," Zoey says. She points at the drawing but doesn't look up at Lily. "Now let's give her some hair and a dress." She dabs at her eyes again and traces a wave of hair around the figure's head before adding arms, legs, and a triangular dress. "There. She's very pretty, just like you, Lily." Zoey glances up and sees Lily has stopped rocking. Her eyes flick to the drawing before glazing over once again.

"Hmm," Zoey says loudly. "I wonder what we should name her. Hmm, maybe her name should start with an . . ." She lets the last word draw out. ". . . L!" She draws a large, capital L above the figure. "Let's see. I'm not sure what should come next. Wait, I think I'm getting it. Yep, it's an I!" She draws the letter beside the first. "But I'm not sure what comes after that. Hmm, what would be a good letter after the I?"

There is a timid smile on Lily's face and her eyes are locked on the letters above the drawing. Her mouth works silently, and Zoey sees her tongue appear between her teeth.

"What did you say? I thought you said something."

Lily smiles a little more, glancing at Zoey. "L," she whispers.

"L? You want L after the I? Okay. That looks familiar. I wonder where I've seen that before? But it's not done yet, is it?" Lily shakes her head, her smile broadening. "Do you know what the last letter is?" Lily nods. "Then come down here and draw it."

Lily hesitates but then slides off the bed. Zoey's throat tightens again at seeing how carefully she moves, how much pain she's in. The girl leans over the drawing and traces a lopsided Y at the end before snatching her hand back as if she's done something wrong. She gives Zoey a wide-eyed look. *Can you believe I did it!*

"Well, that says . . . wait, what does that say?" Zoey asks.

"Lily!" Lily laughs and rocks happily, staring down at the figure in the dust.

"You're right, you got it, Lily." Zoey slides closer to her and gently puts an arm around her. "You got it, and you're safe now. You're going to be okay."

"Kay."

Zoey's vision blurs again and she turns her face away. "I'm so sorry, Lily. It's my fault, my fault." She sniffles, continuing to rub the girl's back. "Everything's going to be okay now. Everything will be all right."

"Aaa rye," Lily repeats.

Zoey lowers her voice to a whisper. "I'll make everything right very soon."

9

When Zoey steps into her room, she sees that the blood has been cleaned from the floor and everything is back in its place.

There is no sign of the struggle that occurred. Zoey strides to the window and stands on her chair. The loose pane of glass has been repositioned, and a new bead of bonding compound has been applied. She rubs her nail against it. It's as solid as steel.

She climbs down and replaces the chair. The numbers on the calendar churn and change. They seem to speak in their own language, repeating the same word over and over. *Soon, soon, soon.*

Zoey readies herself for bed, planning on getting some sleep before the night closes in. There will be much to think about before the sun rises tomorrow. She's returning to the bed when there's a knock at the door.

"Come in," she says. The door clacks and swings inward, revealing the slender shape of Assistant Carter framed there. He wears one of his suits as usual, an ugly brown color, along with a cream-and-red-striped tie that hangs down past his belt buckle.

"Zoey. I hope I'm not intruding."

Her stomach twists, writhing on itself. "Of course not. Come in."

Carter steps inside stiffly, like he's made out of glass, and the Red-eye that Simon struggled with looms behind him.

"No, I don't want him in here," Zoey says before she can stop herself.

Carter blinks, a shallow smile growing on his weaselly face. "I apologize, Zoey, but he is my personal bodyguard and must come with me everywhere." He sees her discomfort, and she can tell he enjoys it. "Please sit," he says, gesturing toward the bed. She perches on the bed's far edge and Carter rests in the chair at her desk. He studies her and though she tries to keep her gaze level and calm, his eyes feel like greasy, probing fingers on her skin. She finally looks away. "How are you faring now that your punishment is finished?" he asks in a softly venomous voice.

"I'm doing very well, thank you."

Carter's eyebrows rise. "That's good to hear, but surprising I must say, considering the amount of time you spent inside the chamber."

She shrugs. "I earned it."

"Indeed." Carter studies her before inhaling sharply. "Pain is an unfortunate necessity in life. It shapes us, defines us, helps us learn." She thinks of Lily's torn scalp and wants not just to hurt him then, but to destroy him, end him where he smugly sits. "What did you learn during your time in the dark, Zoey?"

"I learned that it is important to follow the rules."

"It is. The rules are more critical than you can fathom, especially in a place such as this." He gestures to the walls. "They help the system function, and they keep people alive." Carter tips his head to the side. "Where did you get them, Zoey?"

"What?"

"The books and the chewing gum."

"I found the books where they were in the alcove. The gum was in the bathroom on the first floor."

Carter sits forward, his smile growing wider than it possibly should on his narrow face. "Lies." She holds his sickening gaze until he leans back in his chair and begins to inspect the fading light that coats the inner curve of the outside wall. "You've been witnessed being insubordinate to several Clerics recently. This is unacceptable, Zoey. It would be tragic if you were to continue your current, shall we say, *defiant* behaviors as they would inevitably lead to more punishment."

"I forgot to tell you what else I learned in the box," Zoey says, rage simmering beneath every inch of her skin.

"And what was that?" Carter asks.

"I learned that I'm not afraid of the dark."

His grin falters before returning stronger than before. "That's admirable, Zoey, it truly is. But when I mention punishment, I'm not talking about your own."

Any satisfaction that she felt in their brief exchange evaporates. He sees it in her eyes and nods.

"From now on, Lily will receive your penalty if you break the rules, and I can assure you there will be no leniency shown as there was the first time."

It is all she can do to hold herself back from clawing his smirking face to ribbons like she did Dellert's. "You can't do that. The rules say—"

"The rules," Carter says sharply, "are adaptable to each situation. You would do well to keep that knowledge close the next time you consider breaking them."

They stare at one another for a lengthening span that snaps audibly as Carter stands and turns toward the door where the Redeye waits, expressionless as ever.

"I trust we are at an accord then," Carter says over his shoulder. "See to it that you don't let me down, Zoey." He pauses in the hallway and glances at her one last time before smiling again. "Better yet, see that you don't let Lily down."

And with that, the Redeye swings the door shut and it locks with a clack, leaving her alone once again.

♦ ♦ ♦

When Lee enters her room just before midnight, Zoey is awake and waiting. Carter's visit still hangs over her like a foul smell that won't dissipate. She didn't even attempt to sleep.

Lee steps inside, placing something over the door lock before shutting it.

"What was that?" Zoey asks, pointing at the lock.

"Something I came up with while I was tinkering in the shop. It's a thin piece of steel that molds when the lock striker hits it so it doesn't latch all the way. I put a little reusable adhesive on one side so it will stay in place."

"That's ingenious," Zoey says. Lee beams.

"It was fairly simple once I started working on it."

"And you started working on it because you were planning on breaking into my room at night?"

Lee's face flushes bright red. "Well, I was going to tell you but I thought . . ."

Zoey hides her smile. "That brings me to my next question. How do you get in? Your bracelet doesn't open the women's doors."

Lee brings something out from his pocket, and it takes her a split second to recognize it, mostly because she's never seen one that wasn't wrapped around someone's wrist. She reaches out and takes the bracelet from him.

"Where did you get this?"

"In the guards' dorm. Dad and I were in there the day after Lowe died. You remember him, right?"

Zoey recalls the eldest guard, who passed away in his bed over a year ago. He had been the one who helped Simon carry her to the infirmary when she was fifteen after tripping during exercise hour and twisting her ankle so badly it swelled three times its normal size. She remembered his eyebrows the most, how gray and long they were, their tips nearly touching the fringe of his thinning hair. He had been only second in kindness to Crispin.

"Yes, I remember."

"This was sitting on his bedside table when we went through. I waited until no one was looking and took it. I was almost sure it wouldn't work, but it does."

"But they're supposed to be destroyed after they're removed."

Lee nods. "I know. I think someone assumed that another guard disposed of it after it was taken off of Lowe's body. The code inside the bracelet is still active."

Zoey turns the item around in her hands. Here it is, exactly what she was hoping for. It is literally the key to their salvation.

"So how do you sneak through the halls without Becker seeing you? It seems like he's always in the observation room."

"He is," Lee says, strolling across the room. "He only exchanges duties with another guard once a day, usually around three or four in the morning. He's off for four or five hours before coming back to his post."

"But that doesn't explain how he doesn't catch you."

"Becker sleeps at his desk during the night."

"What?"

Lee smiles. "He props his hand under his chin and faces the monitors, but he's asleep. I watched him for a half-hour one time from the hall, and he kept jerking awake but went right back to sleep. If there isn't an alarm going off in the middle of the night, he's not going to catch anything."

"I always thought they had motion sensors on after dark," Zoey says, looking at the bracelet again.

"Nope. The guards patrol during the night, so they'd be setting them off when they come through."

"So how do you get past them?"

Lee smiles, taking a step closer to her. "I'm sneaky."

"That," Zoey says, shoving him playfully away, "I can vouch for." She moves to her bed and sits. Lee joins her and the mattress squeaks under his added weight.

"I know you have a plan," he says after a long silence. "Tell me."

Zoey takes a deep breath. "I'm going to kill the Director."

10

"What?"

"It has to be done," Zoey says, glancing at Lee.

"You said you wanted to escape, not kill the Director."

"I want to escape, but I want everyone else to be free too." She sees him wince at the word. He's still not used to hearing it.

Lee stands and paces to the door. For a moment she thinks he's going to leave, that she's nudged him too hard toward something he's not ready for, but he stops and turns back.

"There has to be another way," he says, stopping by the desk.

"How? How do we ensure the other women's release and safety if the Director is alive? With him dead, there will be no order, no command except Assistant Carter, and I think half of the guards hate him as much as I do."

Lee opens his mouth, then closes it. He shifts, running his fingertips across the desktop. "It's suicide. There's no way we'll get out alive."

Zoey is on her feet before she realizes it. "This isn't living," she says, pointing out the window at the walls, palely illuminated in the artificial light. "I'd rather die trying to get out than walk willingly into something worse."

"Do all the other women agree? Would they go with you if you let them out? Do you really think Rita and Penny and Sherell are going to band together with you?"

"I don't know, but I can't leave them behind either. They're not my friends, but they don't deserve being kept here any more than I do." Lee shakes his head, staring down at the floor. She steps closer to him, and he raises his eyes to meet hers. "Lee, my birthday is in four days. I'll be gone no matter what then. I want to try. Will you help me?" She's very close to him and can smell his scent. It's a mixture of steel and sawdust from working in one of the shops, a smell of strength and comfort. He puts a gentle hand to her neck and guides her face to his. He kisses her again, and this time she's ready for it.

She presses her lips against his and discovers the feeling that eluded her earlier that day when they were interrupted by Simon. An unfamiliar giddiness blooms within her. She's felt echoes of it before when their hands would brush or when he would smile at her in the hallways, but now it is a force of its own, wild and frightening in its intensity.

Lee pulls her closer along the length of his body. She melds to him, conscious of every centimeter of their skin that's touching, heart picking up speed as she runs her hands up his back. He slides his fingers gently beneath the hem of her shirt, the delicious tactile sensations beginning to resonate in her core, urging her to strip away their clothing as fast as possible.

She breaks away at the last second, one of the hardest things she's ever had to do.

"We have to stop."

"Why?" he says breathlessly.

"Because." She steps away from him and a new sense of weakness encloses her legs and overrides the pain from the box. "I'm afraid, that's all."

He seems to digest this before nodding. "It's okay. I guess I am too." She wonders if they're talking about the same thing.

Zoey moves closer to the window, slowly clearing her mind of the passion that nearly overcame her. She shifts her gaze to the rim of the walls. A sniper turns, and she sees the glowing tip of a cigarette before his face.

"Can you imagine somewhere that we aren't watched or told where to be and at what time?" she says. "Where we could make our own decisions about what we wanted to do or where we wanted to go?

"I used to try to picture what my mother and father looked like by studying myself in the mirror. Do I have my father's eyes or my mother's nose? Does she have dark hair like mine, or is it blonde? How do my father's hands look? I always imagined them scarred and pitted from the fights he had gone through trying to save me from this." She turns back to Lee and rests on the bed. "But I stopped that a long time ago. They're dead, most likely, and if they are living up there on the fifth floor or in the safe zone, then what does it matter? They won't recognize me when we're reunited, and I won't recognize them. We'd be strangers. I've come to terms with that even if it hurts to think I'll never truly know them. What I have is my life and those that I can save."

"What about the greater good? What if you and the other women are the last hope for humankind? What if by leaving you seal everyone's fate?"

She looks up at him. "The greater good isn't what they enforce with rules and guns and punishment. It's being free to decide for ourselves what's best for each of us."

They are both quiet for a long time before Lee comes to sit beside her once again. His head droops forward as if his neck has given up. He closes his eyes.

"Okay. Tell me."

◆ ◆ ◆

"I'll need a weapon to do it," she begins, letting the warmth of Lee's shoulder seep into her own through the point where they lean together. "I'll need a gun."

"You don't even know how to use one."

She snorts. "Dellert does. How hard can it be?"

"Fair enough. But the only place you can get a gun is from a guard, and I don't think they're going to hand you one."

"You said you've been in the guards' dorms. Maybe—"

Lee shakes his head. "They lock their belts up when they're not on duty, in a container beside their beds. It takes a numbered code to open it."

Zoey ponders the problem for a moment. The guns are almost a useless adornment because deadly force is strictly forbidden unless absolutely necessary. Even when death is the penalty, Reaper carries out the sentence. She shivers, thinking of his masked face, only his eyes visible, their color the same as burnished steel knives. No, the guards' weapons are mostly for show. She wonders if they'd even miss them . . .

Zoey inhales, her eyes opening wider.

"What is it?" Lee asks.

"I can just take one," she says.

"A gun?"

"Yeah."

"Are you feeling okay?"

"I'm fine, listen to me. Have you ever seen a guard draw his handgun?"

Lee thinks for a second. "No, I guess not."

"It's because they're forbidden to use them. The prods are what they're allowed to use, especially on the women, because they don't want us hurt beyond repair. The guns are mostly for show and for extreme situations."

"Okay, but how does that help us?"

"Don't you see? If I managed to take one from a belt, they might not notice until that evening or even the next day. There's so many things on their belts—"

"Zoey, that's insane. What if you got caught?"

"They'd probably kill me," she says simply.

"How would you even do it? There's no period of time that you'd be alone with a guard to take it from him."

Zoey falls silent, drumming her fingers on the tops of her thighs. "Crispin."

"What about him?"

"He's the nicest guard here, right?"

"I would say so."

"He hasn't been on duty near the laundry in a while. I'm guessing he'll be there soon. When he is I can jam some laundry in the delivery elevator and ask him for help, it's happened before. If his back is to me, I can take his gun and he won't ever know the difference."

"When he realizes his gun is gone, he's dead. You know that, right?"

Zoey grimaces. *How much is a life worth?* "I know. But he's one of the few guards that won't be suspicious of me."

Lee stares at her for a time. "You're different than before."

"Before what?"

"Before the box."

The memory of the darkness is almost overpowering, and she struggles against it. She hears the scritching of the insects and jumps when something touches her leg. Lee's hand rests there, and he's looking at her with concern.

"Are you okay?"

"I'm fine. And yes, I am different. I don't think I'll ever be the same. But that's not what's driving me."

Lee frowns and fidgets on the bed. "How will you smuggle the gun back up here?"

She thinks for a moment. "I'll need some heavy tape. I can make some kind of a holster in the small of my back. Our clothes are loose enough to hide it. As soon as I get it, I'll find a reason to come back to my room and hide it here."

"Where?" Lee says, motioning to the walls. "They found your hiding spot."

"I'll think of something new."

Lee rubs his forehead and sighs in exasperation. "Say you do manage to do all that, what's your plan to, you know, to . . ."

"To kill the Director?"

"Yeah."

"When is the only time we see him?"

"At the induction ceremonies."

"And?"

Lee shrugs. "That's about it. I never really see him in the halls or anything. And he's always got guards around him."

"He goes for a jog every night around the promenade unless it's raining."

Lee blinks. "Yeah, I guess I have seen him from time to time there."

"Meeka told me weeks ago that she heard a couple of Clerics say they'd love to use the sauna in the exercise room, but it's for the Director only."

"So you think he uses it every night after his run?"

"I do. And that's where he's most vulnerable."

"But how will you get down there? There's at least six doors between here and—"

She cuts him off by holding up the empty bracelet. "After Simon locks me in for the night I'll get out using your trick and sneak down to the exercise room. When the Director comes in, I'll kill him, and the two guards if need be, then use his bracelet to get to the uppermost level."

"Someone will hear the shots."

"Not on that level. You know how loud the mechanical room is."

"You'll never make it up to the fifth floor without someone seeing you."

"Not without the diversion you're going to make."

Lee points at himself. "Me?"

She nods. "You can sabotage a piece of equipment in one of the shops, light a fire, something. Then, when all the commotion starts, you meet me in the bathroom on the second floor. I'll give you Lowe's bracelet back, and you let the other women out of their rooms and bring them to the infirmary. I'll be waiting there. And we'll need some rope, a lot of it."

"What for?"

"For climbing down the side of the ARC once we cross the bridge on the roof."

"Zoey, this is . . ."

"Crazy, I know. It's absolutely insane, but it's the only way. The bridge to the wall is on the roof. The only way to get to the roof is through the fifth floor. You need to take the elevator in the infirmary to get to the fifth floor. It has to happen in a succession. Then when everything is done, and if the Director is dead, we'll be able to slip away."

"You think Reaper and his men will give up that easily?"

"No, he won't. But we'll just have to deal with it when it happens. Maybe they'll leave on another reclamation mission like they did a few days ago."

"And what about my father?" Lee asks. It's the first time throughout their discussion that his voice has taken on an edge.

"Do you think he would help us?"

"No."

"Me neither."

"So what then? We leave him here? Forsake him so that you and the others can be with *your* parents?"

Zoey frowns. "I already said I've made peace with never seeing them."

"But you're asking me to give up mine."

"I'm asking for your help."

"You're asking for more than that," he says quietly, rising from the place beside her. He moves across the room, glancing at the calendar as he goes. "I should get back to my room. It's getting late."

"Lee," she says, standing up. "I don't have much time. I need to know if I can count on you."

Lee pauses at the door, his hand on the handle. "I'll have to think about it," he says without looking back. "Give me until tomorrow. Will you give me that?"

"Yes."

"Goodnight, Zoey."

"Goodnight."

He pulls the door open and is gone in a whisper of clothing. Zoey sits and stares at her hands until she can fight the fatigue pulling at her no longer. She slumps to her side, drawing her knees to her chest, and closes her eyes to the swirling questions without answers.

11

Zoey looks for him the next morning in the halls and in the cafeteria during breakfast, but Lee is absent from the small throng of Clerics' sons who eat quietly in the far corner of the lunchroom.

Rita, Penny, and Sherell stare at her as she sits beside Lily. It's the first time she's seen Penny since the other woman was locked in the box. Other than a fading bruise on the side of her forehead, Penny is unchanged, the same flatness to her eyes.

"I won't ask you what it was like," Meeka says between bites. "I wouldn't want to talk about it so I won't make you."

"Good," Zoey says.

They eat in relative silence save for Lily's slurping of milk for nearly a minute before Meeka says, "Was it really dark?"

"God, Meeka."

"I'm sorry, I'm sorry. I know it was terrible in there," Meeka says, shooting a glance at Lily's wounds. "But you know me, I'm curious."

"Then break the rules and find out yourself."

"You don't have to get nasty," Meeka mumbles. In a lower voice she says, "Where did you get them?"

"The books?"

"Yeah."

Zoey glances down the table at the Clerics. They are all talking to one another. "They were left in my room."

Meeka's slanted eyes open wide. "You're kidding." Zoey shakes her head. "Then you've got someone looking out for you."

"Then where were they when I got put in the box?" Lily has stopped eating and begins to rock, her hands creeping up toward her ears. "I'm sorry, Lily," Zoey says, rubbing the girl's back. "It's okay, we're done talking." She shoots a look at Meeka to affirm the statement. Meeka nods, and they continue to eat quietly until the chime sounds.

The niggling voice inside Zoey repeats the fears that invaded her dreams the night before as she walks through the corridors to lecture. *Lee's going to tell you he won't help. Or worse yet, he'll tell Simon and you'll be at Reaper's mercy. No, Lee wouldn't tell anyone. He wouldn't.*

She walks like a zombie across the lecture hall and past Miss Gwen's smiling face to take her seat. Zoey draws out the hulking NOA textbook and sets it on her desk. She runs a finger up its spine, recalling the feel of the two books that were taken from her. Even though they were much smaller than her textbook, the weight they carried within their words dwarf the larger tome. Her conversation with Meeka clarifies the questions that have been burning in her mind from the moment she found the first book. Who left them for her, and where is that person now? How cruel of them to tempt her with the visions and meaning in those pages, but now, when she needs real help, they refuse to reveal themselves.

Zoey shoves the textbook away from her, and it plummets to the floor with a resounding slap.

The other women glance her way. Miss Gwen jumps, her head snapping around, eyes widening behind her glasses.

"Zoey! What is the meaning of this?"

Zoey rises from her desk to retrieve the book, the pain from her time in the box so familiar now that she barely winces when she bends over. "I'm sorry, it slipped."

"See that it doesn't happen again." When Zoey says nothing, the instructor clears her throat loudly.

"Yes ma'am," Zoey finally replies from between gritted teeth.

Miss Gwen rises from her chair and comes to stand between the first two seats of their rows. She runs her gaze across them all, hovering last on Lily's damaged appearance. Lily gives her a cautious smile. The instructor's mouth puckers as if she's tasted something vile. "Once again I'm obliged to touch on the importance of following the guidance laid down by the Director and his staff. I was hoping not to mention anything like this in my room for a long, long time, because this is a place of learning. But since some of you seem to have a proclivity for stepping outside the rules, I must. I will get right to the point. You are held to high standards for a reason. You are the last few hopes of the human race. Can you fathom what I've just said to you? The *entirety* of humankind depends upon you. And yet you flout your responsibility like it is a joke."

Miss Gwen's voice rises with each sentence until it grates upon Zoey's eardrums. She forces herself not to blink, not to look away from the fevered gaze of the instructor, and in the second that their eyes lock, Zoey sees that Miss Gwen is mad. Not partially. Completely. Insanity dances like a flame behind her irises as she surveys them all once again.

"You're *lucky* to be here," she hisses, pointing a dagger-like finger at all of them. "You have no idea how lucky you are, to be who you are. I'm ashamed of your actions against NOA, and I'm ashamed to call you my students." She favors them all with another burning look before returning to the front of her desk. "Page three hundred seventeen. I want someone to read about the devastating conditions women who were unable to have children endured during the time of war. Maybe that will get it through your stubborn skulls. Who will read?"

Zoey's breath is coming faster and faster. Her muscles twitch. She grips the sides of her desk, and when the others open their books, she remains still. Beside her, Lily finds the correct page and begins to wave her hand in the air.

"Me, I ree!" Lily says.

Miss Gwen flicks a glance at her before motioning to Sherell. "Sherell, begin at the top of the second paragraph and—"

"Why won't you ever give her a chance?" Zoey says. Her voice is low, but it carries well across the room.

Everything is utterly silent.

Miss Gwen looks at her and blinks. "What did you say?"

"I said, why won't you ever give Lily a chance to read?"

The instructor comes down the row, walking fast. "Zoey, you are dangerously close to more punishment. You will apologize this instant for interrupting me."

"No."

"What? What did you say?"

Zoey stands up, a livewire of rage running through her. "No. I won't. Not until you apologize to Lily."

Miss Gwen's mouth works for a moment before the words will come. "I'll have you locked up again, you little—"

"You hate us, don't you, Miss Gwen? I can see it when you look at us. What is it? Why do you hate us?" Zoey moves around her desk, leaving nothing between her and the instructor. Miss Gwen holds her ground for a beat before retreating a step. "You talk about privilege and the greater good, but you don't have a last name either. They took it from you, didn't they? But I bet you remember it, don't you?"

"Zoey, you will sit down." Miss Gwen tries to make the words a command, but her voice falters, and she takes another step back as Zoey advances on her.

"No. I've been sitting all my life. Apologize to Lily."

"I don't take orders from you." Miss Gwen's feet bump her desk, and she puts a hand out to steady herself.

"All she's ever wanted was to read in lecture, and you couldn't even give that to her, could you? Because we have something you don't, that's why you hate us. We have a chance. That's why you're the only other woman here—this is your only use. We can have children, but you're barren, aren't you?"

Miss Gwen's hand moves faster than anything Zoey's ever seen. It whips out and cracks solidly across her face. Zoey's head rocks to the side, and immediately the patch of skin on her cheek begins to burn. The instructor is shaking, her mouth open in an O of horror. Zoey wipes at the swelling of her cheek as if brushing away a fly.

"I saw you," Zoey says in a whisper. "That day in the mechanical room with the guard. I saw you. You think if you can get pregnant, they'll give you everything back. But they won't."

Tears slide from the older woman's eyes in shining tracks down her cheeks. She tries to keep herself upright, but her legs won't hold her and she crumbles to the floor. Zoey stands over her, breathing hard, the place where Miss Gwen struck her throbbing in time with her heart.

"Get out," the instructor says between sobs in a breathless voice. When no one moves, she stares around at them with the same madness as before. "Get out!"

There is a thunder of footsteps as the Clerics approach from the far side of the huge room. Simon is the first to step around the barrier and see the instructor seated on the floor.

"Remand her to her room!" Miss Gwen yells. "Get her out of my sight. All of you, get out."

Zoey walks away from the instructor, heading for the exit. The rest of the women rise from their seats and file out past Miss Gwen's weeping form.

"What happened?" Simon says, catching up to her near the exit.

"Go ask her."

"Zoey, stop." He grabs her arm gently. "What happened?"

"Miss Gwen isn't feeling well."

He glances at her cheek where she can still feel the instructor's palm. "Let's go."

Simon escorts her back to her room. He doesn't speak the entire way, only telling her to get some rest before closing the door.

Once the locks click home, she slumps to the bed. Her hands shake and she holds them out before her, studying their traitorous vibrations.

Miss Gwen deserved it. So why do I feel dirty, like I've committed a crime? It's several minutes before an answer comes to her.

It is because she understands.

For a second she places herself in the instructor's position, and it is enough to create a flicker of empathy.

Zoey stands and makes her way to the bathroom. There is the perfect outline of four fingers gracing her cheek, their tips pointing into her hairline above her ear. She splashes cold water on her face, cooling the sting before scooping handfuls up over the back of her neck.

When she's dried off, she moves around the small space of the bathroom, searching for a place in which she can hide a handgun. She tugs on the sink, but it is immovable. She looks in the toilet tank, but it is too obvious. Dismissing the bathroom entirely, she begins pacing back and forth past her bed. She spends the majority of the next hours finding and discarding a half-dozen hiding places. The closest feasible options are somewhere in the small closet beside the bathroom, or within her mattress. Both will be easily detected if they search her room. But really, she doesn't have to concern herself with it as much as she first thought. If she manages to take Crispin's gun, she will enact her plan that night. And if it works, she and the others, along with Lee, will be free the following morning.

Or I'll be dead.

Either way, she won't have to worry anymore.

◆　◆　◆

Shortly before lunch, Simon steps into her room. She managed to fall asleep in the meantime and feels somewhat rested as she rises from her bed.

"Miss Gwen has requested that you not return to lecture for the remainder of your time before induction," he says.

She had anticipated as much. "Are they sending me back to the box?"

"In light of the fact that she struck you, no. And she hasn't stated what angered her to that point. Would you like to tell me?" Zoey shakes her head. "I didn't think so." Simon watches her for a long time before motioning to the hall. "It's time to eat."

The lunchroom is cold. They file into it together, all the women at the front, their Clerics trailing behind, murmuring to one another. Zoey's sure they're talking about what happened in the lecture hall.

She hears low laughter far behind her and glances over her shoulder. Lee is near the back of the line with several other Clerics' sons. He's smiling at something someone else has said, but he notices her looking and his grin falls away. She turns back to the front, but not before she catches Rita looking at her. The larger woman is directly behind her, and she appears to have regained her swagger from before her time in the box.

They make it to the serving table and begin to gather their food. Rita's elbow brushes Zoey's arm with a soft nudge.

"Oh, sorry," Rita says, not sorry at all. "Hope that didn't hurt. I'm sure you're still sore."

Zoey smiles. "Feeling very well, thank you."

"Hmm. Good to hear. I was worried you wouldn't be the same after that."

Zoey doesn't answer. Instead she places the last few items on her tray and begins to move to the water dispenser.

"It was me," Rita says in a whisper. "I told Dellert to search your room."

Zoey freezes, and all sound falls away in the lunchroom. Everything is in stasis except for her and Rita. She turns her head, eyes narrowing.

"What did you say?"

"I smelled the gum on your breath, you stupid bitch. The day I hugged you I smelled it. It couldn't have worked out more perfect. Especially since the retard got—"

But Rita doesn't finish her sentence because Zoey smashes her tray into the side of the other woman's head.

Rita tries to feint away but the plastic tray catches her in the temple and she stumbles out of the line.

Food flies, and Rita grunts with pain.

The sound comes rushing back to the room, and there is movement again. Zoey ignores it all. Her vision has narrowed to a pinprick with Rita taking up her entire view. She swings the tray again, the remaining food slopping off the top and fanning out in the air before the plastic clips Rita's shoulder. The bigger woman slips in a pool of gravy as she tries to throw a punch, and her fist goes wide. Zoey sidesteps the attack, bringing the tray up over her head. She turns it sideways, making it as much of a blade as possible, and aims for the back of Rita's neck. She hears Lee yelling something. Fingers snag her collar, but the entire world is red with her fury.

As she swings the tray down, there is an explosion of pain in her lower back, her muscles seizing with it. She hears the crackle of electricity as the tray falls from her hands, tumbling down harmlessly to the floor. Zoey opens her mouth to scream, but she's already falling, falling like the tray, into darkness that is enclosing the ceiling from the sidewalls in. It rushes down and covers her completely.

◆ ◆ ◆

Crimson furrows of light brighten somewhere in the distance, but it is like an angry sunrise before a storm. Heavy clouds adorn everything around her and she tries to rise through them but fails. She drifts, weightless, as unfamiliar sounds echo outside the darkness. She is vaguely aware of her body, but it is insubstantial as fog each time she tries to reckon out her position.

Suddenly a voice speaks above her and the drifting ceases. The words are jumbled, but she knows their owner. It is the first voice of memory. It is Simon. It is her father.

She tries to say the word, to call him what she's always wanted to, to give him a title that he's earned, but he falls silent. The red smear of horizon begins to widen with gaps of lightning painful enough to make her moan, and even as she realizes she's struggling to open her eyes, there is a sharp pain in her arm and ice flows outward from the spot.

Zoey tries again to open her eyes, but the storm clouds are unfurling like black sails and coming lower and lower until they smother her in their dark embrace.

12

Boom.

    Boom.

    Boom.

    Boom.

    "Zoey."

    She hides from the pain that each thunderous concussion brings.

    "Zoey, can you hear me?"

    She takes a deep breath, coming slowly to realize that the blows she's feeling aren't being rained upon her head from outside, but from within. Her heartbeat holds the hammer and continues to smash the sides of her skull. Nausea snakes through her stomach and sets up camp there, ready for an extended stay. She groans and opens her eyes.

    She's in the infirmary, but not in the same room as before. Curtains surround her bed, and a machine beeps quietly to the left. A heavy cuff of fabric gradually inflates on her right bicep, almost to the point of pain before relinquishing its grip. There is someone beside her and she cranes her neck around.

Simon peers down at her, his dark eyebrows drawn together. "Zoey, can you hear me?" he repeats.

She nods, forcing herself into a sitting position. Simon steadies her with a hand, and the room spins.

"Going to be sick," she manages. He places a plastic container in her lap, and she vomits into it.

"The doctors said you might get sick from the sedative," Simon says, taking the bowl from her grasp. He produces a white towel and dabs at her mouth. "It'll pass soon, though."

Zoey sinks back into the bed and its pillows. She stares up at the featureless ceiling. "What happened?"

"The guard in the lunchroom shocked you with a prod. He was right behind both you and Rita when you attacked her."

The memory comes flooding back. "She told Dellert to search my room."

"What?"

"The day she was released from the box and she hugged me in the hall, she smelled mint on my breath from the gum I'd been chewing."

"How do you know?"

"She told me."

Simon sighs. "So you attacked her."

She lets the silence draw out. "I couldn't help it."

"Zoey . . ." He shakes his head.

"I'm sorry."

"I know."

"What are they going to do with me?"

"I don't know yet. Assistant Carter is meeting with the Director right now. The only thing you have going for you is the guard overreacted. He's young, and he panicked when the fight broke out. They've already stripped him of his post, and he'll be punished accordingly."

"What about Rita?"

"She was treated for a concussion and released an hour ago."

"What? But she—"

"Zoey, it looked like you attacked her for no reason. And that's exactly what she told Carter."

She turns her head away. There is a slight gap in the curtains around the bed, and through the slit she sees half of Lee's face across the aisle. He is asleep, and a small bandage is stuck to his forehead. She turns back to Simon.

"What happened to Lee?"

Simon glances in the direction of his son, his mouth becoming a thin line. "He tried to wrestle the guard's prod away from him after you were shocked. The guard hit him and knocked him unconscious."

"Is he okay?"

"He'll be fine. He needed a couple stitches, that's all."

She relaxes into the pillows once again. The nausea is relenting, but a thickening ache takes its place in the pit of her stomach. She wonders if the guard also struck her there. If he did, there will be no saving him. She twists her neck, noting that the pounding in her head has come down to a manageable level. "Can I have some water?" Simon produces a cup with a straw and she drinks. "How long have I been out?" she asks when she's finished drinking.

"About five hours. The doctors said you had some kind of reaction to the shock. They had to work on you for a bit before bringing you back here."

"When can I leave?"

"They want to keep you overnight for observation."

"I don't want to stay here. I hate it here."

Simon studies her for a long moment before standing. "I'll see what I can do."

He sweeps out through the curtains, and she listens to the pop of his boots on the tile. Zoey takes several deep breaths, willing the clinging effects of the drugs in her system to go away. She doesn't want to be in this room after dark. Not this close to those shining doors, not until she's ready to step through them. A minute later footsteps return and Simon appears through the curtains followed by a young doctor with a shaved head and a manicured goatee. The doctor is taller than Simon and has dark brown eyes that are nearly black.

"This is Doctor Calvin," Simon says, stepping to the side.

"How are we feeling, Zoey?" Calvin says in a surprisingly high, nasally voice. The way he looks at her makes her want to shiver and hide deeper beneath the blankets, but she steadies herself and meets his gaze.

"Much better. I think I can go back to my room now."

"Hmm." Doctor Calvin moves to the beeping machine and presses a button, bringing up an array of readings and digital lines on its screen. After flicking the button several times, he nods to himself and faces them. "Your vitals look good. Are the effects of the sedatives wearing off?"

"It feels like it."

"Good." The doctor's eyes glint in the light and he cocks a half smile that reveals a crooked canine. "I guess I don't see why you can't spend the night in your room then." He gives Simon a nod and steps through the curtain without looking back.

Once he's gone, Zoey motions to Simon to come closer. When he does she says in a low voice, "Have you ever seen him before?"

"Doctor Calvin? Not that I can remember. Why?"

"Where has he been all these years if not in the infirmary?"

"Zoey, there's a lot of doctors here and they rotate out constantly. It would be easy to not meet one of them since we're rarely up here. Except as of late," he adds, giving her a warning look. "Get dressed. I'll be waiting outside if you need anything."

Simon steps through the curtains, and she hears him cross the aisle to where Lee rests. Zoey gets shakily to her feet and waits nearly a minute with one hand on the steel bed railing until the floor steadies beneath her. She finds a fresh set of clothes stacked on a bench beside the bed and dons them before taking another long drink of water. The place where the guard shocked her in the lower back feels strangely numb, but the pain in her abdomen has become more like severe menstrual cramps. It is as if a smoldering coal has been placed inside her and stokes red every time she moves.

After several deep breaths, she emerges from the surrounding curtain and crosses the tile to where Simon stands at the foot of Lee's bed. Lee is awake now, his eyes slits in his face, but they follow her and a smile tugs at the corner of his mouth. Simon is holding Lee's feet through the thin blanket that covers him, and when he notices her approaching, he releases them.

"Are you ready?" he asks.

"Yes."

"Good." He turns to Lee, squeezing his son's foot one last time. "I'll be back later this evening to bring you home." Lee nods and refocuses on Zoey as his father turns toward the exit. There is something in his gaze that dismantles all the doubt she's carried until now about his allegiance. The warmth and reassurance that radiate from him tell her all she needs to know. He's going to help.

Tonight, he mouths so quickly that she barely catches it. She flashes him a fleeting smile and follows Simon to the doors that lead out of the infirmary, elation carrying her above the pain in her body every step of the way.

◆　◆　◆

The meal she ate in the empty cafeteria sits heavily in her stomach as she lies on her bed. There was barely any hunger to sate, but she ate as much as she could, almost to the point of bursting. She knows she will need her strength for what's to come. It's really happening. Lee is going to help her. They're going to try to escape.

Excitement bristles along her spine at the thought. She dozed for a time, but now she shifts on the bed, wincing as she sits up. Her lower back is bruised from the strength of the shock she received. She examined the area in the bathroom mirror after Simon escorted her to her room, the vague outline of the injury a solemn red, the center beginning to purple like the eye of a storm.

Rita. Rita caused this.

Hatred rises within her at the thought of the other woman. The sneering, smug look she must have plastered on her wide face right now. Zoey clenches her fist. *I should leave her here*, she thinks, shaking with rage. *If the plan works I'll take the rest of them, even Penny and Sherell, but leave her here to suffer alone.*

The thought stokes righteous anger but just as quickly it deflates, leaving her feeling dirty and defiled for having thought something so cruel, even about someone as heartless as Rita. She couldn't leave another woman here any more than she could leave one of her limbs.

Zoey shoves the thoughts away. There isn't time for whims of revenge now. At a later date, if they make it out alive, she and Rita will have their reckoning. Until then the energy is better spent elsewhere.

She uses the next few hours to reexamine her room for a hiding place for the gun she will steal. And at the end of her search, her options are the same: mattress or cabinet. She finds a loose seam on the top end of the mattress that she easily widens, just enough to slip a handgun through. She pulls up the mattress several times, mimicking an inspection, but the torn seam is only noticeable if looked at directly from the end.

Satisfied, Zoey remakes her bed and lies down on it again. She watches the calendar and imagines she can hear the digital numbers ticking off. Three days. Three days until the white dress will appear in her closet. Three days until she'll be led into the assembly. Three days until she'll stand before the shining doors.

No.

That's not going to happen. Until the box she considered herself weak and unimportant, simply another cog in the machine of NOA, an unwilling part of the greater good. But now she knows different. For years the whispers from her inner sanctums spoke of traitorous and forbidden things, actions and words that would immediately receive punishment both swift and fierce if spoken aloud. For the longest time she was full of doubt each time she considered those most secret thoughts. Who was she to put herself above the rest? Who was she to question the authority of those so much older? Who was she to ask the questions that were only answered by penance? Yes, the shame that accompanied the strange obsessions was almost as powerful as the thoughts themselves.

But not quite. Not quite.

And now, with so little time left, with the numbers actually falling away before her eyes, there is no more denying the choices that will become her fate. Her horizon has split into two now, one of freedom and one of death. There is no in between.

Zoey stands from the bed, her body calling out for the sleep it so desperately needs, but the fire in her veins won't let her rest. Instead she showers and dresses in fresh clothes. As she carries her dirty clothing into the bedroom, she imagines the pile of laundry that must be accumulating in the room far below her feet and wrinkles her face in disgust. To never return there for another shift—how would that be? *Wonderful*, she thinks. *Truly wonderful.*

She is just beginning to wonder how long it will be before Lee arrives, or if he will come at all after receiving a head wound, when footsteps begin to approach her door. She glances at the calendar. It is nearing midnight, but it's earlier than Lee's ever come before. Two feet stop in front of her door, creating ominous shadows in the space at the bottom. Even as it registers to her that Lee never made as much noise before, the locks clack open and the door swings inward, revealing Dellert's torn visage.

His face is a landscape of skin patched in several places by black thread. The gaping mouths left by her fingernails have been closed, but their lips still shine ugly and red in the harsh light. The guard smiles, which makes his entire appearance even more foul.

"Evening, Zoey. It's time we had a little talk, you and I."

13

She opens her mouth to scream, but Dellert moves like lightning.

He shoves something between her lips that shunt her jaws painfully apart. Her cry dies in her throat just as one of the guard's hands comes up and strikes her upon the left temple.

The room whips to the side, and before she can gain her balance, she's being hauled out of her room and down the hallway. Zoey blinks, trying to clear her vision, but the blow has left her head spinning, unable to focus completely on anything. She grunts and tries to dig her heels into the smooth floor, but Dellert is strong and has her by both upper arms. Whatever he put in her mouth digs into her tongue, its surface rough and sharp. A rock, maybe. She shakes her head, trying to expel it, but it's stuck fast between her teeth. Her stomach slops with fear as Dellert forces her around the closest corner and stops beside a featureless door she's only noticed in passing. She tries to scream again as he scans his bracelet and the locks open, but his fingers entwine themselves in her hair, and he yanks her through the doorway so hard her head rocks to the side and the bones in her neck pop.

Through the door is a dimly lit stair landing with a set of treads running both up and down. A dome light throws shadows across the other two occupants of the space, and when Zoey focuses on them, she quits breathing for a long moment.

Meeka stands in the closest corner of the landing with Dellert's companion, Baron, beside her. The younger guard has her pinned to the wall and is nuzzling her neck with his mouth. The same type of gag protrudes from between Meeka's lips, and her dark eyes are alight with panic as they meet Zoey's.

"Baron! I told you, nothing until we get there," Dellert says, his voice just above a whisper. Baron snaps away from Meeka as if he's been struck and wipes at his mouth.

"Sorry."

"Sorry my ass. Get moving."

The two guards shove them down the stairs, hands grasping their hair. Zoey's heart beats so hard her vision jumps with each pulse. Her breath rattles in her chest, and she feels saliva escaping her mouth around the sides of the gag.

They go down, farther and farther through the stairway until they reach the lowest level. Dellert again scans his bracelet, his hand loosening some on her hair, and Zoey takes the opportunity to spin and throw a punch at his throat. Dellert sees it coming and turns, taking the strike on the meat of his shoulder. His retribution is immediate. His hand comes out, slapping her on the same place he'd struck her earlier. Her sight bleaches at the corners and she nearly falls, her jaws clenching down hard. The taste of blood fills her mouth.

"You try that again and I'll strangle you to death," Dellert says, emphasizing his words by sliding a callused thumb beneath her chin. His hand clamps down on her throat, and she gags as he releases her. "But first I'll kill her in front of you. Got it?" He jerks a thumb at Meeka and ducks his head so that his face is level with hers, their eyes inches apart. She nods. "Good. Now let's move."

Dellert rescans his bracelet and checks the hall outside before ushering her into it. They are in the laundry corridor beside the mechanical room, the sonorous throb invading her bones. Realization of where they're being taken hits her and she begins to struggle again, but there's no escaping Dellert's grip. He guides her to the mechanical entrance and opens the door.

The reek of oil and hot steel assaults her nasal passages, and she nearly gags again. She prays silently that the yellow flash of a worker's jumpsuit will appear in the tangled rows of equipment, some promise of salvation, but none does. Dellert shoves her to the left, past the hanging worker uniforms, past the stand of lockers and humming electrical panels. Then they are in the narrow passage that Miss Gwen and the anonymous guard occupied only days ago, the end of the bench where the instructor rested still clear.

Zoey scans the rest of the space, but the aisle ends in a cement wall a dozen yards away and there is no possibility that even she can squeeze through the gaps in the cabinets. Dellert gives her a last shove and she stumbles, catching herself on the edge of the workbench. Meeka bumps into her, and Zoey snags her friend's arm as she's about to fall. They stare at one another, wide-eyed, trembling, and even though Meeka doesn't resemble her at all, Zoey feels like she's looking into a mirror. The same terror is etched into Meeka's face, and there is something in her eyes that is beyond panic. It is like a cord has come unplugged somewhere deep in the younger woman's head. Zoey feels the same anchoring pleading to be released within her own mind. What a joy it would be to detach and become an otherness, separate from the all-consuming fear that's rising with shining teeth and a promise of what's to come.

"You can take those things out of your mouths now," Dellert says, standing with his hands on his hips, blocking the only way out of the aisle. "And don't bother screaming after you do, no one's going to hear you."

Zoey reaches up and gets her fingers around the thing in her mouth. She stretches the tendons in her jaw even farther, the pain so bright she whimpers from it. She tugs and pulls the gag out, its rough edges grinding against her teeth. It *is* a rock, the perfect size to barely fit in her mouth. Its jagged sides are coated with a slickness of blood.

"Throw it on the floor," Dellert says. Zoey glances at Meeka, who has also removed her rock. She considers flinging the stone at Dellert's head, but the chances of hitting him are slim to none—and it seems he can read her mind, for he jabs his finger at the floor. "Don't you dare throw it either, bitch. Put it down."

Zoey and Meeka drop the rocks at the same time, the sound of them striking the floor barely audible above the growl of equipment.

"Good girls," Dellert says. His grin stretches the sutures on his face, and his tongue protrudes obscenely, touching his upper lip.

"You can't do this," Meeka says, taking a small step forward. "You'll be executed for even touching us." She spits a wad of blood onto the floor at Dellert's feet, and he looks down at it before raising his eyes to them.

"You don't know what I can do," he replies. He takes a step forward and Baron follows him, the younger guard's face tense with excitement.

"You're insane. You're both on camera taking us from our rooms. We'll tell the Clerics and you'll be dead before tomorrow," Zoey says, forcing back the vomit that has gathered at the back of her throat.

"See that's where you're wrong, girlie," Dellert says. "We're friends with the guard that runs the cameras and it won't be anything to get that little bit of video deleted. Especially since we promised him a turn next time."

"You're lying," Zoey says, but even as the words leave her she remembers the information Lee gave her about Becker sleeping on his shift. If the man is that lackadaisical, perhaps his morals are as well.

"You know I'm not. I wouldn't lie. I'm not like you, keeping con-traband in my room." The guard's voice wavers as he motions to his injuries. "Do you know what the doctor told me? He said the scars will never go away. Never. I'll have to look at them every time I shave or catch a glimpse of myself in a mirror or window. I'll have to remember the pain of your fingernails tearing my skin apart." Zoey backs away as Dellert takes another step, but Meeka stays still, frozen by fear. "So it's only fair that I give you something to remember, too. I'm going to screw you so hard you won't walk right for a week."

"I'll tell Simon. He'll kill you," Zoey says, flicking her eyes to the right. A short length of steel pipe rests on the workbench beside a vise. It isn't overly long, but it looks heavy. Heavy enough to break bones.

"Go ahead and tell him—no one will believe you when there's no video to back it up. It's your word against ours. And you said so yourself—we'd have to be insane to do something like this." His dark eyes glint in the light as he advances another step.

Dellert is almost even with Meeka when Zoey shoots the pipe another quick glance. It will have to be perfect. If her hand slips or she stumbles, there won't be another chance. Dellert stops several feet from Meeka, who hasn't moved. He reaches out and tucks some of her hair behind her ear.

"Think I'll warm up on you, though," Dellert says to Meeka, his eyes swimming over her body. "I want to last longer when I punish your friend back there." His hands drop to the zipper of his pants.

"Hey, you said she was mine, man," Baron says in protest.

"You'll take what you get or I'll bust your teeth off in your head," Dellert replies, without looking back. He continues to dig at his crotch and smiles as he takes another step forward.

Zoey lunges for the pipe.

She sees Dellert's eyes widen but he only has a split second of surprise before Meeka moves as well.

Meeka, always so fast, faster than any of the other women no matter what the activity. No one has ever come close to beating her in a footrace, and Zoey doesn't know how many times she's seen her friend snatch a falling item out of the air with startling reflexes. But the speed at which she moves now defies reason.

Her foot flicks out in a light kick, perfectly aimed at the bottom of Dellert's prod that hangs from his belt. The weapon shoots straight up out of its holder and hangs motionless for an instant between the small woman and the guard before Meeka snatches it and twirls it once. In one motion she depresses the button on its handle and jams it up into Dellert's gaping mouth.

There is the droning crackle of electricity and blue light leaps from between Dellert's lips. His eyes roll up to the whites and his long body jerks backward, arms and legs going rigid.

Zoey is stunned by the violent spectacle but manages to grasp the pipe from the bench as Dellert topples backward. He falls gracelessly and slams into the cold floor on his back. His slackened jaws clack together, and one hand curls into a spasming fist. Zoey steps forward, her eyes locked on Baron, who is openmouthed and frozen in place. She has to incapacitate him before he can draw his weapon. But as she tries to step over Dellert's fallen form, Meeka shoulders past her and brings the prod down in a flash of black steel onto Dellert's forehead.

Dellert's skull crunches with the impact.

It's a wet sound that carries over the noisy equipment, and Zoey sees why as gray mush spurts from a crevice of bone on the side of the guard's skull. Meeka raises the prod and swings it again. Dellert's head cracks wide open in a spray of red that speckles Zoey's bare arms. Meeka brings up the dripping weapon and steps past the twitching corpse at her feet as loud explosions tear the air apart around them.

Zoey flinches, ducking involuntarily as several more blasts fill the aisle with flashing fire. She raises her eyes and sees Baron standing at the head of the corridor, his gun drawn, barrel smoking. Beside her, Meeka stumbles back, darkly wet blossoms appearing on the front of her shirt.

Zoey blinks, trying to reconcile the image, but there is only the pungent smell of gunpowder, the ringing in her ears, and the stillness of the moment. The single second hangs for an eternity before Meeka looks down at her shirt, then slowly crumples to the ground.

"Meeka!" Zoey screams, scuttling forward, all thoughts of the pipe gone as she drops it and crouches beside her friend. Meeka quivers on the floor, her slender neck trying to hold her head off the ground. Zoey reaches out to the front of her bloodied shirt that is becoming wetter by the second, but she stops her trembling hands inches from the gushing wounds, overwhelmed by the magnitude of blood. Instead she cups Meeka's head and grasps her closest hand.

"Got him," Meeka rasps. A small bubble of blood inflates at the corner of her mouth and pops.

"Don't talk, you're okay. I'm going to get you help." Meeka closes her eyes and when she reopens them they are half as wide. Zoey shoots a glance at Baron who has inched forward, his arm still outstretched and holding the pistol. "Go get help!" Zoey yells, but the guard's eyes are locked on Meeka and the spreading pool beneath her body.

"It's okay," Meeka whispers, wetting her lips with crimson. "It's okay now. I'm . . ." She inhales a rattling breath partway and her eyelids flutter like a butterfly's wings before stilling.

"Meeka? Meeka!" Zoey shakes her gently, but the other woman's eyes are already glazed. Drying in the hot air. "No, no, no, no," Zoey keens. There is something expanding inside her, an all-consuming pressure that forces out only sounds from her throat, no more words. She sobs, feeling the warmth of Meeka's blood seep into the knees of her pants.

"Is she dead?" Baron asks. He's standing near Meeka's feet, the gun at his side. Zoey bares her teeth at him. She gently lowers Meeka's head to the floor and glances at the pipe beside Dellert's corpse. As she prepares to leap for the weapon, Baron raises the pistol and places its barrel in his mouth.

The report is muffled, much quieter than the prior shots, but Zoey still jerks with the sound. A dark shower erupts behind Baron's head and he crumples to the floor limply. The handgun clatters once, landing only inches from her hand.

All is still.

Zoey stares down at the pistol, the tip of its barrel coated in red. The machines hum around her, and the scent of death permeates the air. She reaches out a hand and touches Meeka's fingers. They are already cool.

A scream wells up inside her, and it's all she can do to hold it back. The urge to simply lie down next to Meeka and stay there until someone finds her is strong, but even as her muscles slacken to do just that, her eyes fall on Dellert's outstretched hand and the bracelet above it.

Zoey swallows a choking lump in her throat and stands. Her legs threaten to fail her, but she steadies them and moves to the nearest workbench. The wall behind it is lined with various small tools: screwdrivers, chisels, a rubber mallet. She reaches the end of the bench and stops, glancing toward the door to make sure she's still alone. Something catches her attention on a shelf several yards away, its bulk partially hidden beneath a plastic drop cloth. She moves to it, pulling the shroud away before examining it for a moment. She grasps the tool and walks back to the aisle.

Zoey positions herself beside Dellert's body, her feet straddling his arm. She places the long blades of the bolt cutter to either side of his wrist, and raising her eyes away from the sight, brings the handles together.

There is almost no resistance and only a faint crunch as the cutters do their work. When she looks down, Dellert's hand lies palm down and a gush of blood escapes the stump of his wrist. Shoving aside the churning nausea, Zoey kneels and pulls the bracelet free of Dellert's arm. She wipes it on his uniform before unsnapping his holster to retrieve the pistol that rests there. After examining the weapon and determining its safety mechanisms, she slides the gun into the pocket of her pants so that only its grip protrudes.

Zoey moves back to Meeka's side and bends down. She places one hand on the other woman's cold brow and brushes back her hair before leaning forward to place a kiss on her forehead.

"You never would have let me do that before," Zoey chokes out. She tries to say something more, but her throat constricts to a pinhole and she has to wipe away a thick layer of tears that have formed on her eyes. She shudders once with a final sob and sniffles, standing. Zoey grasps the bolt cutters and carries them past the other two bodies, pausing as an afterthought to pull Baron's prod from his belt. There is a small dial on its handle that she turns up to the highest number. She throws a final look back at Meeka's unmoving form before rounding the corner.

The door opens to the outside corridor with a swipe of Dellert's bracelet. She peers into the hallway before hurrying down its length to the laundry door. A frenetic excitement laced with terror runs through her as she stops at the laundry room. There will be someone inside, a guard will come through the doorway at any second, an alarm will suddenly sound, something will stop her.

But none of these things happen, and she slips inside the large room in silence. Without hesitation, she hurries to the laundry elevator and presses the load button. The second shelf extends out over the folding table, and she places the bolt cutters as far back on the telescoping extension arm as possible. The steel is harder to cut through than Dellert's wrist and she tries to ignore the comparison her mind insists on making. Finally there is a snap and the shelf twists, still held up by the other arm. Zoey snips through the second support and the shelf falls to the folding table with a bang. She cringes for a moment before dropping the cutters to the floor. After setting the shelf aside, she crawls onto the table and climbs inside the space left by the absent shelf. The steel is cold, and she has to exhale to slide into the elevator. She tucks her feet close to her body and reaches out, knowing simply by touch which button to push.

The amputated arms retreat past her, and the door to the elevator closes with a click. Then she is rising, her stomach struggling to keep up.

Her breathing is loud and painful, since each inhalation presses her back against the shelf above her. Claustrophobia descends as she imagines the elevator as an enormous vise, slowly and inevitably clamping down on her body. She grits her teeth and twists a handful of her pant leg.

The rising sensation stops, and the elevator doors open onto the inside of the women's and Clerics' clothing cabinet. Before the automatic arms go through their cycle of depositing the nonexistent apparel, Zoey slides out and wiggles past piles of pants and shirts until she is at the doors enclosing the cabinet's front.

Sweat runs freely down her back and neck. She blinks, finding the inside of the doors' handles before turning them as quietly as she can. The doors ease open a crack and she inches forward, pausing to look through the gap. There is only darkness on the other side. She squints, frowning. The cabinet is set beside the laundry chute in an alcove near the head of the stairway. There should be ample illumination from the hallway lights, not this solid blackness.

The darkness shifts, and her eyes bulge.

She is looking at the back of a guard's shirt.

He stands only inches away from the cabinet and adjusts his duty belt with a soft clicking. He begins to hum a low song beneath his breath before striding away down the corridor. Zoey listens to the sound of his retreating footsteps over the base thumping of her heart, sure that he will hear it and return to yank her free of the cabinet. A tremor runs down the length of her body, and she takes several deep breaths before pushing the doors the rest of the way open.

She slides out into the vacant alcove like a ghost, pale and cold as the floor she stands on. One hand grasps the prod and the other the pistol grip. Zoey moves to the corner of the nearest wall and shoots a look down the stairway, then toward the empty hallway. The guard who was standing before the cabinet strolls leisurely, stopping every so often to check a door or dig at the seat of his pants. Finally he rounds the next bend and disappears.

Zoey steps into the corridor and looks up at the black, half-domed camera, the surveillance like a pressure on her skin. She has perhaps a few minutes before another guard comes through. If she's lucky. She has to free Lily, Rita, Penny, Sherell, and Lee before going to the infirmary. How to explain to Lily she's got to stay quiet? She knows Lee could help her but she isn't sure she's fortuitous enough to meet with him by chance in the hall. And what to do with Simon? For he will surely wake when she opens the door to the room he shares with Lee.

She clears her mind, focusing solely on her senses, pausing every three steps to listen for the telltale sound of polished boots. Her eyes dart forward, then back over her shoulder, awaiting the moment when an alarm will sound, waking the entire facility. As she nears the first door on her left she slows and pushes past the void that tries to grow within her chest.

Meeka's room.

She wishes beyond everything that Meeka was beside her now instead of lying on the hard floor of the mechanical room with the would-be rapists. It was a desecration to leave her there, but she had no choice.

Zoey shakes her head, realizing she's stopped moving completely. Meeka would chide her for being so sentimental at such a perilous time. She gives Meeka's door one last look before creeping past it. At the next corner she stops, tilting her head just so one eye can see around the bend.

Four snipers are moving toward her, long rifles slung casually over their shoulders. They talk in low voices and one in the rear of the procession laughs quietly.

Zoey jerks back behind the corner, her shoulders digging into the hard wall. The snipers are relieving their four counterparts from the perches outside. There's no way she can kill them all and there's no place to hide here.

Time slows to a crawl, each breath takes a full minute to complete. She is frozen except for her heart, which defies the shackles of suspension and double times.

Move, Zoey. It is Meeka's voice within her mind.

I can't.

You move right now, you worthless princess. I didn't die for you to get caught.

I can't.

MOVE!

The last thought is a shout, and Zoey breaks from her position against the wall. She pelts down the center of the hall, indifferent to the watching cameras. She comes to a stairway and flies up the treads. Behind her, the footsteps of the soldiers echo in the hall. She rounds the first landing and doesn't stop. Up the next set of stairs, and then she's at the junction of halls that lead to the assembly area or the infirmary.

Which way? Which way? Whichwaywhichwaywhichway?

Voices float up to her from the stairs and she bolts right, toward the infirmary, even as she sees a guard round the farthest corner of the corridor. If she had gone left, she would have run right into him. She waits for a yell to come, but there is only the approaching sound of the snipers. The door of the infirmary is ahead. She slides to a stop and flashes Dellert's bracelet across the scanner. The door takes forever to unlock and she hears one of the snipers call out to the guard.

They're on the top steps.

The door clicks open and she dives inside, ready to tase anyone in her way.

The infirmary is quiet, the rows of beds empty, doorways darkened. The door shuts silently behind her and she moves forward, knees bent, heart raging.

There is the swish of a white coat ahead and she flings herself into the closest room, crouching beside the exam table. A pyramid of light stains the floor from the hall, and she inches backward as far away from it as she can as it flutters and Doctor Calvin strides by. His head doesn't turn to look in the room, and she holds her breath as he stops at the exit. After a long moment there is the click of the locks and a flow of conversation floods the infirmary.

"Was there someone in the hallway outside?" Calvin's voice says.

"Greg was doing rounds," one of the snipers answers. "Why?"

"I could have sworn I heard the door open a minute ago."

"Wasn't Greg, he went past us down to level three."

There is an extended silence. *Search this floor* will be the doctor's next order, she's sure of it. Slowly, Zoey withdraws the pistol and aims it at the empty doorway. She will not make it easy for them to take her. If she's not going to be able to help the others escape, she's going to take out as many of the bastards as she can. They'll remember her at the very least for that.

The thought brings a flicker of a smile to her face before the sound of footsteps wipes it away.

"Must've been hearing things," Calvin says.

"Yeah."

"Well, I'm going off shift, I'll ride up with you all if you don't mind?"

"Fine with us, Doc. Hey, you hear about what the one rat did to Gwennie today?"

"I've asked you not to call them that, Lieutenant."

"Yeah, okay. Anyway, she said something to her, and now Gwen's locked up in her room. Won't come out."

Five figures file past the open door and Zoey aims at each one of them in turn, ready to pull the trigger as soon as a set of eyes lands on her. None do. The last sniper disappears from her line of sight, and their voices fade as they move deeper into the infirmary.

Zoey lets out a shaky breath, deflating with it. Her vision doubles for a brief, sickening beat before refocusing. She stands and sidles to the door. The aisle outside the room is empty. The voices of the men are gone, leaving only the faint hush of wind outside the walls and the buzz of lights in the ceiling.

She glances to the left at the exit. Then to the right. What are the chances of her retracing her steps, unseen, to the women's dormitories, releasing them, and guiding them back to this point? There aren't enough zeroes in the world to place after a decimal point in that equation.

How much is a life worth?

She closes her eyes and begins to excise the traitorous feelings from her mind with a scalpel of cold reason. She is here, the other women are not. She was trying to release them but fate swayed against her. She knows she probably won't escape with her life tonight, and that is the only redeeming quality she feels her actions may grant her. If she manages to kill the Director, then all of this will benefit them in turn.

Zoey abolishes the last traces of guilt, knowing they'll return tenfold if she somehow survives the night.

There will be a guard, she knows, and he will be in front of the doors. The damnable, shining doors, and no other bracelet will allow her to pass besides the one on his wrist. She composes herself for nearly a minute, listening for any movement, but there is nothing. Zoey steps into the open air of the hall and scans the medical beds and their surrounds. She reaches the end of the rows of beds and stops. Across the wide room, which holds dozens of unused gurneys and rolling operating trays, are the elevator doors. They gleam their silver smile as if they have been waiting for her. In a way she supposes they have.

Zoey surveys the entire space once, twice, three times. The guard is not here. She squints and bends low, thinking he may have heard her coming and is hiding beneath one of the empty beds, but there is only bare floor. She pivots, holding the prod in front of her, ready to depress its trigger at the creeping foe behind her, but the aisle is empty.

Faintly she hears a toilet flush.

Zoey spins, eyes darting to the single, unmarked door left of the elevator. It must be a bathroom. She runs, feet barely touching the ground as she slides to a stop beside the door. She brings up the prod as the handle rattles and a man steps out into the light.

Zoey shoves the prod into his neck just as he registers movement beside him and begins to turn, his hand dropping to his own weapon.

She triggers the prod, and the blue electricity crawls across the stunned features of Crispin's face.

The guard's eyes jitter and his body locks solid and begins to fall as Zoey releases the trigger, her hand coming to her mouth to stop the cry from escaping. Crispin hits the floor on his shoulder, his head snapping off the concrete with a horrifying crack.

"Oh no," Zoey says, her voice only a whisper. "Crispin?" The guard lies still, one arm pinned beneath him, the right side of his face pressed to the concrete. She kneels, beside him, placing a hand on his shoulder. "Crispin?" She pushes him onto his side, then his back. The guard's face is slack, lips slightly parted. A smell of singed flesh rises from him, making Zoey's stomach heave. She reaches out and places her palm above his mouth and nose.

No breath touches her skin.

She sits back, turning her head to the side and biting off the scream of fury that rises in her throat. Why? Why did this have to happen? Where was her plan now that everything had been shattered?

But you were going to take Crispin's gun originally and condemn him to death anyway, weren't you? she thinks. *This is simply shortening the means to the end.*

She shudders with revulsion.

There is no time for this. Meeka again.

I can't.

You have to.

Zoey struggles to her feet, hoping against hope that she will feel a pulse in Crispin's wrist as she grasps it, but there is nothing. She muscles past the rage and self-hatred and uses it instead as fuel to drag the man across the floor to the waiting doors. She has to struggle to bring Crispin's bracelet high enough to scan. When it registers, a deep humming issues from behind the doors and she hurries back to retrieve the prod from where she left it. She positions herself to the side of the doors, ready to leap forward if anyone occupies the inside of the elevator.

There is a ticking and a quiet ping, then the doors open.

The inside is featureless and composed of the same glinting steel as the outside. She moves forward, panning the entire interior before stepping in. As soon as she is inside, the doors begin to slide shut. She allows herself one last look at the man lying on the floor, crystallizing the image into memory.

My fault.

The doors close and the floor vibrates beneath her feet. Her stomach drops as the car rises. The anticipation of what will appear on the other side of the doors is almost too much for her.

Will they be there, waiting for her? The two people she never thought she'd meet. Even as she steels herself, exhilaration surges through her. What if? What if it's true? What if they're on the other side of the doors? Will she know them when she sees them? Will they know her? Her thoughts race frenetically but she readjusts herself to the side of the car and draws the handgun as the force under her slows, then stops. There is another quiet ping.

The doors slide open.

14

"Do you remember them at all?"

Terra and Zoey turned their heads toward Meeka, who continued to gaze up at the sky above the wall. The day was bright, the sky blue and completely clear of clouds. They had stopped to sit on one of the benches during exercise hour, even though it was forbidden. Their Clerics were on the far side of the building, and they wouldn't be too concerned if their group took an extra five minutes to complete the loop. Meeka had argued it was too beautiful out not to stop and enjoy it.

Lily scratched a rock across the concrete several inches in front of where she sat, her mousy, brown hair twirling in the breeze.

"No, not really," Terra answered, shifting from foot to foot. Zoey could tell she wanted to move on. Breaking the rules always set the eldest woman on edge. "I remember a smell, something sweet and smoky. Definitely food. Nothing like we have here. I think maybe that was my mom or dad cooking." She shrugged. "How about you?"

Meeka pulled her eyes from the azure above and tucked an errant strand of dark hair behind one ear. "I remember someone lying on the ground, not sure if it was my mom or dad. I don't know if they were hurt or playing." Her dark eyes narrowed. "I think they were hurt. Then nothing. Well, then you freaks, I guess."

Lily giggled and drew a lopsided circle with the rock on the concrete. Terra shoved Meeka playfully on the shoulder.

"How about you, Zoey?" Meeka asked.

Zoey licked her lips, glancing back the way they'd come. She's always told them she remembers nothing of her parents, and it's almost true. Almost. But there is something in the recesses of her mind; a sensation so vague it is beyond any type of distinction. She isn't sure herself if it is truly a memory or something she dreamed in the lonely hours of the night when she was younger and sometimes cried herself to sleep.

The feeling of soft hair sliding between her fingers.

That is all she can remember. The quality of the sensation makes her think that it is a memory and not something her young mind conjured as a coping device to deal with the inhospitable and cold reality of being alone in this place.

She can still almost feel the silky hair gliding between her thumb and forefinger, so soft and smooth it is like water.

"Zoey?"

Terra's voice brought her back and she stiffened, realizing that she had been adrift in the moment, experiencing it all over again.

"We'd better get going," Zoey said, setting off in the direction that would bring them around to the waiting Clerics.

15

The elevator sits in the junction of two hallways.

The first stretches ahead of her while the other runs to the left and right. The floor isn't concrete but some type of filigreed stone tile, the color she imagines moss might be in the spring. The lights here aren't industrial but rather have a softness to them that is easy on the eyes. Zoey steps forward and peers out of the elevator, scanning every direction at once.

She is alone.

She moves into the hall and stops, the shuffle of the doors closing behind her giving her a jolt of pure adrenaline she doesn't need. Again she's faced with the choice of which direction to take. Left has the fewest number of doors and none of them have windows, which gives that direction a distinctly cavernous feel. Ahead, the doors lining the walls are wide and completely clear, made of some thick plastic, she assumes. To the right there are multiple doors set only several feet apart, and the hallway goes on the longest out of the three. Glancing up, Zoey sees there is a single camera above her in the ceiling. She nearly points the pistol at it and fires.

Ahead, one of the transparent doors whooshes open.

She slings herself to the nearest corner, catching only a half-glimpse of a white-smocked doctor coming toward her, eyes locked on a sheaf of papers in one hand. She waits, listening to the footsteps coming closer and closer, as she raises the prod from her side.

The doctor steps out of the corridor and turns the corner opposite her. He is short, with graying hair at the temples, and walks with a slight limp. He doesn't look back or slow. When he reaches the farthest end of the hall, he scans his bracelet, steps through the door, and is gone.

Zoey detaches herself from the wall and looks toward the doors from which the doctor emerged. She flicks a glance at the camera and prays that Becker continues his incompetent behavior a few minutes longer. When she reaches the first door she stops and sidles up to its frame, risking a momentary look.

Inside is a sprawling space of white tile and the jagged shapes of medical equipment. The machines are spaced apart equally and most circle rolling gurneys dressed with white sheets to match the floor and walls. The beds have no occupants.

Zoey hurries past the door and makes her way to the second. She has a better view of more of the same room through the next door. The rows of beds seem endless, yet none of them appear to have had any use. Even as the other hallways call to her, she moves across the corridor to the last doorway.

The room inside is much smaller than its counterpart across the hall. There are banks of computer consoles lining the left wall and a cylindrical tower stands in the center of the room, its surface covered in shifting lights that seem to swim over one another as she watches. There is a pattern to the movement, something almost organic about it. It grates on her nerves to look directly at it but she can't begin to explain why. Just as she's about to turn and hurry back the way she came, she spots something else along the farthest wall.

There are rows of rounded, opaque tanks stacked upon one another. Their bulbous sides appear to be made out of blackened glass. Flexible tubes and bundles of wires grow from each of them and run on the floor beneath a plastic cover to the blinking cylinder.

She studies the room, something about the layout and the shifting lights of the tower so unnerving it sends a cold tingle of fear through her. Just as she takes a step away from the door, a furtive sound meets her ears.

The hairs stand up on the back of her neck.

She doesn't hesitate, only moves.

The gun comes up in an instant as she whirls, and she points it at the person standing a dozen steps away.

A woman.

Her breath hooks in her lungs. The woman is dressed in brown slacks and a dark, long-sleeved shirt that hugs her slender frame. Zoey is a bad judge of age but she guesses the woman is somewhere between forty and fifty. She is slightly taller than Zoey with dark brown hair held back tightly from her brow. She has a narrow, hawkish face, a blade of a nose centered between two luminous eyes that are a color Zoey's never encountered before. They are a mixture of green and brown but instead of looking muddy, they shine.

They watch one another for a long moment before the woman's mouth trembles into a cautious smile.

"Hello," she says.

"Don't move." Zoey takes a step forward, trying to keep the gun centered on the woman's body, but her hand is shaking.

The woman holds up her hands. "I won't."

"Who are you?"

The woman hesitates. "My name is Vivian. I'm a doctor. What are you doing up here, dear?"

"Be quiet," Zoey says, closing the distance between them. "Hold up your hands." Vivian does, showing two pale slices of palm. "Now turn around." The doctor complies, standing stiffly. She glances back, one striking eye finding Zoey.

"You really shouldn't be up here, Zoey."

Hearing her name come from the woman is jarring. "How do you know my name?"

"I'm good with names. I know everyone's."

"I've never met you before."

"No. No you haven't."

Zoey casts a glance past Vivian at the deserted T of hallway beyond. "Go forward, and if you run, I'll shoot you."

"I believe you." Vivian begins to walk, hands now at her sides. Zoey inspects the woman's clothing but doesn't see any telling bulges that could be a weapon. They reach the junction of the corridors and Zoey sidesteps around Vivian to make sure they're still alone. They begin to pass the close-set doors and Zoey slows.

"Stop." Vivian does, but stays facing away. "What's behind these doors?"

"Cells."

"Cells for who?"

"Whoever requires them."

"Open the one to your left." Vivian turns and scans her bracelet across the door's reader. The lock pops. "Now open it, slowly." The woman does, pulling the door wide enough for Zoey to see inside.

The room beyond is barely ten feet deep and slightly smaller in width. There are no windows, only a toilet set in one corner and the staring eye of a camera jutting from the ceiling.

"Step inside," Zoey says. For a moment it seems like Vivian isn't going to obey, but then she moves, and even in the heightened state of stress, Zoey can't help but admire the woman's grace. She doesn't walk, she floats.

Vivian stops at the rear wall and finally turns around. Zoey moves just inside the room's door and studies the woman for a beat. "What is this place?"

"I told you, a cell."

"Not this room, this floor. What are you doing in that laboratory down the hall?"

"We're searching for a cure."

"A cure to the plague?"

"Yes. We're hoping to find a way to not only cure the plague, but also to end the Dearth. We're trying to bring back the baby girls."

Zoey studies her slight features, watches for a flicker in her eyes, but sees none. "Where are the parents?"

"What?"

"The parents. The parents of all the women here. They're supposed to be here on the fifth level, waiting for each of us to turn twenty-one. Where are they?"

Vivian's mouth closes, and her lips tighten into a bloodless line. She simply stares back at Zoey. There are no answers in her gaze, only a coldness that Zoey can feel across the distance that separates them.

Zoey motions with the pistol. "Turn around."

"Why?"

"Because I'll shoot you if you don't."

"Do you know how to use that weapon?"

"Would you like to find out?"

Vivian smiles, and this time there is genuine warmth in it. "I believe you." She pivots, facing the back wall of the cell.

"Put your hands on your head," Zoey says, turning the setting on the prod down to half power. Vivian does as she's told as Zoey moves closer.

"I'm very impressed with you, Zoey. You're an indomitable young woman."

"Shut up," Zoey says, pressing the prod into Vivian's back.

There is the sizzle of electricity and the older woman's relaxed posture goes rigid. Her feet jitter across the floor for an instant, then her legs fold and she slumps to the ground, falling hard to her side. Zoey waits for a ten-count to see if the woman is faking, but when Vivian doesn't stir, she moves forward and inspects her bracelet. She needs it to continue on, she's sure of it. She doesn't want to chance locking the woman in the cell, only to find that Dellert's bracelet won't open any of the doors on this level.

Zoey checks the doorway before kneeling beside the woman. How to get it off without cutting the strap? She has nothing to sever the woman's hand with like she did Dellert's, though she's not so sure she could do such a thing to a living person. The thought of cutting through living flesh and bone sickens her.

She stands and hesitates between Vivian and the door. She has to think of something, and soon. It's only a matter of time before someone comes across evidence of the path she's taken to get here.

Zoey turns toward the door just as something strikes her in the stomach.

The blow catches her so completely by surprise, she doesn't even cry out. She registers with horror the gun and prod flying from her grip as she falls to the ground, the pain in her abdomen flourishing up into her chest.

Assistant Carter stands in the doorway, fists held at chest height, weasel face wrinkled around eyes that are aflame with rage. He wears his customary suit and long tie, which, she registers through the fog of pain, is the ugliest shade of orange she's ever seen.

"Zoey, Zoey, Zoey," Carter tuts as he stalks forward. "I was almost sure you were smarter than this. We had our chat, remember?" She is finally able to draw in a breath and with it, lunges toward the fallen pistol.

Carter is faster.

He steps on the gun and spins it away with one foot. Then he is on top of her, his spider-like hands encircling her neck.

The cell takes on a watery quality and she coughs, but isn't able to draw a breath back in. Carter is above her, his weight pressing down, thumbs punching into the soft flesh of her throat. She feels her eyes bulge and she scrabbles at the ground, her fingernails shredding, trying to feel for the prod's solid length, but it's not there.

"You little bitches never learn, do you?" Carter breathes into her face. His breath is hot and her stomach rolls with revulsion even as stars begin to dance in the corners of her vision. But there is something else that catches her attention. The flailing part of her brain that clamors for survival shrieks and points at Carter's tie, which is no longer hanging down, but is over his right shoulder at an angle.

Zoey manages to bring one of her knees up, and grinds it into Carter's crotch. It isn't a blow, but it's enough to make the man's eyes squint and his grip lessens. She draws in a quick pull of air and reaches under his left arm.

Her fingers snag what they're looking for, and she yanks as hard as she can.

Carter's long tie cuts hard into his windpipe and he gags, his eyes widening. Zoey pulls harder and the fabric tightens into the man's skinny neck. He releases her with one hand and tries to wriggle his fingers beneath his collar, giving her enough room to bring both legs up between them.

Zoey plants her feet on Carter's chest and shoves, releasing the death grip she has on his tie.

He flips off of her and lands on his hip, a wheezing honk coming from his throat. Zoey rolls as he reaches for her, her hand stretching for the pistol a few feet away. She feels his fingers entwine in her hair as she dives forward and her scalp erupts with a thousand points of pain. Carter says something in a grating choke, and a blow lands on her lower back. She whimpers but manages to kick out and catches something solid.

Her hair separates from her skull, and she's free.

Zoey snags the gun and rolls onto her back as Carter launches himself at her, one hand still holding a tangle of her dark hair.

The gunshot is so loud it forces her eyes shut. Carter's weight falls on her, his forehead meeting her own in a painful collision. His hands claw at her neck, and she feels his fingernails scraping away skin. When she opens her eyes, his face is inches from hers, teeth bared behind bloody lips.

"Missed me, bitch," he grunts and tightens his grip once again around her throat. Zoey tries to bring the gun up, but its barrel is snagged on something and she can't get it free. Warmth blooms in her stomach and lower legs. *So this is how it feels to die. Who would have thought it would be warm. It's really not so bad.*

Carter struggles above her and slowly, she relaxes beneath him. Darkness grows like a mold in the edges of her vision.

You weakling, Meeka says.

I'm sorry. I'll be seeing you soon.

I won't speak to you. I don't talk to quitters.

I'm sorry.

Quit saying that and fight!

I can't. I'm too tired. So tired.

The darkness is almost complete. All she can see through the tunnel is Carter's horrid face. What a thing to die looking at. But there is something wrong. His features have slackened, the tautness of hatred no longer there. More blood seeps from between his teeth and drools down his lower lip. The pressure recedes from her throat, and the floating sensation that was enveloping her gives in to gravity.

The darkness flies away as she breathes in.

Carter shakes above her, his entire body convulsing as if he is hooked to an electric cable. Slowly he looks down, and Zoey follows his gaze.

The front of his button-up shirt is muddied with dark crimson. His jacket is slick with it. He tries to stand, but more blood pours from the hole in his stomach and he tips to the side, slumping against the wall.

Zoey manages to slide away from the dying man, the floor beneath her hands wet, and now she sees the warmth that had flowed across her lower body was Carter's life running free of him. She gains her feet, wobbling to the right so hard she bounces off the wall before steadying herself. Carter's eyes swim up at her. Blood coats his lower jaw like a red beard. His lips try to form words, but instead they merely create several crimson bubbles. His eyelids flutter, and his head sags forward onto his chest.

Zoey stands, watching his body for movement as she sucks in air over and over, and it has never tasted so sweet. The hot wetness of Carter's blood is cooling and the clamminess of it seeps through to her skin. She finds she's still holding the pistol and that its front sight is hooked on her pants. She frees it and stares at the corpse for a long second as Vivian begins to moan.

Zoey moves forward and kneels by Carter's side even as her head tries to float away in a swarm of dizziness. She pulls the dead man over so that he lies on his back and drags his arm out straight. Standing, she centers herself over his arm, brings her leg up, and smashes her foot down on his hand.

There is a soft crunch of bone. She resets herself and slams her heel down again.

And again.

The lump of Carter's hand softens more each time. She stomps five, seven, nine times, and stops. She bends down and tries not to focus too much on the pulped, bleeding thing that used to be an appendage. Zoey grasps the bracelet around Carter's wrist and works it down over the softened mess at the end of his arm. It comes off easily.

Vivian stirs again at the end of the cell. Some of Carter's blood has run toward her in a dark pool and is soaking into her slacks. Zoey retrieves the prod and gives the waking doctor a final look before stepping into the hallway and slamming the door.

The corridor is still empty. Carter mustn't have called anyone before finding them in the cell. The slick weight of her clothes stuck to her skin makes her gorge rise. She looks down and sees that the few steps she's taken into the hallway are marked by bloody footprints. If someone happens upon the hallway now all they'll need to do is follow her trail.

Zoey moves down the corridor, passing dozens of other cells, all of which are deathly quiet. She approaches the steel door at the end of the hall and stops, risking a quick look through the narrow pane of glass set in its side.

Beyond the barrier lies another short hall marked by only four doors. Past them is a set of wide stairs that rise to a landing before turning out of sight.

The way to the roof.

Zoey scans Assistant Carter's bracelet and pulls the door open. The short hallway smells different than any other she's been in. It's a fresh scent, one of rain and outdoors as well as something else. A flowery odor mingled with cooked meat hangs in the air like someone has just prepared a delicious meal nearby.

She lets the door swing shut without a sound behind her and moves on to the first room. The door has a small, square window barely five inches across set in its center. Inside is a space slightly larger than the cell she left Vivian and Carter in. There is a narrow, plain bed as well as a toilet and a bedside table with a single drawer, but there is no occupant. She moves quickly across the hall, performing the same search of the next room, and freezes.

Terra lies on her side in the center of the bed within the cell.

Her long, blonde hair is ratty and unkempt, its shine long since departed. Large, dark bags hang beneath both her eyes, and she's wearing a shapeless, teal smock that comes down to her ankles. Her feet are bare.

Zoey almost says her name out loud but catches herself. Instead she scans the bracelet and the door opens. She steps inside but Terra doesn't so much as twitch.

"Terra," Zoey whispers, her bruised vocal cords protesting their use. The older woman lies completely still, so still Zoey wonders if she's dead. She shoots a look into the quiet hall before hurrying to the bed's side. "Terra, look at me," she croaks, shaking her shoulder. Terra jostles with the movement, and slowly her eyes drift to Zoey's face. They are unfocused and dim—the dark, flashing intelligence Zoey knows so well, gone.

"Zoey?" Terra says. She speaks as if in a dream, and Zoey realizes in a heartbeat what's wrong.

"They drugged you, didn't they?"

"What are you d-doing here?"

"I'm getting you out. You have to get up."

"Can't, too tired."

"Come on." Zoey conceals the pistol in the pocket of her blood-soaked pants, grasps Terra's limp arm, and pulls her upright on the bed. "We don't have much time. We have to go."

"There's nowhere to go," Terra mumbles, but her voice sounds steadier, more there. Zoey hauls the other woman to her feet and stabilizes her until her balance takes over.

"Can you walk?"

"I—I think so."

"Let's go then."

"Why are you all bloody?"

"Terra, we don't have time for this. We need to leave."

"We can't get out. It doesn't matter anyway. You were right, Zoey, right all along. Our parents aren't here. They never were."

The poisonous suspicion had always stalked at the edge of her thoughts, and seeing the empty cells in the prior hallway only strengthened her wariness. But hearing the certainty in Terra's voice brings the horrible doubt into reality. And beyond that the implications are too immense to fathom. If NOA was lying all this time about their parents, what else was being kept from them?

Zoey nods numbly. "Okay. Okay, we need to keep moving."

Terra shakes her head as if trying to clear it. "Don't you get it? We're alone, Zoey. We've always been alone. They lied to us."

"I know. But we can change things now. You and I." She grabs the other woman's arm and tries to guide her into the hall, but Terra pulls away, swaying in place.

Terra blinks and swallows, her gaze going hazy again. "There's no safe zone. The woman doctor told me. There's only this. They're using us. Trying to find the keystone."

A chill courses down Zoey's back. "What do you mean?"

"We're just experiments, Zoey. They're trying to breed a female baby. That's all we're here for. They raise us up and lie to us about a safe haven, then they bring us here when we're old enough and . . ." She loses her voice for a moment. ". . . experiment to see if we can have girls or not."

The creeping horror of Terra's words tears Zoey's breath away. No safe zone. Just test animals. Being used.

"If there's no safe zone, where are all the other women?" But she already knows the answer. She can feel it deep in the marrow of her bones. It is the black whisper that has been there for years, telling her the acidic truth.

"They're dead. They're all dead. They kill them if they can't have a girl. They need the keystone." Terra's voice drifts again as she says the last words.

"What's the keystone?" Zoey hears herself say.

"I don't know. I've heard them say it over and over. They're looking for it. They need it."

Zoey comes out of the daze and bites down hard on her lower lip. The pain clarifies everything around her. "Come on. We're going." She hands Terra the prod after turning the setting back to full power. "You know how to use this, right?" Terra stares at the weapon as if she's never seen one before but finally nods. "Good. We see anyone, you use that, okay? Let's go."

Zoey leads the way out and hurries down the hall, pausing every few steps to make sure Terra is following. Her friend wobbles as she walks, but with each stride she becomes more sure-footed.

They come even with the last door before the stairs, and Zoey pauses. There is something different about the door. It is wider for one, and for another there is a keypad below the scanning device to the side of the jamb. She moves to it, placing her hand against the cold steel.

"The Director's quarters," Terra murmurs. "I saw him go inside one day when they were bringing me back to my room." Zoey scans Carter's bracelet, and the number pad glows bright. She pushes four random numbers, and the display above the pad turns red and emits a quick buzz before quieting. "What are you doing?" Terra hisses.

"I'm going to kill him," Zoey says.

"You need a code."

"I know." She punches in another set of numbers, and the pad's crimson tone brightens. "It's going to trigger an alarm," she says almost to herself. So close. She can see the Director's handsome face just beyond the sights of the gun, feel the trigger squeezing beneath her finger.

She steps away from the door and motions to the stairs. "Come on."

They climb the stairwell and stop on the landing to peer around the corner. There are another four stairs and a door blocking the way, all lit by a glowing alarm handle set in the wall. A large window is mounted in the upper half of the door and stars blaze in countless clusters of light beyond the glass, their glow almost too beautiful to look at. Zoey jogs up the last set of stairs and waits for Terra to join her.

Beyond the window is the roof. Several lights affixed to steel poles illuminate the ARC's top. Its expanse is flat save for the occasional bulk of unidentifiable equipment. Fifty yards away the two black helicopters wait like silent birds of prey. Beyond the aircraft the bridge ascends to the outer wall that rises above the ARC's roof by at least forty feet. She spots a single sniper in his perch with his back facing the roof, a dozen paces from where the bridge meets the wall.

They will have to be fast.

Zoey unlocks the door before turning to Terra, the other woman just an outline beside her in the shadowy stairway. "Okay. This is what we're going to do." She explains the plan without stopping as Terra's eyes widen. When she's finished, Terra drops her gaze, turning the prod with delicate fingers.

"I can't go with you," Terra says.

"What do you mean?"

"I told you they tested on me to try to make a girl baby. They're keeping me until they know if it worked."

Zoey shakes her head. "I don't get it. That's all the more reason to come. We're going to escape, Terra. When we're free they can't hurt you or your baby."

"You don't understand," Terra says, and now Zoey can see tears glistening in the corners of her eyes.

"What—" Zoey begins to say, before she can finish the question, Terra turns and pulls the alarm lever, sending a shrilling electronic shriek out of every speaker in the ARC.

"Go!" Terra yells, shoving Zoey out the door. She says something else, but Zoey can't hear it over the alarm, she only sees Terra's mouth form the words before she spins away and rushes in the direction of the bridge. They play on an endless loop in her mind as she runs.

You were always the strong one.

16

Yells fill the night and blend with the keening of alarms.

Flashes of high-powered lights sweep the darkness away, though it rushes in again as soon as they pass. Zoey tastes metal, the tang of fear mixed with adrenaline. She smells old grease and dried sweat. Her heart slams inside her chest and she regrips the gun, terrified that she'll drop it. After what seems like an eternity, the alarms stop and she can hear a familiar voice yelling something. The voice is punctuated with sobs. It's repeating the same thing, and she can just make out the words over the low hum of wind that buffets the ARC.

"She jumped over the side! She jumped over the side!"

Zoey closes her eyes, waiting for what she knows will come now that Terra has done her part. It wasn't supposed to be like this. But nothing has gone how she planned. She tries to calm herself, empty her mind of everything save for what she must do.

Other yells now, echoing off the walls. Men calling out to one another.

"Can you see her?"

"No, nothing!"

"How did she get past you?"

"She didn't, couldn't have."

"Then where the hell is she?"

"Shut the auto-guns off, they'll tear her apart if they track her movement!"

Zoey listens, the talk doing nothing to soothe her anxiety. The fear is a solid tumor inside her. She is beyond reckoning now, beyond punishment. She has disobeyed, maimed, killed. There is only one direction for her, and that is forward, no matter the cost.

Heavy boot steps hammer the ground closer and closer. They're going to see her, they're going to drag her, kicking and screaming, back inside the ARC. They'll put her in the box for a week before they execute her. The footfalls stop only feet away, and a voice begins to speak. Her bladder nearly releases.

"Use infrared and the tranqs," Reaper says. "She can't have gotten far. Go downstream. Radio contact the whole way. Do not injure her if at all possible."

"Yes, sir!"

There is the creak of metal, and then two slams that vibrate through her palms. She risks a glance to her right and sees polished boots three feet away. They shift and step out of view. Something heavy bangs down near her, and she bites hard on her first knuckle to keep from crying out. There are several snaps and clicks before a high, whining sound begins to fill the air. Steel pulses beneath her body and she readjusts herself, trying to rotate farther onto her side. The whining increases to a pitched scream that punishes her eardrums. She resists the urge to plug her ears and brings the handgun close to her face. She can smell the cordite and oil of the weapon and focuses on it as a deep howl rises above the whine.

Wait. I have to wait until the perfect moment.

There is a shudder all around her, and her stomach lurches as the helicopter leaves the roof and becomes airborne.

Zoey slides to the farthest end of the steel bench she's hiding under, inching along because there is barely any room to crawl, even for someone her size. A garble of conversation erupts in the cockpit but no words are clear over the chuff of the rotors. Night air courses through the helicopter and she realizes they've left one of the large sliding doors open. She slides another foot and stops, her head and shoulders protruding from beneath the bench.

She is near the very rear of the helicopter beside several locked panels and a medical gurney that is strapped to the sidewall. The entire aircraft rattles and pitches as the pilot makes a turn. There is one Redeye standing at the open doorway, gazing out into the night. Another sits opposite him in a foldout seat, a rifle propped across his thighs. The pilot guides the helicopter alone, the chair beside him empty. She is about to wriggle completely free of her hiding place when the sight outside the open door freezes her.

They have risen high above the walls and she sees past them for the first time in her life.

An enormous concrete structure sits a quarter mile from the ARC, its wall-like appearance in contrast with the compound's round shape. It is slanted upward at an angle, its ends built into the surrounding landscape. A bridge runs its entire length that she judges must be at least a mile long, and water sheets down its front in milky translucence fueled by the moon's light. It is a dam, she realizes, one so much larger than those she's read about in the NOA textbook that she can barely conceive it. The rushing sound they always thought was wind wasn't air at all, but water cascading over the spillway.

The helicopter banks, and she receives another angle of the ARC, surrounded by a wide river flowing below the dam. Suggestions of buildings stud the banks, their forms only darker shadows on the land. Rough hills grow above the shores and continue to rise into rounded peaks in the distance, but the sight beyond the dam is what makes her temporarily forget where she is.

A body of water extends out in a massive sprawl that defies her idea of space. The amount of it is staggering and her eyesight shimmers simply from looking at it. The moon reflects in a broad channel of light on its surface, which fades to an inky darkness near the banks of the reservoir.

She isn't prepared for the sight. She reels with it. The hugeness of the world is blinding.

The helicopter turns a last time, giving her a final look at the ARC hundreds of feet below, its bowl shape lit by countless lights, the figures gathered on the roof like slow-moving insects.

The aircraft drops in a pocket of air, and the thud of the rotors consumes all else in the cabin. Zoey comes back to herself, realigning with what she must do. She slides soundlessly out from beneath the bench, keeping tight to the wall and floor. The Redeyes' focus is outside the cabin, their goggles centered on the passing river and land beneath.

Zoey crouches low, gathering strength in her legs though they feel distinctly separate from her.

She aims the pistol at the Redeye leaning out of the open door.

Slowly squeezes the trigger.

Squeezes.

The Redeye turns his head toward her in the instant that she fires, his goggles flaring with bloody light in the muzzle flash.

The recoil surprises her and she blinks at the noise. The shot takes the soldier in the center of the chest as he struggles to draw his side-arm from its holster. He topples sideways into open air as the helicopter slews, and a cable attached to a harness around his torso snaps tight, leading to a ring in the ceiling, as he disappears with a short cry.

Yells erupt in a cacophony of sound, the motors screaming to meet the pilot's sudden demands.

Zoey stays low, managing to keep her balance, and turns the gun on the next Redeye, who is bringing up his rifle. He should have her dead to rights, but the angle at which he's belted to his seat is wrong, and in the second that it takes him to readjust his position, Zoey fires again.

The bullet sings through his left shoulder and travels up his neck.

Blood splashes the wall behind him, and he slackens against his restraints, his rifle spinning and sending off a chatter of bullets.

Ricochets blaze by her, their hot passage splitting the air beside her face. The pilot screams incoherently and the helicopter rips to one side. Zoey tumbles onto her shoulder, then to her belly as the aircraft stabilizes. She's got to get to the pilot, force him to fly her far away.

She makes it to her feet and sees the pilot struggling within his seat by the light of the controls. The side of his jumpsuit that's visible to her glistens with blood, and there is a patch of darkness above his right kneecap that is growing with each second. She rushes forward, grasping a protruding handle beside her as the pilot glances over his shoulder.

With a spastic jerk, he tips the helicopter hard to the left, and she feels herself thrown toward the open door and the ground a hundred feet below. Her grip on the handle tightens, the metal in her hand slick.

I'm going to fall, she thinks even as her fingers slide free of the bar. She tumbles toward the open air and snatches at the taut safety cable extending from the ceiling. Her skin flays open as the cable glides through her hand, but her momentum slows as one leg falls free of the aircraft.

Zoey yanks her leg back in as if she's been burned and the helicopter levels out, a looming hillside tumbling away as they fly past. She leaps toward the slack form of the second Redeye and snags the belt that holds him to his seat.

A gunshot rings out in the cab and for a moment she thinks she's accidentally discharged her own pistol. Then she feels blood spatter her face and a gaping wound opens up in the dead Redeye's chest. She turns and sees the pilot aiming a handgun over his shoulder while trying to maneuver the craft closer to the ground.

She aims as he glances out the windshield, knowing either way she's going to die. These are her last seconds of freedom, her entire stint bathed in violence with only a shining moment of moonlight on water to remember.

Zoey fires.

The bullet misses, spider-webbing the glass past the pilot's head.

The helicopter rolls, but she holds tight to the strap and shoots again.

This time the round goes through the back of the pilot's seat, and he chokes out a moan before slumping forward.

All is movement, a tandem of gravity and floating.

The entire helicopter rotates, spinning sickeningly counterclockwise. Zoey catches a glimpse of something tall and silver, glowing in the night. The engines shriek and the rotors take on a slower, more powerful chopping that batters her ears.

The shadow of a hill out the window spins past.

Moon.

Sky.

Ground.

A slight shudder, then a hissing snap.

An explosive boom that makes her feel as if her heart has detonated.

There is a colossal impact and then flooding darkness.

17

Zoey wakes to the sound of a helicopter and knows it was all a dream.

Dellert never took her from her room. Meeka is still alive, as are Crispin and Assistant Carter. She never escaped to the roof and stowed away on the helicopter. She is in her bed in her room, and for some reason Lee wasn't able to come the night before, and she fell asleep waiting for him only to dream of her escape. Yes, that's what happened. She tries to roll over and fall back to sleep when the pain hits her.

It is a rolling wall of ache that begins in her skull and penetrates deep into her spine. She's left breathless from it. The pain is so powerful she can see it. It is a red, blinking light that flashes in strobes of agony with each heartbeat. It is only when she finally manages to drag some air into her lungs that she realizes the light is mounted in the helicopter's dashboard barely a foot away.

Zoey shifts, trying to determine how long she has left on Earth. There is no way she can survive the pain that consumes her, it must be a result of a mortal wound. She manages to sit up and places a hand to her head. Her hair is wet with blood. She moves her arms and closes her hands into fists. Wiggles her toes and draws her knees up, which sends a bout of pain through her midsection. Looking down at her stomach, she sees why.

There is a gash in her shirt several inches above her waistline that reveals a long cut in her flesh. It seeps blood steadily, and when she moves the gap widens, releasing more crimson onto her already ruined clothes. She hisses through her teeth and blinks as her vision seems to tip to one side. When she can see straight again, she takes in her surroundings.

She is sitting on the ceiling of the helicopter.

The red light blinks continuously, and a pale illumination leaks from a crack in the control panel to her right, shining on the dead face of the pilot whose neck is cranked at nearly a ninety-degree angle.

Zoey gazes around at the wreckage, tasting blood, smelling death.

The sound of a helicopter rises again in the distance, a low and even chop that's growing louder.

They're coming.

She searches frantically for the pistol, but it's gone. A nylon strap catches on one of her fingers as she's looking and a rattle accompanies it. She pulls the strap closer and makes out the shape of the rifle at its end. The helicopter is louder, the rotor more insistent. Her bracelet, she's almost forgotten. They'll be able to track her as long as she wears it.

She yanks on the plastic around her wrist, but it doesn't break, so she runs her hand over the dead Redeye's belt until she finds the handle of a knife. Zoey slides the blade beneath her bracelet and gives a sharp pull.

It cuts through without resistance, and the bracelet she's worn since she can remember falls away. She has no time to appreciate its departure. Instead she tosses Dellert's and Carter's bracelets away as well. Without hesitating, she rolls to her side and cries out at the strafing pain. Each movement sends a shower of sparks through her vision, but she keeps her eyes locked on the open door six feet away.

The night air is a blessed relief on her face, and she can feel her sweat cooling as she drags herself free of the crash. The ground is rough and gritty with dry, crackling grass growing sporadically everywhere. Zoey crawls for a dozen paces before climbing to her feet.

She is in a narrow valley created by two rounded hills that rise several hundred feet into the night. The shining silver tower she saw from the air stands a hundred yards below her and thick cables extend from its distant pinnacle to the helicopter. They appear to be huge electric cables of some type, their lengths shredded and tangled in the ruined helicopter blades. Above her position is the uneven horizon beginning to lighten with morning.

The immensity of the space around her, the utter openness of it all, yanks her breath away. She could stay here for days, examining the jagged outcroppings of rock that protrude from the sides of the hill, feeling the texture of the plants at her feet, letting the gentle breeze coast across her skin, but the second helicopter is getting louder. Any second it will rise from the river valley below and swoop up to her. They will surely shoot her after what she's done, there will be no second chance.

Zoey moves away from the overturned aircraft and heads into the thicker darkness to the west. The going is rough, mostly because each step rings a bell of pain in her side where the gash continues to bleed. She concentrates on breathing, pausing after a hundred yards to hoist the rifle's strap over her shoulders.

The helicopter's beat thickens, the air thrumming with it.

She hurries up the grade, legs burning, air turning to acid in her lungs. She makes it to a low stand of brambly brush and sinks behind it as the helicopter slides into view from the south. Its running lights glow red and green, a white strobe on its tail flashing. It flies past the crash site before banking hard to the left. A white spotlight shines on the downed chopper's jutting landing struts.

They think you're still in there, Meeka says. *Now's your chance. Go! Go! Go! Go!*

Zoey climbs to her feet and shoots the helicopter one last look before breaking from her cover. She flits to the next stand of bramble before cresting the last hundred feet of the valley. A long plateau extends away from her toward a flat, winding trail that's barely discernible in the growing light. She has to get away from here. How long until they land and discover that she's not in the wreckage? Minutes? No more than that.

She hobbles onward, wooziness growing and receding in her head. She breathes evenly, blinking to keep her vision straight and locked on the path ahead. As she nears it, the helicopter's solid thud begins to slow. They're landing.

She forces herself to run.

When she makes it to the path, she sees that she misjudged its width. It is more than a path, it's a road. The hard pavement beneath her feet is covered with layers of dirt and grime. Thin branches crumble under her shoes and she skids, nearly falling as her foot slides over a large pebble.

She has to find a place to hide, there is no chance out in the open. The road extends up the side of another hill before turning to the left and out of sight. The light is taking on a grayness as if everything is wreathed in smoke. Her air puffs from her mouth, a ghostly cloud before her. Only then does she feel the cold that has wormed its way inside her destroyed clothing.

As she crests the top of the hill, the sound of the helicopter winding back up reaches her. She glances back, but its form is hidden below the edge of the valley. Soon it will rise into the air and fly toward her, the spotlight stabbing her to the ground.

She breaks out into a full sprint.

Gravel crackles under her feet.

Air courses past.

She gasps for breath.

On the other side of the curve a stand of houses begins. They are dainty and gapped apart only by strips of brown lawn. Their paint has faded to muted versions of the colors they were before, now dismal blues, greens, tans. Beyond them the road continues by a larger metal building with some type of awning covering rows of boxy shapes with hoses looping from them. Past that is a small bridge and more houses lining the edge of a narrow stream.

Zoey turns to the right and rushes down the alley between the last of the two houses. Her footfalls echo off their sides before she emerges into a flat yard. A low fence borders the back of the property, and beyond that is another line of larger homes. She hurries to the fence as the chop of the helicopter takes on another pitch.

They are airborne again.

She scrambles over the fence, the hole in her shirt catching on its top. She rips it free and runs to the nearest house as lights appear above the farthest hill. She slides to a stop at a door with a partially broken window. The handle holds fast when she turns it, and panic climbs to a new level within her as the spotlight lances the top of the houses she passed. She reaches inside through the broken window and finds the interior door handle. She spins it, and the door pops open. Zoey swings inside as the thud of the helicopter grows so loud she imagines it coasting directly over the house.

She stands in a narrow entryway that is littered with rubbish. Broken glass and water-stained paper cover the floor. The walls flake paint in long, drooping strips, and the air smells of old dampness. Zoey makes her way to the doorway ahead, glancing back to make sure her footprints aren't visible.

The next room is devoid of any features. There are spaces against the walls containing shadows of dirt that give her an impression of the objects that rested there for years. Tangles of spiderweb dance from the ceiling and there is a dried pile of what appears to be feces in one corner. To the right a narrow set of stairs extend up to a second floor. Zoey sweeps up them and finds two rooms at the top, windows shattered, sills warped with rain. A stained blanket lies in the center of the second room before an open closet door holding darkness.

"Where. There's got to be somewhere to hide," she whispers to herself. She emerges into the hall again and is about to return to the first floor when she spots a short chain hanging from the ceiling. It trails to a square outline of a panel large enough to climb through.

She shucks the rifle sling off her shoulder and manages to hook the steel ring hanging from the end of the chain with the gun barrel. She pulls and the panel opens.

A moving shape descends from the darkness above, and she nearly screams before seeing it's some type of a wooden ladder. It unfolds in front of her, bracing against the floor.

The helicopter cruises over the house again as the first rays of sun leak through the windows.

Tentatively, Zoey climbs the ladder, sure it will collapse under her weight at any moment. Brisk air meets her as she pokes her head and shoulders through the ceiling. There is a flashlight attached to the rifle but it takes her several tries to find the switch before clean, white light blinks on.

The space above the ceiling is low and filled with some type of fluffy material. She touches it and its coarseness surprises her. She scans the area before descending the ladder again. In the second bedroom she grabs the blanket, grimacing at the stench that rises from it. It smells as if something has died in its folds, ingraining death into its very fibers. Ignoring the odor, she climbs the ladder once again. When she's steadied herself on the edge of the hole, she pulls on a handle set near the top of the stairs. She strains for a moment before the ladder refolds itself into a neat bundle above the panel that locks back into place.

Darkness rushes into the space, pressing upon her skin like a physical force. She reaches for the flashlight as the helicopter draws near again, and Reaper's voice booms outside of the walls.

"Zoey, I know you can hear me. You need to come out in the open so we can take you home."

She trembles and nearly loses her balance. Grasping a rough beam, she holds her breath.

"One way or another we're going to find you, Zoey. You can make it easy on yourself, or very hard." The helicopter flies past the house, and the roof shakes with its passing.

They're very low, very close.

"If you come out now, you won't be punished."

She huffs a derisive laugh that sends bolts of pain through her stomach. How stupid do they think she is?

"You're weak and wounded. I saw the blood myself, Zoey. Come out before it's too late."

She pulls herself across the material, which she realizes is some type of insulation, and settles into a low depression. From her vantage point she can still make out the trapdoor and the ladder, but someone would have to climb fully into the attic to see her. Her body aches everywhere, and a thirst has begun to build in the back of her bruised throat. She checks the wound on her stomach, the crusted blood almost black in the harsh glow of the flashlight. It's stopped bleeding but still hurts as if it happened seconds ago.

The helicopter sounds as if it's getting farther away, the blades no longer concussive. She spreads the stinking blanket over her and settles into the nest she's made before clicking off the light. Sleep immediately begins to pull at her with claws of fatigue. She has to hold on and wait until she's sure she's safe. Wait until she can't hear the copter at all.

"If you refuse to come out now our only choice is to punish Terra and the other women when we return. Do you want that on your conscience, Zoey?"

She blinks at the darkness, trying to ignore Reaper's voice. "I'm going to kill you," she whispers, her words ragged and venomous. The helicopter's sound is fading, or maybe she is, she can't tell now. She only knows that her eyes won't stay open a moment longer, their weight too immense to hold up.

As she drifts deeper and deeper away from the world, Reaper's voice comes one last time, filtering its way through the old boards of the house to where she lies.

"Think about what you're doing, Zoey. Think of the repercussions. There is nothing out here for you. You need us."

♦ ♦ ♦

She comes awake to the sound of footsteps on the stairs below her. Her eyes pop open, and for a precarious second she doesn't have any idea where she is. Several pinholes pour thin cones of light across the space, and Zoey resists the urge to move.

The crackle of boots passing under her is loud. A door swings open, bangs against a wall. Whoever it is clears their throat and spits.

The rifle lies across her stomach and hip. Slowly she picks it up, straining her eyes to see how the weapon actually functions. In the low light the details are extremely hard to make out, but she finds a switch marked with the words Safe, Semi, and Auto. She turns it to Semi.

The footsteps retrace their path, closer, directly below her, and stop. There's a short click and a man begins to speak, his voice so loud and sudden that she nearly yanks the rifle's trigger.

"This is D two. In the second to the last house on the northern side. What's the next move after I clear the final? Over."

A crackle of static, then a garbled reply that she can't discern.

"Received. Heading that way now. Over."

There is the scuff of boots on the treads, the squeak of a stair, then silence.

She waits, heart steadily picking up rhythm as the stillness draws out.

The footsteps come back up the stairs and pause.

"Zoey?"

Her name being spoken sends a violent spasm of fear through her. How? How could he know that she was here? What did she leave behind?

Carefully, she adjusts the rifle so that its muzzle points directly at the ladder and the opening below it. She barely breathes.

There is a creak and she watches the ladder unfold and disappear as the trapdoor is opened. She swallows, vision jangling with each heartbeat. If she kills him, they'll know, they'll find her and catch her before she has a chance to run.

The ladder squeals in protest of the heavy weight ascending it.

Zoey slides the blanket up and over herself, covering her entire length along with the rifle. She keeps the barrel pointed at where the soldier must appear and leaves the tiniest gap through which she can see.

The top of a helmeted head inches into view. Then the red reflective goggles, as well as a rifle barrel. The Redeye flicks on a flashlight and shines it around the space. Zoey eases the blanket down completely as the light passes over her. She hears the soldier sniff and snort in disgust. He utters a quiet curse, and she sees the light pass by her before winking out.

The ladder barks again as he descends. A second later it rattles up into place, and his passage down the stairs is marked by much quicker footsteps. A door slams, and all is quiet again.

Zoey pushes the blanket away, silently thankful for the rancid odor it gives off. She sits up, wincing as her entire body cries out. It feels as if she is a rusted piece of iron that's meant to move but hasn't in years. The wound in her stomach throbs. Hunger is a storm that fills up her insides, and the first inklings of thirst she felt before falling asleep is now a burning that screams to be put out.

Zoey manages to get her feet beneath her and moves as quietly as she can to the door. She listens for a long while before unfolding the ladder down to the second floor. When there are no shouts or movement below, she clambers down until she stands outside the first bedroom. She moves to the second bedroom, seeing the muddy outlines of the Redeye's boots. It must have rained while she was sleeping.

She looks out the window toward the next house over, keeping herself hidden but for one eye and a sliver of face. The day is in early afternoon, the sun hidden behind a sky veiled completely in clouds. The neighboring house is still, windows dark. Water drips off the eaves. Nothing moves in the space between the buildings or in the following yard. Distantly there is the whup of a helicopter.

She settles onto the floor of the room, letting some of the adrenaline leach from her as she stares at the dusty walls and listens for noises. The helicopter comes closer, but not near enough for alarm. After a time it fades away completely, and she wonders if they've moved on to another area for their search. She's sure they've left several soldiers in the vicinity just in case they somehow missed her. She looks down and finds that her hand is rubbing lightly at her opposite wrist, realizing only then that there is a phantom feeling of her bracelet still there. She looks at the place where it has always rested, and tears gradually fill her vision.

Zoey curls into a ball and cries silently beneath the grimy window. She sees Meeka bleeding on the floor of the mechanical room, Lily's scab-encrusted scalp, Crispin's lifeless eyes, Terra's broken and hollow-eyed stare. She cries for them all until there are no tears left.

She drifts in and out of consciousness, sleeping even as an internal voice tells her she can't, that they'll come back to the house and find her. If they do, she will die. She will end herself before ever returning as a prisoner to the ARC, to suffer the same fate of all the other women before her, to become NOA's experiment.

It is late afternoon when she wakes again. She can tell the rest did her some good. Her muscles still ache as if she'd fallen down the side of a mountain, but she can move easier and the gash on her stomach hurts less.

Zoey stands and surveys the small neighborhood again. Everything is unchanged. There are no soldiers in sight, no sound of the copter.

But her hunger and thirst are so vivid it's painful.

She has to leave the house before full dark. In the dark they will have the advantage with their night vision. And she has to eat and drink. Her mind starts to retrace the last time she had a meal and she stops it. Knowing will only make it worse.

Zoey gives the window another cursory glance before moving to the hall and refolding the ladder up overhead. She moves down the stairs and into the kitchen area, pausing at each window before going on. The door she entered through is ajar, the same muddy footprints as upstairs trailing in and out of the house. She finds a small room at the rear of the structure that has some type of torn and rusted screen covering its sides. The wind passes through it creating a mournful hum. Beyond the enclosure is a flat expanse of brown grass that merges into a low set of rolling hills dotted with scrub and bramble. A single scraggly pine tree grows fifty feet away, its needles a shifting, green curtain.

Zoey studies the houses to the left and right before easing onto the porch. She sidles through a long gap in the screen and before her courage can escape her, she sprints to the pine tree, sure that any moment a sniper's round will rip through her back. But she makes it without hindrance and surveys the rear of the houses through the sweet-smelling needles. The structures remain still in their rotting solitude.

She counts to three hundred before breaking cover again. Her legs burn as she pumps them, holding the rifle before her in case she needs it suddenly. The wind howls in her ears, and dried twigs and grass crackle beneath her feet.

Zoey doesn't stop when she reaches the first of the hills. She continues on, keeping low, climbing the incline even as the air in her lungs turns to fire. They could be right behind her, running to catch up. She was silly to think they would take her out with a rifle shot. They want her alive. At the very least she's useful as an example to the other women in the ARC.

She crests the hill and spots a slanted piece of rock the size of her old bed jutting from its top. She slides behind it, laying the rifle across it, ready to fire if need be.

The slope is empty below. Nothing moves but the grass stirred by the breeze.

Slowly her breathing comes back to normal and she slumps to the ground. Her stomach is bleeding again, and she stanches the light flow by pressing part of her shirt to it with her palm. The earth is cool and she prays that the sun will come out, even for a moment to warm her, but it remains concealed by the clouds like the gray-scrimmed eye of a dead man.

18

Zoey watches the silent farmhouse and barn beyond the flowing stream, trying all the while to ignore the rasping thirst in her parched throat.

It is an hour before full dark, and the sky has taken on a beaten look, the clouds becoming waves of purple tinged with threatening veins of black. It is going to rain again.

All afternoon she trekked across the brambled hills in search of water. She found only two shallow, muddied puddles that were so choked with silt she more or less chewed down several mouthfuls. Everywhere else there was the evidence of rain, but the earth had already gotten to any standing water, its barren topsoil greedily drinking down the moisture. No one pursued her, as far as she could tell, and only once she spotted the helicopter as it skimmed across the horizon miles away, its passage soundless and menacing as a stalking predator.

In the hours she walked, the vastness of the world kept distracting her from her vigilance. She would be watching the skyline of a nearby hill, and a fathomless sense of the world would press upon her. How large it truly was. There were no words for it.

She had heard the brook before she saw it, the babbling of water like a half-remembered song. It revitalized her lagging senses, sending her traipsing up the side of a small rise and almost into the farmhouse yard.

Her eyes fall from studying the two structures and trace the level path leading away from the property. It runs over the nearest hill and cuts to the right down and out of sight. She brings her eyes back to the shining, silver water that flows barely a foot wide from the side of the bank before disappearing into a slight, curving channel that winds to lower ground. She waits another minute before she can take it no longer and breaks from her cover to rush to the stream's side.

Zoey falls to her hands and her knees, the rifle dropping to the ground beside her. She plunges her face into the water and nearly shrieks at how cold it is. The water burns her face, so shocking that all the hairs stand on the back of her neck. But nothing can keep her from sucking up huge mouthfuls and swallowing them.

It is bliss beyond words.

Just when she thinks she's slaked her thirst, she drinks again, the water more sweet, more satisfying than anything she's ever experienced. She drinks until dizziness swarms her head and she gasps for breath; face barely an inch above the stream. Her stomach is swollen and heavy but still her throat aches. She takes several, more measured drinks before finally settling back on her haunches. The first drops of rain fall on the stream's surface, creating expanding silver rings. She gazes up at the sky and shakes her head in disbelief.

"Great timing," she says.

The storm coalesces quickly, and soon a torrent of water falls from the sky, soaking her meager clothing. She watches the dark windows of the farmhouse for another minute before heading toward it.

Keeping the rifle level on the door that sits above a sagging, covered porch, she creeps up the steps and leans her back against the wall beside the jamb. Lightning arcs across the sky, sizzling to the ground a mile away. Thunder echoes the flash, and beneath its cover, she turns the knob and steps inside.

The air is dank but dry. She can make out only a dozen feet in front of her before darkness consumes everything. She shuts the door and steps to the side, kneeling below the closest window. With a flick of her fingers she turns on the flashlight and sweeps the room before her.

It is large, with wooden floors that run to walls covered by garish, green paper that peels and hangs like dry skin. There is a strange, long chair in the center of the room, its hide dark brown with tufts of white poking from a dozen holes. A huge desk stands in the farthest corner, a chair toppled and broken to pieces before it. A stone alcove, pitted with ancient soot, is centered on the right wall and a set of stairs extends up to a darkened hallway above.

Zoey stands and hurries to the closest doorway. Inside is an empty kitchen, long counters covered with black dots and dust. A mane of green mold adorns the far wall and extends nearly to the floor. She turns and moves through the first larger room, finding an empty bedroom with cracked windows on its other end as well as a bathroom with a pedestal sink and a huge tub made of white stone, its inside obscured by a torn plastic curtain.

The upstairs holds a strange, wild smell that reminds her a bit of Zipper. One wall is buckled, the wooden structure beneath bared like bones in a wound. There is a scatter of insulation trailed across the floor and a rounded nest of papers and cloth in one corner. She picks up the cloth, which turns out to be a stained, long-sleeved shirt. She puts it on, noting it's slightly too large for her but happy to have it nonetheless.

Zoey stands in the quiet of the empty room, listening to the flow of wind through broken windows. It seems to have its own voice out here, not like the breeze that blew over the top of the ARC.

She shivers and finally slings the rifle over her shoulder. There is no one here. Not that she truly expected anyone. The plague did its work and moved on like all things. She is cold, but the hunger in her stomach is somewhat quelled from all the water. She feels sleep tugging at her again from the miles she covered to get here. She gives the room a last look in the dying light and makes her way back down the stairs, pausing only a second at the door before going outside.

The barn is well built, with heavy timbers that have weathered time with ease. The double doors are open, one of them battered and nearly broken from its hinges. Inside is cavernous night, a musty scent drifting from within.

Zoey approaches the opening and shines her light inside. There are wooden partitions that section the barn off into quarters with an alley that bisects them. Cobwebs churn against the ceiling, and broken chaff of some sort litters the concrete floor. The back of the barn has another set of doors that are slightly open. All is still.

She makes her way inside, sweeping the light around the space just to be sure nothing hides within the shadows. At the rear of the structure she finds moldy straws of some type of grass, their lengths scattered in piles that have turned the color of the stormy sky.

Zoey sits in the largest pile and pulls the heady-smelling grass up over her. The rain drums on the roof, splashes in puddles outside the doors. She clutches the rifle close, turning off its light, and darkness rushes in to embrace her. She closes her eyes to her first day of freedom and is asleep in seconds.

19

Blades of sunlight force their way beneath her eyelids and she groans, turning her head to the side.

She is warm and comfortable, and there is nothing else she would like to do but lie there, affirmed by the knowledge that if she moves it will hurt.

A faint popping floats through the open doors, and it takes less than a second for her to leap to her feet, eyes wide, fully awake.

The helicopter is coming.

She scrambles to the front doors on legs made of wood, hobbling so badly she almost stumbles. The world outside is bathed in golden light, the storm long since departed to the east. Everything shines with moisture, and a vaporous fog rises from the ground in hazy tendrils. The rotors continue cutting the air, louder than before. Zoey grips the rifle so tight her knuckles crack.

Where? Where is it? How close?

She strains her eyes against the blinding light, frantically searching. She has to know which way to run. The copter is closer, she can feel its beat in her ears like a second heart.

It emerges from behind the farthest hill she can make out, its shape detaching from the land to steadily grow. She waits two seconds, confirming its direction.

It's coming straight for the farm.

Zoey runs.

She scrambles to the rear doorway and explodes through it into the morning light. Legs pumping, hands clutching the rifle, the sound of the copter mounting between each hurried breath.

The land dips hard behind the barn, and she nearly loses her footing as her momentum takes her faster and faster. There is a dotting of pines and sage to her left. Not enough cover for her to hide. Ahead the ground falls away harder, the land becoming more and more rocky. She risks a glance over her shoulder, but the barn is almost out of sight, the chopper hidden behind it.

When she looks forward again, the ground has disappeared.

Zoey releases a small cry of terror and jams her feet to a stop. The rocky outcropping ahead ends at a razored edge that leads into open air. Beyond is the twist of a narrow river far below.

She slides over the brink, falling hard to her side, feet flying into nothing.

She drops the rifle, her hands scramble, slide on stone, slip free, catch again.

Zoey jerks to a stop and flops against the side of the stone wall she hangs from. Her feet pedal but find no purchase. She squints through tears that turn the sunlight into a thousand bleeding prisms. She pulls, trying to hoist herself up, but the strength is gone from her arms. Slowly it leaches from her hands as well.

The skin of her palms tears.

She utters a hoarse cry as her fingers rip free of the rock and she falls.

Her feet land a foot down, jarring her to a stop.

The arrestment from her fall is so sudden and unexpected she can't breathe.

Eyes bulging, she turns around. She stands on a narrow outcropping of rock. Below the drop is at least sixty feet, straight down with no hand- or footholds. To her right the outcropping widens and descends in a ramp-like fashion to a silt washout that ends just before the riverbank.

Zoey glances up and sees the rifle sling hanging over the edge. She leaps and snatches the loop, yanking the weapon down to her. The helicopter's thrum is slower.

They're landing.

She sidles close to the cliff wall, her shoulder blades rubbing against the rough rock, until she can walk comfortably. As soon as she's able, she runs. She jogs down the path and descends to the washout of loose rock and sand. Her feet sink in the softness of it and she slogs on, falling twice before making it to clearer ground.

How long until they check the house? A minute? Two? Will they see her footprints from her inspection the day before? She's nearly sure of it.

Zoey runs between the flowing water and the sheer cliff face, the land chunky with broken rock. The unstable footing tries to turn her ankle twice but she remains upright, skipping along as fast as she can while the sound of the copter slowly lessens to nothing until she can only hear the rush of the river.

She stops beneath the shade of a lone pine tree after what feels like a lifetime of running. The sun has risen high enough to shine into the river valley and its warmth is now uncomfortable. Zoey sits on a wide, flat boulder below the tree's heavy branches and lets her heart come back to a normal pace. She's thirsty again and makes her way to the river's edge to drink. The water is a pale greenish-blue in the light of the sun, a color she's never seen before. She lets herself marvel at its beauty for a moment before stooping to drink. The river tastes clean with a slightly chalky undertone. When she's finished she returns to the tree and sits once more, gazing back the way she came.

"Maybe they didn't see the footprints," she says aloud. Her voice is coming back to normal, but she can still feel Carter's hands there, squeezing the life from her. She grunts, placing her fingers beneath her chin, traces the tender flesh. "Never again," she murmurs. Her eyes unfocus and she stares through the opposite valley wall, not seeing anything that surrounds her.

After another five minutes of rest, she hauls herself to her feet, wincing at the pain in her stomach as she straightens. When she checks the wound beneath her shirt, her mouth goes dry.

It is bleeding again, but that isn't what concerns her. The edges of the gash are an inflamed red and a milky coating rims the borders of dried blood. When she places her palm over the wound it is hot, much warmer than the flesh surrounding it.

Zoey blinks, swallowing the knot in her throat. She considers washing the cut in the river, but thinks better of it and simply covers it again. The sun ripples across the water, blinding and harsh.

She continues on throughout the morning, climbing over ragged boulders and the odd trunk of a decaying tree that has washed up on the bank. Several times she has to wade into the river to circumvent a cliff face that is so sheer it actually curves out as it rises. The wound gains a heartbeat of its own, throbbing in time to each step she takes, but the pain is nothing compared to the hunger that gnaws at her stomach like a starving animal. More water does almost nothing to stop the pangs that fill her. She begins to imagine the food being served now in the cafeteria. All disgust she harbored for the mostly tasteless meals is gone. It is replaced by the certainty that she would shove handfuls of the food into her mouth if set before her now. She wouldn't even bother with utensils.

She is so engrossed by the fantasy of consuming a buttery pile of potatoes, she doesn't hear the rotors until the chopper appears over the rim of the canyon.

It erupts into sight a hundred yards ahead, its black form like the carapace of some flying beetle. Zoey reacts immediately, collapsing to her left behind a slanted piece of rock twice her height. She squeezes into the angle created by the boulder and the valley wall, pressing her shoulder into its uneven hardness.

Did they see her? Oh God, did they? Are they making a turn right now? Maybe priming some type of tranquilizer to shoot her with? She risks a glance around the side of the rock and sees the copter disappear over the opposite ridge of stone that rises a hundred feet into the sky.

She waits, her senses screaming for her to run. How far does she have to go before they quit searching? How far until she's out of their dominion?

The copter's sound fades before vanishing completely. Again she's alone with only the sun and the steady rush of the river.

◆　◆　◆

Near mid-afternoon the river widens out into a flat, calm stretch, and the harsh cliffs give way to gentle rises covered with more trees than she ever thought existed. Her legs ache, and the back of her neck is burned from the sun. The hunger has taken on a new life, something wholly separate from the burning fist it was that morning. It now seems to speak to her directly from her center. The small plants that grow from the banks have become delicacies, the moss from rocks delectable appetizers. Even the bits of brown flotsam that bob along the river's edge tempt her.

She tries to ignore the hunger's voice, but her body is beginning to tremble with each step, and soon her steady pace slows to a hitching plod. She stops to rest beneath the closest tree, leaning against its bark, its smell enveloping her. How long since she last ate? She can't stop herself from remembering this time.

At least forty hours ago. Almost two days.

The thought increases her trembling, and she closes her eyes. She can still taste the last bites she had, how the bread crust crunched between her teeth, the soft vegetables in the soup sliding down to the pit of her stomach, warming it, and . . .

"Stop it," she says. Her voice is weak, and she hates the sound of it. A gust of wind rustles the branches of the tree, and several pine needles brush her hair. She reaches up and grasps a handful, tearing them free. And before she can think about it, she shoves them into her mouth.

The taste is a lot like the fresh smell they give off, but much thicker. It envelops her senses, clogs her nasal passages. She chews until the needles are a sludgy paste and swallows, managing to get them down before she gags. Zoey shudders, both at the pleasure of swallowing something solid and at the revolt of her stomach. It twists upon itself, trying to send the needles back into her mouth. She breathes deeply, and to distract herself, climbs to her feet and begins to walk again. She makes it a dozen steps before she stops in her tracks.

The end of something red pokes from around the next bend in the river.

She raises the rifle, sighting down its length at the object and slowly approaches. With each step more of it is revealed, and soon she sees she's looking at a strange boat. She's seen boats before in the NOA textbook, but this one is narrow and long, with an oddly curved front and rear. It is maybe large enough for two people.

As she studies it, she notices more of them farther back in the woods that have thickened in the last several miles. It appears they were once on some sort of rack, but time has weakened its structure and sent the boats into a pile, the paint on their hulls dull in the afternoon light.

Zoey's heart quickens. Past the boats is an overgrown trail, barely visible, extending through the trees. It twists out of sight, but between the large trunks she can see the side of a building that it must lead to.

She listens for a long moment before hurrying away from the river. Pine needles crackle beneath her feet as she climbs the trail. There are portions of manufactured stones protruding from under decades of dirt and refuse of the forest. Stairs—these used to be stairs.

Zoey steps into a clearing before a row of very small houses, all painted the same drab brown and speckled with moss and mildew. They all share identical steel roofs that are slanted hard in upside-down Vs. All the windows are whole, the doors closed.

As she stands at the edge of the small clearing, her stomach growls so loudly, if anyone were nearby, they would've heard. Food. There has to be some kind of food here.

She moves forward and begins to search.

There are five "cabins," as she learns they're called from a small wooden sign in the first of them. It says *Welcome to Pine Ridge Resort. We hope you enjoy your stay in our nostalgic cabins that offer the antiquity of former years and all the present amenities of today.*

The only amenities she can find are beds with decaying quilts nestled across them and old video screens mounted on the walls that reflect her dark image through a layer of dust.

She looks in every cupboard, every closet, every nook and cranny.

There is nothing.

The last building she searches sits above the other structures and is three times the size of the cabins. The door is wide open, and it appears that animals have made it their home in the past. All manner of branches, grass, needles, and brambles cover the floor. She moves through the rooms, opening doors, checking beneath beds, but there is nothing that even resembles food. Not that she would know exactly what she's looking for. All of her meals have been served to her, always waiting to be eaten whether hot or cold. She curses the dependency that has been forced upon her. Just another form of control. Reaper's words float back to her then, eerily disembodied.

You need us.

Zoey returns to the front of the lodge and sits on the broken porch. She stares out at the forest. How ironic—to escape imprisonment and a certain fate, to overcome all odds and elude capture, only to starve to death here by herself.

She begins to laugh. She can't help it. The giggles become belly laughs that hurt her stomach both inside and out, but she can't stop. She succumbs to the insane mirth that pours from her. The rifle drops from her hands and she holds herself, quaking with the gales that aren't funny at all. And before she can register it, she's sobbing.

After a time the tears slowly stanch as a memory rises within her. Terra, stricken with fear, and something else. Some unspeakable secret behind her eyes. She was absolutely terrified the night Zoey escaped, and something kept her from leaving. What could have enough power to hold her in that place?

Her sobs slacken until they are gone completely. She clenches her hands into fists, and though the weakness is still there, rage overcomes the sorrow, batters it, beats it into an insubstantial feeling that no longer has meaning. There is no use in regret. What's done is done. There is no changing her actions, who she has become in the last weeks.

Zoey clenches her teeth. She's not going to die out here, alone and for nothing.

She rises from the porch, grasping her rifle, because it is hers now, no one else's. She stalks back to the river, steps steadier even though the hunger still rages on. There has to be something here, some way to find food. She approaches the cabins again but pushes past them toward the riverbank. She stands, watching the water flow by, searching its aquamarine depths for an answer. She's about to turn over the boats to see if there's anything useful beneath them when she spots something floating near shore.

It bobs there, white and out of place among the drifting sticks and muddy scum that extends the first six inches from the bank. Zoey moves toward it, stopping a few paces back when she realizes what it is.

The fish floats belly up, nestled among the water's accrual. She can see one of its dark eyes looking sightlessly through a layer of algae. Its scales shine muted silver in the late sunlight, and as she watches the current tugs at the detritus around it.

Without thinking, Zoey snatches it from the water and walks back to sit down on the nearest overturned boat.

Its scales are wet and clammy, and a thin layer of slime covers its length. She doesn't know what kind of fish it is or how long it's been dead, but she's eaten baked fillets before. At least once a week they were served a meal of fish with steamed vegetables. Nutritious, always nutritious.

Zoey wipes the creature off on her filthy pant leg. She brings it to her nose and sniffs. Definitely fishy. She hiccups a laugh.

How to do it? The hunger beckons. She searches the nearest rocks and finds a suitable one almost immediately, one edge blunt and rounded, the other curved like the moon and thinner than a fingernail.

Zoey holds the fish belly up and, before she can think about what she's doing, slices through the white flesh of its stomach.

Pink and red ropes pool out over her hands, and she nearly yelps with surprise. She's vaguely aware of the animal's anatomy, but no text could prepare her for the sensation of its innards falling into her palms. She swallows her revulsion and cuts some more. The insides of the fish look nothing like the baked fillets she's eaten before. She carefully extracts the intestines and small organs with shaking fingers. The cold slickness of the job nearly breaks her resolve. She can taste pine needles again.

Once the inside of the fish is relatively clean, she pries the bones free. It is a messy job, and she knows she isn't doing it right. Her hands shake, and she utters a small cry as a particularly sharp rib bone slides beneath her fingernail. Gradually she scrapes the last of the bones away, revealing grayish-white meat. Despite the tangy smell and slime that covers her fingers, saliva pumps into her mouth. Slowly, she cuts through the scales and pries out a portion of meat that clings to her fingers in a translucent blob. She should cook it, but how? She understands the basic premise of cooking, how you need to heat food perhaps by fire, maybe by another method . . .

Without meaning to she shoves the dripping flesh into her mouth and chews.

The flavor is sour, the texture gooey and gelatinous. The fish had been rotting, she knows it now. She can taste it. Zoey squeezes her eyes shut as they begin to water. *Just get it down, get it in your stomach and you're set.* She thinks of mashed potatoes, of warm bread, a ripe apple full of tart juice, a mouthful of walnuts.

She tries to swallow, and a scale sticks in the back of her throat.

Zoey lurches to her feet and is sick beside the small pile of offal. The milky blob of fish comes up, as well as a strikingly green mush of needles. She stands with her hands on her knees, trembling, hair hanging down with strands matted by her vomit. She spits out the offending scale that somehow remained stuck to the roof of her mouth, and shakes as a full-body tremor runs through her.

Try again, Meeka says faintly.

"No, I can't do it," Zoey answers out loud. She glances around, almost expecting to see the other woman standing yards away, arms crossed over her chest, a disdainful look in her dark eyes.

Quit saying you can't. You've done the impossible, and now you're quibbling over a little raw fish?

"You don't know how bad it tastes." Zoey stumbles back to the boat and collapses onto it. Her head hangs down, and she doesn't have the strength to raise it.

Does it taste worse than death?

"I don't know."

Well, you're going to find out if you don't eat it.

"Go away."

I already did, don't you remember?

"Shut up, shut up, shut up!" Zoey raises her head and scans the little clearing beside the river. Meeka isn't there. She never was, of course. Zoey stifles a sob and leans forward, already feeling the tears in her eyes. The fish's carcass lies at her feet. The baleful dark eye staring up at her.

She bends lower, grabbing it from the ground, and snatches her cutting stone from beside her. With an angry slash she cuts another small hunk of meat from the fish's side, studies it for a second before placing it in the side of her mouth.

Zoey chews slowly with the steady determination of a machine performing a task. She doesn't stop even when a stray bone jabs her gum. She bites harder, cracking it like a splinter until it is mixed with the rest of the meat.

She swallows.

The morsel travels down to her stomach and doesn't rebound. Somewhere in the forest she hears Meeka's laughter.

Zoey eats everything she can off of the fish. She strips the scales away to get to the meat better and devours it without thought. Her stomach accepts each bite, and soon her mouth is coated with an oily flavor she's sure will never fully leave her taste buds. When she's finished, the fish is only a head with a few scraps of skin and vertebrae hanging from it. She tosses it into the woods behind the closest boat before eyeing the intestines on the ground.

"Now you're pushing it," she says to herself.

Her stomach is full though she's only eaten a few handfuls of meat. Weariness invades her like some type of parasite feeding from her strength. She makes her way back to the cabins, carrying the gun by its strap, thinking only of rest.

Zoey flops onto the bed in the first cabin after locking the front door. The fog of sleep surrounds her, and she barely has time to drape the rifle across her chest before it carries her away into a soundless slumber.

◆　◆　◆

She wakes to a soft scuffling of movement in the next room. Her eyes come open, and the darkness that meets her is impenetrable. Zoey shifts on the bed, mind scrambling to associate where she is. The cabin beside the river. She's in the bedroom, and there's something outside the door.

Her heart steadily picks up speed until it hammers against her breastbone at a frenetic pace. She manages to sit up and grasp the rifle's stock with one hand.

Something slides across the floor and falls silent.

It's Reaper and his team. They've found her.

She releases a held breath and pivots to her feet, the rifle tucked against her shoulder. How did the helicopter not wake her? They must have landed miles away and moved in on her in the dark.

A bang from the other side of the door stops her in her tracks and clenches her guts into a cold mass. Why are they making so much noise? She doesn't have time to think about it. There is a window to the left, but the chances of her opening it and climbing out without being detected are infinitesimal. If they're in the next room, they're outside as well.

She won't go back to the ARC.

Zoey sets her jaw and crosses the room silently. She can't remember if she left the rifle's safety on or not. She feels its position and thinks it's ready to fire but can't be sure. She takes several calming breaths that do nothing to slow her racing heart before reaching out to find the doorknob. Her fingers graze it, clutch it.

She'll have less than two seconds.

She hesitates, listening to the quiet in the next room, counts to three in her mind, and flings the door wide.

There is a terrifying second where her fingers scrabble around the flashlight's switch before the beam lances the darkness away.

Eyes shine close enough for her to see the detail in the irises, and she nearly yanks the trigger, but their height is all wrong. The eyes hang only a foot above the floor.

Details register to her as they are revealed by the light.

A fluff of dark fur, rounded ears, black rings that fill up most of a pointed face.

The animal lets out a harsh shriek and lunges away toward the corner of the room. Zoey follows it, still pointing the weapon in its direction, but now more curious than anything. There is a small rotted area in the floor beside the bathroom wall that she missed earlier and the animal slides through it. There is the whip of a black-ringed tail that reminds her of its face, and then it is gone.

Zoey stares at the hole, waiting for the creature to reappear, and when it doesn't, she steps to the window to see if she can get another look at it. A foot from the glass she stops, turning the light off as quickly as she can, and watches, wide-eyed, for a dozen breathless seconds.

The flickering of flames dance against trees past the lodge above her, and through the silence of the forest, comes the steady chatter of voices.

20

Zoey stands at the farthest corner of the lodge, watching the sinuous way the light rolls through the trees.

She holds the rifle ready across her chest, finger just outside the trigger guard. The voices echo to her through the forest in eerie layers, words lost in the distance. It sounds like several people all talking at once. She even catches a snippet of what could be song, the melody there and gone in the cool air.

She shifts in place, a chill creeping through her light clothing. She'd been warm and full upon falling asleep but now her belly aches again, the meal of fish no match for the strenuous pace at which she pushed herself for most of the day. The wound on her stomach throbs in time to the jumping flames. The voices are unmistakably male, and the knowledge fills her with dread. Why are there people here? The country is barren from the plague, and those still alive would be few and far between. She should've been able to travel for months without encountering . . .

But that's it, isn't it? She's relying again on the information given to her by NOA.

Zoey shakes her head. The flames dance, beckoning.

She moves up the hill through the massive pines, their bark full of menacing faces created by the firelight and shadows. The rest of the woods are quiet save for the odd creak of branches far overhead moving in the wind's embrace. Zoey steps over a fallen log heavy with moss and crouches on the other side. The voices are closer, words clearer.

"Bullshit, David. You seen it once, I was with you all day."

"—ee times, at least. They're . . . for someone."

Laughter peals out, ricocheting off the trees.

"—aranoid!"

More laughter.

Zoey jogs thirty yards up to the top of the rise that sits between her position and the fire. There is a massive stump jutting from the ground at least three feet wide that towers over her, and she slides behind it before gazing around its far side.

The hill descends in a steady grade through a spattering of trees to a clearing that levels off before falling away again down the side of the slope. A small ring of younger pine trees grows to the left, while a line of sage curls in a half-circle opposite the conifers. Beyond the sage, the fire burns in orange tongues that lap the air. Around it she can make out the heads and shoulders of at least six men. Their faces are in shadow, but it is plain that most wear beards, and their hair is unkempt and falls to their shoulders.

Zoey watches them, studies their movements, how they gesticulate at the air. Their words are slurred, and they speak of things she doesn't understand. "Fae Trade" is mentioned several times, and for some reason the term sends a shiver of fear through her. She is about to search for a better position from where she can listen to their conversation when the breeze changes, and with it comes the smell.

It is glorious. The odor of cooking food, its delectable scent nearly maddening in its potency. She can't pick out a singular smell among the mélange of mouthwatering odors that coast on the air, but it is unlike any food she has smelled before. While the cafeteria meals always had a muted scent of boiled vegetables and bland rice, this food has life to it. She doesn't realize her mouth is open, tasting the air, until a runner of drool drips over her bottom lip.

Her stomach growls, and she comes back to herself.

She focuses on the line of brush that hems in the little clearing. Through one gap there is a bag slumped onto its side, within reach if someone were to crawl partially through . . .

No. It's too risky. They would catch her, and do God knows what to her. There are six of them, probably armed. She would be insane to try it.

Zoey shoots a glance to the other side of the stump and runs, bent over, to the following tree. She pauses there for a second before hustling on to the next trunk. Gradually she makes her way closer to the flames, their light shoving the darkness back only to let it flow forth again. She stops at the final mature tree before the line of young pines. Checking in both directions, she breaks cover, runs, and slides to a stop behind the thick, intertwining branches, listening for calls of alarm.

Only raucous laughter.

The fire is maybe forty yards away, and the smell of food is so intoxicating she sways with it even as she curses herself. This is too close.

She worms her way into the thick cover of the pines, gently pushing aside the prickly branches until she is only several feet from the open space on the opposite side. The sage still blocks most of her point of view, but the men's words are more pronounced than ever.

"Just be sure you duck and cover if that chopper comes over, that's all I'm sayin', Reg. Never know what those black ops bastards will do if they track us back to the group."

"Don't worry about me, you old coot, I'm faster than all of you."

"Yeah, and dumber too." Laughter fills the night again.

"You wouldn't say that if my uncle was here."

"Listen, boy, the only reason you're on this little scouting mission is because of your uncle. If not for him, we would've chucked your whiny ass into a ravine a week ago."

A new voice chimes in. "Yeah, except then the ravine would've been full of bullshit too." This is met by high, crazed laughter.

"Ahh, where ya goin', Reg? We was only messing with ya."

"Screw you guys."

"Well, at least leave us the bottle, you little pig, you've been sucking off it all night like it was your momma's teat."

The loudest eruption of laughs and calls yet comes from near the fire, and Zoey realizes the men are drinking alcohol. Lee's told her about it before, how it's forbidden except for once a year in the middle of winter since it makes people act strangely, unlike themselves. But he also said the guards don't abide by that rule either and it's easy to find a bottle of the concoction at any given time being passed around in the guards' dorm.

Lee. How she wishes he were here now. He would know a way to get food. He would find a plan that would work. Maybe some type of diversion. Zoey nods to herself. She has to figure out a way to get the men away from the fire so she can steal the bag on the ground. There's bound to be food inside it, not to mention other useful things that could help her survive. Maybe she can—

But all thought goes dark as a large shadow approaches the line of pines, coming straight toward her with a single purpose. He's so close she can see long, tangled hairs, lit by the firelight, sprouting from the sides of the man's head, hear the crunch of his boots, smell him over the delicious odor of food.

He is five steps away.

Three.

Two.

She brings up the rifle, readying herself to break cover the moment she fires the first shot.

The man stops a few feet to her left and sighs. He fumbles with his belt, hawks and spits into the tree over her head. If she wanted to, she could reach out and touch the toe of his scarred boot.

A spattering of liquid startles her, the warmth of it speckling the fabric on her arms and shoulder. She turns her head away, silently gagging as the urine cascades down through the thick branches and pools a few inches beside her. Reg grunts, shifting his boots farther into the soft soil. Every nerve in her body screams for her to move, to burst from her hiding spot and run. She has to get the urine off her, scour it away. She can almost feel it crawling on her skin, infecting her.

Slowly the man's stream lessens and dribbles to a stop. He coughs and spits again and Zoey can't help but flinch, sure that the phlegm will find its way through the cover to her face. And then she will scream, there will be no stopping it.

The man buttons his pants and turns partially away, scratching at his ass before meandering down the lane created between the young trees and the sage. Zoey loses sight of him in the cajoling shadows at the edge of the clearing.

She scuttles backward as quietly as she can, rubbing the urine-spattered sleeve of her shirt in the soil as she goes. When she reaches the opening behind her she crouches, eyeing the way opposite where the man was heading. A diversion, that's exactly what she needs. Something to send them all scurrying away from the fire for a few seconds, just enough to allow her to snatch the bag and disappear again into the darkness.

She ponders her options as she sneaks back the way she came to the safety of the larger trees, scooting from one to the next to circumvent the open ground. Zoey stops beside the stump once again to catch her breath. There has to be a way to get the bag, she just needs to find it. Be like Lee, be a problem solver. Her gaze hovers on the flames, almost entranced as a niggling sensation crawls through the back of her mind. The man who'd relieved himself on her hasn't returned to the fire yet.

She registers movement to her left a half-second before something strikes her hard on the side of the head.

The fire pinwheels as she rolls from behind the stump, and she nearly cries out when the rifle slips from her fingers. Her vision wobbles as she comes to a stop at the base of a tall pine, its exposed roots digging into her back.

Reg is there in the flickering dark. One side of his face is bathed in firelight, and a single hard eye gleams at her as he stalks forward, his hand on the butt of a pistol strapped to his thigh. His lips glisten with moisture as he stops and licks them, the eyebrow she can see rising in surprise.

"Holy shit. It's a girl," he says in awe. "Where the hell did you come from?"

Zoey works her jaw, but nothing comes out. Her eyesight is steadying, and the strength that fled her limbs with the blow is returning. Her skull pounds from where Reg struck her.

"Aren't you something?" Reg says, his voice husky. "I've never seen one so young." Zoey claws her way backward up the slope, fingers digging into the fallen layers of pine needles. "Where you going?" He follows her, slowly, carefully.

"Stay away from me," she whispers, searching the ground behind him for the rifle. Reg tips his head to one side, wild hair floating in the breeze.

He lunges for her but Zoey is already up and moving, legs pumping up the slight hill. She can't hear him but knows he's right behind her, any second his fingers will clamp onto her shoulder and he'll drag her down.

Darkness invades the trees, their trunks deeper shadows as they flash by on either side. Panic is a living creature in her chest, tearing at her heart and lungs, weakening her legs. She jags to the left in a ninety-degree turn, using the base of a deadfall to launch off from. Reg curses and there's a soft snapping of branches and twigs as he flies past. She sprints lateral to the crest of the rise, eyes searching for a hiding place, a weapon, anything.

There is only the trees and wind.

Ahead a rough outcropping of rock appears, piled up on the inside of a bowl where the rise turns in on itself. She leaps up the first three boulders and releases a short yelp as the fourth gives beneath her foot.

Her knee slams into granite, the burst of pain a lightning strike behind her eyes. Her lips pull back from her teeth as she tries to force herself up the rock tumble.

Fingers snag her hair and yank.

She loses her footing and falls backward, tumbling once on an unforgiving boulder before rolling over the softer mass of Reg, who plummets with her.

Zoey flips once in a clumsy somersault and comes to a stop on a bed of needles. Before she can pull herself up, Reg is above her. One booted foot plants itself in her stomach, hard.

Her air rushes out and refuses to return.

"Why you gotta run, girlie? Why you do that, huh? Make it hard on yourself." Reg stands near her feet as she struggles in vain to get her breath back. "God, you're a pretty one. Best I've ever seen." He begins to fumble with his belt. "I'm gonna be a rich man, you don't know the price you're gonna bring for me." He lets out childlike laughter. "Can't believe my luck. Go to take a piss and find a girl. Knew I heard something when I was walking away."

"Please," Zoey manages. Her lungs are two limp bags inside her chest as she tries to scoot away.

"Oh, I'm not gonna hurt you. Well, maybe I will. Guessin' you're a virgin so it'll hurt a little." Reg lowers his pants slightly and moves forward, crouching down over her like a bearded spider.

Zoey swings an arm out but finds only rumpled piles of needles. No rock, no stick, nothing to defend herself with.

Reg falls upon her, splaying her legs apart hard enough that her pelvis emits a pop. His face is inches from hers, hands fumbling for the waist of her pants. She is paralyzed, unable to even scream. The smell he gives off is a mixture of stale sweat and onions. The coarseness of his beard scratches her face, and she whimpers as his breath washes over her.

21

Zoey nudged the small clump of gristle toward the owl that watched her with its luminescent eyes.

"You need to eat," she said, pushing the morsel another inch closer to the bird's hooked beak. She had saved the bite of meat beneath her tongue during dinner, daring to spit it out only after Simon said good-night and locked the door to her room. She'd waited until after midnight before pulling the loosened piece of glass out of its casing to find the bird still in the small alcove where she'd left it that morning.

Its wing hung at an ugly angle away from its body, and its beak opened and closed in small movements as if it were panting. It hadn't drunk any of the water she'd poured into the divot in the alcove's floor.

"Just try a bite, okay?" She picked the soft piece of meat up and extended her arm farther out. The owl nipped at her fingers, pinching the tip of one hard in its beak. "Ouch!" Zoey squealed, unable to stop herself. She dropped the chunk and drew her hand back, examining the shallow cut the bird had made. It oozed a line of blood, and a sudden overwhelming fear flooded her. What if the owl was infected with the plague?

She stepped down from the chair and went to the bathroom, running the cut first under steaming hot water, then under cold until the bleeding stopped. She wrapped it carefully in toilet paper before returning to the window. The bird hadn't touched the meat.

"You don't look sick," Zoey said. "I don't think there's anything wrong with you besides your wing." The owl tilted its head at her words as if considering them. "But you'll starve if you don't eat something."

She glanced away from the alcove and its occupant, looking into the night sky.

The darkness above the wall was buffeted by some of the exterior lights, but beyond the pale glow, stars glistened in a billion flickering points.

"How high have you flown?" she said, not breaking her gaze. "Have you tried to reach them?" She looked back at the bird before remembering Simon's words from earlier that day. "I bet you can fly really fast. Faster than that bird that flew past us today. Zipper. Is that an okay name?" The owl cocked its head the opposite way. "I'll take that as a yes. Zipper, if you don't eat or drink anything, your wing won't heal and you won't ever fly again. And if you can't fly, you can't leave this place. If you'll just eat and let me help you, I know you'll get better. I can fix your wing, I'm sure of it." She licked at the dryness of her lips, studying the sky again. "Otherwise you'll die here."

Zoey checked the cut on her finger and tossed the toilet paper into the room. The slice didn't look infected, but it was really too soon to tell. Maybe she'd wake up with the plague. If she did, she was going to cough all over Rita.

The owl shuffled to one side and made a low, mournful croak. She watched it try to fold the broken wing tighter to its body, but let it flop back to its original position after a moment.

"You can't give up," she said in what she hoped was a soothing voice. "The second you give up is when you start to die. You have to fight to make it. You have to want to live. Do you want to live?" The bird blinked. "Then let's try this again."

Zoey picked up the meat between her thumb and forefinger and slowly extended it toward Zipper again. In a quick, darting motion, it stabbed its beak forward and snapped back. She nearly yelped with the anticipated pain. She'd pushed the animal too far, been too excited by its presence, too determined to keep it alive, and now it had taken a piece of her finger for payment. She should have left it alone, even if it was going to die. That was the way things were. If you didn't fight, you died, either in body or in mind.

She brought her fingers back into the better light of the room, ready for the sight of her torn flesh, but they were unscathed save the prior cut.

Zoey blinked and looked back at where the owl rested.

Zipper's beak worked in quick, pinching motions, the scrap of meat she'd been holding vanishing down his throat with a bob of his head. His eyes flashed and he shuffled forward, dipping down to scoop up some of the water she'd left that morning.

Zoey smiled.

22

With a single motion, she grasps Reg's beard with the arm he doesn't have pinned and yanks his head forward to bury her teeth in the soft skin of his face.

Hot blood squirts into her mouth.

A gurgling cry comes from the man's chest and the reaction is immediate. He shoves away from her, and she feels his flesh tear from her mouth. The gap between them widens enough for her to launch a kick at his groin. The muffled, mewling sound he makes as he tips to one side lets her know she found her mark.

Then she's on her feet and running, hoisting her pants back above her hips. She flies up the rockfall, not looking back to see if Reg is pursuing her, only moving, running from the feeling of his body on top of hers. Her mind attempts to rip itself from its moorings, to hide away behind a sudden memory of Lee's fingers sliding over her hand, but she flings it away, bringing herself back to the present.

A branch snaps behind her, close, and her bladder threatens to release itself. She can hear his breathing now, ragged and hoarse. She won't be able to outrun him.

Zoey catches a glimpse of a barren pine to her right a dozen paces ahead. Its branches are different from the other trees, and it takes her a split second to realize it's dead. Its limbs snake out in a thousand directions, and even in the faint light she can see their pointed ends scratching the sky.

She changes course for the dead tree, leaping over a knee-high rock. She trips as she reaches the tree's base and skids to a stop with its crumbling bark crushing into her shoulder. Reg's footfalls are right behind her, and she barely has time to climb to her feet and face him.

He is ten steps away, coming full bore, an outline of fury against the backdrop of forested night.

Zoey reaches up over her head.

Stretches high.

Grasps the lowest, wickedly pointed branch and pulls it down.

The branch shudders in her hands and she lets go, cringing against the impact she knows will come.

But it doesn't.

She opens her eyes and stares at what she's done.

Reg jitters at the end of the razored branch, and it takes a heartbeat for her to recognize its tip protruding from the back of his neck. Reg chokes and splutters something as he makes feeble grabs for the branch impaling him. His fingers slide in a bony rasp down its length to where it disappears under his chin. His legs shudder before they fold, and he drops to his knees.

Zoey moves out from under the dead tree's cover, taking care to keep far out of the man's reach. She stares, transfixed as Reg's shirt and jacket darken with the unending current that pumps from his ruined throat.

He turns his head to look in her direction, to follow her movement, but instead slumps to the side, the branch snapping off to follow him to the ground, where he lies utterly still.

The sounds of the night come rushing back in. Zoey blinks, the silence that had gathered in the seconds before Reg impaled himself on the tree branch washing away.

No, she tells herself. *He didn't do it, you did. You've done it again, killed again.* But even the guilt-fueled voice can't drown out the lingering feeling of his hands on her, trying to tear her clothing away. The urge to spit on his corpse comes and goes as she steps past it.

Zoey moves through the trees, climbing carefully back down the rocky embankment and retraces the path of her flight. Soon the woods begin to jitter with firelight again, and she makes out the stump she hid behind earlier.

The fire still wavers in bright, lapping tongues. The men's voices are there, but lower now, almost conspiratorial. She drops to her hands and knees, fingers hovering across the ground, searching for the hard composite of the rifle stock. It has to be here. She remembers it falling away when Reg struck her. It was only feet from the right side of the stump. Couldn't have gone far.

She crawls a little farther down the slope, a sense of unease multiplying within her. Where is it? Where, where, where? She rotates to her left, and her hand brushes something hard. Her heart leaps. No, just the end of a rock. She fumbles past it, and something snags her thumb. A strap, the rifle sling. Zoey nearly moans with relief as she drags the weapon to her, its weight so comforting she nearly hugs it. She starts to rise to her feet as a sound makes the hair on the back of her neck stiffen.

Quiet footsteps to her right.

A small but bright light flashes on, which partially illuminates the man holding it. His face is stained with smudges of dirt beneath a pair of very thick glasses with black frames. Where Reg was heavily bearded, this man is almost clean-shaven with only a slight stubble covering his cheeks and chin. His mouth is a round O in the lower part of his face.

They are both hypnotized for a brief second by the sight of one another, held in the stasis of shock. Then the man's mouth opens wider, and he inhales to release a shout.

Zoey levels the rifle and yanks the trigger.

When she dropped it the selector switch on the side must have gotten bumped from the "Semi" setting to "Auto," for the rifle kicks and chatters in her hands, and tufts of needles fly into the air several feet in front of the man before the bullets walk a line up his left leg and continue on to his stomach and chest. He quakes with the impacts, vibrating in a strange dance, his yell lost in the gunfire. Blood blossoms in the holes of his clothes and mists the air behind him, crimson rain lit by the fire. The rifle continues to rise in her grip until the rounds are no longer hitting him and strafe the trees over his shoulder.

Zoey stops firing and her ears chime a single tone, but above it are the yells of the men by the fire, their forms spilling from behind the sage ring.

The man she shot falls to his back and rolls down the decline toward his companions.

Zoey runs.

She pelts away from the voices, the lights that begin stabbing the night around her. Tree trunks zip by, her footfalls echoing back like a dozen heartbeats. Something tangles her feet and she nearly falls but keeps going, down a small ravine that washes out below a high ridgeline of staggered rock.

The sound of an angry insect sings past her head and she ducks instinctively. A second later she hears the gunshot as the ground before her is bathed in the glow of a flashlight.

"Here! I got him over here!" a voice booms. Another shot splinters the bark of a pine a step to her right. Sap sprays her face and hair and she remotely wonders how she'll ever clean it off.

The ground descends, dropping sharply at a bank of trees. The cliff is only a dozen feet tall but too much for her to leap from. Through the dark, the calm expanse of the river winds away in a sharp bend. Booted feet thud on the ground behind her and she turns, crouching, and fires at an indistinct shape coming through the trees.

The rifle spits flame, and the man is lit in the muzzle blast. He dives to one side, vanishing from sight even as the weapon goes silent.

Zoey glances down. She's out of bullets.

She drops the gun and runs again, keeping even with the cliff to her right, which slowly levels down to the shore of the river. The inky water moves at a steady pace, gurgling as it rounds the bend she stands at. Her eyes flick across its width but the far bank is too distant to swim to even if she knew how.

Branches crack in the forest, voices yelling to one another.

Closer.

Bobbing against the shore thirty yards downstream is a length of driftwood, its bulk bigger than she is around. Zoey runs to it, ankles trying to turn on uneven rocks. When she reaches the log she sees that its end is lodged in the crook of a boulder. She yanks on its length, and it shifts toward her but doesn't come free.

"The river! He's at the river!"

A light appears on the ridge she came down, and she slides over the top of the log and into the frigid water. A gasp escapes her and her feet slip, submerging her completely for a moment. When she surfaces, the light is sweeping the riverbank below the ridgeline, coming closer. Zoey braces her feet on a slick rock beneath the water and hauls on the log again. This time it unhooks from the angled boulder and comes free. Its weight surprises her but she's able to move it into the flow of the stream. She slings one arm over it like she's embracing a friend, and begins to float.

The light on the ridge has traveled down to the riverbank, and now there is another beside it. They sweep the current and the rocks with precision, pausing here and there before continuing on. The distance between them and her is growing by the second. In less than a minute, they'll be out of sight.

Zoey readjusts her hold on the log and kicks gently with her feet. Her body is growing numb from the water, and her teeth threaten to chatter so she clenches her jaw. The voices are fainter, the beams heading the opposite way. She releases a sigh and tries to turn so she can grasp the log with both hands.

Ahead of her, a light flashes on a dozen yards away.

She doesn't think, only acts.

Slipping below the water, she grasps the underside of the log, finding a knobby handhold of an old branch. She forces herself beneath its mass, closing her eyes to the blinding cold. The water roars around her and she wonders if she'll even feel the bullets when the man fires or if she's already too cold.

The air in her lungs begins to smolder.

Then burn.

How far? How far has she floated? Far enough?

She starts to shake against the log's length, shuddering with the need for air. Finally she can stand it no longer and rolls to the far side of the log, coming up only enough to peer over its top but still not daring to breathe.

The light is fading behind the nearest corner, its beam cutting the dark in quick slashes. He's running in the opposite direction.

Zoey sucks in a huge lungful of air, drinking it, gasping with ecstasy. The river picks up speed as she manages to get both arms over the log, then a leg. She hauls herself mostly free of the water, straddling the driftwood like the people she's seen in the textbook riding animals called horses. The log rocks, threatening to spill her back into the river each time she moves, but she keeps her balance.

She shivers, the air, so wonderful to breathe moments ago, now an enemy as it invades her soaked clothing, running icy hands across her numb skin.

A shout echoes from far behind, but she doesn't bother looking back. They've probably found Reg. Good.

She stays on the log as the river bends three more times. With each corner the current seems to gain speed, and somewhere ahead the sound of water rushing over rock filters to her.

With arms that have been dipped in lead, she paddles to the left side of the river, the log scraping bottom after an eternity. Zoey tumbles from it into thigh-high water, managing to keep her head above the surface. She slogs to land, legs faltering twice before they fail her completely, dropping her onto all fours.

Overhead a pale slit of moon emerges from behind a cloud bank, its light enough to make out a tall stand of dry grass lining the bank ten yards away. She crawls to it, hands abrading on rocks, until the shush of the grass surrounds her. Even though it is dry and brittle, it feels like the softest thing she's ever touched.

Shaking, she flounders to the center of the dead growth that would come up to her waist if she were standing, and rolls to her back. Feebly she pulls armfuls of grass close, down over her like a braided, rustling blanket.

The last thing she sees is the cold wink of the moon disappearing once again behind a veil of clouds.

23

An alarm is going off.

Its incessant call repeating over and over. The shrillness of it drags her from a mired sleep so thick it feels like she's deep underwater.

The alarm. Something's happened. Someone's finally broken out of the compound. Or someone's broken in. The thought excites her, but she still can't get her eyes to open. She's warm now, even her ears flare with heat, and the sun is shining through her window onto her bed. Simon hasn't come to bring her to breakfast. She must be sick, but she doesn't feel it.

There's something wrong with the alarm. It's not as loud as it should be, and the end of it turns up in a sort of sweet tone she's never heard before.

Zoey cracks her eyes open.

A bright yellow bird with black-and-white wings sits on a tree branch above her. It leans forward, and with a little bobbing motion, sings its song again.

She watches it, letting reality seep back in. The night before, her escape down the river, how cold the water was. She tries to sit up, but it takes three efforts before she manages it. The sun shines down on the river and shatters there into a million fractures of gold. There is no wind, and the brown grass around her is still.

She climbs to her feet, wincing at the new injuries from her latest flight. Above them all the gash in her stomach is the worst. It's as if someone poured salt into the wound while she slept. She starts to peel back the still-damp hem of her shirt, but stops, afraid of what she'll see.

The yellow bird continues to sing and she watches it for a time, swaying a little on her feet as a bout of dizziness comes and goes. It tips forward and back on its branch, balancing on such thin legs and feet, she's amazed it can stand at all. It calls again, and somewhere in the trees beside the river a quiet answer returns. The bird cocks its head and flits away, leaving the branch it rested on swaying.

"I could've watched you all day," Zoey says. Her voice sounds like she swallowed gravel and feels like it as well. She listens for a bit longer, the bird's intermingling song getting farther and farther away until it is quiet again. At least she can't hear the men—that's something. Though that doesn't mean they aren't nearby.

He's at the river!

She sneers at the memory of the men's shouts. Of course they thought she was male. How could a woman kill two of them and escape? Though it's probably not a bad thing to let them think they're chasing a man. The alternative would be worse. For a man, they might look for several days before giving up.

But for a young woman?

What had Reg said right before he tried to force himself upon her? *I'm gonna be a rich man, you don't know the price you're gonna bring for me.*

She casts off the panic that tries to descend on her and begins to walk along the river but stops, flexing her fingers. She's forgotten something. Zoey turns back to the place where she laid overnight, but there is nothing but the crushed shape of her form there in the grass. Something, something isn't right. She realizes what it is after another minute of thinking. The rifle. It's gone, and her hands feel strange not holding it. She turns away from her makeshift bed and moves on.

The rushing water she heard the night before appears in the form of a tumble of rocks cutting into the current a half mile downstream. They shine with moisture and gush foam as the river tumbles past them, faster and faster until it drops twenty feet in a waterfall to a swirling pool below. Zoey watches the place where she would've been dashed to pieces for a time, swaying drunkenly. Then she keeps walking for another hour before she has to sit and rest.

The woods have thinned out to nearly nothing on either side of the river and the lack of cover makes her feel vulnerable. She leans against a toppled boulder that has broken into a spray of rock either with the impact of its fall or the onslaught of time. She picks through the pieces, seeing if they fit together, tossing them back down when they don't. The wind pushes against her face and for the first time since waking she realizes she's very warm. Too warm. She strips off the long-sleeved shirt, realizing she has a fever, there's no denying it anymore. She recalls the only other time she came down with one; when she was ten and had caught a cold that traveled deep into her sinuses before compacting inside her right ear. It had only lasted a day after an injection from one of the doctors, but for that brief period the world had taken on a hazy quality and her head had tried to drift away from her body.

That same sensation grips her now, but its intensity is threefold. Unconsciously she places a hand over the wound on her stomach and holds it, as if mere pressure can draw away the sickness it's spewing into her bloodstream. She supposes she should feel grateful for the infection. Without it she might have frozen to death the night before. Appreciate the small things.

She coughs out a laugh. That's what Lee would have told her. Lee. How she wishes he was beside her now. She can almost feel his arms around her, holding her. Why didn't she let him do that more before?

She swipes at her eyes and notices how taut the skin of her face feels, how warm. But her hands are warm as well, as warm as Lee's always are.

Zoey forces herself to her feet and is about to continue on when she stops. A faded spot of blue protrudes from between two rocks several feet away. When she moves closer she sees it's some type of clear container, its cap the blue she spotted. She picks up the bottle and looks through its scratched and clouded side. There is nothing within it and when she twists off the top only a slightly stale smell escapes. She rinses it in the river several times before filling it. The icy bottle is such a contrast to her burning skin it forces a shiver from her as she continues parallel to the river.

It is past midday when she stops again. The trees are completely gone save for distant patches miles from the river, across the humped plains that have taken over as scenery. Everything is brown with only suggestions of green here and there. Zoey drinks from the bottle, letting the cool water slip down her throat in little sips. Her stomach is hollow but doesn't ache anymore. She wonders if that's good or bad. The thought of potatoes slathered in butter rises in the back of her mind, and she shoves it away. There's no time for fanciful ideas now, it's a dangerous distraction. She needs food, shelter, better clothes, and most of all a shot like the one she received all those years ago to take away the sickness. She'll have to find a house and hope there will be something to help her inside, and she can't delay any longer. The sun is already in its descent and the day will be gone before she knows it.

She begins to rise from the rock she's sitting on and freezes.

The day.

Today.

Today is her birthday. She is twenty-one.

It is past midday. If she were still in the ARC she would be wearing the white gown now, listening to the Director's speech. She would be walking past all the watching eyes, seeing them for the last time before being taken to the elevator, and then to the lab with the beds and machines. They would put her to sleep and violate her and, and . . .

Zoey nearly faints but catches herself at the last second, biting down hard on her lower lip. The world comes back into the hazed focus of the fever and she braces her hand on a nearby stone. After several calming breaths she raises her head, letting the sun shine down on her ratted hair.

She isn't in the ARC anymore. She won't be going to the upper level again. Ever.

She starts walking then. Away from the river, across the dry and crusted ground, and she doesn't look back.

◆　◆　◆

She smells smoke in the late afternoon as the sun is slanting shadows hard against the ground. There is an acrid taste in the air, its stinging bite sour in the back of her throat. The horizon to the west is a strange orange, the air above it pale and shimmering. Beyond it are bizarre shadows far in the distance, their rising outlines something that must be a trick of the light, some type of illusion born of the afternoon sun and perhaps her own wavering vision.

Zoey stands on the highest rise she's seen so far, the land sprawling out below her in waves of tan speckled with darker scrub. A bird glides far above in spirals that never end. It's been there for the last few hours, hovering, watching. There is a hump rising up from the landscape perhaps a mile from where she stands that might be a structure, though it looks crooked and odd. It is her only option. She needs to rest, somewhere out of the sun and wind. Needs to eat. The instability of her limbs is increasing along with her temperature. What happens when she can't walk anymore? When she runs out of water? When she collapses from fever?

She supposes she will die.

But she will die free.

She is about to set out again toward it when a sound slowly begins to rise through the air.

It's a low humming and at first she thinks it is the helicopter returning, but soon she realizes it's too even, too uniform for the chop of the rotors. It climbs in volume, and Zoey lowers herself closer to the ground.

A line of vehicles appears from behind a grade to the west. They emerge from the land like a herd of trundling beasts, a fog of blue smoke trailing behind them. One, two, three, four of them, and now she sees they are following a faint depression she initially mistook as a natural wash in the land. The road they drive on is covered in silt that kicks up into the air with their passage. A man pokes from the top of the first vehicle as well as the last, their indistinct shapes holding black silhouettes of rifles.

Zoey drops lower and hugs the ground, only the top of her head visible above the rise. She curses herself for being so stupid. Why is she walking on the highest point where she's visible to anyone passing by? She isn't thinking straight. She watches the convoy pass and then slow before stopping at a low hill. Another vehicle emerges then from the opposite direction, its shape almost identical to the others. It coasts to a stop, nose to nose with the lead vehicle.

Doors open, and figures get out.

Four of them, all armed, vaguely familiar.

They are the men from the night before. She stares at them as the passenger in the convoy's first vehicle climbs out and approaches the group of four. They speak for a long time, their gesticulations becoming more and more emphatic. The flash of something near the tail end of the convoy catches her attention.

A man is standing on the roadside holding something to his eyes. Again the flash.

Zoey slides down completely out of sight. Binoculars. He was scanning the area. Did he see her?

She inches backward, sliding down until she's sure she can stand without being seen. She hurries away, hunched low despite the pain that radiates from her stomach. The land dips and rises before falling away to a narrow, rocky valley. On its far side, the house she spotted before comes into view. Its strange shape is due to the fact that most of the roof has caved in and one wall is entirely gone. Rotted boards protrude from the wreck like broken teeth into a weed-choked yard.

In the distance, engines rev and slowly fade away until there is only the sound of the plains and the smell of smoke.

◆　◆　◆

The house is even worse than it appeared from a distance. She approaches it at a slow limp, throwing looks back in the direction of the road every few steps. She's visible here, but the convoy has moved on. Each step is becoming a laborious event. The ground doesn't feel solid, instead her feet seem to sink into it and stick each time she tries to move.

The house stinks of mold and the musk of an animal. She pulls herself inside through the gaping hole left by the collapsed wall. She is in a wide room held up by interspersed wooden beams traveling from floor to ceiling. A chair, its cushions black and bloated with moisture, sits across the room. All manner of nature coats the floor and walls—dried moss along the baseboards, dark mold crawling across the ceiling, old nests of unknown creatures.

The stairway to the second floor is collapsed, and the door leading off the large kitchen won't budge no matter how hard she pushes against it. She slides down to sit on the floor, the exertion overwhelming.

Her temples beat in time with her heart, face dry and swollen with heat. Even as she sits it feels like she's still moving, still walking on the rolling plains.

Eyes barely open, she stares across the kitchen at another door she didn't notice before. It is open a crack that is pure darkness.

Zoey hauls herself to her feet and crosses the buckled flooring, pushing the door open. Broken stairs descend into a basement. Water drips metronomically. No way for her to get down.

She moves back along a row of buckled cabinets, their doors hanging weakly off like broken wings, and stops beside a grimy window. The yard outside is a mass of twisted bramble, dried and withered. To one side there is a path leading away that might've once been a road of some kind. The thought of leaving the house to continue on is too daunting, and Zoey settles to the floor again. This time she knows she won't be getting back up.

"This is it," she whispers to the empty house. "Good effort, Zoey, good try." She closes her eyes to slits and stares at the warped wood of the kitchen. What would Meeka say to her now? Her friend's voice has been silent for a long time. But she already knows. Meeka would call her weak and pathetic. Brought down by something as common as a fever. She can almost hear the disgust in her words, but it makes her smile.

"Soon," she says, reclining farther on the floor. "You can tell me what you think soon." The warmth of the fever surrounds her like a blanket. It isn't that unpleasant. She's sure there are worse ways to die. She knows so. Her only regret is not being able to help the other women escape the ARC. She was their only hope, their one chance. But what could she really do? What was her plan? She is one small, insignificant woman in the wide world. NOA has guards, weapons, and, most importantly, control. What had she hoped to accomplish? It is a miracle she made it this far.

She settles into a more comfortable position. Yes, she will go to sleep thinking of her regret. That is penance for failing them all. Failing herself. Failing her parents, whom she will never meet. She sighs. She really would have liked to know her last name.

As she rolls to her side and tucks an arm beneath her head, her eyes come level with a gap in the closest cabinet door. Something silver glints in the darkness, far back, like distant starshine. She nearly dismisses it but out of curiosity, tugs the door all the way open, letting the failing light invade the space.

A gray, rusty can sits at the back of the cupboard on its side.

Zoey stares at it for a long while, unmoving. When the can doesn't disappear, she pulls herself up and snags it from its hiding place.

"Corned beef and hash," she reads from the water-stained label. The top of the can has a steel ring flattened against it and she struggles for a long moment to get her fingernail beneath it before prying it up.

The can pops and a smell comes out that makes her want to weep as hunger resurges in her stomach. She yanks on the tab and the top comes completely off. Congealed fat covers a brown and gray mash. She pokes a finger into it and finds it's moist. Hesitantly she brings the finger to her mouth and tastes it.

Salty, starchy. So good.

Zoey scrapes a handful free of the can and shoves it in her mouth. Her taste buds explode with flavor. It is a little mealy and there are some chewy grits that smash between her teeth, but it is by far the best thing she's ever tasted.

She feasts, gobbling down the entire can in minutes. She scrapes the bottom with the tips of her fingers, licking the rim of the last remnants before setting the can aside. Her stomach is bloated, gurgling, wonderfully full. She drinks several long swallows of river water from her bottle but stops before all the taste of the corned beef and hash is washed away. She savors it, running her tongue around her mouth and across her teeth.

The daylight continues to fade and she drifts with it, her head light and floating with the meal and fever. Wind pushes gently against the house's eaves, creating a mournful tune that she closes her eyes to, and falls asleep as darkness eats the world up from the east.

◆ ◆ ◆

Zoey . . .

She wakes to her name being whispered, sometime in the early morning hours. The wind has died and all is quiet in the house, outside on the moonlit plains. Her body is something insubstantial, it merely surrounds her in an aura of heat. But it isn't the raging fever that woke her.

She listens, hearing nothing for minutes that seem to stretch into hours. But there is something here. She can feel it.

She sits up, her stomach a mass of glowing embers around the wound. Spangles of light lace her vision, and she blinks them away. Her mouth is dry, so dry, and everything in the room sways. She tries to steady herself but realizes she's still sitting on the floor—the movement is all in her head.

Zoey . . .

She flinches. The voice.

She knows that voice, but it's impossible.

She stares into the shadow-clotted corner of the kitchen. There is something there, something watching her. Even as her heated brain tries to refute it, she knows, and a scream tries to escape her throat.

Assistant Carter's bloodied face slides from the shadow, and grins.

24

"No!" Zoey yells.

She scrambles to her feet, shoes sliding on the floor, kicking up dust and debris. She stumbles from the room, throwing a horrified glance at the corner, and he is there, still smiling his dead smile and bleeding from where she shot him. He reaches for her and begins to follow, detaching himself from the darkness.

Zoey pelts toward the open air outside, tripping once over an animal's nest. She leaps to the ground and falls hard to her side, pain erupting from her wound. But the terror overrides all else. There is only the need to flee, to get away from the grinning abomination that shouldn't be there.

She runs.

The sky is a hammered plate of steel barely lit by the first strands of daylight, the ground ruddy and uneven. To the left the horizon is aglow with the same alien orange light as the day before, and the smell of smoke is thicker. Fire. There is fire that way. She doesn't care. She will gladly run into an inferno if only to escape the thing chasing her.

Zoey runs until she collapses near a long cut in the land that is pooled with shadows. She gasps for breath and manages to gaze back through bleary eyes at the direction she's come.

The house is hidden behind a low rise, and nothing pursues her across the plains. Her pulse hammers in the base of her skull, each beat a detonation of pain. She sags against the rough ground, grit biting into her hands and face as she lies down.

He wasn't there, couldn't have been. She imagined it, hallucinated. She'd killed him, watched him bleed out and die. Or was that all a dream? Was everything a dream? Is she still in the box, locked in the darkness? Was everything that had happened an imagining of her broken mind gibbering to itself as she wastes away in complete isolation?

Zoey sticks her tongue out and touches it to the dirt. Tastes it, feels it between her teeth.

Slowly she rises, the world a blurred fog at the edges of her vision. She stumbles on into the beginning of a new day.

◆　◆　◆

The fire consumes the land with a hunger unknown to her before. She stands watching it from a rock outcropping that protrudes from the hillside like a dying tongue. The fire might be over a mile away but she feels its heat over the din of her fever. It is a dry, cruel warmth that speaks of obduration in its purest form. There is nothing that can stand against it.

She is in awe. Never has she seen something so powerful in all her life. Everything pales in comparison. The tongues of flame leap and snap at the air as if they would like nothing more than to devour it as they do the land. Atop the fire is the smoke, a solid wall of churning white and gray that twists up until it blots out the sky.

She saw the first suggestions of fire an hour before noon, the acerbic sting of its scent trying to choke her until she was forced to cover her mouth with her shirt collar. Until then the plod of her movement had been static; one foot after the other, try not to fall, don't look back for fear of seeing *him* again through her deteriorating vision.

Zoey blinks, each one longer than the last. To sit here and fall asleep—how nice would that be? She is more akin to the fire now than to anything else. Her body glows with heat. She could embrace it when it rushes up the rise she sits on, walk down to it and meet it halfway.

She coughs again and the pain in her stomach echoes with each convulsion.

With a last glance at the sea of flames, she trundles away in the opposite direction, head hanging down, studying the ground that will soon be ash.

◆ ◆ ◆

The white forms rise high above the ground, high enough for her to see them long before she reaches the field atop the rise, where they grow like feral trees stripped bare of any bark. They are strange in a way she can't describe, their giant, steel columns rising up hundreds of feet, blunt heads holding three massive blades pointing in opposite directions.

There are dozens of them stretched out in a long, staggering line.

The blades on one situated in the center of the field turn in a lazy circle, emitting a short, rusty shriek with each revolution.

It hurts to look up at them for too long, so she makes her way around the field, giving them a wide berth. She imagines the towers uprooting themselves to lurch after her, blades turning much faster like whirring teeth. Zoey throws quick looks at them as she passes, making sure that they haven't moved each time. At one point she thinks she sees a figure standing on one of the structure's tops, but when she looks again it is gone. She tells herself that it's too far away for her to see what she thought she saw, too far away to make out the maniacal grin and blood drenching the front of its suit.

◆ ◆ ◆

In the late afternoon she finds a field of flowers. She crossed four different highways in the hours after leaving the field of white giants, scuttling over their broad expanses with hurried looks in all directions. Twisted signs peeled of their paint dotted the roadsides like stolid sentries. What would they have told her years ago? What secrets did they keep now that time had erased their messages? Before fleeing the openness of the highways, she caught herself staring at one of the stripped signs and noticed the sun had dropped much closer to the horizon since she'd last looked.

Past the intersecting roads, over the next rise cluttered by cracked rock, and through a stand of high bramble, all of it a delirious shade of yellow now.

But the flowers—the flowers are blue.

They send lances of pain through her eyes, but she can't stop looking at them. Her vision is a corridor that she peers down, all else watery and fog-hewn shapes. But the flowers are sharply contrasted compared to the rest of the world. The field is full of them, their blooms like miniature bells, all tolling a scent she drinks in. Beyond the field, the monstrous shadows rising from the ground are more prominent, their edges taking on definition that eluded her before. The mountains are reflected in thunderheads that cluster above them, angling down to fill their valleys. The flowers contrast against the storm in a cerulean of dreams.

It is the most beautiful thing she's ever seen.

She lies down to die amongst the flowers.

She's lucky, she thinks. To have a place such as this to lie down in, to pass from. How many others in this world would have given anything to find such a place of peace, of beauty? But before she can truly appreciate this final gift, she thinks of the other women—of Lily, Terra, and even Sherell, Penny, and Rita. She thinks of Lee.

"I'm sorry," she says. At least she thinks she's speaking aloud. Now it is hard to tell.

The faraway sound of thunder coming down from the mountains falls across the plains, and it is gentle, something to fall asleep to.

Zoey closes her eyes.

A whistle snaps them open again.

She gazes up, expecting the blue flowers but they are gone. In their place are wicked loops of dead thistles and thorns. They bite through her shirt and pants and how did she not feel it before? Zoey forces herself up when the whistle comes again. It isn't mechanical but comes from human lips, that she's sure of. Again the thunder grumbles, sliding over the peaks to the west.

A loud bark meets her ears.

Her vision is still tainted yellow and her heartbeat is in her hands and feet. She stands up in the thicket that tugs at her clothes, urging her to lie back down, but she pushes through.

The whistle again. Closer.

Long scratches appear on her bare arms. She moves through the last of the dead bramble that was once blue flowers and steps into a clearing before a tree-studded foothill.

A man sits on a log with his back to her. Long, gray hair hangs down between his shoulder blades. A large black dog runs to and fro, ears laid back, tail whipping, as it rushes after a stick the man tosses into the tall grass. When the dog doesn't reappear immediately, the man whistles and it comes back, dropping the recovered stick at his feet. He pets its head, smoothing down the long, pointed ears.

Every instinct within her is screaming to hide, to dive back into the thicket and lie down. It was comfortable there, even with the thorns, and she should not trust this man for that is what he is—a man.

But there is something in the calm way he strokes the dog's head, how he seems to be communicating without words. Even his whistle is soft and patient.

Zoey tries to take a step forward, but the horizon slews and she loses her footing. She catches herself on her knees. "Help me," she says, but her words aren't even a whisper. She swallows, grimacing at the pain, and tries again. "Help."

The dog's ears prick up and it looks in her direction. The mane of gray hair twists before she falls forward and the world tips again.

Years later a hand grasps her shoulder and rolls her onto her back. The figure is outlined against the approaching storm above, gray hair blending with the swelling clouds. She cannot see his face. Wetness brushes her cheek and she jerks to the side, seeing only a dark mass several feet away in the grass.

"Get back, give her some air." The voice is the grinding of rocks. The man stoops lower and Zoey blinks, trying to focus on his face, but it is lost to her. "Where did you come from?"

She tries to tell him as the clouds behind his head swirl and begin to rotate, faster and faster. She licks her cracked and ragged lips.

"Are you God?"

He is a long time answering, and now the sky is a cyclone bearing down on them, much lower than before.

"Not even close," he rumbles.

Arms scoop her up from the ground, and at the same time the sky comes down to meet her in a collision of white that fades to a deep and soulless black.

25

Time loses cohesion.

There is no way to judge its passage, so she can only label different periods when she drifts into consciousness. There is moving, stopped, day, and night. All else is a muddled wash of dreams that have no true form. Figures move in and out of the light, a smile full of bloody teeth, the warm touch of fingers brushing her own, Lee's voice murmuring something she can't understand, Simon's eyes soft and sorrowful, the feel of Zipper's feathers, pain in luminous flashes of red.

At one point it is day and they are stopped and she smells something bitter before it touches her lips. Zoey turns her face away, grimacing.

"Drink this now, it's not too hot. There you go, little sips." The liquid is lukewarm and acidic and tastes of the earth. She lets the brew slide down her throat until there is no more. "Good, good," the voice says.

Night and moving again.

Harsh breathing and the pain in her side is tremendous.

The whup of a helicopter, close. Some type of light blooming her vision red beyond her eyelids. Then stillness and the noise fading. She moans something but can't form the words. There is nothing but the pain radiating from her stomach and the jolt of movement again.

"Hush now, we're almost there. You hold on. Don't you die after all this way."

The dog woofs and the voice scolds it.

Dreams again that pour fear into her like ice water. She is in the black box, unable to move while a crawling sensation covers her body. It is as if her nerves have been exposed to the air. She tries to struggle but her control is gone. She is stuck lying on the biting nubs of the floor while her skin crawls.

But then there is light through a strange, shifting gap. She isn't in the box after all. There is some type of room beyond. The gap closes and reopens again, flickers of movement around the narrow tunnel of sight. She is in the operating room on the fifth level. The equipment is huddled around her, machines and lights everywhere. The gap closes again, and a dark inkling begins to grow in the back of her mind. There is something horrifyingly familiar about the way the scuttling sensation moves across her body, how it sounds. When she can see the room again, her very soul quivers with revulsion.

She is covered in the bugs from the shower drain.

They move over her in waves, breaking apart momentarily so that she can see. Their legs scratch against her skin for purchase, antennae fluttering in feathery violation. She opens her mouth to cry out and their legions flood inside her like a black tide.

Zoey sits straight up and releases the scream.

She gags, the feeling of a million segmented legs trundling down her throat so vivid she almost doesn't see her surroundings.

Almost.

The room she's in is small, with a single window in the right wall. It is daytime, and a clouded light shines in, landing in a crooked rectangle upon the clean floor beside the bed she rests in. The room is bare save for a wooden chair a few feet away, one of the thin spindles in its back missing. On the wall opposite her is a picture framed in amber wood of a boat caught in a gale, resting upon a heaving wave crowned with foam. A glimpse of dawn streams from a distant horizon and a dark figure is at the ship's wheel, steering toward the light. Beside the picture is an ebony stained door that is partially open to what looks like a hallway.

Zoey gazes at her surroundings with something that borders on shock. Her mouth is parched but her bladder bulges painfully. She places a hand to her forehead. Cool and dry.

The fever is gone.

Slowly, memories come creeping into the light: her flight from the broken house across the plains, the great fire, the field of giants, and finally the meadow of flowers that weren't flowers at all, then the man and his dog. Even as she thinks of the animal a steady clicking comes from the hall, growing louder until the door to her room is pushed open from the other side, revealing the large mass of dark fur and two deep brown eyes that study her with uncanny intelligence.

"Uh, hello," Zoey says. The dog watches her for a long moment and glances around the room before disappearing back down the hallway. There is a deep grunt and the sound of its considerable weight dropping to the floor.

She stares at the empty doorway for several seconds before taking inventory of herself. Her face feels clean, as does her hair, but her body is a different story. There is another layer of sweat and grime beneath her clothing, which she inspects. She is wearing a type of dress, long and softer than any of the clothes she's ever worn. A lace filigree rings the neck and cuffs as well as the bottom hem. There is a six-inch slit in the fabric over her stomach and she looks at it for a beat before pulling it open.

The wound on her stomach is still bright red, but now a colorless thread has been stitched through it, holding it shut. The skin around it is a mottled blue-black, but the injury itself doesn't throb anymore.

Zoey swings her feet over the edge of the bed, the movement causing a ripple of dizziness in the back of her skull. She waits for it to pass before standing up. Her legs hold her, though the weakness in them frightens her for more than one reason. The wood floor is cool but very clean and the air is full of a sharp chill that's not unpleasant.

She makes it to the door without falling and peers into the hallway. It is short with only two other rooms branching from it. One door is shut while the other is ajar. Beyond the hall is a wider room she can see only part of, but it resembles a kitchen. The dog lies at the foot of a counter on a brown sack. Its head is up and it watches her as she emerges from the room.

She tries the door that is closed but the knob stays unmoving in her hand. The other room holds a sort of low toilet and shower stall so confined she's not sure if she could turn around within its borders. She relieves herself and notices there is no flushing device, only a blue sand that fizzes a little at the touch of her urine. Beside the door is a simple sink with only one handle attached to a nozzle. The water that comes out is warm but not hot.

Zoey makes her way out through the hall and into the rest of the house. A compact kitchen takes up half of the space, the front wall broken by a solid wooden door and two windows looking out into a small clearing lined with immense trees. The other half of the room is dedicated to a set of overstuffed chairs, a stone alcove with a steel tube extending from its top, and a rickety table in one corner holding some sort of lamp with dark liquid inside its base. But these adornments only warrant the briefest scrutiny, for the wall behind them makes her forget to breathe.

Shelves and shelves of books stretch from the floor to the ceiling.

They are all sizes and colors, stacked haphazardly atop one another and lined neatly in a row. Some of their spines are wider than her hand while others are only the breadth of a fingernail. Covers that look solid, covers that curl almost in a circle, titles in bold and scrawling script. So many. She never dreamed there were this many books in the world.

Zoey steps forward and stretches out a hand, hesitant but unable to stop herself. Her fingers graze the first row of tomes, large, leather bound with gold writing on the spines. *Encyclopedia*, she reads, mouthing the word. She moves down the stacks, eyes spilling over authors' names as well as titles. Shakespeare, Chaucer, Cervantes. They are like a foreign language. Two shelves down she reads King, Koontz, McCammon, Matheson. Below that Hawking, Einstein, Nietzsche. So many names, so many, too many.

She sinks into one of the chairs, unable to take her eyes from the books. There is more than anyone could read in a lifetime, ten lifetimes. The words and stories from so many minds, all here, contained in one place. She runs her gaze across them again, a fluttery faintness washing over her. This is only *some* of what had been in the world. Maybe even a very, very small fraction of the work produced. She remembers first stepping from the overturned helicopter into the world, marveling at its size, but seeing the shelves of books rivals it. The sheer mass of knowledge, of creation, of life before, all of it gone now. She had no idea.

Her vision fractures with tears, and she blinks them away. She didn't know because they kept it from her, kept it from all of them. She wonders how large the stash of books was that the guards and clerics were allowed to read, and anger stokes within her from the constant glowing ember to an all-encompassing firestorm.

She needs to find her clothes and get out of here. Now that she is well again, she can start planning for her next move. She has no idea who the man is who took her in, though his intentions seem good enough judging by the care he's given her. He could have done something to her while she was unconscious, but she doesn't feel he did. Regardless, she can't stay here.

Zoey makes to rise from her seat when a book lying flat atop two others catches her eye.

The Count of Monte Cristo.

She reads the title over and over as if she's never seen it before, her jaw beginning to tremble. She reaches out and gently lifts it from its place, turning it in her hands. This copy is tattered, much older than the one she used to have, and it is heavier, thicker. With a held breath she opens the cover and begins to page through it, the words igniting a bittersweet ache in her chest.

The dog shifts on the sack across the room, raising its head, ears up. She follows its gaze to the door leading outside but it is several seconds before she hears it.

Footsteps.

Zoey starts to rise but before she can, the door swings open, revealing the gray-haired man standing there. He wears dark pants and a green, threadbare jacket with many pockets. A bag is slung over one shoulder, and he holds a long rifle in his hands. He doesn't move except for his eyes, which travel across her and around the room before coming to rest upon the book in her hands. He lets the satchel slide from his shoulder before moving his thumb to the rifle's safety, and flicks it off.

26

Zoey has a split second to register that she's going to die before the man brings the gun up and spins in the doorway.

The rifle booms, filling the house with a thunderclap before the report echoes throughout the forest. Zoey drops the book and a bird cries out in a strangled voice somewhere outside, then all is quiet again.

The dog is at the man's side in a black flash, but stops short of the doorway, muscles taut and flaring beneath its coat. The man is still sighting down the long barrel, both eyes open and staring. Slowly he lowers the weapon, makes a quiet nicking sound in the back of his throat, and strides out of the house, leaving the door wide open. The dog follows.

Zoey closes her mouth, unable to process what just happened. She manages to stand, her legs holding a bit more strength than when she first woke, and crosses the room to the door.

The yard outside is small, spanning perhaps forty yards in a semi-circle. Beyond it, giant pines grow sixty feet or more into the air and form a canopy of branches. The ground is a carpet of fallen needles and moss. Everything is a light shade of green. The man is walking straight across the clearing, the dog at his right heel. The rifle is still pointed into the woods but he no longer holds it at his shoulder.

Zoey steps outside onto a narrow deck shaded by a slight overhang. She moves down two carved chunks of wood to the ground, unsure if she should try to run into the forest or follow the man. She scans the thick blending of trees to either side before glancing down at her feet. She has no shoes and nothing on under the thin garment. The air holds a clean, biting edge to it that she's sure will become much colder once the sun falls below the horizon. Without thinking anymore she moves away from the house and trails the man and the dog.

They enter the forest in earnest fifty yards from the house, the trees closing in in an almost claustrophobic way, their trunks blending together, branches shielding all sight of the sky. Zoey hangs back several steps behind the man, watching the way his long hair swings from the band at the back of his skull. Neither man nor beast acknowledges her as they move and she's about to speak when they both come to a halt.

Zoey glances down to where they're looking and stifles a short cry.

A dead man lies slumped on his side behind a large pine tree. His face is mostly gone above the bridge of his nose, the too-white glare of bone mingled with congealing blood all that is left of his forehead. He is dressed in ragged clothes that look oily in the low light. Several feet away from his outstretched hand is a pistol.

The dog approaches the corpse, sniffs once and huffs a sneeze. The man stares down at the body for a long minute before glancing over his shoulder at her.

"Go inside," he says, the words guttural.

Zoey gives the dead man one last look and backs away before turning to hurry to the house, which she now sees is mostly built into the side of the hill they're on. It has an aged look and blends with the cascade of greens and browns that make up the forest and its floor.

She rushes inside and moves to the room she awoke in. Her clothes have to be here somewhere. She will get dressed and climb out the window of her room, get away from the man before he decides to use the rifle on her as well.

She finds her clothes folded neatly beneath the bed. The tears have been sewn with what looks like the same thread that holds her wound shut. She hesitates only a moment before stripping off the dress and pulling on her pants and shirt. Her shoes are nowhere to be found, but she can't worry about that now—there is no time.

Zoey pulls the quilt from the bed, folding it as tightly as she can beneath her arm before moving to the window. When she looks outside, expecting the slope of the hill dotted with trees, she finds herself staring up a tunnel of dirt and rock that opens to the tree canopy beyond. She curses silently, having forgotten the house is mostly buried. Even if she could get the window open, she's sure she couldn't squeeze out through the narrow tunnel.

Zoey spins to exit out the front and stops dead seeing the man blocking the doorway. She didn't hear his approach or the door opening, and the sight of him there makes her jerk.

"Leaving so soon?" he says.

Her mouth works for a moment before she's able to speak. "What do you want?"

He watches her before glancing down the hallway. "I think I'd like a cup of tea."

The man leaves the doorway and a few seconds later she hears him moving things around in the kitchen. Zoey wavers in place and glances at the window before dropping the quilt back to the bed. She leans into the hallway and sees the man standing with his back to her, busy with something on the counter. The dog, in its customary place on the floor, raises its head as she enters the room. She looks at the door leading outside before glancing at her host.

The man shuffles to a cupboard and brings down two cups with small handles on them. He doesn't move like he did outside when approaching his kill. Instead he looks all of his years, which Zoey judges are many.

A steel kettle begins to hiss, and he pulls it from the top of some kind of appliance with dials before pouring a brownish liquid from it into both cups. There are two chairs on either side of the counter, and he motions to the one closer to her as he sets the cups down.

"Have a seat."

Zoey hesitates, searching his clothes and hands for weapons. Slowly she slides into the chair opposite him. The man picks up his cup, blowing steam from its top as he studies her. His face is lined around the mouth and eyes. Faint stubble that matches his hair flecks his cheeks, but his nose draws her attention the most. It is crooked and smashed to one side, almost to the point where she wonders how he can breathe through it.

He motions to her cup. "It's willow tea with a little honey. It's quite good, though you always have to watch out for a few bits of bark." When she doesn't move to pick up the tea he tilts his head. "You've drank about two gallons of the stuff since you've been here. It's not going to hurt you."

Zoey keeps her eyes fastened on him, but picks up the cup and sips from it. Immediately she remembers the taste from her fever dreams. The bitterness is less now, dulled by a hint of sweetness, but there's no mistaking that she's had it before. She swallows and sets the cup down. "Who are you?" she asks.

The man closes his eyes and sips his tea before cupping it between his hands as if he's chilled. "My name is Ian, but I suppose you're asking for a little more than what to call me." A twinkle shimmers in his eyes, there and gone in an instant. "This is my home, and that is my friend, Seamus," he says, pointing at the dog. At the mention of his name, Seamus raises his head, licks his chops and huffs. "I guess you could say I'm an old man living in the mountains. May I have the pleasure of your name?"

She feels her brow furrow, indecision rising within her. "Zoey," she says finally.

"Zoey," he says, tasting her name. "Why, that's beautiful, if I may say so."

"Why did you help me?" The first drink of tea soothed her throat and she wants another, but doesn't reach for the cup.

"Because you needed help." He glances out the closest window before returning his gaze to her.

"Who was the man you killed?"

"I don't know. Someone who followed me here. Someone who was foolish enough to think I couldn't hear him trailing me. Someone who wanted to take away what I have."

"Do you mean me?" she asks.

Ian chuckles. "No. I mean my home, my possessions, as meager as they are. You are not mine, nor would I guess are you anyone's."

She blinks. "How long have I been here?"

"About a week. It took me two days to get you back here after you passed out. Didn't know if you'd live or die. To be honest, I figured you'd die. That wound was septic, and I don't have much in the way of anti-biotics. I fed you willow tea day in and day out, along with a few other herbs that are good for fighting fever and infection." Ian sits back from the counter, appraising her with unblinking eyes. "You're a tough one. Most wouldn't have pulled through."

Zoey takes another sip of tea, the bitterness almost addictive in a way. She looks out the window at the yard and the trees beyond. "Where are we?"

"Well, that depends on whether we're speaking of now or what was."

"What do you mean?"

"Right now we're simply in a little house built on a hill. If we're speaking of before, then I'd tell you we're in the Pacific Northwest, Washington State to be exact, in the foothills that border the Cascade Mountains."

"I don't know what that means."

Ian nods. "Of course you don't."

They stare at one another for a time before Ian glances out the window again as if he's looking for something.

"What did you do with him?" Zoey asks.

"Who? The man I killed? Dragged him off the path for now. I'll bury him later so he doesn't attract any wildlife. Isn't that right, Seamus? Don't want any of your kind coming to visit." The dog sighs but doesn't raise his head. "He's part wolf, you know. I found him when he was little older than a pup. He didn't trust me for a time, but slowly he realized I meant him no harm." Ian pins her with his gaze as he speaks.

Zoey finishes her tea and sets the cup down. "Thank you for the tea."

"You're welcome."

"Where are my shoes?"

"I'm afraid I had to dispose of them. They were falling apart. They seemed not to be designed for cross-country travel. I should be able to get another pair for you, though."

"I appreciate you helping me, but why did you?"

"Because there was nothing else I could do," he says simply.

"I think I would have died if you hadn't."

"I think you chose to live. I wouldn't have known you were there if you'd kept quiet." Ian purses his lips. "May I ask you a question?"

"Okay."

"How is it that you came to be miles and miles out in the middle of nowhere?"

She looks down at the countertop, which is scuffed and pitted. She finds a smooth portion and runs her fingertip over it. Ian's eyes press upon her, his waiting a physical presence in the room. When she doesn't answer he stands from his seat and retrieves her empty cup. He places both cups into the shallow sink and walks out of the kitchen, stopping by the chair she was sitting in when he appeared in the doorway.

Ian stoops and retrieves the book from the floor, keeping his back turned to her.

"Do you know what kept Dantès alive and fighting to free himself while he was imprisoned in Château d'If?"

"His need for revenge."

Ian remains motionless. "Maybe. I like to think it was something more along the lines of hope. Hope of redemption and a true second chance. Revenge was a choice he made after he escaped." The old man turns toward her, thumbing the well-worn pages of the book. "They were looking for you, Zoey. Many times the helicopter passed over us while I was bringing you here. I know of the compound built in the river. I've seen it myself."

She doesn't realize she's standing until her hand is on the doorknob, her muscles tensing to run. "Why do you know about the ARC? Who are you?" The volume of her voice rises until she's nearly shouting. Ian remains placid as ever.

"I've already told you who I am, and as for your other question, that requires a bit more time to explain. I'll tell you if you give me the chance." He motions to the chair beside the bookcase and begins to busy himself near the stone alcove. Zoey falters in the entryway, half of her longing to run out the door while the other half demands she sit and hear what he has to say. Slowly she moves to the chair and lowers herself into it.

Ian crumples several pieces of bark into a pile at the center of the alcove and adds a layer of sticks to its top. There is a pop, and a flame blooms from a lighter in his hand. Within a minute, a hardy fire crackles and smoke rises to vanish in the pipe above the stone setting. He adds a larger log to the blaze after a short time before sitting in the other chair. Heat seeps into the room, and despite her apprehension she can't help but relish the warmth.

"I was in the army when I was a young man. That's where I learned how to stitch someone up," Ian says, gesturing at her stomach. "I fought in several skirmishes before the Dearth, but I wasn't convinced that the higher powers truly had America's best interests in mind when they sent young women and men such as myself off to die. So I retired from service after five years and became an engineer. Do you know what that is?"

"Someone who designs things," she answers, an image of Lee so clear and poignant coming to her she has to look away.

"More or less. I fell in love with a woman named Helen, and we were married. We had a son and a daughter. We were happy." The old man begins to knead his knotted fingers together. "Our son entered the military, just as I had, several years before the Dearth began. Following in my footsteps, I suppose. He lived on a base not far from here. Our daughter loved animals and became a veterinarian, that's a doctor for animals. She was very successful but never found someone she could share her life with." Ian falls silent, and the only sound comes from the fire gnawing the wood into flame.

"When the Dearth came, there was utter panic. Uprisings, murder, chaos, it was a horrible time to live through. Our daughter was deeply opposed to the government's action and, against our wishes, she traveled with a group to protest the National Obstetric Alliance in the country's capital."

The mention of NOA here in this small house, in the middle of the woods, sends goose bumps flowing across Zoey's arms. She steadies herself and waits for Ian to continue.

The old man's fingers stop moving. "She was killed by riot police sent to put down the protest. Someone threw a stone, and that was all it took for the authorities to unleash their violence against them. Our son's army base was overrun by a marauding group of thousands. He barely made it out alive and was on his way here when he was attacked again. All that was left of his car was a burned husk by the side of the road."

Zoey swallows the lump that has risen in her throat. She has to stop herself from reaching out to the old man. Instead she focuses on the weaving flames within the hearth.

"I'm sorry," she says quietly.

"Thank you." Ian composes himself and takes a deep breath. "Helen and I remained here as the world fell apart around us. The Dearth became an epidemic and to be honest, at that point I didn't care if anything or anyone else survived. My children were gone, and we were alone."

"Were you immune to the plague?"

Ian's silver eyebrows draw down. "Plague?"

"The virus that caused the Dearth. It killed almost everyone else. Were you and your wife immune?"

The old man studies her for a long moment. "Zoey, there was no plague. They never determined what caused the lack of female births, but there was never a plague."

The room takes on a hazy appearance at the corners of her vision, and she pinches the skin of her forearm. "Then how did all the people die?"

"They were killed by our own military. At a certain point there was an enormous uprising by the populace. The rebel forces fought for years but were never able to gain any ground. They were crushed under superior firepower, and those that defected from the military in protest of what was happening were executed as well. Millions fled the country or died trying. The atomic blast that killed the President was a last-ditch effort by the rebels, but to no avail. By then it was too late. Over the years, many more perished by one another's hands, starvation, illness. But it all began with genocide."

The enormity of what Ian is saying hits her like a slap.

Lies. Everything she has ever known. Lies.

She suspected that the entire truth wasn't being told to them for years, that Miss Gwen and the others were twisting facts to meet their own needs, but this, this is unfathomable. If Ian is telling the truth, it means that the population of the United States wasn't decimated from without, by an uncontrolled virus, but from within, by its own government.

"Is that what they told you?" he asks. "That a plague was responsible?"

Zoey can't answer. She simply nods.

Ian drops his eyes to his lap. "So much lost. Not only life but truth as well. It's unforgivable." He glances up. "Perhaps it would have been better if there had been a plague. At least our humanity, or lack thereof, would have gone out in a graceful way. Maybe something resembling compassion would have shined through." He shrugs. "I don't know. It's so hard to understand."

"Why? Why would they kill everyone?"

"Because they were afraid. That's why so many kill. Fear feeds the worst in all of us. It drives the most despicable of our natures to the surface. The masses disagreed with NOA and the soldiers that came to take away the women, so they were slaughtered in fear they would overrun the powers that be, or were, as it is. Not to say the rebels were in the complete right either. People panicked and lashed out. At times there was no rhyme or reason to it."

"'Hatred is blind, rage carries you away; and he who pours out vengeance runs the risk of tasting a bitter draught.'" Zoey recites from memory. She gazes into the fire and only looks at the old man when she realizes he is staring at her.

"Who gave you a copy of the book?" Ian asks, gesturing at *The Count of Monte Cristo*.

"I don't know."

"How did you escape, Zoey?"

"I killed," she says quietly. "I killed and I died there."

"How many other women are imprisoned?"

"Why do you want to know?"

"Let me answer that question with another question. What were your intentions after escaping?"

Zoey blinks and looks away toward the windows. The afternoon is growing darker. Somewhere in the distance the sky chuckles with thunder. "I don't know."

"Were you going to go back?"

"I don't know."

"Don't you want to save the others?"

"I don't know!" She thrusts herself up from the chair, hands clenched. Dizziness assaults her and she reels with it, stumbling one step to the side. Ian is on his feet in less than a second, hands held out to help steady her. "I don't need your help! Just—just back off!"

"Okay, I'm sorry."

She stabilizes herself against the warm stone surrounding the fire. Ian watches her, his hands still out before him. Suddenly his eyes flick over her shoulder and back.

Zoey spins, looking out through the window. Only vivid green and brown bark. But was there movement between the trees down the hill? She turns back to him.

"What's going on?"

"Zoey, calm down. You're stressing yourself too much."

"Who's outside? Is it them? Is it Reaper?"

"I don't know who that is."

"You're lying." She staggers away from him, head hissing with static. She has to get out, get away from the house and off the mountain.

"Zoey, please. No one's going to hurt you. I invited some people who want to help you. That's where I was coming back from when you woke. They're friends. Please calm down."

"No, I won't go back. I won't." She tries to rush down the hallway, but her feet tangle and she falls hard to the wood floor. All of her wind rushes out in a gust that leaves her empty, powerless. The grayness at the corners of her vision multiplies as she tries to rise. She falls again, the strength in her limbs ebbing to nothing. Ian shouts something as she feels her consciousness slip away like a stone dropped in a pool, but the sound of booted feet on the stairs outside the house reaches her even as her pleas die in her throat and the world fades away.

27

She becomes aware of a susurrus of low voices, very much like the sound of wind in the big pines.

"Absolutely amazing that she made it this far." Deep, throbbing bass voice.

"I'm still having trouble believing it." This voice smoother, quieter, but still definitely male.

"You and I both." Ian.

So, three of them. Zoey tries moving her arms and legs. They are unbound. She'll have to be fast, they'll all be armed, but they think she's still asleep.

"Are you sure about her?" The softer voice again. "Maybe she came from a camp down south. I've heard rumblings of several girls being born there. Or maybe from the city itself."

"We all know those rumors are just that," Ian says, closer to her now. "Rumors. NOA would have raided them years ago."

Zoey pauses. She has their locations in the room pinpointed and is almost ready to leap from the bed, but their conversation doesn't make sense. They're speaking about NOA as if they aren't associated with it.

"Where's our good doctor?" Ian asks.

"She's changing clothes. Fell in a stream on the way up. Madder than a wildcat when she came out," the deep voice says. His words are followed by rumbling laughter.

"Okay, you guys, there's not enough room in here for all of us, and besides, we don't want her waking up to a roomful of people. The poor thing's probably scared enough as it is, so shoo. Get moving."

There is the clunking of footsteps retreating from the room. When they're gone, Zoey cracks her eyelids just enough to survey her surroundings.

A woman stands at the end of the bed. Her hair is a dirty red and is tied back from her face, which is oval-shaped and long. Her lips are crimson against her pallid skin, their edges pressed together to form a straight line. She is tall and thin, her frame covered in a pair of dark pants and a gray, button-up shirt.

The woman moves closer to her and pulls a strange rubber apparatus from a bag she carries. One end is split, with two curving metal pieces, while the other ends in a silver disc. She places the split ends in each of her ears and moves forward, the disc gripped in one hand.

Zoey snatches her wrist when she's close enough, yanking the woman off balance. With her other hand she grasps the woman's throat and squeezes with all her strength, which isn't much. The woman's eyes pop wide and she issues a quiet squawk.

"Who are you?" Zoey asks. The woman jerks away, yanking herself from Zoey's grip. She takes a breath and begins to rub at the place on her neck where Zoey's fingers sank in.

"My name is Chelsea Tenner. I'm sorry for startling you. I'm a doctor, I wanted to check to see how you were healing. Ian tells us that you had quite a trip."

Zoey studies her for a long time before licking her lips. "What did you say your name was?"

"Chelsea."

"No. You said something after that."

"Tenner. My last name is Tenner."

"You have a last name?"

Chelsea squints at her. "Yes, of course." A look of dawning overcomes her features, and she shakes her head. "They never told you yours, did they?"

"No."

Chelsea sighs and returns to the bedside, pulling the wooden chair with her. She sits, combing back an errant strand of hair that's escaped its tie. "We mean you no harm whatsoever, Zoey. Ian told us about finding you and asked if we would come."

"Who's with you? How many?"

"There's five of us, and I'll let them introduce themselves once you feel up to meeting them."

"Who are you people?"

"Survivors, just like you. Look, I know you're scared and suspicious—you have every right to be. We want to talk with you, that's all."

Zoey watches Chelsea's eyes, searches for a tell in her body language that reveals a lie or even a half-truth. She sees none. Slowly she nods.

"Okay. Is it all right with you if I check you over? Make sure Ian did a good job of being a nurse?"

"Go ahead."

Chelsea places the silver disc on Zoey's chest. She listens and asks Zoey to take several deep breaths, moving the device around to different areas. She inspects the wound on her stomach, clucking with an apparent disapproval of the stitches. Lastly she takes a small, digital wand from the bag and has Zoey hold one end beneath her tongue. The unit beeps after only a few seconds and Chelsea nods.

"Generally you seem to be okay. You don't have a fever, your wound is healing, though you're going to have a nasty scar thanks to Ian's sloppy hands, and your heart and lungs sound very healthy. You're a little malnourished and dehydrated, but that's easily fixable. I think you're going to live." Chelsea smiles, and there is something in it that reaches out to Zoey and instantly sends an inkling of appreciation through her. She's not at all like the doctors at the ARC.

"Thank you."

"You're welcome. Now one thing I did notice is that you smell quite rank—not your fault, of course, bathing facilities were probably scarce in the wild. You'll find a new set of clothes that should fit in the bathroom. There's soap in there as well. I had Ian turn up the water temperature so it should be fairly hot. Let me know if you need anything else. We'll be waiting for you in the living room."

Chelsea stands and exits the room, leaving the door wide open. Zoey crawls from the bed and follows her into the vacant hallway. There is a murmur of voices in the living room but she slips into the bathroom before she catches sight of anyone else.

A stack of clothing rests on a short stool inside. The pants are a tough and beaten canvas the color of sand, and the shirt is a thick button-up of faded blue. There is a folded pair of woolen socks and even underwear that feels freshly washed. She tries not to think of where the underwear came from or who's worn them before.

Zoey strips and turns the nozzle on the shower, which produces a weak stream, so unlike the blast of hot water she's used to, but when she steps under the flow it is glorious. She finds the bar of soap on a little shelf built into the shower surround and washes away weeks of grime. After what seems like hours, she finally feels clean. She climbs out and dries off with a threadbare towel hanging from a nearby hook. She dresses slowly, taking her time to get used to the clothing. It is much rougher than all the prior garments she's worn but it feels good against her clean skin. An ivory-colored brush rests on the edge of the sink and she picks it up, seeing for the first time that a small mirror has been set on a ledge above the drain.

A drawn and shrunken version of herself stares back from the glass. Her cheekbones are more pronounced, and there is a strange look to her eyes that at first she mistakes for hollowness. After a long moment of staring, she sees that it isn't a void that has taken up residence in her gaze but a sharp, feral wariness. They are the eyes of an animal.

She brushes her hair without looking in the mirror again, the tangles in it so tight she's not sure they'll ever come free. It takes her the better part of a half-hour to release all the knots and loops that have formed in the time since her last shower. Thoughts of meeting the others waiting in the living room send a bristling fear lined with excitement through her. She still has no idea if they can be trusted, but if she were to judge them by Ian and now Chelsea, she would have to concede they mean her no harm.

Zoey opens the door, the cool air from the rest of the house making her shiver after the warmth of the shower. She moves down the corridor and stops at the threshold of the kitchen.

There are six people in the living room and one dog. Ian, Chelsea, and Seamus she knows. Then there is a black man who looks to be only a few inches taller than she is but is broad through the shoulders and thick through the chest. His skin is twice as dark as Crispin's or Sherell's, almost to the point of being purple, and his eyes are deep-set and unblinking. He stands beside a stout woman of perhaps fifty. She wears a black cloth over her head that's tied tightly in the back and her face is round and full. Her nose is unnaturally flattened, indicating that it's been broken at least once and never fixed, while her lips are pale and almost nonexistent. In one of the chairs rests a dark-haired young man maybe a few years older than Zoey. He is very handsome, with brown eyes and a square jaw dusted with whiskers. He picks at a tear in his pants with one fingernail over and over. Behind his chair, speaking with Ian, is a tall man wearing a black vest with several pockets lining its front. He has even darker hair than the boy and it hangs lank and straight down to his ears. The muscularity and power of his body is apparent even through the clothes he wears. His arms rest languidly at his sides, but he shifts on his feet with an easy grace that suggests he could spring into action at any second.

She is about to retreat to her room to compose herself when the boy in the chair nudges the tall man's arm and points to where she stands.

The room hushes, and the crackle of fire and gentle tap of rain against the house are the only sounds.

"Hello, Zoey," the tall man says. "Please come in and join us."

She steps around the wall and stops beside the hearth, the door to outside still calling her even though no one looks as if they have any intention of moving from their places.

"My name is Merrill Grayson. I'm sorry we alarmed you earlier."

"That's really my fault," Ian cuts in. "I was trying to get around to telling you that they were coming, but an old man tends to wander when he begins a story." He smiles sadly and pets Seamus's large head with one hand.

"This is Tia Ferrone," Merrill says, motioning to the woman with the black fabric tied on her head. "And that's Eli Weston beside her. You've already met Chelsea, and this guy here we call Newton." Merrill claps the boy on the shoulders with two large hands. Newton stares up at her with wide eyes before jerking his gaze down to the floor.

"What's his last name?" Zoey asks, nodding to Newton.

Merrill frowns, glancing at Chelsea before tipping his head to one side. "We don't know. We found him, or he found us a few years back."

"Fell out of a tree and almost crushed my boy Merrill here," Eli says, his deep voice booming easily throughout the room. "That's why we call him Newton."

Zoey frowns and shakes her head. "I don't get it."

Merrill smiles. "No, I suppose they wouldn't have had much purpose in teaching you about gravity, would they?"

"I know what gravity is."

Merrill nods. "Well, we'll fill you in on the rest some other time." He surveys her, his eyes losing some of their lightness. "I suppose you're wondering why we came to see you."

"Yes, I am."

"If I may," Ian says, glancing at Merrill. "I told you I'd enlighten you on how I knew of the ARC, but I didn't have a chance to finish my story. You see, Helen passed away over fourteen years ago. It was cancer, though we never had a formal diagnosis. She slipped away in the night while I slept beside her. I didn't get to say goodbye properly." Ian's voice falters but he clears his throat and continues. "Merrill here was my son's best friend, and after Helen passed he came to me asking for my help. My soul was full of vengeance for the government that took away my children, because if NOA hadn't enforced the mandatory draft of women who had given birth to females, the rebels may have never have had their uprising and all of this might have been avoided.

"Helen made me promise," Ian continues, "to never seek out revenge on those we felt were responsible. She was a wonderful woman, my wife; strong, beautiful, and much wiser than I'll ever be." The old man hesitates and glances at Merrill, who pauses for a moment before beginning to speak.

"I came to him with a force of people that were like-minded. We all had lost someone because of NOA and had learned of the ARC in the eastern part of the state. There were forty of us, and we had a plan along with weapons, equipment to scale the walls, everything we thought we'd need. Ian was to be our lookout and sniper."

"Sniper?" Zoey says, shocked though she realizes she shouldn't be after seeing how the old man dispatched the intruder a hundred yards away in the trees. Ian nods, though there is no hint of pride on his face.

"We executed the plan perfectly," Merrill continues. "We went in at night in boats and on land, but they knew we were coming. There was a spy in our ranks who had been keeping tabs on us for months while we prepared the assault. He tipped the soldiers off days before we attacked. They wanted to draw us out, wanted us to come to them." Merrill swallows loudly and grimaces. "It was a slaughter. Thirty-five of our forty died, and only a few of us got away unscathed. Myself not included." Merrill draws up his right pant leg, and Zoey blinks at the shining aluminum shaft protruding from the bottom of his knee joint. He drops the material, hiding the amputated limb and shrugs. "There's no excuse. It was my fault. I trusted the wrong man."

Zoey studies the group while something rises in her memory. *Her hands pressed to the glass in her room, looking out at the white streaks of fire burning in the night sky. The gunfire, explosions, distant screams. Simon bursting in with Lee, the gun in one hand. She and Lee huddled in the bathroom while something neither of them understood raged on outside the walls.*

"It was you," she says, looking at Merrill. "That night, I remember it. It was you attacking the ARC."

Slowly he nods. "I didn't know if any of you girls would be able to see the flares or the gunfire. The interior layout of the ARC was one thing we knew nothing of."

"We could see," Zoey says. For some reason, this seems to upset Merrill. He bites his lower lip and paces away from the group before coming back.

"How many of you are there?" Merrill asks.

Zoey hesitates. The thought of revealing something about the ARC, about the other women, gives her pause. But the stricken look that's overtaken Merrill's face nudges her forward.

"Six besides me," she says finally.

"What are they doing with all of you?" Tia asks. It's the first time she's spoken, and she has a smooth voice that is striking in comparison with her smashed nose and aggressive stance.

"They're . . . they're using us. Trying to have one of us give birth to a girl."

The entire group grows rigid. Even Newton sits stock-still in his chair.

"Are you pregnant, Zoey?" Chelsea asks.

"No. I got out before my birthday. They take you when you turn twenty-one. It's called the induction. They take you to the fifth level and that's where they . . ." She can't bring herself to go on. The words are hooked inside her.

"Take your time," Eli says.

Slowly she begins to speak again. She tells them of the ceremony, of the fifth level, of the lies. It pours from her as if a dam has broken. Years of insecurities, misgivings, mistrust, theories, all of it comes rushing out. When she's finished, there is a stunned silence that hangs in the room like fog against the mountains. Merrill and Chelsea exchange a look and Ian moves to the corner of the room, where he opens a glass decanter and drinks from it before handing it to Tia.

"We suspected as much," Ian says as the bottle is passed around. "We knew NOA would go to great lengths to try and find a solution, but this is simply monstrous."

"A plague and a safe zone," Eli rumbles after taking a long pull from the bottle. "Those bastards."

"How did you get out, is what I'd like to know," Tia says. She takes a second drink from the bottle before handing it back to Ian.

"I took a guard's bracelet and made it up to the fifth floor. After that Terra helped me get onboard one of the helicopters and then lied to the guards about me jumping over the side of the wall. The helicopter crashed and I made it out alive." Zoey keeps her eyes locked on a spot on the wall over Tia's shoulder.

"I think there's a bit more to it than that," Tia says. "You don't have to be ashamed of what you did. Whoever you hurt deserved as much and more, don't worry about any of them."

Zoey nods, but in her mind she sees Crispin crumpling to the floor, his last spasms and the look of disbelief on his kind face.

"They're looking for something, too," she says, mostly to rid herself of the horrid vision. "Something called the keystone."

"Keystone?" Ian says. The old man rubs his jaw and glances around the group. "Does that term mean anything to the rest of you?" There is a chorus of 'No's and a shaking of heads. "Do you have any guesses as to what it is, Zoey?"

"No. Terra didn't know either, and I didn't really have a chance to ask anyone else." She glances at Merrill, who has been staring at her intently since she started speaking about the inner sanctum of the ARC. His jaw is trembling, and he swallows before addressing her.

"You said they take the women when they turn twenty-one?"

"Yes," Zoey says.

"Do you know why?"

"No."

"I need to ask you something, Zoey, and please, this is very important. Did you ever know a girl by the name of Meeka?"

The house starts a slow spin around her and she grits her teeth to keep from toppling over. "Why?"

"Please!" Merrill yells, startling everyone. The group gives him a look and Eli places a hand on the tall man's shoulder. "Please," Merrill says again, quietly this time. "Just tell me if she was ever there."

"Yes," Zoey says, unable to say anything more because she sees something in Merrill's eyes that she's seen before. When Simon held Lee's foot for a moment in the infirmary after his injury, the same look had been on the older man's face.

The face of a worried father.

Merrill sags a little but doesn't drop his gaze. "Is she alive? Is my little girl alive?"

Zoey reels internally, a thousand abject paths opening before her, her choice limited to one and one only. She hovers over the thousand forks and finally chooses, plunging headlong and screaming inside.

"Yes," she says evenly. "She's alive."

28

The storm comes in layers from over the mountain, each harsher than the last.

First there is the rain, then the stitching slash of lightning through the great trees with its counterpart of thunder following close behind, then the wind that blows so hard it's as if it intends to tear the mountain from the earth and crumble it back to whence it came.

Zoey sits in her bedroom and listens to the sounds of the tempest, more muted since this part of the house is mostly underground. Every so often she glances at the window that has grown almost black, then to the closed door, then back to her hands that lay in her lap. She turns them over, looking at their creases, the cuts that are healing into fine, red lines that will scar. All the while the words she spoke to Merrill echo in horrifying clarity through her mind.

Yes, she's alive.

She puts her palms to her eyes, pressing the tears away that threaten to come spilling out. How could she have done it? How? The immensity of the lie hangs over her, pressing down as if she is buried beneath a million tons of rock instead of resting upon it. But the question is an easy one to answer, isn't it? It's easy, because its answer is the same that she would have given to Ian if she had been honest with him before.

Do you want to save the others?

Yes.

She wants it more than anything else in the world. The hatred she feels for herself over leaving the other women behind hasn't dulled with the days since she escaped. Instead it has increased like a spark being constantly fanned until it bursts into flame. Running so far from the ARC was her way of dodging the guilt, but the distance hasn't helped.

She always knew she would go back. It was that or die.

And in Merrill she sees her chance.

Here is a group that will either help her or leave this place broken, for she can tell that Merrill is the one who binds them together. He is the knife edge and the driving force. The love for his daughter is the fuel that kept his will burning through all these years.

And now she has used it against him.

The tears come, and she can't stop them this time. She sees Merrill's face after she told him the lie, how he couldn't bear to look at her, at any of them. How he strode out into the rain, so overcome with emotion that he didn't bother to grab his coat from the hook by the door.

How much is a life worth?

Zoey sobs into her hands as quietly as possible. The grief wracks her in time with the storm outside, the gale within her just as powerful.

It is a long while before the tears taper off, and even longer before sleep takes her and folds her away from the storm.

She wakes to a knock at her door and sits up. She is still fully clothed and on top of the covers. Daylight streams down from outside and flattens itself against the floor.

"Zoey?"

Merrill.

"Yes?"

"Can I come in?"

"Sure."

She gathers herself to one end of the bed, wiping the sleep from her eyes as Merrill enters. He wears the same clothes as he did the day before. His eyes are narrow, weary, and bloodshot. He leaves the door partially open and lowers himself into the wooden chair beside the bed.

"How did you sleep?" he asks.

"Good. How about you?"

"Not so good, but that's okay."

"I'm sorry."

"Not your fault."

"And I really should have given you guys my room. Where did you all sleep?"

"Ian made us comfortable. Believe me, this is very nice compared to some of the places we've had to bed down in."

"Where do you live?"

Merrill stretches back, and the chair creaks with his weight. "Outside a city, really just a town. There's only one real city now that I know of. Seattle, or what used to be Seattle."

"Where is it?"

"Over the mountains."

"And your town, how many people live there?"

"A hundred, maybe a few more."

"And the men there don't bother Chelsea or Tia?"

"I didn't say that."

"Oh."

"That's why we live outside of town. We have to be especially careful because you never know who's watching or what they want. It's amazing that Chelsea and Tia are still alive and free, really. We keep them hidden very well, and they only come into the open when it's absolutely necessary. Eli, Newton, and I travel into town for supplies about once a month. It really pisses Tia off that she isn't able to go." Merrill utters a short laugh.

"She doesn't seem like the type who would be afraid."

"She's not. I once saw Tia knock out a two-hundred-fifty-pound man with one punch. She's as tough as any of us."

"And what are you? Really?"

Merrill studies her. "We're survivors."

"That's what Chelsea said."

"She's right. Sometimes that's the best you can do. But you already know that, don't you?"

Zoey nods. They both fall silent. She struggles with a question she knows she shouldn't ask, but can't help herself. "How did Meeka come to be at the ARC?"

Merrill visibly stiffens, and he casts his eyes across the floor. "She was taken from me."

"When?"

"It was two years after the Dearth began. She was just a little over a year old. I met her mother on a trip to China ten years before." Merrill still isn't looking at her, but his lips quiver with a sad smile. "Jia was a software engineer for a large company that was adjacent to my hotel. I bumped into her the first day trying to leave the parking lot. Literally bumped into her, with my car." He shakes his head. "Man, I felt like such an idiot, even though she wasn't hurt. I insisted on taking her to the hospital, and she kept saying things in Chinese and I knew she was swearing at me." Zoey can't help but smile. Merrill sighs and rubs at his brow. "I went to her office the next day with flowers, and the day after that. Finally after a week her workspace was so full of roses and lilies she agreed to go to lunch with me just to get me to stop." He pauses and bobs his head several times. "She was beautiful, just like Meeka."

Zoey's throat tries to close as she sees Meeka lying in a spreading pool of blood, her eyes vacant and staring. Merrill's voice snaps her back to the present.

"When I saw what was happening, the road the government was going to take, I started working on a place in the Canadian wilderness fifty miles across the border near a glacial lake. It was five miles from the nearest road, and I didn't own the land, but there was nothing but woods and mountains as far as I could see. I built a little cabin there, large enough to hold the three of us, and hauled supplies up with each trip. We had plenty of fresh water, food, shelter, everything we needed to survive. We were planning on leaving the next morning when they came."

"Merrill, you don't have to tell me this," Zoey says in a soft voice. She doesn't want to hear it.

"There were five of them, all armed, black ops by the look. I knew the signs from being in the military for a few years when I was younger. I tried talking with them at the door, stalling for another day because I knew we could be long gone by the time they came back, but they weren't having it. They were there to take Jia and Meeka both." Merrill's voice grows flatter and colder with each word, his eyes glazing over. "I had a gun hidden underneath a chair in the living room. I went for it as they were carrying them away. I shot one of the soldiers before they were able to open fire." He points to his left shoulder and lower abdomen. "The bullets hit me here and here, but one of the other soldiers must not have had his rifle on safe. Jia grabbed it—I could see her from where I was lying on the floor. She grabbed the gun and it went off." Merrill grimaces and looks at the ceiling. "It hit her directly in the heart, there was no way of saving her, so they just left her there in the doorway like a piece of trash. I managed to crawl to her but she was already gone. When I looked out through the door, they were climbing into their vehicle, and one of them was holding Meeka and she was looking back at me. But she never cried, she was always such a good girl."

Zoey shudders with a restrained sob and blinks away the tears that have doubled her vision, the memory of Meeka telling them what she recalled about her parents flooding her mind.

I remember someone lying on the ground, not sure if it was my mom or dad. I don't know if they were hurt or playing.

"I'm so sorry," she whispers without raising her head.

"Thank you. I don't mean to put all this on you after everything you've been through."

"It's okay."

"When I learned about the ARC, I knew that's where they'd taken Meeka. The birthrate for girls had dropped to almost nothing, and I had already scoured every other possible place she could be. When I failed to get her out, I wanted to die. I knew I'd never be able to raise another army that was like-minded. Most men nowadays are either in league with NOA, or religious fanatics, or worse, they're part of the Fae Trade."

Zoey flinches at the mention of the Fae Trade, the slurred voices of the men coming back to her from the night in the pine forest.

"I gave up," Merrill continues. "I was wounded and could barely get around by myself. I drank for years and tried to forget my family, even tried to kill myself a couple times, but couldn't do it properly. Chelsea found me after my last attempt. I'd swallowed a bunch of old painkillers and had wandered out of town. She got me to throw them up and nursed me back to health.

"Slowly our group came together, mostly out of necessity. I found Tia living in an industrial complex. After she held me at gunpoint for the better part of a day, I learned she was a welder—one of the best in the world, if the truth is told. She built me this." He raps on the fake leg beneath his pants. "Eli came later, wandering into our camp delirious with some kind of fever. Chelsea helped him, and he stayed with us. He'll tell you it's because of the danger and that he's a thrill-seeker, but he's got the biggest heart of anyone I know. And of course, we kind of adopted Newton. He didn't have any family that we could find. I'm guessing they abandoned him."

"What's wrong with him?" Zoey asks.

"He's mute. Never said a word to any of us. He communicates sometimes through gestures or grunts, but other than that he can't speak."

Merrill watches her for a time, and with each passing second she grows more uncomfortable under his gaze. It's like he's looking inside her, and soon he'll discover the lie she told to him. Maybe he'll kill her right where she sits, and truthfully she deserves exactly that.

"I'm sorry, you need your rest," Merrill says, standing. "There's food in the kitchen if you're hungry." He turns to leave.

"How do the others feel about the ARC, about NOA?" Zoey asks.

Merrill pauses at the door, looking down. "You know how I said I was sure I'd never find another army?"

"Yes."

"Well, I did." He gives her a fleeting smile and is gone through the door.

♦   ♦   ♦

The hours pass in a gray-tinged impression of day. Zoey ventures into the kitchen when her stomach refuses to quiet and finds a plate of dried meat that is tangy and very salty, along with some fresh bread. The house is vacant, though she catches flashes of movement out in the trees from time to time. She is about to retire to her room again when Newton steps through the front door. He freezes in the entry, eyes wide and unblinking.

"Hi, Newton," she says. He stands his ground for a second, his gaze flicking to the remaining meat on the plate, before he flees back outside, as skittish as some small animal. Zoey watches him sprint into the woods past Tia and Chelsea, who only stare after him. Both of them glance at the house, and Zoey moves away from the window and back to her room.

She remains there for the rest of the day. No one comes to disturb her, and she sleeps off and on, fatigue still taking its toll on her body. She dreams of the greenish-blue river, of flying over its surface. It is dawn and she skims over the water without resistance. Ahead the shape of the ARC solidifies in the early light. She slows as she nears it, hovering in place a good distance away.

There are five forms hanging by their necks from ropes over the side of the wall.

Slowly the swaying corpses raise their arms and point directly at her.

Zoey wakes to the early dusk of evening with a strangled scream bubbling from her that she manages to stave off. She grips her pillow and twists it until her heart returns to a normal speed. The dream's hold on her slowly loosens, decaying into a softened memory, leaving her with only a paralyzing sense of dread.

She doesn't want to go back, she realizes. She's terrified of returning to that place. A greed-plated voice begins to speak in the back of her mind, telling her that she has every reason to stay away from the ARC now. It was a miracle she escaped at all and little as she knows about the outside world, she can learn. She can learn to live, learn to have a life.

Zoey rises from the bed on unsteady legs, a burning thirst sending her in search of water. She leaves the darkly seductive voice behind in the room and moves to the front of the house.

It is quiet and empty, as it was earlier when she encountered Newton. Outside the sun has disappeared behind the mountain and a surreal shade coats the forest. She pours a glass of water from a pitcher beside the sink and drinks until her stomach is full and sloshing. When she moves to the farthest window she sees a fire burning a short distance from the house. The hunched outlines of the group sit around it.

Zoey slips out the door without a sound and creeps down the steps. She stops a dozen paces from the border of firelight and listens.

"Might be wasting our time, you know," Tia says. "I'm not taking anything away from her, but I don't think she's willing to do what we want."

"You don't know that," Merrill says from across the fire. He holds a long stick that is singed black at one end from prodding the flames. "She's very strong. Determined."

"I'm not saying she isn't," Tia replies. "I'm saying she may have zero interest in helping us."

"When I asked her what she wanted the day you all arrived, I saw something in her even though she declined to answer me," Ian says. He is smoking some kind of long pipe, the white smoke trailing up from its bulbous end to mingle with its kin from the fire. "There is a deep hatred burning inside of her, more so than I've ever seen in anyone, including you, Merrill. She may have an incredible fear of NOA and the ARC, but her anger is stronger, I believe."

"Anyone who can do what she did and survive is okay in my book," Eli says. "Tough girl, you know?"

"Look, I want to go, you all know that," Merrill says, staring into the fire. "But to actually have a chance, we need her help. No one else has seen the inside of that place, no one knows the layout and security. Without her it's a suicide mission."

"It's probably a suicide mission regardless," Tia grumbles.

Merrill shrugs. "Probably. But every one of us has our reasons to go." He gazes around at their firelit faces. "All we can do is ask her."

"I'll help you," Zoey says, stepping into the ring of light.

Every head snaps toward her and Eli even reaches for something beneath his coat.

"Holy hell, girl, you scared the bejeezus out of us," Eli says. "Try making some noise next time."

"Sorry," Zoey says, coming closer. Ian gazes at her with a knowing look. He doesn't appear surprised by her presence in the least as he continues to puff his pipe.

"How long have you been standing there?" Tia asks, scowling over one shoulder.

"Long enough."

"Look, Zoey, we were only discussing some options. There's nothing written in stone yet," Chelsea says, throwing a look at Merrill, who hasn't moved since Zoey stepped into the light.

"I understand," Zoey says. "But you were talking about trying again, weren't you? About attacking the ARC?"

"Yes," Merrill says. "We want to try again."

"You want to destroy it?"

"We want to rescue the remaining women," he says, glancing away into the shadows that drape the forest. "If we save them, that will be enough to destroy NOA."

"This is all noble and good," Tia says, shifting on her seat. "I hate the idea of what they're using them for as much as anyone, but have you guys considered the sheer mechanics of getting into that facility and out with half a dozen women in tow? We would need a miracle."

"Miracles are just really good plans with a little luck," Merrill says. Tia makes an exasperated sound and leans back in her chair. "If anyone doesn't want to be a part of this, tell me now, because I'm going ahead with it regardless." He gazes around at the circle. Tia casts her eyes downward into the flames but doesn't move otherwise. "Okay," Merrill says after a long moment of silence. "We do this. And as far as miracles go, we already have one of those." He points to Zoey. "She's standing right there."

29

Ian brings out the glass bottle from the house and they pass it around.

When it comes to Zoey she tries to hand it off to Eli, who pushes it back.

"Nah, see, this is how we celebrate, girl. You're twenty-one now, so you're legal and everything."

"What do you mean?"

"Twenty-one was the legal drinking age for alcohol before everything fell apart," Chelsea says. "But you don't have to try it if you don't want to."

Zoey frowns at the bottle but brings it to her nose to sniff. The smell bites her sinuses and makes her eyes water. "Wow, that's really awful."

"Yeah, but it tastes so good," Tia says. Eli laughs.

Zoey musters some courage and puts the bottle to her lips, tipping some of the liquid into her mouth. The liquor burns a fiery path down her throat and detonates in her stomach. She gasps, sitting forward, and shoves the bottle into Eli's waiting hand. The entire group chuckles as she sits back, fanning her mouth.

"It's horrible," she chokes out, and this only makes them laugh harder. Even Newton smiles and tries to hide it behind one hand. The night deepens, and the fire grows higher as Merrill adds more wood. The small conversation dies down and trickles to a stop. The pines creak and crack with the wind that never seems to cease. Zoey sits forward, holding her hands out to the flames. The fire feels good on her skin, but something is different. It takes her the better part of a minute to realize what it is.

She's relaxed.

The constant hammering of fear and trepidation that she's felt over the last two weeks is gone. But it is more than that. It's the relief of years of control as well. The last two weeks were the culmination of her entire life, but the time before that is what is leaving her now. She can almost feel it peeling away like dead skin, revealing a new, healthy pink tissue beneath. She allows herself to bask in it for a moment before the guilt comes flowing back in with the images of the other women asleep in their small rooms right now. The quiet halls of the ARC, the pacing of the snipers on the walls, as well as the new weight she carries.

She glances at Merrill but he is focused on the fire, moving the logs around systematically with his stick.

"Man, why you always gotta mess with the fire? Shit's gonna burn whether you poke it or not," Eli says, not unkindly.

Merrill doesn't respond for a long time. He shifts the burning wood again, sending a shower of sparks upward in defiance of gravity. "Because there's a perfect way to set the logs. You can construct a fire to burn slow and low or fast and hot, but you have to learn how the flames move, how the air fuels it." He looks up and fixes Zoey with a stare. "There's a way to do everything if you want to learn it." He turns another piece of wood over, and the fire leaps high from the pit, licking at the night air. Merrill sticks the poker in the ground and sits. "When we attacked the ARC before it wasn't only the foreknowledge of the guards that destroyed us, it was their position high on the walls, the way the building is situated in the river, the auto-guns mounted on the sides, everything. They picked the perfect location to build it: defendable, unlimited power from the hydroelectric dam. If we're going to succeed this time we not only need the element of surprise, but the perfect way to infiltrate the compound."

"Explosives," Eli says. "My main lesbian over here knows a thing or two about blowing shit up, am I right, darlin'?"

Tia smiles grimly. "I could set a trip wire in your bed that would blow off your legs. Is that what you mean?"

"Mmm, wish you'd just climb in there with me some night, I could show you what you've been missin'."

"Pretty sure you don't have anything I'd miss, unless not being able to see it counts?"

"Ooooo, deep burn!" Eli says, throwing his head back and laughing. Tia rolls her eyes but smiles and shakes her head.

Merrill is unperturbed by the banter. "No, explosives won't work. They'll know right away that we're inside. It's not an option. We need to slip in and out as quickly as possible. Some sort of distraction would be good."

"Without blowing a hole in the damn place, how are we going to get in?" Eli asks.

"We could cut through," Tia says. "The plasma cutter I built would do it."

"The concrete is two feet thick or more in most places," Zoey says quietly.

Tia pats her on the knee. "Did I mention I built the cutter?" She gives Zoey a quick wink.

"Okay, we can cut through, but where?" Merrill says. "The outer wall only leads us to the gap between it and the building, correct, Zoey?"

She nods. "Yes. You'd still have to get through one of the doors and inside, which would trigger an alarm without a bracelet with the right clearance."

"Then we need to come up from the bottom," Merrill says. "Come in under it in a boat and cut through the floor."

"How do we know where's a safe place to cut?" Chelsea asks.

"I know where it's safe," Zoey says after a pause. "The laundry room has a blind spot beside the folding area. We could come up there."

"How would we find it?" Eli asks.

"The washing machine dumps its water out through the floor. I've listened to it a thousand times. If we can get under the ARC, I can lead you to the exact spot."

The group hushes, and looks are exchanged. "Okay, if we get in through there, how do we get to the women?" Merrill says.

"They're on the third floor, but Terra is on the fifth. We'll need a guard's bracelet to get through all the doors."

"Not with my cutter," Tia says. "I can zip through a lock in under two seconds, guaranteed."

"But then we face setting off an alarm, like Zoey said," Chelsea says.

"Not if we cut the power first," Eli says.

Merrill shakes his head. "That won't work. We tried that on our first attack. We managed to cut the power, but they had backup generators that kept some of the lights on and the auto-guns working."

The group falls into a brooding silence. The wind has increased to a low roar and the trees are talking more and more, their branches creating an eerie cadence.

"We'll keep at it," Merrill finally says. "The plan has to be perfect for it to work. We'll start up again in the morning."

They all rise, and Ian produces a shovel to toss dirt on the guttering fire until it is snuffed out. Zoey hugs herself, the cool air caressing her bare neck and face. She begins to follow the others to the house when Merrill speaks from the opposite side of the fire pit.

"Zoey?"

"Yes?"

"Thank you for helping us."

She tries to form coherent words but they wither before she can utter them. Instead she nods quickly, hunches her shoulders, and hurries away.

◆　◆　◆

Zoey lies in the dark quiet of the room on her back, listening to the distant howl of wind. Each time the memory of Merrill thanking her rises in her mind, she thrusts it away, concentrating on the obstacles that face them as a distraction. The plan seems plausible to her, even more so now that she's escaped. If someone had laid out the idea months ago she would have told them they were insane. But now, in the darkness of the room with people who are willing to help her nearby, there is another feeling tingeing her emotions.

Hope.

She rolls to her side, smelling the soft cotton of the quilt that she's sure Ian's wife, Helen, stitched. She closes her eyes, but sleep refuses to come. There is something about the generators that keeps surfacing in her mind. Something about the power itself that she should know. It is like some wispy material being drawn through her fingers that she's trying to grasp but can't. Lee would know. He would have a quick answer to nearly every question. That's the way his mind works. He is a solver, a walking solution to problems. Zoey recalls the way his lips felt against hers, and a hollow need fills her unlike ever before. It is beyond the hunger that nearly consumed her on the plains, above the fear when the helicopter was plunging to the ground, larger than the sorrow of knowing her death had been close during the fever.

She closes her eyes again, breathes in the old smell of the fabric, and falls asleep imagining the warmth of Lee's fingers intertwined in her own.

◆　◆　◆

There is only darkness. She is lost in it, suffocating from it. She can't breathe, can't see, can't feel. She floats in a sea of midnight, towed by an invisible force toward something that slices through the black far away. Soon it is closer and she sees it crawling like a serpent overhead. It is everywhere and gone all at once. The lightning emerges from the dark like a living thing, rippling down closer and closer to where she is. It is going to burn her, blacken her bones, and she will die with the language of electricity on her tongue, blue flame dancing from tooth to tooth like the worker the guards killed with their prods. Now she can feel it, straightening her hair, lifting it from her skull as the charge builds above her. The crackle of it starts, not far away, but in her ears, climbing in decibels until the sound of fire is all around her.

The lightning arcs down out of the blackness and doesn't branch out but comes like a spear that slams into her chest.

♦ ♦ ♦

Zoey jerks, kicking the covers away as she tumbles off the side of the bed to the floor. She lands on her hands and knees, breath coming in pants between clenched teeth. Her hair is sweaty, as are the clothes she fell asleep in. There is a taste of bile in the back of her throat. The room is still mostly dark with only a hint of pallid light spilling in through the window. She rises to her knees and stares at the corner where the shadows hold sway.

"That's it," she says in a whisper.

She climbs to her feet, swiping her tangled hair away from her face. She half runs down the hallway and bursts into the kitchen, where Merrill, Ian, and Chelsea sit huddled around steaming mugs.

"The lightning," Zoey says as they all look up at her in surprise. "That's how we get inside."

30

"Tell us again, Zoey, now that everyone's awake."

The group sits in the living room chairs and on the floor opposite the low fire Ian built before waking Eli, Tia, and Newton. Merrill leans against the wall beside the bookcases and nods to her encouragingly.

Zoey takes a deep breath, looking around at her audience. She shouldn't be nervous, she's fought and killed before, been in extreme peril, but the multitude of eyes watching her makes her stomach slowly flip. "Okay. There was a storm, I don't know how long ago, that I watched from my room one night. I remember the power going out, not just the main lights, but almost everything. There were emergency lights on in the halls, but that was it. It was a complete blackout outside. It took them a couple hours to get everything back on, so all I can think is that a lightning strike must've knocked out the power as well as fried their backup generators." She waits, glancing from one person to the next. When Eli frowns and shifts in his seat, she holds out her hands before her. "If we can figure out a way to create a big enough power surge during a storm, they'll think the lightning is responsible."

A slow realization dawns across the group. Tia purses her lips and squints at Merrill. "You think that would work?"

"Yeah," Merrill replies. "I do."

"What would we use for a surge?" Chelsea asks. "EMP?"

"No, an EMP has a specific signature, they'd know they were under attack right away. We want them completely oblivious to what's happening until we're on our way out. The ARC runs off of the power created by the dam, right? In the first attack we were going to cut the electricity, so we researched how the power system was set up. There's a relay station beside the dam that the electricity runs through. It's basically a control hub where they can change the power influx to the compound. If we could disrupt the supply for a split second and change the power settings to full, the subsequent surge would blow their generators no problem and it would look just like a lightning strike."

"What do you think, Tia?" Eli says.

Tia shrugs. "It's sound in theory. All we'd need to do for the delay is hook an inverter into the main power relay. It would destroy the inverter, but it would give us the disruption we'd need." She smiles, and there is a gleam in her eyes. "And I happen to have such an inverter at the warehouse."

Merrill nods. "I was hoping you'd say that. So, the emergency lights run off of batteries, but the auto-guns and the big floodlights on the walls are hooked to the main power and generators, from what Zoey's saying. They'll be off along with any alarm systems if we do this right."

"So we just cruise up under the ARC in a boat? What about the snipers on the walls? They'll have night vision for sure," Eli says.

"They will, but that's a risk we have to take. With the power going out, they'll be distracted. We can use the boat you built, Tia," Merrill says, motioning to her. "That will hold everyone."

"We'll have to use an electric motor, can't have any sound," Tia says thoughtfully.

"Right. We'll wait for a storm to brew at night before going in.

Shouldn't have to wait long, since it's spring and there have been a considerable number already. Now we need to decide who's going into the ARC and who's handling everything outside."

"I'll have to run the cutter to get us in," Tia says. "So you'll have to create the disruption, Merrill."

"No. I'm going in. I have to," Merrill says quickly. "There's—"

"There's no one else here who knows how to disrupt the power," Tia says, cutting him off. "There will have to be at least two people, and you're going to be one of them."

"I could do it," Eli says.

"Honey, no offense, but this isn't like running a football through a gap in the line," Tia replies.

"You really hurt me so," Eli says, wiping away an invisible tear. "I forgot I was just a simple colored boy."

"You're going to have to come inside with us," Tia says, ignoring Eli's bait. "It'll be dannngerouuuuus." She draws the last word out in a singsong way and waggles her eyebrows up and down.

"Can't resist when you do that," Eli says smiling widely. "I was just tryin' to help out my boy here."

Merrill's lips move, but no words come out. He struggles for a long moment before his shoulders drop slightly. "You're right, Tia. As much as I hate to say it, you're right." He seems to consider something before glancing around the room. "So that's settled. I'll take Newton with me to the relay station, and we'll kill the power. Tia will take Chelsea and Eli inside and bring the women out. Ian, you'll be our overwatch, if you don't mind?"

Ian nods solemnly. "I do mind. I swore off killing a long time ago, but I haven't been able to keep my promise very well." He frowns. "I'll do it."

Merrill shoots a last look around the room. "Okay. We know what we need. We head out in a couple hours to get everything. Let's pack up what we have to take and move."

Everyone stands and begins to shuffle out of the room, but Zoey steps in front of them. "Wait. I'm going into the ARC, too."

"No. That's not an option," Merrill says. "You can guide them via wireless microphones."

"I'm going in, or I won't help you," she replies, without breaking eye contact with him. He towers over her but she stands unmoving, blocking the doorway. Merrill swallows and stares at her, searching her face. The seconds stretch into a minute before he finally sighs and looks away.

"Okay, you go in. I wouldn't be any better than NOA if I dictated what you could do," Merrill says in a quiet tone.

"Merrill, I—" Chelsea begins, but he holds up a hand, silencing her.

"There's no one in this house who has more right to decide what she wants." Merrill runs his eyes over Zoey's face one last time before stepping past her. The group slowly files out, leaving only Newton and Ian behind in the living room. Newton catches her gaze and he opens his mouth. For a long beat she thinks he's going to speak, but after a few seconds his lips come together and he rushes from the room, sidling past as if he doesn't want to touch her.

Zoey watches the group amass in the yard beyond the windows. They are in discussion again and Tia makes a harsh gesture inches from Merrill's face.

"Don't worry about them," Ian says, moving to the kitchen. "They've been a family for years. They'll be completely in tune before long, you'll see."

"What's the world like out there?" Zoey asks, eyes still locked on the window.

"Unfortunately it's very much the same as it used to be. Now there's just fewer people and more killing."

Her eyes travel up and land on a red, white, and blue flag pinned to the wall above the window. She's seen miniature versions of it in the

NOA textbook, mostly emblazoned on the sides of army vehicles or in the form of patches sewn onto soldiers' uniforms.

"What does it mean?" she asks, pointing at the flag.

Ian gazes at the faded material. "Freedom," he says in a tired voice. "Or at least it used to."

"Do you think it will again?"

"You mean, do I think things will change?"

"Yes."

The old man drops his eyes to the pitted countertop. "I'm not sure, but I hope I live to see it. The world wasn't perfect before. It had its darkness, and there were always people willing to help spread it. The defeatist in me says it's already over, and that it's for the best."

"But that's not what you really believe."

"No. Hope still holds sway in this old man. I'm a romantic at heart."

Zoey moves to the opposite side of the counter. "If we succeed, where will we go?"

"You mean you and the other women?"

"Yes."

"Well, I suppose you'll stay here. It's the safest place I can think of. If you're not opposed to it, of course," he adds quickly.

She smiles. "I'd like that." The wrinkles in Ian's face deepen as he grins.

"We'd obviously have to expand. This little abode won't do as it is," he continues, beginning to bustle about in the kitchen. "The north wall could be knocked out and we could build that way, it's fairly level. Yes, that would work."

Zoey watches him clean, the plans for creating a larger household floating back to her over his shoulder. She lets herself imagine a life here with the others. What would Lily make of the trees? The thought broadens her smile. She would love them, she decides. And the rift between her and Rita, Sherell, and Penny? It would have to be mended somehow. They didn't have the luxury of remaining enemies in the outside world.

And Terra and her unborn child. The thought of Terra being a mother, free and unhindered here to raise her son or daughter, is all the resolve Zoey needs.

Leaving Ian to his cleaning, she steps outside into the mountain air that she thinks she'll never get tired of breathing.

31

The warehouse becomes more distinct, its borders sharpening as the distance closes between it and the approaching vehicle.

Zoey stares at its broad bulk in the afternoon sunlight. She sits on the driver's side of the last seat in the "Suburban," as Chelsea called it. It is a massive vehicle that's lost nearly all of its pewter paint, the places where rust has accumulated patched with a series of steel plates riveted beside one another. The top has been cut off, leaving only the windshield to protect the passengers. The large rear compartment holds the group's meager supplies, as well as Ian's green bag, which he packed before leaving the little house on the mountain.

Zoey had watched him shut the door after everyone was outside, lovingly stroking Seamus's broad head while murmuring something under his breath. The dog had watched him with complete attention, lying down on the porch as Ian had turned and walked away. Then they'd been off through the tangled web of undergrowth that lay like a haphazard carpet beneath the trees. It took them nearly two hours to reach the suggestion of a road where the Suburban was parked, concealed beneath three heavy layers of pine boughs. After they'd driven down the narrow and treacherous road, Zoey's teeth and nerves were jangled to the point of coming loose. The foothills soon appeared thereafter, and they coasted through them, fallen branches and needles crackling beneath the tires of the machine.

There would be two stops, Merrill had told her before they left. The first would be at an intersection on the outskirts of the nearest town. There were several things they needed for the expedition, and of course they couldn't risk Zoey or any of the other women being seen by the residents there, so they let Merrill, Eli, and Ian out at the intersection, promising they would rendezvous at the same spot in three hours' time. They had all agreed they wanted to be far away from any type of civilization before nightfall. To Zoey's surprise, Chelsea had pulled Merrill into a quick embrace before he'd jumped from the vehicle, and a reassuring softness in his eyes was directed at her as he walked away.

The second stop was to be at Tia's warehouse. From what Zoey understood, the building was a storage place for the group's more important equipment and supplies.

Now, seeing it in person, the excitement of the journey down the mountain diminishes to almost nothing.

Besides the ARC, the warehouse is the most imposing structure she's ever seen. Its steel walls are mottled dark, stained by time and rain. The windows in the upper story are shattered mouths of glass teeth. Its length sprawls across the plain it's built upon and rusted heaps of equipment decorate the clearing before the large, double doors set in its front.

Tia steers the vehicle up to the side of the building away from the road and shuts it off. In the quiet that rushes in with the absence of the motor's growl, a new sound takes precedence. It is unlike anything Zoey's ever heard before, a gentle and eerie fluting that makes the hairs stand on her arms and neck.

Tia glances at her and smiles. "Wind chimes," she says, opening her door. "When I lived by myself out here, I got tired of the silence."

Zoey, Newton, and Chelsea climb out and round the vehicle. Tia stands before a door cut into the side of the building. She works at the handle for a moment before the door swings inward with a creak.

"How do you know someone's not inside?" Zoey asks as they approach the entryway.

"Tia always tucks a strand of wire on the side of the jamb so if someone got in, the wire would be on the ground," Chelsea says.

They step into the warehouse and Zoey stops, unable to move any farther.

The building is immense. Seeing it from the outside did nothing to prepare her for the staggering openness of the interior. The ceilings hang forty feet above her head beyond a series of catwalks and ledges on a second floor that's partially obscured by the lack of light. The floors are cracked concrete and stretch away for hundreds of yards with only the occasional interspersing support beam to break the expanse. Some of the larger rooms in the ARC gave Zoey pause at times and she knew that their daunting size and emptiness were intended to be filled by women such as herself, but the warehouse dwarfs them all in comparison.

"It's something, isn't it?" Tia asks.

"Yes. It's unbelievable." Zoey glances at the older woman. "You lived here *alone*?"

"Yep. For about ten years it was just me and the wind. Chelsea, why don't you and Newton get the guns? I'll have Zoey help me gather the rest." Chelsea nods and takes Newton's hand gently in her own, leading him away to a set of stairs that rises to the second story.

"This way, girlie," Tia says, moving toward the opposite end of the building. There are piles of iron, all lengths and widths, stacked beneath the second-story overhang to either side. Tools, their uses unimaginable to Zoey, lie on crowded benches, and here and there a decayed sign displaying half its message pokes up through the refuse.

Tia produces a small flashlight from her pocket, shining it through the gloom that deepens the farther they walk.

"What was this place for?" Zoey says.

"They used to repair industrial combines here. Combines are huge machines that cut and process different plants. Some of them would barely fit through those front doors."

"Is this where you worked?"

"No. I was on a crew in Seattle when everything fell apart."

"Merrill called you something in Ian's house? A welder?" Zoey asks as they walk.

"That's right."

"What is that?"

"Basically someone who can bind things together."

"Oh. And lesbian is another name for welder?"

Tia's raucous laughter peals out so sudden and loud that Zoey flinches. She stops beside the older woman, who has halted and is bracing her hands on her knees for support. Another gale bursts from her, and Zoey can't help but smile.

"Eli called you that. What? What did I say?" Zoey asks.

Tia wipes at her eyes and continues to chuckle for another moment before she can answer. "Nothing, honey. But that's the best damn laugh I've had in a long time. Another name for welder!" Laughter erupts from her again, and she shakes her head. "No, I suppose they didn't bother to educate you on people like me," she continues after the final squalls of mirth depart. Her voice grows suddenly serious. "Of course. Why would they care to explain something like that if they were only after your eggs?"

They move toward a very dark alcove cluttered with heaps of glass panes and thin squares of metal stacked opposed of each other. "I don't understand," Zoey says, following Tia through the maze. They arrive at a cleared area at the rear of the space. There is a long, neatly organized workbench that is completely at odds with its surroundings.

Tia hands Zoey the light. "Hold this." She bends low and yanks a steel frame out from beneath the bench. Attached to the frame are two cylinders, one pale yellow, the other green. A long, thick hose extends from a dual connection at the top of the canisters, ending in a gun-like tool at the opposite end. Tia hoists the equipment off the floor easily, though to Zoey the steel appears thick and heavy.

"Bring that light here and hold it so I can see," Tia says. Zoey watches as the other woman begins taking apart the connection apparatus, pausing to clean several small pieces as she works. "Were there any boys about your age at the ARC?" Tia asks after a short time.

"Yes. There were the exact same number of them as us."

Tia stops cleaning and looks at her. "Really?"

"Yes. They were all sons of our Clerics."

"And these were the only boys there your age?" Zoey nods. "Weird. Okay, well, your Cleric's boy, what was his name?"

Heat begins to grow in Zoey's face and she's secretly thankful for the relative darkness. "Lee."

"And is Lee a good-looking boy?"

"I don't know."

"Bullshit, you don't. Is he good-looking, or did he give you the creeps?"

Zoey laughs. "He . . . he's, yeah . . ."

"Okay, okay, I get the idea. So, the way you feel about Lee, that's pretty well defined, right? You know you like him, and you think about him when he's not around. It's the same for me, but with women."

Zoey blinks, thinking Tia is making a joke. The older woman stops cleaning and glances at her. "You're serious?"

"Yes. I grew up being attracted to girls, just like you did with boys. I know that might sound strange to you, but lots and lots of people were that way before the Dearth. Men fell in love with men, women with women, it was fairly common." Tia begins putting the apparatus back together, slowly, deliberately. "But it wasn't always welcomed.

Lots of people like me were ostracized, beaten, even killed. Nowadays it's twice as bad."

Zoey frowns, trying to absorb the idea of two women falling in love. For a second it seems odd to her, very foreign. But then she thinks of the absolute darkness of the box, the phantom bugs, the thing with the red eyes.

"It's not any different than being a woman now," Zoey says finally. Tia twists the last bolt tight but doesn't look up from the tanks. "They kept me controlled just because I was born a girl." Zoey shifts in place, glancing down at the cluttered floor. "No one should tell you you're wrong for who you are. I don't think you're strange at all."

Tia remains motionless for a time, still not looking at her before standing and hauling the tanks up onto her shoulder. "Let's head back," she says quietly.

They move back through the length of the warehouse, and Zoey spots Chelsea and Newton at the far end carrying a satchel between them down from the second floor. Outside the day is a filmy gray, the sky scudded with thickening clouds. Zoey watches Chelsea and Tia open the satchel on the ground.

It is full of guns.

There are several pistols like the one she used in the ARC, rifles of different lengths, and a long, padded case lying at the bottom that barely fits in the bag. Ammunition jingles in a second bag that Newton sets down in the dirt.

"Enough to kill everyone in the ARC three times over," Tia says. "Hope we don't need a quarter of it."

"We'll need it," Zoey says, looking down at the weapons. When she glances up, both Tia and Chelsea are watching her. "You've never been there, it's unlike anything you've ever seen," she says.

Tia nods, still looking at her. "Chelsea, you want to help me load the boat in the trailer on the other side?" Chelsea gives Zoey and

Newton one last look before following Tia out of sight around the corner of the building.

Zoey glances at Newton, studying the boy again. His eyes are locked on the distant lines of the mountains, his mouth open a little. "They're really big, aren't they?" Zoey asks. Newton closes his mouth and shoots her a look before shifting his eyes back to the blue-black smudges farther away on the horizon. "I never imagined that the world was this big," she says, absently wondering if Newton is registering anything she's saying. "I always knew there was more out there, but these last few days have been almost too much to understand." Newton blinks in rapid succession. He's listening. "Merrill said that you don't have your parents anymore. I don't either. I never knew them." Newton's hand lifts from his side, and he gently presses it against his ear. "I'm sorry, Newton, I didn't mean to upset you, I was just trying . . ."

But he is gone before she can finish the sentence. She sees the black streak of his hair disappearing around a pile of scrap iron, and then she is alone. ". . . to talk," she says under her breath.

◆　◆　◆

Within the next hour they gather the last remaining items they need. Tia shows Zoey the inverter that will interrupt the power flow to the ARC. It is an unremarkable steel box containing a mass of electrical components and a shining coil of gold wire so thin it looks like hair. After all the other supplies are packed within the Suburban, Tia backs it up to a two-wheeled trailer, which holds a cupped length of aluminum nearly twenty feet long.

"The sides fold out here and here," Tia tells her, pointing to several hinged flanges that are bent over the main body of the boat. "You flip them out when you launch it and then it can hold more people."

"It won't sink if we're all riding in it?" Zoey asks, running her hands over the smooth aluminum hide.

"Not a chance, girlie. I modified it myself. This thing would float in a hurricane."

Zoey moves up beside the Suburban to where Chelsea stands, sweeping the heaps of junk with her eyes.

"Are you looking for Newton?" Zoey asks.

"Yes. Have you seen him?"

"Earlier when you went to get the boat ready. He went that way." She points in the direction of the road.

"Damn it. He does this sometimes, just wanders off. Once about a year ago we stayed out all night looking for him. He was hiding behind a chair in our house. He must've crawled behind it and fallen asleep there. We were worried sick."

"I think it might be my fault he ran away," Zoey says.

Chelsea looks at her, eyebrows drawing together. "Why would you say that?"

"I tried talking to him. I told him I didn't know my parents." She shrugs. "I guess I didn't know what to say, but it upset him."

Chelsea looks toward the road once more before turning to Zoey. "You didn't do anything wrong, but just so you know, Newton does seem to react strangely when the word 'parents' is mentioned. We think he may have seen something, something terrible happen to them and that's part of the reason he doesn't speak. Don't feel bad, it's just one thing about him you should be aware of." She jerks her chin over Zoey's shoulder, and when Zoey turns she sees Newton making his way between the piles of scrap toward the Suburban. "He never goes far, though," Chelsea says.

Zoey is about to return to the vehicle as well when Chelsea stops her.

"I never got a chance to say thank you for helping us," she says. "For helping Merrill. It's the greatest gift you could give him."

Zoey can't stand the warming gratitude the other woman exudes, so she drops her gaze to the ground. "It's nothing."

"It's everything."

"You care about him very much, don't you?" Zoey says.

"Yes, I do."

"I didn't know that you were . . ."

"Together?"

"Yes."

"We didn't mean to be. When I found him, he was a broken man. Hopeless, destructive, filled with so much hatred it came off him like heat. But I saw something in him that made me keep trying. Underneath all the hurt was a deep love. That's rare in this world now." Chelsea smiles and Zoey realizes she's quite beautiful when she lets go of the serious façade that normally resides on her features. "Come on, it's almost time to go."

As Zoey follows Chelsea back to the vehicle, she tries to leave the singeing sting of guilt behind in the refuse, but it follows her like a predator that's tasted blood.

32

"Something's wrong."

They're sitting in the Suburban pulled to the side of the road at the rendezvous intersection. The wind sweeps over the foothills to the west and fans eddies of dust across the plains creating a multitude of capering waves that speckle Zoey's face hard enough for her to shield it down in her collar.

They'd waited nearly an hour before Tia said the words that were growing inside them all unspoken until then.

Tia turns in the driver's seat, glancing back at Zoey and Newton, who sit behind her, before picking up the binoculars that rest on the center console to scope the surrounding area for the tenth time in as many minutes.

Chelsea clears her throat. "They're just running behind. They might've had trouble getting the gear."

"That's what I'm afraid of," Tia says, still passing the binoculars slowly over the land. "Town's rough, always has been. They had to be careful getting the things we need. The wrong people see what they're buying—"

"Tia, enough. They're fine. They'll be here soon." Chelsea is like a stone in the passenger seat, but Zoey can see her eyes playing across the land, searching. Newton fidgets with his hands in his lap, winding his fingers into and through one another over and over. There is a strangely beautiful pattern to it, almost as if his hands are dancing.

"We're going to have to go in after them," Tia says quietly, dropping the binoculars from her eyes. "I say we give them another fifteen minutes and then we go."

"Are you insane? We'll be captured within five seconds of stepping into town. They'd sell us into the Fae Trade by nightfall."

Tia is about to respond when Zoey breaks the silence she's held since leaving the warehouse.

"What's the Fae Trade?"

Chelsea and Tia exchange a glance, a conversation taking place within seconds without words. Finally Tia looks away, picking up the binoculars again, and Chelsea turns so that she's facing the rear of the vehicle.

"The Fae Trade is a traveling market that deals in women," Chelsea says. "It roams from coast to coast, north to south, seeking women of all ages and those that harbor them. They're bought, sold, traded for, treated like breeding stock or worse at times."

"Why?" is all Zoey can manage.

"Because they can," Chelsea says. "Before everything happened there was a myth in Africa that if a man raped a virgin he would be cleansed of all diseases. The Fae Trade is built upon the same ideals. Every woman sold could be the one that will give birth to a girl, and you know how valuable that woman would be then? Men pay the highest for the youngest women they can find, but most of them are in their mid-thirties or early forties. Someone younger . . ."

Chelsea stops talking as if she's hit a wall.

"You mean someone my age," Zoey says. Chelsea starts to reply but is interrupted by Tia's shout.

"There they are!"

All eyes turn to the direction Tia points. Three figures have emerged from a cut in the land. Merrill's height is unmistakable along with the gray swinging of Ian's long hair. But there is something wrong. Zoey can feel it the second she sees them.

"Oh no," Tia says quietly. "They're running."

She throws the Suburban into drive and they launch forward toward the ever-growing figures. They slide to a stop several feet from the three men but Merrill barely slows his run. He tosses a large bag into the rear of the vehicle and swings himself up into the very back seat.

"What is it?" Chelsea asks, twisting around.

"Trouble. We need to go. Now."

As soon as Ian and Eli climb aboard, Tia guns the engine and they cruise up a low hill back to the suggestion of the road running east.

"Gotta get off the highway as soon as you can," Merrill says. Tia nods and takes the next gentle grade that leads up to a series of lonesome pines growing from a low ridge.

"What happened?" Zoey asks, running her gaze from Eli to Ian to Merrill. All of them look haggard and exhausted.

"A few guys started following us after we made our first stop. We were casual, but more kept joining their group until there were six of them. After we got the last of what we needed, we lost them behind the row of abandoned houses on the north side and ran the rest of the way here. I didn't like the looks of them, though."

"Why? Were they NOA?" Chelsea asks.

"No. But one of them had a radio that he was talking on."

The sound of the wind is nearly deafening as it howls through the open cab. Tia guides the Suburban over a rough track that might've once been a well-maintained trail that winds through another patch of trees. They climb higher into a foothill, the electric green of the blooming foliage almost too bright to look at. Merrill busies himself in the rear hold of the vehicle and after a short time produces several dark hats with long bills. He passes them out to Tia, Chelsea, and Zoey.

"Wrap your hair up and put them on," he says.

Zoey tries twice unsuccessfully to bind her hair tight enough to hide beneath the hat, cursing the tangled curls all the while. Finally Chelsea motions her closer and helps tame the locks into a bun that they're able to tuck beneath the hat. As soon as Zoey sits back in her seat, Merrill pushes a pistol into her hand.

"You know how to use that, right?" he asks.

"I think so. Where's the safety?"

"Next to the trigger. Down is safe, up is off. There's a round ready to go." Zoey flips the safety down and up several times, getting the feel for it. Merrill continues to pass out weapons until everyone is armed.

"You think we'll need these?" Chelsea asks.

"God, I hope not," Merrill says.

The trailer and boat rattle loudly behind them as Tia steers off the small trail and into a field carpeted with sprouting grass. In the distance a machine with huge wheels and a tall cab lined with shattered glass sits mired in the ground, a broken barn and matching house rising up behind it like ailing parents watching over their child. Zoey turns and gazes at the mountains that are growing more indistinct with each mile, their tops fading into an oblivion of clouds.

"We'll see them again," Ian says from beside her. The old man gives her a smile out of the side of his mouth. She nearly reaches out to grasp his wrinkled hand, but instead she clutches the pistol tighter.

Tia brings them down several overgrown back roads that pass decaying properties. Yards tangled with dead weeds, a smattering of trees growing in to hide the roofline of a home, washed-out driveways that gape like broken mouths.

As the sun is nearing the westernmost peaks of the dwindling mountaintops behind them, Merrill tells Tia to return to the highway.

"I think we're okay now," he says. "We've traveled quite a ways." Tia takes a right, bringing them down out of the bruised hills and onto a dirt track that spills them into the edge of some rolling plains that are still tinged with brown amidst the growing green. After several miles of bumping over a barely discernable road, the Suburban rises onto a wide slash that cuts through the countryside, winding beside a twin artery separated by tangles of scrub. Here and there the sediment that covers the road breaks and Zoey sees ghostly lines of yellow and white.

Her face stings from the constant wind and she's slightly chilled, but she can't help the awe she feels looking at the land washed in the last rays of the day. The openness of it all induces both terror and exhilaration as her eyes drink the world in. How would it feel to just run across the open plains and hills without fear of being followed or killed? How would it be to sit quietly on the side of Ian's mountain without some other place to go?

She stanches the wistful thoughts. They are leaks in a boat and if too much water comes in, she'll drown. She focuses again on the highway ahead, readjusting her grip on the gun, but not before the image of the other women and Lee standing beside her on a hill takes shape in her mind.

The road curves into an incline, cutting through the hill instead of climbing over it. To the right the matching highway drops down almost out of sight to the bottom of the ravine.

"We'll stop somewhere soon for the night, there's enough ground between us and town now. You don't know of any other settlements out here, do you, Ian?"

"Not that I can—"

The old man's words are cut off as they round the next corner and two trucks come into view, blocking the center of the road.

Men stand in the truck beds holding guns, and several lean casually against the bumpers.

Tia jams on the brakes and Zoey feels herself being flung forward. Ian grips her arm and holds her in her seat as they slide to a stop ten paces from the front of the right truck.

"Oh no," Chelsea whispers.

Three men detach from the group and saunter forward; rifles nosed to the ground, fingers on the triggers.

"Everyone buckle their seat belts," Merrill says through clenched teeth. Ian drops a belt attached to the seat into Zoey's lap and motions to her opposite side. She digs for a moment and finds a metallic end that she snaps into the buckle that Ian gave her.

"Tia, keep it in drive and be ready," Merrill murmurs. Tia's head tips forward a fraction of an inch. There is a metallic ping from the back seat where Merrill sits.

Zoey's heart double-times as she slides the safety off her pistol. To their left is the high embankment of rock and dirt, to the right the steep decline to the other highway, a sagging steel rail guarding the drop. Nowhere to go.

"Keep your heads down," Merrill whispers, and Tia as well as Chelsea glance at the floorboards, letting the bills of their hats cover their faces. Zoey follows suit. She tilts her head just enough to keep one eye trained on the armed men that are now at the bumper.

"Where you guys headed?" one of the men asks, stopping several feet from Tia's door.

"Out on a supply run for our settlement in Easton," Merrill says.

"Yeah?"

"Yeah."

"Hmm." The man walks closer, and Zoey catches a glimpse of piercing blue eyes and scraggly red stubble covering hollow cheeks. "You wouldn't have been the ones back in town gathering up some interestin' supplies, now would you?"

"Haven't been to town in months," Merrill says, his voice steady.

"Yeah, I figured. You all look like you've seen better days."

"Everyone has."

"True, true. We're keeping an eye out for three guys who stole something from friends of ours in town."

"What did they look like? Maybe we saw them on our way out here," Merrill says.

"Well, they kinda look like you, blackie there, and the old man."

Time stops and Zoey's stomach seizes with ice. The hand holding the gun shakes against the side of her leg.

"But they was on foot, and you all are in this big ugly piece of shit, so it couldn't be you, am I right?" The bearded man's voice has taken on a mocking tone that sends ripples of goose bumps up Zoey's arms.

"Right," Merrill says.

"Say, you all wouldn't know of any girl wanderin' around, would you?"

"No."

"Okay, just askin', cuz we're hearin' all sorts of strange tales. That maybe she's the youngest woman been seen in over twenty years."

The man is closer to Zoey's door now, approaching with inevitable clunks of his boots on the road.

"Heard crazy stuff, like she's real pretty, and might be still around here."

Zoey registers the flicker of movement even as the man lunges forward. She leans away, bringing the handgun up, but his hand is quicker, knocking her hat up and off her head.

Her hair drops in a cascade around her shoulders.

"It's her!" the man has time to yell before the side of his face vaporizes in a puff of blood that mists her forehead and cheeks. The report from Merrill's gun rolls off the rock wall beside them.

"Now, Tia!" Merrill screams, but she's already punched the gas and they're ripping forward. Gunfire chatters, and there is a hot channel of air suddenly beside Zoey's face that makes her skin shrink in on itself.

Out of the corner of her eye Merrill throws something small and black toward the closest pickup.

Tia jerks the wheel to the right and they smash through the rail at the same time the closest truck shudders with a concussive whump.

Gravity ceases.

The Suburban floats down the embankment, engine roaring, and Zoey can't help the cry that boils up from inside her.

They land with a bone-jarring bounce as wind shrieks past them. Grass and sticks fly up from the wheels and Zoey clutches the back of Tia's seat as they rip down the side of the hill. It feels as if the vehicle is going to tumble forward, the rear end flipping up over them, but it doesn't, they only go faster.

Ahead a stand of trees loom, and beyond is the other road, clear and open.

Tia turns the wheel, the tires leaving the ground again. Zoey's stomach floats.

They miss the last tree by inches, bark shredding against the Suburban's fender. The boat and trailer behind them bang hard against something, but then they are flying up the ditch and skidding onto the highway.

Tia floors the throttle and there is the screeching of rubber before the vehicle slews and straightens out.

Chelsea turns in her seat. "Is anyone hurt? Anyone get hit?" Zoey sits frozen in the seat, unable to even look down to see if she's been shot. She can't feel any pain, only a surging numbness that drains away all her strength.

"Merrill? Merrill?" Chelsea says. But she is already climbing back to him.

"I'm okay. I don't think it hit anything major," he says. Zoey manages to turn enough to see bright crimson coating the lower part of Merrill's jacket. His face is white above his collar but his eyes are clear.

"Shit! They're following," Tia says. Zoey stretches her neck up, looking past the supplies behind Merrill.

The other truck is bouncing down the same path they took, men crammed into the rear of the bed. As she watches, one of them is wrenched free by a savage bump and he tumbles bonelessly down the hill before a rock halts his motion so suddenly she can almost hear the crunch of shattering bones.

"Flip over, you bastards," Eli growls. "Flip over."

But the truck races through the ditch and skids onto the road behind them.

It accelerates, closing the distance.

Ian turns in his seat and calmly points to the weapons bag. "In the bottom, Chelsea. The long, black case, please." She glances up from her inspection of Merrill's wound and yanks the bag into Ian's reach. The old man draws out the case and unbuckles several clasps even as the roar of the truck's engine begins to rise.

"Ian?" Merrill says.

"Lie down, Merrill," Ian responds, pulling out the largest rifle Zoey's ever seen.

It is solid black with a thick, fluted barrel. A magazine juts from its bottom, and a huge scope sits atop it. Chelsea slumps to the side with Merrill in her arms as Ian lays the rifle over the back of the seat.

"Steady now, Tia," he says.

The truck is a quarter mile back and gaining. There is a muzzle flash from the passenger window and a bullet sings past Zoey's door.

Everything is movement and sound, but Ian is like a stone beside her. One eye nearly pressed to the scope, finger on the trigger.

The wrinkles in his face smooth to nothing.

The rifle shoves against his shoulder and a split second later Zoey hears the shot.

The windshield in front of the truck's driver spiderwebs and the wheels whip to the side. It rumbles down a short embankment and collides with a tree in a cataclysm of glass and steel.

Bodies pinwheel in all directions. There is a short bleat of the truck's horn and then only the wind coursing through the cab as the Suburban cruises onward.

Ian carefully replaces the rifle into the case and stows it away in the weapons bag. Zoey watches the placidity of his face. It is not simply calm, it is devoid of emotion. She stares at him for a long time as Tia brings their speed down to a reasonable rate and Eli climbs back to check on Merrill's wound. The old man finally glances at her and now there is naked shame in his eyes.

Zoey reaches out and slides her hand into his. The barest of smiles touches his lips, and he squeezes her fingers once.

"Tia, find us a safe place for tonight," Merrill says. "Get us off this goddamned road."

33

The house looms above them in haunted splendor.

They had to drive for another hour before Tia was able to find a passable road branching off from the main highway. By then the air had cooled and they were all shivering in their seats. The road split several times leading toward a segmented hill populated with pines. Tia had guided the protesting vehicle up through a crumbling neighborhood full of desolate homes. Garage doors gaped open, windows were shattered and dark, cars sat abandoned, some of their doors still ajar as if their owners were only seconds from returning. At the end of the last street another paved drive cut up into the side of the hill behind a stand of trees. Tia had eased them up the grade that switchbacked several times until they came to an iron gate lying flat in the center of the road. They passed over it, and after another hundred yards the house came into view.

It is three stories, made of cut stones interlocked together, their gray fronts speckled with moss and mildew. Most of the windows are intact, and the ones that aren't have been boarded over. The solid oak doors in the entrance don't budge when Eli tries them. He gives them all a look before Merrill nods and motions toward the building.

Eli blasts the doors inward with a kick and goes in low, his rifle out before him. After a drawn minute of waiting he returns and nods once. "Looks empty."

They move their gear inside, making trip after trip to the Suburban until its rear hold is empty. After they've packed everything in the large entryway so it will be ready to go at a moment's notice, she steps into the main body of the house.

Even without adornments, its grandeur overwhelms her. Everywhere there is marble, both dark and light. The walls are polished stone and the floors are deeply stained wood. While Tia and Eli examine the rest of the house, Zoey walks through the main floor, reaching out to touch filigreed cabinets, an ornate light switch that does nothing, a marble statue, nearly as tall as she is, of a woman in an elegant dress. The closets she checks are bare, as are the cabinets in the kitchen. There is evidence everywhere of possessions removed in haste—long scratches on the floor, a cleaner place on the wall where something once hung, a single sock lying in a corner. She marvels at the idea of taking time to save inanimate objects, of holding belongings so dear it would be unthinkable to leave them behind even in a time of chaos.

She has trouble imagining it.

Zoey moves through a hallway off the kitchen that runs parallel to the biggest room on the main floor. The hall branches, one doorway leading to the high-ceilinged room where a few of the others are talking, one to an empty bedroom with only a heavy steel bed frame left in its center, and the last to a wide room with high windows looking out into the forest behind the house. There is something large in one corner hidden beneath a dark cloth, its shape suggesting a table. She almost doesn't go to it, but then does, tugging the cover from it.

Zoey stares at the object, not entirely sure what it is. It is like a table, its top a smooth wood as black as night, but the closest side is stepped down, and there are long white and black rectangles set in the lower level. She frowns, placing a fingertip on one.

She jumps back as a solid note rings out from the table's center. A second later Eli is in the doorway, his characteristic smile firmly in place.

"Look what you found, lady."

"What did I find?" Zoey asks.

"You don't know what this is? You're shittin' me. It's a piano, girl. An instrument. Here, watch." He leans his rifle against the nearest wall and runs his fingers over several keys. A discordant tune peals out from within the piano. "Hmm, 'course I can't play worth a shit, but you get the idea."

"So it's for music?"

"Yep. Suppose you never heard proper music before."

"No. Just some songs we sung when no one was around. Singing was forbidden."

Eli's face hardens, but then he smiles again. "Well, you go right on ahead and sing as much as you want, I'm sure you got a beautiful voice." As Eli reaches out to pick up his weapon, Zoey spots a dark string of writing on his forearm, barely visible against his ebony skin.

"What's that on your arm?" she asks.

Eli pauses before slinging his rifle over his shoulder. "A mistake," he says quietly, and walks away, turning in the hallway and moving out of sight.

She stands looking after him for a moment before glancing at the piano. She touches a key again, liking the sound it makes. She tries putting several different notes together, but after hearing the dissonant tones she draws her hands away. The notes should fit with one another, and she wishes she knew how to do it. Zoey covers the piano with its sheet again before returning to the largest room to find Merrill seated in a wooden chair at its center. He is shirtless and Chelsea kneels by his side, her medical bag open on the floor.

"Is he going to be okay?" Zoey asks, coming even with Chelsea.

"I'll be fine," Merrill says without looking up. "Got the best doctor in the world working on me."

"I'm nowhere near the best, and you know it," Chelsea says, pulling thread through a hooked needle.

"You might be, now that there's only a few left. Ouch!" Merrill flinches as Chelsea pokes him gently with the needle. "Real nice, stab the injured guy."

"Oops," Chelsea says, shooting Zoey a wicked smile. Zoey begins to smile back, but her eyes land on the oozing wound in Merrill's lower right side. The hole is ragged and dark, the skin around it coated with dried blood.

"It went right through," Merrill says, following her gaze. "Don't worry. Maybe you want to help Tia gather some firewood for tonight. By the time you get back I'll be right as rain and we can go over the plans again."

"Okay," Zoey says. It takes effort to pull her eyes away from the bullet hole. When she manages to do so, she leaves the house through the front door, spotting Tia across the small clearing at the border of the woods.

"How much more do we need?" Zoey asks, seeing that the other woman's arms are nearly full of sticks.

"If you get an armful, we should be good for the night," Tia says, motioning with her head toward a broken deadfall on the ground several feet away. "Pick up a few of the bigger ones and we'll head back." Zoey is turning to do it when she sees movement on the roof of the house. She's about to cry out a warning when she notices long gray hair blowing in the wind.

"What's Ian doing up there?"

"Think he's figuring out if it's going to rain or not."

"How can he do that?"

Tia shrugs. "He's old as hell."

Zoey looks to the roof again but he's disappeared. She turns and begins picking up broken sections of dry wood, stacking them in her arms. She steps over the tree trunk, set on getting one last hunk that looks like it would burn for a long time, when she stops.

The ground beyond the fallen tree is speckled with blue.

It takes her a beat to realize she's looking at flowers sprouting through the dead leaves and dry grass. They are very much like the ones she saw in her fevered state before collapsing, but much smaller, so delicate she's sure a strong breeze would tip them over. The blue transfixes her, and it's only when Tia says her name that she snaps out of her reverie.

"Sorry," she says, stooping to pick up the piece of wood. When she rises, Newton is standing a few paces away, watching her. As soon as they lock eyes he ducks away, hurrying out of sight down the length of the clearing.

"Why does he run away like that?" Zoey asks Tia as they make their way back to the house.

"He's afraid. He takes his time with people. It took him almost a year before he would sit beside me at the fire. Don't worry, he'll warm up to you."

Zoey looks for Newton as they enter the house, but the yard is empty.

Inside, Merrill has his shirt back on and is standing over the kitchen counter, one hand on the marble, the other pressed to his side. A wide piece of paper lies beneath his gaze and his eyes burn into it as if he's attempting to read a different language. Zoey and Tia join him at the counter and a moment later Ian enters along with Chelsea and Eli, who carries a bucket of clear, shimmering water in one hand.

"Found a stream about a quarter mile into the woods," Eli says. "Should be able to refill our stock before we head out."

Merrill doesn't look up from the paper but says, "Good. Thanks, man." Zoey approaches the counter and studies the document. It's a strange layout of squares and intersecting lines, and she wouldn't have recognized it if she hadn't seen something similar within the NOA textbook.

"That's a map," she says, tracing a highway marked "90."

"You're right," Merrill replies. "This is approximately where we are." His finger drops on a place labeled "Westin." "And this is where we're going."

"Grand Coulee," Zoey reads. "That's where the ARC is?"

"Yeah, and I'm guessing it hasn't been called that in a while," Merrill says. He glances up at Ian. "What do you think?"

"I think it's going to rain tomorrow, though I'm not certain it will last into the night."

"We'll have to plan like it will." Merrill searches the map and points to a spot over a squiggly, blue line. "The boating group will launch here into the river. It's about ten miles downstream from the ARC. This is the relay station where Newton and I will be. If I remember the landscape correctly, there's some very tall hills surrounding the dam. Am I right, Zoey?"

She thinks back to the night when she escaped, a lifetime ago. The ground zipping past beneath the helicopter, the glimpse of the enormous reservoir beyond the dam, dirt under her fingers as she crawled out from the crash.

"Zoey, are you okay?" Merrill asks. She comes back to herself, swallowing the acidic fear that's risen in her throat.

"Yeah, sorry. Yes, I remember hills and valleys."

"Good. We'll park the Suburban a mile away from the dam if it's possible, farther if there's a patrol. Ian, you'll be our distraction and cover our escape when the time comes. I seem to remember an observation perch above the dam."

Ian nods. "It's made out of concrete, as I recall. It should still be standing." Something passes between the two men, and Zoey sees a flicker of the same look in Ian's eyes that she'd seen in the vehicle.

"When you're all clear of the ARC, we'll lay down cover fire and make sure you get to shore. Then we'll lose them in the hills on our way back to the Suburban," Merrill continues. "Tia, you're going to have to sacrifice your boat, I'm afraid. We'll need the trailer to haul everyone."

"Knew that already. But you're going to buy me another one," Tia says, crossing her arms.

"Deal."

"The helicopter will be following us," Zoey says. "As soon as they know something's wrong, they'll be in the air."

"Don't worry, we've got that covered," Merrill says. He shoots a look at Ian before proceeding. "So we get into position by evening tomorrow night, and we wait. If the storm comes, we'll move ahead. If it doesn't, we'll wait until one arrives. As soon as it's a go, we'll communicate by the headsets we got in town."

"Is that what you stole?" Zoey asks.

A hint of a smile tugs at Merrill's lips. "No. That was something else."

"Are you sure you're up for this?" Eli asks Merrill. "You did just get a hole blown through your dumb ass."

"I'm fine. It was barely a flesh wound. I think it was a ricochet anyways."

"Yeah, probably shot yourself," Eli says, snorting laughter. The rest of the group chuckles, and Merrill feints at his friend playfully.

"You're probably right," he says. "Okay, any questions?" The room is silent as they look from one to another. Zoey is suddenly overcome with emotion for these people. How strange to have no one, to know that you must rely solely upon yourself, and then abruptly find people to care for. And those that care for you. It nearly overwhelms her.

"Okay," Merrill says. "Let's get some food in us and sleep. We'll need it tomorrow night."

◆ ◆ ◆

They start a small fire in the marble fireplace in the great room once night falls in earnest. The food is simple but good, canned meat that Chelsea tells her is venison, and cold peaches that are so sweet Zoey's teeth tingle.

They are very quiet all through dinner and the feeling in the room is as if everyone is holding their breath. She looks from one face to another. All wear the same thoughtful expression, minds elsewhere as hers has been all evening.

Tomorrow. She will see the ARC again tomorrow.

It feels both so recently and so long ago that she escaped. She imagines climbing the stairs to the so familiar hallways and stepping inside her old room. Would she be there? The old Zoey who had conformed, obeyed, died more and more each day until she couldn't stand not to think the thoughts that were forbidden?

Because she is someone new now. Someone different.

"Who wants first shift?" Merrill asks from beside the fire.

"I'll take it," Tia responds.

"We switch every hour until dawn. Everyone should try to get some sleep."

Zoey helps Chelsea spread out the sleeping bags they brought from Ian's and lies down to the right of the fire. Merrill is propped up against the wall, staring across the room at the jittering shadows thrown by the flames.

"I wanted to thank you for saving me today," she says after a time.

Merrill cocks his head toward her. "You would have saved yourself."

"What do you mean?"

"You had your pistol up in that guy's face the moment he knocked your hat off. You would've pulled the trigger if I hadn't. Am I right?"

Zoey swallows, her throat very dry. "Yes."

"Then there's no need to thank me," he says, and slides himself down onto his side opposite his injury. Chelsea lays her sleeping bag between them, giving Zoey a quick smile before climbing beneath the thick cover. Eli sits in the wooden chair in the corner of the room holding his rifle. He is no more than a shadow amidst the gloom.

"Chelsea?" Zoey whispers.

"Yes?"

"What is that writing on Eli's arm?"

"It's a tattoo. Ink under the skin."

"What does it say?"

"It says 'Ella.'"

"That's a name, isn't it?"

"Yes, I think so."

"Who is she?"

"I don't know. Eli told Merrill who it was when he first came to us, but he made Merrill swear not to tell anyone else."

"Not even you?"

"Not even me. But everyone's entitled to their secrets, even in the world that's left."

Zoey's stomach clenches, and she gazes past Chelsea to where Merrill lies. "Someone he's lost," she says, when she's able to speak again.

"Yes, I'm sure it is. He covers up his hurt by being upbeat and laughing, but it's there. It's there for all of us."

"Did you lose someone?" Zoey asks tentatively.

Chelsea sighs. "Yes. My younger sister, Janie. She was fifteen when she was taken by NOA. It was at the point of no return for the country. There was fighting in every street of America. Our parents were already gone then, thank God—they wouldn't have been able to handle it if they'd been alive. We only had each other. We were living in an abandoned house outside of Tacoma—that used to be another big city. We had a special hiding place we made in the house's back wall, kind of a false panel that swung out. There was enough food and water there for a few days and flashlights. We had to spend a couple nights in there when we saw either government forces or rebels coming. One night a rebel faction stayed in the house and never knew we were there."

"You must have been terrified."

"We were, but we had each other, and that made it bearable." The older woman seems to go somewhere else for a moment before blinking. "One evening when things were quiet we decided to go out scavenging, just in our neighborhood. We'd found some bottled water and a can of tomato soup. I remember we were laughing because Janie used to hate tomatoes, but after we found the soup she couldn't wait to get back home and warm it up."

Chelsea pauses, and Zoey hears her sniffle quietly. "A group of soldiers were making a sweep on foot when we got back to the house. They spotted us from down the street, and we tried to lose them through a couple backyards, but they were too close. We barely made it into the house and to the hiding place when they busted in the front door. Before I could stop her, Janie ran out the back and drew them away. I was already inside the wall, and she knew they'd find us both if she tried getting in too." Chelsea sniffs again. "She said, 'I'll be right back.' And that was the last time I saw her."

"I'm so sorry," Zoey whispers. "You didn't have to tell me."

"I wanted to. Each time I talk about her, it gets a bit easier. Time helps too, you know. It softens the edges, but memories almost always slice you open a little." Zoey stares at the flames, each one a swirling blade of orange. "We better get to sleep," Chelsea says. "I'll wake you after my shift."

Zoey lies still for a long time, waiting for sleep to come, but it eludes her. The shadows on the wall become faces, figures moving menacingly through a dark landscape, intent on evil. Her mind keeps returning to the ARC, and each time she thinks of entering the compound again, her stomach curdles with fear. She has to make sure they can all escape together, and the iron assurance of what she will do if she's captured is still strong.

She'll die before she returns to the room she spent all her life in. Kill herself before they violate her like they did Terra.

Zoey tries to focus on the plan, searches it for flaws but can find none other than the obvious danger and the luck they balance on to complete the task and get everyone to safety. The nagging feeling that she's forgetting something keeps returning, but she knows it isn't a lapse in her memory. It's the thought of what will happen if they succeed.

How she will have to face Merrill, face all of them with the lie she told.

The prospect of it is nearly as frightening as being captured again.

She rolls over to her side and thinks of Meeka, of how much the man lying only feet from her now loves a daughter who is already dead.

Sleep finally comes without her knowing, and with it nightmares of clawed things that speak in choked voices, and beneath it all the sound of locks snapping shut in metallic finality.

She wakes later to a gentle sound that draws her up out of the black box of her nightmares where the skitter of bugs is all she can hear. It is vaguely familiar and she isn't sure it's truly real until she sits up and surveys the room.

Tia and Ian stand in the far doorway, their figures barely discernable. The fire has burned down to a pulse of embers and Chelsea and Merrill are still sleeping, their hands locked together on the floor separating them. Eli is a large bulk beside the farthest wall, snoring softly.

The sound comes again and she pinpoints it to the direction from where Tia and Ian are, from the direction where she found—

—the piano. Someone's playing the piano.

The music floats throughout the room, gently echoing off the walls, and the sound of it fastens her to the floor.

It is beautiful beyond words.

She can't begin to contend with or unravel the feeling that the music creates within her. Slowly she rises and crosses the room, carefully stepping over bags, around a rifle, worried that the slightest interruption will make the piano stop and the music go away. Zoey is carried toward the door by the melody, which is so haunting and breathtaking that she wonders if she is actually awake.

But even as she nears the doorway, Tia and Ian parting enough for her to see the moonlight-dappled room beyond, she is already taking inventory, her mind telling her who is playing before it fully registers.

Newton sits on a low bench with his back to the door. The silver illumination pouring in through the high windows lands across his bent neck, back curved over the keys, along with his hands.

His hands.

Zoey watches them, transfixed as they flutter across the keys, their movement so elegant and practiced they are like separate entities from the man. The notes, so soft and low when Zoey first woke to them, are gradually picking up speed. The intricacies and pattern growing until Newton's fingers fly in the moonlight and it seems he plays the beams themselves instead of the keys.

She doesn't realize she's crying until Ian puts a hand on her shoulder. She doesn't make a move to wipe the tears away. There is nothing but to listen, listen to the magic that pours from Newton across the room in the moonlight.

The melody lessens again, growing slower, quieter, until only one of his hands teeters between two notes that sound like heartbreak.

Then he draws his hands back and sits still.

Zoey moves to the side of the bench, her throat completely closed to words. She kneels and waits until Newton looks down at her. His face is lost in the darkness but she can feel his eyes on her, hesitant but probing.

Zoey reaches out and touches his fingers.

They stay that way for a moment that stretches out, and she is about to speak, about to try to convey how beautiful the song was when he stands and rushes out of the room past the crowd that is gathered there. Merrill, Chelsea, and Eli all stand in the hallway behind Ian and Tia. They part like water around a stone as Newton moves through them.

Then he is gone and the house is quiet once again.

Zoey stands her watch looking out into the darkness beyond the front door. She waits until the end of her shift to see if Newton will return, but as the sun begins its birth in the east there is still no sign of him.

Merrill tells her to rest again and she lies down on her sleeping bag, sure that sleep won't come, but she falls into a dreamless slumber almost immediately.

When she wakes there is a delicate fan of blue flowers lying next to her on the floor.

34

"Press the button on the grip. Good. Now switch the magazines out. Press the lever beside the slide. And now there's a round in the chamber."

Merrill guides her through the pistol again, having her load it and unload it twice more before Zoey nods.

"I think I've got it now. I never had to reload before."

"Let's hope you won't have to tonight. Line the three dots on the sights up when you aim, and keep both your hands on the grip when you fire." She holds the gun out at arm's length and gazes down the barrel while Merrill turns to survey Eli, who is tightening the last of the cargo down in the back of the Suburban.

"Thank you for showing me," she says, bringing the pistol back to her side.

"You're welcome. I know you can shoot, otherwise you wouldn't have made it out of that place alive."

"I was lucky."

"No one in that place is lucky," he says, studying her. She hesitates, the words almost sliding off her tongue. *I lied. Meeka is already gone. I'm sorry.* But she steps back from the precipice and drops her gaze to the weapon in her hands, flicking the safety on once again. She can still feel his eyes on her, but after a taut moment Eli's voice breaks the tension.

"Good to go there, Captain!"

"Don't call me that," Merrill says, and starts toward the vehicle.

"What should I call you, then? Major Douche Bag?"

"You can ride in the boat the rest of the way."

"You're very nasty in the morning, anyone ever told you that?"

Zoey follows them to the Suburban, where Ian already waits in one of the rear seats. The rest of the group files out of the house, and together they give it a final look.

"Beautiful place," Chelsea says. "Actually feels safe here."

"Too uppity for me," Tia says, testing a strap holding down the boat. "Give me a hole to crawl into and I'm good." Eli opens his mouth and Tia jabs her finger in his direction. "Don't even think about it." He grins.

Newton climbs into the vehicle and sits in front of Ian. No one has commented on his performance the night before. It is like something delicate that they are all afraid will crumble if even mentioned. Zoey begins to hum the melody under her breath, and the slightest of smiles curves Newton's lips.

"Let's go, people," Merrill says, climbing behind the wheel. "Lots of ground to cover."

◆　◆　◆

They drive through the day that began bright and becomes a dusky orange by afternoon. Zoey can't help but look back in the direction they came from, the mountains long gone now. Clouds dominate the sky to the west, their bellies low and swollen. She watches for lightning but sees none.

It is late afternoon when they reach a turnoff that Merrill guides them onto, coaxing the rattling Suburban off the side road on which they're traveling. The land has become rockier again, the smooth roll of the plains slowly giving way to jutting outcrops that tower a hundred feet over the vehicle at times.

They follow the winding road through several caverns, a sapphire lake appearing and then fading to their right behind bunched hillsides. A herd of deer flees from the sound of their passage as they crest a final rise in the road, white tails flicking indignantly as they bound away. At the bottom of the hill they round a bend, and Zoey finds herself looking at the rushing blue of the river.

The sight of it solidifies what they're going to attempt later that night, and when Merrill pulls to a stop parallel to the water, she has difficulty rising from her seat.

"Stiff?" Eli asks, hauling himself out.

"Yeah," Zoey says, unbuckling her belt.

"Me too. Damn long ride." When she still doesn't make a move to leave the vehicle, Eli draws closer. "Hey, you okay, girl?"

"Yeah, I'm . . ." She glances at the rushing river over his shoulder.

"You don't have to do this, okay? You can still go with the others, join Ian way up high and guide us through the radio."

"No, I need to go," she says, steeling herself. She jerks herself free of her paralysis and jumps out of the Suburban.

"You don't owe anyone anything," Eli says, placing a large hand on her shoulder.

"You're wrong. I do."

The next hour is spent loading the correct equipment into the boat before Merrill backs the trailer into the river. There is the vague shape of a ramp disappearing into the current and he guides the trailer down it, letting the boat float free. Tia uses a rope to pull the boat to the shore and ties it to a large boulder. They split into two groups, one that stays, the other that will go. They say their goodbyes punctuated with the occasional hug and handshake. Ian embraces Zoey gently. He feels thin and fragile beneath his coat.

"I will see you very soon," he says, his voice rougher than usual. "I'll be watching over you the whole time."

Newton rubs at the dirt with his shoe and shoots her a glance. "Thank you for the flowers," she says. He tips his head to one side, and the suggestion of a smile is there again as she turns to Merrill.

"Be vigilant—we're in their territory now. Don't take any chances," he says, putting out his hand to Zoey. She places her hand in his, and he squeezes it with callused fingers. "We stick to the plan, everyone makes it out fine."

"I'll do my best."

"I know you will."

Zoey moves down to the water's edge. Looking back once, she catches a glimpse of Merrill and Chelsea beside the Suburban, their embrace fierce and full of passion. Chelsea holds Merrill's hand until he begins to drive away, their fingers sliding free of each other. All of them wave as the vehicle glides around the corner.

Then they are gone in a cloud of dust, the rumble of the engine quieting into nothing and there is only the sound of the river.

35

They use most of the afternoon traveling up the winding river.

The electric motor Tia brought hums with next to no sound, propelling them along faster than Zoey would have expected of the little apparatus. It is nearing evening before they leave the water, pulling the boat up onto the bank and covering it with a tarp roughly the same color as the gray rock surrounding it.

"It's barely a mile around the next corner," Tia says in a low voice after they finish securing the boat. Zoey stares upstream, the knowledge of how close she is thrumming in her veins with adrenaline-fueled bursts.

The sky begins to glaze with a thin coating of clouds by evening, but there is no smell of rain in the air and no thunder in the distance.

They make a rudimentary camp at the base of a hill behind a towering rock shelf and eat a cold meal of biscuits and sweet jam. Zoey sits with her back to the stone and wishes for a fire to stretch her feet and hands out to.

"When did you last talk to Merrill?" Eli asks Chelsea.

"About twenty minutes ago. He said Ian's in position, and they're stationed behind the relay building. From what he could see, he thinks there's only one worker and one guard. It should be easy for them to get in undetected."

"What do we do if it doesn't storm?" Zoey asks.

"We might have to stay here for another day or so," Tia says.

"What if it doesn't storm for a long time?"

"Then we'll have to regroup, try again. Don't worry, Merrill won't give up, not as long as Meeka's alive."

Zoey rubs her finger against the nearest rock. Part of it has been smoothed by the river at a time when the water was much higher. She is like the stone, pieces of her eroding away. The parts that are most important.

They wait late into the night but there is no activity from the sky, only a mockingly calm quiet that grates on Zoey's nerves. Eli offers to take first watch and the rest of them bed down, the river a rushing lullaby that does nothing to help Zoey sleep.

◆　◆　◆

The morning dawns in a brilliant cascade of reds that give way to a hazy blue sky. They spend the hours before noon checking in with Merrill and Ian, inspecting gear that has been gone over a dozen times, and casting glances at the traitorous blue canopy overhead. The sound that Zoey fears the most, the chop of helicopter blades, doesn't come, even though she expects it to at any moment.

The afternoon and evening pass in a moldering of time that grows from minutes into hours, and slowly night creeps in like an assassin from the east.

As the last light fades, Zoey settles herself beneath a heavy overhang of flat rock that leans against another boulder near the edge of camp. The stone creates a natural shelter from the wind and weather.

The weather.

She glances up at the mottled sky. The wind that was nearly non-existent in the afternoon has risen to a constant pitch that sweeps over the hills and hums between rocks. The first clouds appeared just before dark and have taken on a poisonous shade of gray. But there is no thunder, and more importantly, no lightning.

For supper they had eaten dried meat and drank what Chelsea called "coffee." It was black and bitter, but hot from Tia heating the water they used to make it over a hand torch from her bag.

None of them had commented on the activity in the sky.

Now the tension is something that Zoey can feel in the air. With each degree the sun falls, the river is leeched of more color. Soon it is a dark ribbon cruising past them, its constant rush adding to the apprehension instead of calming her nerves.

Zoey looks up as the other three come to sit with her beneath the overhang. She can no longer see anyone's features in the gloom.

"Sure wish we could have a fire," Eli says. "Could almost pretend we were camping out."

"Yeah, maybe a couple cold beers to go with some hot food," Tia murmurs.

"Okay, gotta stop talkin' about it. Shit'll drive me nuts," Eli says.

"Did people used to go camping for fun?" Zoey asks.

"Oh yeah, all the time," Eli says. "People used to do a lotta shit for fun, before everything went to hell."

"Like what?"

"Like go swimming," Chelsea said. "Janie and I would swim almost every weekend in the summer. Our parents used to take us when she was really little, and I kept doing it after they passed."

"I miss the movies," Tia says. "Used to go a lot. We had a big theater near our place in Seattle, one of the kind that had the screen that was curved. I can still taste the butter on the popcorn. It probably plugged up a few of my arteries, but I'm pretty sure I'd drink a gallon of it straight right now."

Eli shivers. "Nearly made me throw up."

"Weak constitution."

"Ain't nothin' weak about me, woman, you know that."

"Besides your mind and sense of humor," Tia says.

"Don't know why you don't just confess your love for me. Could be a beautiful thing."

Chelsea nudges Zoey and laughs quietly. She smiles and gazes at them in turn. At first she thought that the group was made of companions depending on one another simply for survival, but as she spends more and more time with them, it's clear they are so much more than that. She's imagined what her life would have been like if she had grown up with her parents, how different everything would seem, but she could never get a true handle on what it would be like to have a family. She still doesn't, but she realizes now a family is exactly what she's looking at.

"Think we should check in with Merrill?" Zoey asks Chelsea, pushing away the bittersweet sensation.

A rumbling almost imperceptible to the ear comes from the west. Zoey feels it in her chest before she registers what it is.

Thunder.

They stiffen and wait for the sound to repeat itself. After another minute it does.

Chelsea fiddles with the headset hanging around her neck. Her eyes widen. "Are you sure? Okay." She stands. "Ian said he just saw lightning not more than twenty miles away. The storm's coming."

"Let's get ready," Eli says.

They move to the boat and uncover it. Zoey fumbles in the dark, trying to help where she can, but stays out of the way mostly. The handgun Merrill gave her is heavy in its holster on her hip. She grips the handle, feeling a modicum of comfort from its heft.

As quietly as they can, they lift the boat from its mooring and walk sideways with it into the water. Several times the aluminum bumps a rock and Zoey cringes. Thunder rolls again and this time it has more power, lingering longer in the sky. Then there is a purplish jump of light, the lightning blooming in the bowels of several clouds. It is getting closer.

Without speaking, they climb into the floating vessel, and Eli shoves them into the current.

Tia starts the motor, its sound all but muted now by the wind and the murmurs of the storm. They begin to glide up the river, their speed barely enough to keep them moving against the current.

"Remember, Tia and Eli at the front, me at the back," Chelsea says, touching Zoey's arm. "You guide us, and we don't stop for anything, we keep moving until we're back out and into the boat." Zoey nods, her heart beginning to pummel her rib cage. The muscles in her arms and legs have become water. She flexes her hands and rotates her ankles, all the while trying to keep her breathing under control.

The dark landscape slides inexorably past, the bend in the river coming closer with each minute.

A glow begins to fill up the sky above the closest bluff facing the water.

The floodlights. *Oh God*, Zoey thinks, *I'm home.*

Chelsea hands her a small headset of her own and she dons it, poking the single earpiece in her left ear. "You'll be able to hear everyone and if you want to talk to us, just start speaking, okay?"

"Okay."

"Zoey, that you?" Merrill's voice says into her ear as if he's only feet away.

"Yes."

"Good. We're all set here. Newton and I are in position."

"No trouble with the guard?"

"No. We're inside the station, but it won't take long for them to know something's wrong after the power goes out. The guard had a radio attached to his uniform. The first thing they'll do is try to raise him on it, and when that doesn't work they'll send out a repair team along with more guards just in case. You'll need to be very fast. The storm's almost above us."

As if on cue, a light patter of rain begins to fall, dropping in cold points on her exposed skin.

"Tia," Merrill says. "As soon as the lights are out, that's your signal to get into position. If a sniper spots you, Ian will take him out."

"Probably not before one of us goes down," Tia says.

Merrill ignores the comment. "Wait for the signal. Good luck."

They all tell him the same, and the earpiece goes silent.

Thunder booms, so much closer, shaking the extended sides of the boat. The lights continue to burn, creating a halo behind the bluff.

Time seems to still, stretching out, punctuated only by Zoey's rapid heartbeat. How long will they have to wait? Minutes? Hours? Her jacket begins to plaster to her back, moisture running down her sides into her waistline. She grips the seat under her.

There is an incandescent flash so bright it blinds her for a split second. She can see the afterimages of the electricity imprinted in her vision.

Zoey blinks, straining to look past the bluff.

Darkness.

"Go," Merrill says in the earpiece.

The boat leaps forward silently and Zoey clings to her seat. The black shores scroll past as another sound begins to build. A raw gushing that she remembers so well it forces her eyes shut.

They round the bend, and the ARC comes into view.

It is a monolithic shadow rising above them. The outlines of the walls towering over the straight line of the dam behind it is enough to suck the breath from her lungs. There is only the faintest glow emanating from what she knows is the landing pad on the roof of the main building.

The boat closes the distance, the ARC growing taller and wider with each second. She hears Eli swear quietly in her earpiece, and she agrees. It is something to be cursed.

The wind cuts across the water, tugging at her hair, and one of the collapsible sides folds toward her. Without thinking, Zoey jams her arm into its path, stopping it from clanging against the interior of the boat. Pain blooms from her elbow up. It's so sudden and sharp, a bout of nausea boils in her center. Then Chelsea is lifting the side back into position and the aching pressure is gone. She rubs at the place where it struck her but she's not bleeding.

She mouths *I'm okay* to Chelsea and the other woman nods, turning back around toward the approaching compound.

The huge concrete stilts the ARC is built on hold it nearly five feet above the water. They will be able to pass underneath its base, barely.

Zoey watches the walls as more and more detail becomes clear. There is the closest sniper nest, along with the man occupying it. He's yelling something that is lost in another blast of thunder, and she cringes as lightning rips across the sky. They are held there for a second, pinned beneath the light in the center of the river fifty yards away from the structure.

If he looks down now, we're dead, she thinks. *There's nowhere to hide.*

The boat keeps moving and darkness floods back in, blanketing them.

She holds her breath.

Forty yards.

No shots.

Thirty.

Twenty.

Another shout from the wall.

Ten.

Five.

They slide beneath the ARC, its mass above them like some colossal animal standing on many legs.

"We're under," Chelsea says into her headset.

Tia guides the boat between the massive supports, and Chelsea turns on a flashlight that shoots a soft, red beam out several yards. The sound of the river's passage is magnified beneath the structure, the water falling from the dam's spillway a roaring that fills the air. At the corner of her vision, movement catches Zoey's eye. She squints through the darkness but can't make out anything until another stuttering pulse of lightning cuts the night.

Several long boats bob in the current beside a platform that's mounted to the ARC's wall. What looks like a small service elevator runs up and out of sight. That's how the repair team would reach the shore. But with the power out, they'll have to find another way down to the boats. That will buy them time.

"Zoey, where's the laundry room?" Tia asks in her earpiece. Zoey brings her gaze back from the boats and searches the smooth concrete ceiling above them. Here and there are small ports that dribble water that looks like blood in Chelsea's red beam. Zoey imagines the interior layout, positioning herself in the doorway of the laundry room. She twists in her seat and points to the left.

"Go around the next support and it should be right there." Tia pilots the boat in a smooth turn that brings them past the thick stilt. The ARC's base is unbroken for a dozen yards, and Zoey's about to say they must have missed it when a large plastic pipe appears in Chelsea's light. It drips water, and when she glances to the right there is another, smaller port she knows is the drying vent.

"There," she says, pointing again. "Stop ten feet or so to the right of them." Tia brings the boat beside the pipes and Eli stands, sliding his palm against the rough concrete before bringing them to a halt. Tia drops something into the water and ties off a cord as Chelsea does the same.

"Are you sure this is it?" Tia asks, donning the pack over her shoulders that is attached to the steel tanks. "I really don't want to cut into the guards' barracks, but I'd pay good money to see the looks on their faces if I did."

"Tia, focus," Merrill's voice says in their ears.

"Yes, I'm sure," Zoey says, moving out of the older woman's way. Tia braces her feet on the bottom of the boat and slides a pair of goggles over her eyes.

"I'd look away, this is gonna get bright." Zoey turns her head to the side just as a brilliant blue light illuminates the boat and the water surrounding it. The hiss that accompanies the cutter barely competes with the spillway, the sound lost amid the flowing water and thunder that continues to roll above them.

Tia works for minutes that feel like hours. Zoey chances a look up and is nearly blinded by the plasma cutter's light. In that brief glance, three quarters of a smoking circle is illuminated, and even as Zoey looks away, Tia makes a sign with one hand to Chelsea, who pulls up the front anchor and swivels the boat to one side of the hole Tia's making.

The blue light abruptly stops and there is a brief pause before a huge chunk of concrete several feet across drops free of the ARC and splashes into the water beside the boat.

"Easier than I thought," Tia says. "Eli, give me a boost." Eli moves up beside Tia and stabilizes her as she places one foot on his thigh and climbs upward through the hole she's made. "Bastard's still hot," she says as her legs and feet disappear. "Watch yourself."

"Chelsea, you next," Eli rumbles. In a moment the other woman climbs up and out of sight. Eli turns to Zoey and motions to the hole. "After you, my lady." She stands on the boat's seat, trying to balance as it rocks beneath her. She reaches up and finds two hands extended and waiting. She grips them and is lifted up with a quick boost from Eli, then she is on her knees, scooting away from the hole several feet from the table where she spent more hours than she can remember folding never-ending amounts of laundry.

She stands up and draws her pistol.

She is inside again.

The thought sends a ripple of dread through her. It is like she's just been swallowed by an enormous beast and with each minute is being slowly dissolved in its cavernous belly. She steadies herself against the wall as memories wash over her, nearly making her stagger. Zoey blinks, pulls air into her lungs. Expels it.

"Are you in?" Merrill asks.

"We're in," Eli replies, standing up next to the hole. "Leaving the laundry in a second."

"Good. I think I bought us more time. They asked the guard if everything was all right, and I responded that we were working on it. Think they fell for it."

"Perfect. We're moving now," Tia says, stepping up to the door leading out of the laundry. Chelsea and Eli flank her, weapons up. There is a flicker of blue, and the door opens.

"I'll be in front," Eli says. "Zoey, you're behind Tia. Talk us through it." Then he steps through the doorway into the hall, and she follows close behind.

The hallway is awash in the yellow glow thrown by the few emergency lights mounted on the walls. Their footsteps are too loud in the quiet that grips the corridor, and after a beat Zoey realizes why. The mechanical room is silent behind the door to their right, all of the machinery stilled by the lack of power. The quiet is eerie.

"Through the next door and up the stairs to the third floor," she whispers. Eli barely nods, sidling up to the closed door at the end of the hallway. Tia places the plasma cutter even with the lock and triggers the blast of blue flame. The door clicks open, and Eli rushes through.

Zoey gets a glimpse of a black uniform and the surprised face of a guard before the butt of Eli's rifle smashes into his open mouth.

The man drops to the ground, one arm twitching as blood courses out past his ruined teeth and over his broken jaw. Without words, Chelsea unbuckles his belt, stripping his weapons from it in an instant. Zoey peers up the stairway, waiting for a shout of alarm or another guard to appear, but none do.

"Everyone okay?" Merrill asks.

"Fine here. Moving up to the second floor," Tia whispers, dropping back behind Eli. They move in a line up the stairs, turning so they can see past the handrails to the landing above.

Empty.

"Go, quick," Tia says, and they hurry up the treads, pausing at the next landing. Somewhere above them are voices. Zoey listens but can't make out what they're saying, but the words aren't frantic, and there's no thunder of boots rushing down to meet them.

They move again, stopping at the second floor. Two guards stand halfway down the hall with their backs to them, their voices low. Zoey waves the others on, keeping her eyes locked on the two men, until Chelsea taps her on the shoulder. They fly up the next two sets of stairs, halting at the top as a door opens and closes somewhere below them. They wait for an agonizing second to see if there will be a cry of alarm, but nothing comes.

Zoey's stomach clenches as they stop on the third third-floor landing while Eli takes up position beside the hallway entrance. He holds up one finger and points to the waiting corridor. Thunder rumbles, vibrating the air. Below it is another sound.

Boot steps.

Eli waits, his large chest heaving before he spins and sprints through the opening.

There is a strangled cry that cuts off as quickly as it began. Zoey sidles past Tia and into the hallway she knows so well.

Eli crouches over a guard who's lying flat on his back. The man's feet drum for a second and then he is still. Eli stands, drawing the long, thin knife from the guard's neck in a quick movement. A dark pool is broadening around the prone man's head, and Zoey looks away.

"Which doors?" Tia asks, moving past Eli. Zoey follows her, swallowing the fear that taints the back of her throat with the taste of blood.

The doors. She can see hers already, the scanner beside it dark. Lily's is next. She guides them to it, throwing a look down the length of the hall as Tia places the cutter to the lock.

The blue flame ignites.

The door opens, and Zoey pushes through it.

Lily sits on the edge of her bed, her small form barely visible in the single emergency light. Her hair has grown back some in the time Zoey's been gone, and the stitches have been removed from her forehead. The sight of her there, so innocent and delicate, floods Zoey's vision with tears as she holsters her pistol and moves forward. Lily cowers back onto her bed as Zoey approaches.

"Nah, nah, don' 'urt."

"Lily, it's me. It's Zee." She takes another step forward, the light spilling over her.

Lily freezes, and her mouth slowly opens. "Zee."

"I came back for you, Lily." She barely manages to get the words out of her constricted throat before Lily launches herself into her arms. Zoey hugs her fiercely, and Lily squeezes her in return.

"Zee, Zee, Zee," Lily repeats in a hoarse voice. "I sorry, sorry."

"You don't have to be sorry," Zoey says, running her hand over the back of the girl's stubbled scalp.

"Zoey," Eli says quietly.

Zoey nods and brings Lily to arm's length. "You're coming with me, okay, Lily?"

"Kay."

"You have to be quiet, all right?"

Lily nods her head. "Qui."

"That's right, quiet. Let's go."

Eli leads the way with Zoey steps behind, her arm around Lily's thin shoulders. The hallway is still empty, but there is a great pressure building inside her. It is as if she can feel the walls beginning to crumble inward on top of them.

Zoey brings them to a halt at the next door around the corner, and Tia pops the lock. Zoey steps past her and pushes the door open.

Rita stands in the center of the room, hands balled into fists before her. Her narrowed eyes blink once as Zoey enters, leaving Lily in the entrance. They stare at one another for a long second before Rita's hands fall to her sides.

"You," the other woman says. Zoey waits, unwilling to drop her gaze. Lightning flashes, bringing a hyper-glow to the room before diminishing. Each of them stands like a statue. Rita's eyes flick to the hallway, scanning over the others waiting with their rifles. The hardness around her mouth slackens and with a barely perceptible nod, she puts on a pair of shoes beside her bed.

Zoey takes Lily's hand and points to the door directly across the hall. Tia burns the lock and shoves the door inward.

Sherell sits at her desk, a pen and a piece of paper before her. Her mouth is partially open, and her eyes widen as they step into her room.

"The hell—" she manages before Rita moves into view.

"We're going," Rita says, motioning toward the hall. "Get your shoes." Sherell hesitates but then folds the paper she was working on and tucks it away into a pocket before sliding her shoes on.

In the hallway, Zoey brings them to the last door, and Tia opens it with the cutter. Inside, Penny is at her window, staring out at the storm. She turns, and even in the almost nonexistent light, Zoey can see the dark glint in her eyes. Penny glances to each of their faces, hovering last on Rita.

"Penn, we're getting out of here. C'mon." Rita jerks her head toward the hallway. Penny's lips twist up in an awful smile and she moves forward, brushing past Zoey.

"Okay, two more, right?" Chelsea says a little breathlessly. Zoey moves past her without answering. The group follows close behind, their footsteps sounding much too loud.

"Are you almost out?" Merrill's voice says in her ear.

"Close," Chelsea replies, coming even with Zoey as they near the main stairwell again. "We just have to get Terra and Meeka."

Zoey pulls the headset off before she hears Merrill's reply. The group comes to a halt at the quiet stairway, and she runs her gaze across everyone.

"Take them down to the laundry. Get them in the boat," Zoey says, backing away.

"What are you talking about?" Chelsea says.

"Just go." Zoey continues to retreat.

"Where are you going?" Tia says. But then her eyes glaze, as do Eli's and Chelsea's.

Eli places his fingers against his earpiece. "What did you say, Merrill?"

Zoey turns and sprints up the stairs.

Their voices hiss after her, but she doesn't hear any sounds of pursuit. She turns the corner and bounds up the next flight, stopping short before the fourth-floor hallway junction. She draws her pistol and looks around the corner.

The corridor is clear all the way to the infirmary. She sprints down its length, coming even with the infirmary door, and peeks through the glass set in its frame.

The palm of a man's hand presses against the small window.

Zoey flings herself to the side, crouching in the shadows as a metallic scrape comes from the lock. The door opens a second later.

"—such a pain in the ass when the power goes out," the first guard says, stepping past her. "I've gotten so used to the electronic scans that using keys is like work."

"You're one lazy bastard," the second guard says, tight on his heels. Both chuckle. "Now what was Richards going on about?"

The door begins to swing shut behind them as they walk down the hall.

Zoey tenses, watching it slowly close.

"He said Perry didn't come back with his booze from ground level or some shit."

Almost shut.

"We're checking on a booze run? We'd better get some this time."

The guards turn the corner toward the stairs.

Zoey leaps forward, stabbing her fingers into the closing door's gap.

It shuts on her hand hard enough to spring tears from her eyes. Standing, she drags it open and slips through, letting it swing shut behind her.

A flicker of lightning coats the infirmary in a monochromatic flutter. The doorways of the exam rooms are all closed, operating beds beyond empty and waiting for their next patients. Zoey moves without pause down the center aisle, the gleaming elevator doors appearing out of the gloom.

Alongside them stands a guard she's never seen before cleaning his fingernails with a small knife. She raises the gun from her side, but the guard doesn't look up.

"You guys forget something, or was Perry already on his—" He glances up from his cleaning, eyes going wide at the sight of her striding toward him through the semidarkness.

He starts to reach for his sidearm but she speaks, her voice surprising even to her at how level it sounds. "Don't or I'll shoot you."

"Holy shit, what the hell are you doing here? You're dead."

"Is that what they told you? Makes sense. They wouldn't want everyone knowing I got away."

"What do you want?" She moves closer, and it's then she can see that he's terrified. The man trembles, the folded collar of his uniform shaking.

"Call the elevator for me."

"I can't. They disabled the bracelets for clearance on it after you got out." He flashes his bracelet in front of the elevator's sensor. Nothing happens. Zoey glances around the room, mind whirring.

"Give me your radio."

"I don't have one." She raises the gun even with his forehead. "Okay, okay." He digs in his pants pocket and draws out a small radio with a blunt antenna on its top. "Here," he says, extending his arm. Zoey reaches out to take it.

The guard lunges forward.

She fires.

The gunshot is deafening and sends a shrill whining through her eardrums, but she barely notices. She steps forward, pistol aimed at the center of the guard's chest. He's sitting on the floor with his back against the wall. Blood pours from between his fingers where he clutches his shoulder.

"Ahh! You bitch, you fucking shot me!" Zoey bends down and retrieves the radio from where he dropped it.

"I told you I would. Now, how do I contact the Director with this?"

"I'm not going to tell you anything."

Zoey shoots him again in his other shoulder. The report as well as the guard's cry is drowned out by a blast of thunder that reverberates through the floor.

"How?"

"Turn the switch to seven and press the button," the guard says through clenched teeth. He holds both wounds now with opposite hands, his arms crossed over his chest. Zoey flips the small dial on the radio's side to seven and triggers the button.

"Director?" She waits. Lightning slashes the sky outside, and thunder growls its reply.

"Who is this?" The voice is polished and smooth. She would know it anywhere.

"It's Zoey. I'm in the infirmary, and I've come alone, but before you call your guards, know that I have one of your men and I'll kill him and then myself unless you do what I say."

There is a long pause, then a low laugh. "You did this, didn't you? The power outage. Very clever. Our technicians were sure it was the storm."

"Bring me Terra. If you come with someone other than Terra, I shoot your guard and then you along with anyone else I can kill before I die."

"Now Zoey, let's not get hasty. We can all come away from this amicably if we listen to one another."

Zoey pushes the button and pulls the pistol's trigger again. The guard's pant leg jumps just below his knee, and he bellows out a guttural scream until he runs out of breath.

"The next shot you hear will be the one that goes through my head," Zoey says.

"Okay, all right, Zoey, but you'll have to give me some time. The elevator won't work without power, so I'll have to find another way down."

"I don't believe you'd leave yourself stranded up there. I think the elevator runs off of another power source if the main goes down. Maybe your guard here will tell me before he dies of blood loss." She aims the gun at the panting man again.

"It does," he moans. "It runs off of its own backup generator that's not hooked into the system."

"Hear that?" Zoey says into the radio.

There is another brief pause, then the Director speaks again, and the syrupy smoothness is gone from his voice. "I'll bring her down."

Zoey tosses the radio to the floor and strips the guard's handgun from him. He doesn't move an inch, only breathes raggedly with his eyes closed. She puts the new gun in her own holster and waits. Every moment she expects the door at the far end of the infirmary to fly open and a dozen Redeyes to rush in, fully armed. It was stupid to come here, stupid to endanger herself, the mission, but she couldn't leave Terra behind, not when she is so close.

And she couldn't tell the others about Meeka. Not until they were clear of the ARC. Then they can beat her, kill her, whatever they want. At least then the other women will be safe.

She's snapped from her thoughts as the soft rumbling of the elevator comes from behind the doors. Zoey raises the pistol, holding its sights on the doors until they slide open.

Terra steps out into the emergency lighting, the Director holding her arm. There is a small pistol in his hand, its barrel pointed at Terra's temple. Behind him there is more movement. Reaper and the female doctor she'd left locked in the cell with Carter's corpse move into the room as well.

"I said come alone," Zoey says, aiming at the small target of the Director's face over Terra's shoulder.

"We're unarmed, Zoey," the woman says. *Vivian*, that's her name. She holds up her hands to reveal their emptiness. "We just want to talk."

"Then take the gun away from her head." The Director lowers the pistol but doesn't release his hold on Terra's arm.

"Terra, are you okay?" Her friend's eyes swim in the low light. There is a blankness in her stare, a catatonic glaze that's like a brick wall between them. "What did you do to her?"

"Zoey, why don't you put down the gun, and we'll talk," Vivian says.

"Why don't you shut your mouth before I put a bullet in it?"

The scientist looks stunned for a second before she tries to smile. "I know you're upset, but we can work all this out."

"Listen to her, Zoey," the Director says. "You are all precious to us. We don't want any harm to come to you, so why don't you put the gun down, and we'll talk."

She ignores him, focusing instead on Terra, who still seems unaware of her surroundings. "Terra? Can you hear me?" The other woman's lips part at the sound of her name. She blinks and looks in Zoey's direction. "I'm taking you out of here, okay?"

"Zoey, please. Listen to yourself. You're in the middle of the facility with two handguns and no possible way of escape. I'm not sure how you managed the little trick with the power or how you gained entry, but there's no way we're letting you simply walk out of here," the Director says, his gun rising toward her.

"Zoey, listen to him," Reaper says. His voice sends a shiver through her, since it's the first time he's ever spoken to her in person. The tall soldier brings both his hands up and she points her weapon at him, but he continues moving until his fingers touch the sides of the black mask covering the lower part of his face. He unsnaps the straps, and it falls away.

Zoey draws in a quick breath.

His face is a torn landscape of scars.

Most of the left side of his lips are gone, revealing white teeth and red gums. His cheek is puckered flesh, pale and rippled as if from a great heat. Part of his nose is also missing, the left nostril sunken into a dark hole while the other side is only partially formed.

"I look like this because I defended a woman just like you, Zoey. I would have died for her and almost did. Don't rush to conclusions so fast that you miss the truth."

Terra murmurs something, and Zoey glances at her. She is blinking more rapidly, as if she's coming awake from a deep sleep.

"What did you do to her?" she asks again.

"Only what we had to," the Director says.

"Why do you wait to do this to us? Why do you wait until we're twenty-one?" When no one speaks she takes a step forward, thrusting the pistol out before her. "Answer me!"

"At twenty-one years of age, women are most fertile," Vivian says. "We need every advantage to try and cure what's happening."

"Who are the fathers?" Zoey asks. "Random guards? You?" She gestures at the Director with the gun barrel.

"The Clerics' sons," Vivian says. "Their fathers were chosen specifically for the purpose that they serve. They are genetically sound, healthy, virile. Their sons carry the same traits. We use their semen and the women's eggs in the most perfect conditions we can create."

"All is for the greater good," the Director says. "Everything you see around you is in an effort to save humanity."

"Even impregnating us? Using us all as breeding stock? Violating us to see if we can give birth to a girl? There's a line and you crossed it years ago."

The Director's face hardens. "There is nothing more important than the continuation of our species. Anything else is simply selfish." His eyes narrow. "You should be ashamed of yourself, Zoey. How many died so you could traipse off on your own? How many more since you've come back? You accuse us of being monsters, but we work for life, and all you've accomplished so far is bringing death to those around you."

She rages against his words, struggles in them as if they are deep water and she is draped in chains. She grits her teeth and slowly shakes her head.

"No."

"I'm afraid *yes*, Zoey," the Director says. "You know it's true. We saw it in you during your time in the box. The 'creature' that was sent in to test you, that was a man, Zoey. Just a man in a costume, and you killed him."

She tries to find a lie in the Director's eyes but can see none. Somewhere deep inside she knew it all along, knew that it wasn't an animal she'd killed, at least not in the sense it had been presented.

"Now, why don't we end this before someone else gets hurt because of you?" the Director purrs.

"Blame, walls, locks, shame, it's all control. All of it. You use our insecurities and fears against us to keep us in place. But no more," she growls. "No more."

"Zoey?" Terra says, her eyes the clearest they've been.

"Terra, everything's going to be all right."

Terra's chin trembles, and she gazes down at the floor. "It was a boy, Zoey. I was going to have a little boy."

Zoey watches her friend for a long moment before shifting her eyes to the Director, a burning realization surfacing within her. "You kill them, don't you? The boys. You kill them and then kill the mothers."

"You don't understand, Zoey," Vivian says.

"You stripped him from inside her! Look at her! That's why she's like this!" Zoey screams. She is a millimeter from pulling the trigger, from killing them all. It's better than they deserve and there's nothing more she would like to do.

"I never got to carry him," Terra says in her ghostly voice. Zoey blinks, thinking that her friend is so deep in shock she has made herself believe that she gave birth and was never able to hold her son.

But then the words take on a different meaning.

The black tanks in the room above them. Cords running out and into the central computer.

The image cauterizes all thought for a moment before the reality of it sinks home like a thousand pounds dropped on her shoulders.

"She was never pregnant," Zoey breathes. "You *grow* them. You grow the babies in the tanks." She knows it's the truth by the way Vivian's face changes. "You wait to see if they'll be female, and if they aren't, you flush them away. You tell us we're the only hope, that we hold the last chances of life, but you don't even allow us to carry our own children. We're pieces in an experiment. That's the only value you've ever given us."

"Zoey, you have to believe us," Vivian says. "We couldn't tell you certain things—"

"You told us nothing but lies. There was never a plague. You lied to us all, about everything."

"You're right, there was never a plague," Vivian says. "We couldn't isolate a single factor for why females weren't being born anymore. All

we know is that for some reason an embryo, that is in all rights supposed to become a female fetus, changes near the one-month stage."

"What do you mean, 'changes'?"

Vivian grimaces. "They shift and become male. We've never found
a reason why."

Even through the bafflement at the other woman's statement,
Zoey's seething anger emerges. "So this is what you did? Captured us?
Stole us from our parents and raised us to experiment on?"

"We didn't have a choice."

"No," Zoey says, her voice barely above a whisper. "That's what we
never had."

She's going to kill them. She knows it a heartbeat before she aims
the pistol. Just as she's centering the sights on the Director's forehead,
the door to the infirmary opens.

Footsteps come down the aisle, and she spins toward the sound.

Lee stands beside the closest bed.

He stares at her, such longing in his eyes that she nearly drops the
handgun. Even in the dim light, punctuated by the staccato bursts of
lightning, he is handsome beyond measure. All at once she realizes how
much she's missed him, how much she's held back the feelings she didn't
truly understand until now.

"Zoey," he says. Out of the darkness behind him, Simon appears.
Her heart surges at the sight of him as well. She searches his face for
any malice or blame but finds only a gentle relief mingled with sorrow.
They move forward and stand beside her. Lee's fingers trace her cheek.

"Can't believe it's you," he says. She tries to speak but can't. Instead
she shifts her gaze to Simon, who gives her the barest of smiles.

"You see, Zoey. This is your home. We are your family. Put the gun
down," the Director says.

She looks at him, at his hand still holding Terra's arm, at Vivian's
cold expression and Reaper's ruined visage.

"No. You're going to let us go," she says.

The Director sighs. "I was afraid you'd say that."

With a quick movement he raises the gun to Terra's head and pulls the trigger.

Zoey's scream is drowned out by the gunshot. Terra's beautiful, blonde hair flies out from the side of her head and is suddenly streaked with crimson. Her legs fold beneath her, and she crumples to her back.

The room erupts in movement.

Lee leaps in front of her, as does Simon. Vivian steps toward the elevator, avoiding the spreading pool of blood coursing from Terra's head. Reaper moves forward, hands out before him.

"Cleric, apprehend your charge and return her to her room!" the Director yells. He holds the pistol at his side, but it is pointed in Simon's general direction.

Reaper is closer, and now there is something glittering in one hand. Something sharp and pointed.

"Cleric, this is your last warning. Disarm your charge. Now!"

Simon turns, brushing Lee out of the way, as Reaper moves in on her other side. Simon's gaze is steely and dead as he takes a step forward.

"Simon, no," Zoey says, bringing the handgun level with his chest. He stops a pace from her and freezes. His eyes thaw, and she doesn't understand what she's seeing.

"I hope you liked the books," Simon says, and launches himself at Reaper.

He is a blur of motion, faster than she's ever seen anyone move. He strikes Reaper in the side of the head, and then the two men are locked in a struggle for the knife.

Lee yells something she doesn't understand.

The Director moves forward, first aiming his weapon at Simon and then at Lee, the whole while he grins, and there is something unearthly about the smile. It is like seeing past a tattered mask covering pure evil.

"Don't shoot her!" Vivian yells. The Director's attention falters, head twitching toward the doctor's voice.

Zoey brings up the gun and fires.

The Director's grin melts and he stumbles, dropping to his knees. A stain is spreading across the belly of his white dress shirt. He places a hand to the wound and brings it back before his eyes in disbelief. Slowly he tips forward, landing hard on his face, and lies still.

Lee grabs her by the arm and begins to pull her toward the infirmary exit, but even as he does so the door is yanked open and several guards spill inside, lights and weapons pointed at them as they advance.

Zoey turns back just as Reaper and Simon fall to the floor. Simon rolls on top of him, using his knees to pummel Reaper's sides while holding the knife in the other man's grip at bay.

They struggle, their arms interwoven, muscles bulging with effort. Reaper's destroyed face grimaces and he releases a grunt. The tip of the knife slowly rotates between the two of them.

A drop of sweat drips from Simon's forehead.

He shifts his eyes to where Zoey and Lee stand. "Run," he says.

Simon's hands slip as Reaper twists the knife and buries it to the hilt beneath Simon's chin.

He twists and Simon's body goes limp.

"Dad!" Lee screams and tries to run forward, but Zoey grasps his shirt, the material tearing as he drags her forward. Behind her comes the crackle of a prod, and she fires blindly over one shoulder.

"Don't shoot her!" Vivian screams again from near the elevator. "Don't shoot her!"

Reaper thrusts Simon's body away and withdraws his knife, the blade an electrically red smile.

Lee lunges forward again, and Zoey pulls him back. An inhuman howl comes from him and he shudders. She guides him back from where Reaper gains his feet, the soldier moving forward lithely.

"Don't do anything stupid, either of you," Reaper says, flicking the knife back and forth. Droplets of blood fly from its end, their redness amplified by a flash of lightning.

The guards advance from the left, Reaper from the right. Vivian stands in the center.

"Don't shoot her," she repeats.

Zoey backs away, tugging Lee with her. Her hip nudges something and she reaches back, her fingers finding what they search for.

Zoey brings up the gun and fires at Reaper. He dodges, but not fast enough, and the bullet catches him in the side. The guards rush forward and Zoey turns.

She throws the lid on the laundry chute up and pushes Lee in.

He tips backward, eyes bulging, and falls, headfirst into the dark tunnel.

Zoey throws a final look at Terra, at Simon, *never forget*, and dives after Lee.

Vivian screams something and hands grasp her ankles as she slides down. They slip off.

Then she's falling.

Pure darkness surrounds her. She accelerates, the smooth steel polished by thousands of laundry bags hums past. The chute skims her shoulders and she prays that Lee doesn't get stuck. The flesh on her arms heats up, then burns, then blisters. She tries to scream but the velocity sucks her voice away.

A sickly light fills her vision and she flies out into the huge laundry bin. There is a glimpse of Lee within hundreds of uniforms, then she lands on him and he cries out with pain.

The top of her head is on fire and she rolls to the side, struggling in the giving folds of laundry. Lee wheezes and his hand grasps her arm.

"What the fuck," a deep voice says and she blinks away the cobwebs of unconsciousness to gaze up into Eli's face that is hovering over the side of the bin. "I mean, really, what the fuck."

"Help us out," Zoey manages, and Eli grasps her outstretched hand, dragging her up and over the bin's side. Lee sits up, his face a mask of pain, one hand over his chest.

"I'm sorry," she says as they haul Lee out onto his feet. He doesn't respond, only limps away from her. She's about to ask if he's okay when a humming grows from the mouth of the chute and a guard erupts from it into the bin.

Eli fires a burst from his rifle, and blood sprays across the uniforms. "Let's go," he says, shoving her and Lee toward the hole in the floor. Zoey kneels and drops her legs through the dark circle, only then realizing she lost her pistol in the ride down the chute. Hands find her feet and she lets herself be lowered outside into the cool, damp air.

The storm still rages around the ARC. She finds herself being held steady by Chelsea and Tia, who usher her away from the hole as Lee drops down next. Zoey passes Penny and Rita sitting side by side, and Sherell gives her a quick nod as she takes a seat beside Lily, who is shaking, huddled beneath a dark blanket. Zoey places an arm around the girl, holding her close.

"Shhh, it's okay now. We're going to be okay."

There is a loud crack to the west, and for a second she thinks it is the beginning of another bout of thunder, but then it is answered tenfold by more gunfire and streaks of light that zip across the water's surface.

The boat rocks hard, and with a solid thud, Eli drops into the bow. "Let's go!" he yells as Tia scrambles past. There is a cry from where the other boats are docked, and Chelsea releases a curse before the barrel of her rifle spits fire. She empties her magazine and drops down behind the upraised sides of the boat as several bullets sing through the aluminum.

Then they are moving, the ARC's bottom sliding away as they cruise around two sets of concrete supports. A shot whines off the gunwale to Zoey's right and she hugs Lily harder, pulling her down. Thunder detonates above them, and wetness patters against her back.

They are out from beneath the ARC.

The shoreline is only thirty yards away now and coming up fast. The river water leaps up in a million splashes with each raindrop. Eli fires several rounds past Tia's hunched form as lightning splits the sky into two halves.

"When we hit the shore, everyone get out and follow Chelsea up the hill!" Tia yells. "If any of them come after us we can lose them up there." Zoey catches a glimpse of Penny as another branch of lightning splinters in the clouds. The woman's face is flat and empty, eyes like two holes.

"Brace yourselves!" Tia says.

There is a grating screech of metal and the front of the boat thrusts upward, nearly flinging Chelsea out into open air. Everyone slides forward and gathers themselves as Eli hops the side and starts waving them forward. They climb out one by one, Eli hoisting them over the side and onto the rough ground. Zoey jumps out after Lily and grabs her hand tightly. She turns, squinting through the dark and rain back at the looming shadow of the ARC.

"They're not shooting anymore," she says as Tia hits the dirt beside her. "They don't want to hit us."

"That's good for all of us then," Tia says, snagging her by the shoulder. "Now let's get the hell out of here."

They run as a clustered group, a wounded animal, loping awkwardly up a small hill and over a rusted string of fencing that fell decades ago. They climb another rise onto what was once a roadway and find a cut in the next hillside that brings them up through the rising bluffs. As they reach the top of the grade, a sound begins to grow from behind them that makes the hair on the back of Zoey's neck stand on end.

The helicopter is starting up.

"Run! We have to hide!" she yells, yanking Lily along as the girl protests weakly. "They're coming in the helicopter," she tells Eli as they draw even with him.

He wipes the rain from his face like tears and points to the south. "Run that way. Merrill should only be another few hundred yards."

"You can't stay, they'll kill you," Zoey says, trying to pull the big man with her. He pries her fingers from his shirt gently.

"Go," he says. She sees the set of his eyes and turns, dragging Lily with her.

The ground heaves and drops before them. In the strobing light she spots Chelsea far ahead and Tia off to the right. The other women are strung out between them. Lily stumbles on a loose rock and falls hard to her knee. She cries out, face constricting in pain. Zoey slings an arm around her, pulls her back up, and moves them on, much slower than before.

On the rise to their left, a building grows out of the night, and Zoey begins to move toward it just as she registers the darkness a few feet ahead.

A chasm at least forty feet deep drops away in a narrow draft in the land. Tia missed its closest end by only a step or two, and several of the other women are coming toward her, trying to find a way to cross.

"Come on! This way!" Chelsea yells back to them, only a dark figure ahead in the night. Zoey starts moving slowly with Lily parallel to the drop, the other women coming up behind her. The sound of the copter is louder, the rotors beginning their deep thud.

There is a streak of lightning, and at the same moment bright pain rips across her back. *I've been struck*, she thinks absently as she releases Lily. *After everything I've gone through only to be struck by lightning.*

She falls forward, hitting the ground on her hands and knees. Lily shrieks, rolling away from her, and the darkness of the chasm tilts like an open mouth ready for a feast. Warmth rolls down her back, the cold rain a bright contrast. Feet come into view, and she looks up.

Penny stands above her, water dripping from her hair. She's smiling the cold smile that's always chilled Zoey. There's something in her hand, and slowly she brings it closer to Zoey's face, waggling it like a toy.

A knife.

She wasn't struck by lightning. Penny cut her.

"What are you doing?" Zoey asks, trying to regain her feet.

"Something I've wanted to do for so long," Penny says. "And now I'm going to."

"I came back for you."

"I don't want to be out here," Penny says. "I'm going back to the ARC as soon as I slit your pretty throat."

The chopper howls in the darkness.

Chelsea yells something Zoey can't make out.

Rita appears by Penny's shoulder, gazing down at Zoey as she tries to stand.

"We're going back," Penny says, and Rita's eyes flick from the knife in her friend's hand to Zoey's upturned face. Zoey tenses, the skin on her back screaming, ready to lunge forward as soon as Penny moves.

Penny raises the knife.

And flies sideways as Rita pushes her hard.

The chasm swallows Penny in a mouthful of darkness. A second later there is a short cry followed by a bone-snapping impact. Then nothing but the sound of the helicopter becoming airborne.

Rita grabs her by the arm and hoists her up. To her right she sees Sherell helping Lily back to her feet.

"I always knew she was crazy," Rita says.

"Thank you," Zoey says.

Rita nods and glances back the way they came. "Doesn't really matter. Chopper will be here in a minute, and we're all fucked."

"Zoey!" Tia comes bursting through the darkness and grabs her shoulder. "What are you doing? Come on, Merrill's waiting."

They continue around the deep cut in the land and up to the building that she realizes must be the relay station. Automatic gunfire explodes from the top of a hill to the right as the helicopter's lights cruise over the river and curve toward their position.

"Eli will distract them. Come on!" Tia yells in her ear. Ahead Zoey makes out the forms of Chelsea, Lee, Merrill, and Newton waiting a dozen yards from the building. When they reach them, Merrill points to a dip in the land illuminated for a brief span by a flash of lightning.

"Down there! Get down below that rock shelf!" He drops to a knee and unzips a bag, pulling out two long sections of steel that he twists together to form a T. The rest of the group begins to run toward the small drop but Zoey hesitates, glancing toward the approaching helicopter.

"What are you doing? We have to go!" she yells over the storm.

Merrill draws a pointed steel tube out of the bag and affixes it into a groove in the T. There are three fins attached to the cylinder and she spots the gleam of a cable strung behind it.

Merrill stands, pulling the T to his shoulder and aiming at the black form of the chopper that is coming steadily toward them. "You asked what I stole from town," he says. "This is it."

A blade of light lances from the helicopter's bottom and stabs the ground as it turns sideways to them.

Merrill triggers something on the apparatus and there is a sharp twang as the tube zips up and lodges in the side of the chopper.

A pulse of white light emanates from where the projectile hit the aircraft. Zoey blinks at the brightness that is there and gone in an instant. The helicopter's steady beat changes, and the engine suddenly goes silent. The body begins to spin in the opposite direction of the rotors, and the entire craft cruises past them overhead, eerily quiet.

It rotates two more times, a high whistling coming from the slowing blades, before it crashes to the ground a short distance past the rock shelf where the rest of the group took shelter.

The rending of steel makes Zoey wince, and she waits for an explosion, but there is only the hiss of steam and the rain beating on the crumpled body of the chopper.

"What was that?" she asks, trying to shake the disbelief at what just occurred.

"EMP grenade that I attached to a crossbow bolt," Merrill says, dropping the empty weapon to the ground. A small flame pops to life in the nose of the chopper, illuminating part of the wreckage through the storm. "Come on," Merrill says, guiding her down the slope to where the others wait.

When they are within several paces of the group, Chelsea breaks away and sprints to Merrill, nearly bowling him over. He starts to laugh but is cut off as she kisses him. He holds her, and Zoey looks away to take in the others.

They stand in a semicircle, hollow-eyed and ghostlike in the flickering light of the storm. She moves forward to where Lee stands looking at the helicopter's burning carcass. She touches his arm gently but he doesn't respond.

"Lee, are you okay?" The firelight is reflected in his eyes, the flames dancing across his face. She starts to ask again when a tall figure looms out of the darkness. She nearly draws the pistol she took from the guard, but then notices sopping gray hair in full disarray around a lined face.

"You made it out, my girl. Bravo," Ian says. Zoey grins and takes two steps into his arms. He hugs her and strokes her hair before holding her at arm's length. "Are you injured?"

"Just a cut on my back. It's nothing." She looks over his shoulder into the dark. "Did you see any more guards coming?"

"I managed to deter their progress across the river. Eli was covering your trail, and he should be along soon."

"He's okay?"

"Right as rain." This strikes him as funny and he chuckles, holding his palm out to the storm.

"We should get to the Suburban and put some distance between us and the ARC, just in case they send out a larger party on foot."

"I agree."

They walk together back to the group, the rain tapering off slightly as more thunder booms to the east. Merrill is looking from Rita to Sherell to Lee and back again, and Zoey's stomach shrivels. It's time. She begins to walk toward him, to finally face the lies she's told, when movement catches her eye near the downed chopper.

Lily is rocking from foot to foot in the light of the flames. She turns slowly, her head thrown back into the rain, and Zoey realizes she's dancing.

"Lily, come on. Let's go and get somewhere dry."

"Zee! Burr! Burr!" Lily begins to move her arms up and down. *Like wings*, she thinks.

"You're a bird, Lily, you're free," she says, stopping a few steps away from the dancing girl.

"Burr!"

"That's right. Okay, come on, Lily, we've—"

Zoey's words die in her throat.

A form is crawling out of the burning helicopter, the red shine of its eyes reflected demonically as it pushes itself to its knees. And there is something in its hand, something dark that is aimed directly toward Lily.

"Lily! No!" Zoey screams, running forward as she yanks the handgun free at her side. Lily stops dancing and time takes on a distended shape, each second bloated, lasting for eternity.

Zoey brings the pistol up, trying to aim as she runs.

Lightning sizzles across the sky.

Lily is there in front of her, her small face tilted in question.

Flame leaps from the Redeye's weapon and Lily jerks, her eyes going wide.

Zoey fires a round that misses, hitting the steel behind the soldier's head. His gun bucks again and Lily falls to her knees, mouth open in a silent scream. She tips to the side as Zoey shoots three more times, one of her rounds finding its home below the Redeye's chin.

He tips back, a final burst coming from his weapon.

Something tugs at Zoey's shirt beside her belly button. The strength goes out of her legs and she tumbles forward, landing in the sodden ground beside Lily.

The night becomes a cacophony of shouts. There is more gunfire that cuts the air over them, but she can only stare at Lily's face, which has slackened, her beautiful eyes filling up with rain. Zoey drags herself closer to the girl, using her arms because there is something very wrong with her legs. She clutches at Lily's shirt as strong hands roll her onto her back.

Merrill's face hovers over her and then Lee is on her other side, gripping her hand. His fingers are as warm as ever. Or maybe hers are cold.

"You're going to be okay," Merrill says.

She blinks rain from her eyes and draws in a shaky breath. "I'm sorry," she says, the words as heavy as stones on her tongue. "Meeka, she's, she's . . ."

"I know," Merrill says, his eyes locked on her. "I knew as soon as I asked you about her at Ian's. I could see it in your face."

"Why? Why did you help?" she gasps. Now the pain is coming. It's building like the fever she nearly died from, the heat of the agony growing exponentially from her center outward, but her legs remain alarmingly numb.

"Because I wanted to," Merrill says, and he gives her the barest of smiles.

Lee grips her other hand harder, his fingers beginning to stroke the side of her face. Behind him Chelsea comes closer, her red hair fiery in the glow from the helicopter.

The sky begins to swirl beyond them all. The cloud's color bleeds from black to gray to a wispy white. Zoey tries to swallow but loses the strength halfway through. Voices say her name, over and over, but they're growing faint, her name nearly meaningless. The numbness in her legs spreads past her stomach, snuffing the pain there with its frigid touch, and she's grateful for it. It flows upward, cooling her skin and draining away the panic.

She floats in the whiteness, alone on a soft bed that she can't see.

The voices still say her name, and she wonders if it is her parents, finally calling her home.

36

Zoey opens her eyes to the ceiling of the little bedroom.

Her mouth is scorched with thirst, and pain near her navel throbs with each heartbeat. She tries to swallow, but there is no saliva to lubricate the process. Her small cough sharpens the pain in her stomach to a knife's edge.

"Zoey? Can you hear me?" Ian's worn face slides into her field of vision. She turns her head slightly and waits for her eyes to focus.

"Yes." Her voice is as quiet as a draft through a window.

"Here," he says, placing something between her lips. "Drink."

She does. The water is cold and sweet and she's sure that she will drink for the rest of her life, there's nothing that could come close to the ecstasy of it. But Ian draws the straw away after only a dozen sips.

"You don't want to make yourself sick," he says. "You've been hooked to an IV for the past several days, and we've been giving you water through a sponge, but I'm sure you're still thirsty."

"Why am I here?" she asks.

"Do you remember what happened after the ARC?"

She tries. She recalls the scene in the infirmary. Terra's and Simon's deaths. Their escape. Penny trying to murder her. Then a veil of darkness in the form of storm clouds obscures her thoughts, and no matter how hard she tries to circumvent them, she comes up with nothing.

"Somewhat," she finally says. "The helicopter was chasing us, and then . . ."

"It crashed," Ian finishes in a gentle voice. He watches her, pensive, as if there is something he needs to tell her.

But then the veil parts and she sees Lily's staring eyes, the rain glazing them like liquid diamonds.

"Lily," she manages, and tries to curl in on herself, but her stomach erupts into a bed of hot coals and she gasps with the pain and the memory of Lily's death. It hollows her, drains her of everything but the grief and the guilt. She's sure she must die then, that there's nothing for it. Terra, Simon, and Lily—all of them gone.

"It wasn't your fault," Ian says. "No one thought that anyone could survive that crash. We thought we were safe for the time being."

Zoey clenches her eyes shut. She won't open them ever again. Never. Seeing the world while it was ripped away so quickly from Lily isn't fair. She would blind herself if she had a tool to do so.

"Are you in much pain?" Ian asks. "We medicated you with what we had but ran out of the more powerful painkillers after the first forty-eight hours."

"Was I shot?" she asks, keeping her eyes shut.

"Yes. In the stomach. I won't lie to you, Zoey, you nearly died. If Chelsea hadn't been there, you would have."

"The others? Lee?"

"They're here. Safe. Lee has barely left your side since you were wounded."

The memory of telling Merrill about Meeka surfaces, and she slowly opens her eyes. "Merrill?"

"He's okay. He knew, Zoey. I think he might've known in his heart even before he met you. He blames himself for not trying another attack earlier."

"He wouldn't have made it." A bout of dizziness washes over her and she blinks, attempting to arrest the room's spinning. Gradually it comes to a stop.

"That's what I told him. Without you, we wouldn't have had a chance."

"Do the others hate me?"

"No. They understand why you misled them, why it was so important to you. And I'm glad you did, because who knows how things would have turned out if you had been honest."

"I need to sit up," she says, reaching out. Ian grasps her hand but doesn't help her.

"Zoey, you have to lie still, you're very weak and—"

"Why can't I move my legs?" She tries again to bring her right knee up, but the command from her brain fails and her leg remains motionless. Her heart begins to pick up speed as dread flows through her. "Ian, why can't I move them?"

"You need to calm down, Zoey. You were badly injured, and there were complications."

She tries to sit up, tries to see her legs to make sure they're still there, but spangles of darkness appear at the edges of her vision and flood inward. She reaches out, the sensation of falling almost bringing a scream from her, and the last thing she feels is a warm hand that she knows so well gripping her own.

◆　◆　◆

Moonlight streams in through the tunneled window, splashing in silver puddles on the man who sits beside her bed. His head is bowed, but she knows he's awake because of the way he rubs her hand softly every few seconds. She shifts on the bed and his head comes up, though she can't see his face for the shadow that drapes it.

"You're awake," Lee says, scooting his chair closer.

"Yeah. How are you?"

"I'm not the one that got shot."

"I know." She lets the silence between them hang.

"I've been better," he says after a long time.

"I'm so sorry. It's my fault."

His head dips forward, but he doesn't refute her words. "I keep seeing him right before . . ." Lee's voice strangles in his throat and he clears it. ". . . and I can't get it out of my mind."

She watches him through the dappled darkness. She wishes she could rise and hold him, kiss his hands and face and lips, try to pour whatever comfort she can into him, but her body resists even the slightest movement.

"He was all I knew," he says after a time. "And now he's gone, along with the only life I had."

"I understand."

"I'm not sure if you do."

She has nothing to say back.

They sit silently for a long while, hands still linked, until Lee says, "What you did was incredible. I always knew you were strong, but I had no idea until I saw you in the infirmary. They told us you were dead, that you'd killed guards and Meeka to get free and that you died outside the walls, but I knew better. I knew you'd never hurt Meeka, and I could feel that you were out there, alive. And I know you're going to survive now."

Lee rises from his seat and bends over her. His whisper tickles her ear as his lips brush gently across her temple to her forehead where he lingers with a long kiss. He draws his fingers gently over her cheek, and then moves away through the shadows of the room to the waiting door, and passes through it out of sight.

37

6 Weeks Later

Zoey sits in the small front yard, a knitted blanket covering her legs.

The fresh scent of pine fills the air that is warmer now. The greenness of the forest is almost too brilliant to look at. A southern wind tips the tree branches and makes them talk in cracks and groans, with the feathery rasp of needles a steady undercurrent to the conversation.

She watches Rita helping Ian weed the garden that he's expanded to nearly double of what it was last year. He's said more than once he might have to double it again if she, Rita, and Sherell keep eating like they do.

Zoey glances over her shoulder to where Sherell sits on the narrow porch, head bent low over her latest drawing. By tonight she's sure that it will join the half-dozen others that Ian has made frames for and hung over the mantel in the living room.

She adjusts herself in the chair, the last of her bedsores itching almost to the point of madness, and cranes her neck around to see down the narrow path that she knows leads to the road. Merrill said that they would return today with a few more supplies and promised that they'd have a fire tonight, complete with something he called hot chocolate, but wouldn't elaborate on further.

Zoey knows the enthusiasm he infused in his voice before they left was for her. She knows he's worried about how quiet she's become over the last several weeks. She should try to put his concerns to rest, but somehow she doesn't have the energy.

Maybe it's because he's right. There is something wrong with her.

Ever since the night at the ARC, there's been a void inside her that's only grown. No matter how many times Sherell tries to get her to draw with her, or how Rita tries to involve her in chopping vegetables or making dinner, she can't pull herself fully away from the deadened grayness inside.

The sun moves between two of the biggest trees in the yard and shines onto the place where she sits. Slowly she pulls a piece of paper from where it rests beside her in the chair. She unfolds it and reads the words again, even though she memorized them the morning after Lee sat in the moonlight next to her bed. The letter had been tucked beneath her pillow, and the moment she saw it, she knew.

> *Zoey,*
> *I know you won't understand why, but I have to leave. The world is too strange for me here, and each time I look at you I see my father dying on the floor. It is too much for me to bear.*
>
> *I meant what I said tonight; you are the strongest person I know and you'll survive. You have friends here who will always take care of you and keep you safe the way I wish I could.*
>
> *Goodbye, Zoey. Maybe someday we'll see each other again. Until then, know that I love you with all my heart and that there won't be a day that goes by I won't think of you.*
>
> *Yours always,*
> *Lee*

She refolds the paper and places it by her side again. The trees shush one another, and a bird trills somewhere farther down the mountain. Ian and Rita approach the house, their hands stained with the rich soil. Seamus trails behind them, huge head hanging low.

"Would you like some water?" Ian asks on his way by.

"No thanks."

"Are you sure?"

"Yeah. I'm fine."

He gives her a long look before moving up into the house. She hears Rita and Ian murmuring to one another for a time, their voices low, and she knows they're talking about her.

Seamus places his chin in her lap, and she strokes his fur. The dog has become a near constant companion since she returned, his soulful eyes finding her whenever they're in the room together.

"I'm okay," she tells him, but it's a lie neither of them believe.

Zoey folds the blanket up tighter around her legs and unlocks the brakes on the wheelchair that Tia brought her on their last supply run into town. The older woman refitted the wheels with wider treads that roll well over the uneven ground of the mountainside.

Seamus steps aside as she pushes herself across the yard, pausing at the border of the forest before rolling deeper beneath the canopy of branches. She stops near a rock that's she's dubbed "the lookout," since she can see for hundreds of feet in all directions, the ground falling harder away from the natural point. The air is cooler in the forest, and she re-spreads her blanket out, covering herself all the way down to her woolen socks that sit on the chair's footrests.

Everything is still before her save the sway of the branches and the silent flitting of a bird here and there, only shadows that move in bursts of flight. She doesn't know how long it is before she hears footsteps behind her, but she can tell who it is simply by the gait.

"It's beautiful, isn't it?" Ian asks as he stops beside her. "I love spring in the Cascades. There's nothing like it anywhere on Earth." She doesn't acknowledge him, only continues to stare out through the melee of green. "You miss him, don't you?"

Zoey blinks and turns her face toward the old man, who gazes down at her. "Very much," she says finally.

"As much anger as I harbor toward him for leaving you, I understand it just as well. And understanding breeds empathy, and empathy leads to forgiveness, which is the ultimate gift you can give someone. Sometimes it's the hardest gift to give to yourself."

Tears well up in her eyes but she looks away into the breeze to let them dry. A weight settles on her arm, and she sees the copy of *The Count of Monte Cristo* there in his hand.

"I thought you might want some reading material."

"I'm tired of that story."

"Hmm, well, I can see that. But I was thinking the other day and meant to tell you that I realized you're more like Edmond Dantès than you know."

"Why? Because so many people were hurt and died around him, because of his wrath and rage?" Suddenly she's shaking, the brake handle on her chair rattling. "Don't think I haven't thought of that."

Ian remains silent beside her for a time before saying, "No, that's not the similarity I was thinking of. You're right, though, Dantès was full of anger at those who wronged him, and his revenge was momentous. But I was thinking of another aspect of his character that you share with him. He never gave up. Even when all seemed lost, he continued on. And that's what we all must do if we want to survive."

"What if I don't want to survive?" Zoey asks, the tears now flowing free. "What if I don't want to live like this?" She gestures at her legs. "What if I can't stand thinking about Terra and Simon and Meeka and Lily every day?" She tries to say more, but a soft sob wracks her, and her throat closes.

Ian kneels down, one wrinkled hand squeezing her shoulder. "There are prisons of all kinds, Zoey, they take every shape imaginable. They aren't just concrete, and steel, and stone. They're everywhere. And even when you've escaped one, there's always another waiting. But you must remember that the first step to freedom doesn't always start with picking a lock." He reaches out and touches her temple. "It begins here."

Slowly he rises, tucking the book into her chair beside her and moves away through the soft pine needles.

It is a long while before her crying tapers off to a few hitching sobs, and even longer before her vision is no longer blurred. She gazes out at the expanse of forest for a time before bringing her eyes back to the two outlines of her feet beneath the blanket. She draws the woven material up until she can see the knitted socks on each foot. She has tried thousands of times over the last weeks to make them move—the moment they transferred her out of bed and into the chair, she made a silent vow that she would walk again. But each time her efforts have failed, no matter how long she concentrates or visualizes the movement that she wants so badly.

What a princess, Meeka's voice says quietly in her head. *Giving up already?*

I've tried.

You haven't. You only started to. Try again.

No.

Good, feel sorry for yourself.

I will. Get out of my head.

Done. Who wants to hang around a worthless, sniveling, weak princess like you?

Shut up.

All of that effort, all of us dead so you can sit in that chair and feel sorry for yourself.

Shut up!

I always knew you were weak. No wonder Lee left.

"Shut up!" Zoey screams, pushing herself forward in the chair. Her breath comes in heaving blasts, her upper body trembles with rage, and sorrow and a self-hatred so thick she can taste it like bile in the back of her throat. She screams again, this time without words. It is a raw, primal sound that sends the birds zipping away down the mountainside.

Zoey sinks back into her chair, utterly drained, shuddering with the turmoil that burns within her like acid. She's about to close her eyes when she notices something that freezes her where she sits. She waits, her anger still simmering amongst the disbelief and the thrill of excitement that spiked in the split second before she told herself she was seeing things.

She sits forward again, gazing down at her sock feet, bringing back the concentration that she knows intimately from all the failings.

"Move," she whispers.

And the big toe on her right foot listens.

ACKNOWLEDGMENTS

So many people helped with the shaping of this book, it's hard to remember everyone, but I'll definitely try.

Thanks first and foremost to my wife, Jade. You are always the number one person who I write for, and this book is no exception. Thanks to my editor, Kjersti Egerdahl, for the excellent suggestions and helping me see different sides of the story as it was created. Thanks to Jacque Ben-Zekry for all the encouragement as well as Tiffany Pokorny, Alan Turkus, and the rest of the team at Thomas & Mercer. I couldn't have done it without you! Thanks to Tegan Tigani for all the great insight! And thanks to Blake Crouch for the best writing advice I've ever gotten—no more small ideas.

ABOUT THE AUTHOR

Photo © 2015 Jade Hart

Joe Hart was born and raised in northern Minnesota. He's been writing since he was nine years old in the horror and thriller genres. He is the author of eight novels and numerous short stories. When he's not writing, Joe enjoys reading, working out, watching movies with his family, and spending time outdoors.

Learn more about Joe by following him on Twitter @AuthorJoeHart or connect with him on Facebook at www.facebook.com/pages/Joe-Hart/345933805484346.